THE PARISH

WAYWARDEN

ℂ NICK COWEN

Privately printed in 2023 for
   Nick Cowen
   trustharrison@kingsoflounge.com
   (all enquiries to the author at this email address)

by The Hobnob Press
   8 Lock Warehouse, Severn Road
   Gloucester GL1 2GA

Design and typesetting by John Chandler. The text is set in 12 point Doves Type leaded 3 points. Doves Type is a digital facsimile, created by Robert Green, of the celebrated face made by Edward Prince in 1899 for the Doves Press, based on Jenson's 15th-century Venetian type.

© Nick Cowen 2023

All illustrations by the author.

ISBN 978-1-914407-50-5

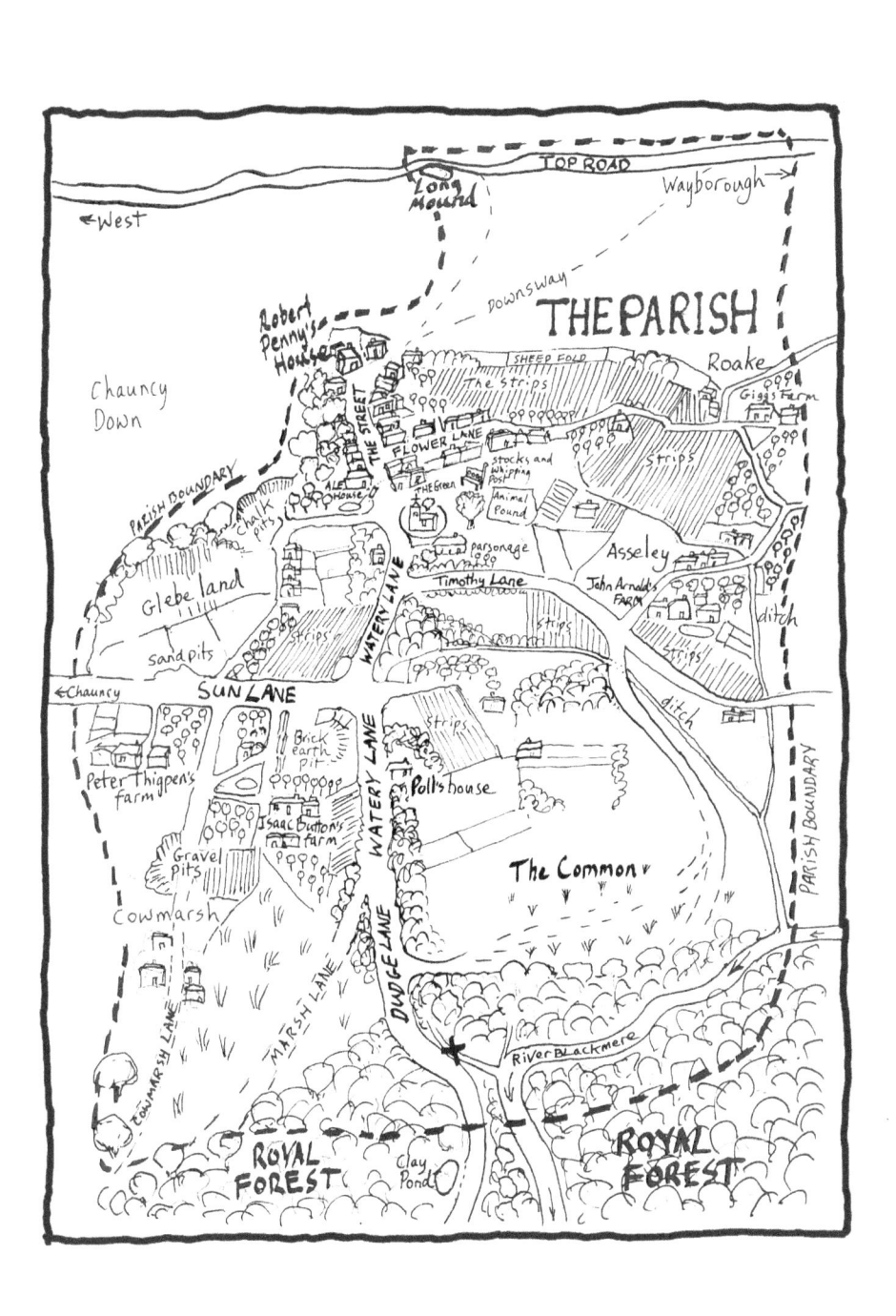

THE PARISH

West →

Top Road — Wayborough →

Long Mound
Downsway
Chauncy Down
Robert Penny's House
The Street
Sheep Fold
The Strips
Roake
Giggs Farm
Parish Boundary
Chalk Pits
Flower Lane
Ale House
The Green
Stocks and Whipping Post
Animal Pound
Strips
Asseley
Parsonage
Timothy Lane
John Arnold's Farm
ditch
Glebe land
Watery Lane
strips
strips
ditch
sand pits
Sun Lane
← Chauncy
Peter Thigpen's farm
Brick earth pits
strips
Isaac Button's farm
Poll's house
Gravel pits
Watery Lane
Parish Boundary
Cowmarsh
The Common
Cowmarsh Lane
Marsh Lane
Dudge Lane
River Blackmere
Royal Forest
Clay Pond
Royal Forest

1633
Autumn
A Parish in South East Wiltshire.

He resented the task for which he had been volunteered and grumbled on his way in the early morning, beyond the church, away from the chalkland, to the south of the parish where the tracks and paths became victim to the clays, sands and water seepages, the shitty land, as he called it. Robert Penny had always lived on the chalk. Chalk collected in the kettle and the pans and Robert wondered whether it collected in the body in the same way and when his first wife Bess was alive, she would shake her head at such nonsense. But chalk looked after itself, it drained itself and the flints from the fields could be thrown into the track ruts. Gate posts stayed upright longer in the chalk, it was dry land and the wooden posts below ground would not rot. A hole dug in the shitty land would fill up with water by the next morning and they say that was that why the church was built where it was, because no one wanted corpses floating about in their graves on the morning of a funeral. He had thought about this and believed that the foundations of the old stone building needed the solid chalk to rest upon and that was why it had been placed on the edge of dry land. He kept these thoughts to himself as it was considered ill-manners to pretend to know more than your neighbours.

Yesterday evening, Edward Loper, the parish constable had knocked on his door with a warrant from the vestry to inform Robert that he had been appointed the parish waywarden. Robert had shaken his head slowly in response at which the parish constable had shrugged and smiled, knowing that Robert had no choice in the matter. The parish vestry members had agreed and that was that.

Back before harvest Robert had objected in church that the incumbent waywarden only served himself and never even cut back his own hedges, hedges that had encroached upon the highway but also the access to Robert's field and which Robert had to clear himself. Robert was certainly not a complainer or a gossip and it was only frustration that had caused him to speak out. He wished now that he had kept his mouth shut, but all householders within the parish were obliged to take on the onerous duties of either parish waywarden, overseer of the poor or parish constable, for a tenure of one year, or two if you were unlucky.

"Accounts'll be passed to thee at next vestry," the parish constable had said, before departing, "oh ah, n' a cart broke a wheel on Top Road by Long Mound and Poll says he 'eard that Dudge Lane be flooded bad."

For the most part, Robert did not really care what happened elsewhere in the parish and certainly not down in the shitty land which he had little cause to visit except to collect fallen branches and cut furze for the fire. Dudge Lane was the track

THE PARISH WAYWARDEN

that he used himself to gain access to the wood and the common and so he would begin his thankless task there. He had not slept well the previous night, thinking and then dreaming about being presented with this insurmountable problem and responsibility. Consequently, shortly after the cock's crow, he found himself sloughing southward through the dun-coloured mire that was Watery Lane, climbing upon the bank to let a half dozen cattle pass. He nodded silently to the boy walking at the rear.

"Mornin' Mr Penny," said the boy.

It had rained a lot this summer, during and after harvest. A week ago, a great storm had flashed overhead and the rains had ceased for now but the fallen water from weeks gone by had pooled across the fields and settled in the lanes.

Further on he passed Timothy Lane, the turning to Asseley, a small hamlet of not many dwellings with more cows than people. A little further on Sun Lane joined Watery Lane, this was the way to Chauncy, the neighbouring and larger parish. Robert carried on down Watery Lane and the geese in the lane hissed as he passed Poll's house but Poll did not come out. Poll seldom came out but he seemed to know more about what was going in the parish than anyone else. Dudge Lane began beyond Poll's house, when Watery Lane turned down towards the marsh and Dudge Lane continued South, towards the Royal Forest. Robert could find no serious flooding in the first part of the long lane, the section that he had cause to use to reach the Common, and he was about to return home.

"Christ's teeth," he said loudly, his shoulders slumping in frustration.

He knew that he would have to continue to follow the long lane, until he reached the parish boundary, if he were to fulfil his new and burdensome responsibilities. He cursed again.

Oak trees favoured the shitty land and clustered to make

a wood in the very south of the parish. Beyond the boundary the Royal Forest spread all the way to the sea and they say that it was more than two day's walking down to the coast. He could not recall when he had come this far south in the parish, perhaps when he last beat the bounds, before he had moved away, when not yet a man to live with his sister Ann in the neighbouring parish of Chauncy. Springs abounded in the south of the parish and there were ponds also, places where not even beasts could wander. It was gloomy under the spreading oak wood and near the lane the River Blackmere flowed with some purpose, accepting draining water from the wet land as it snaked through the wood and into the forest beyond. He wandered in between the oak trees and the alder to peer down at the dark sepia coloured river flowing in its deeply incised channel. A little further on there was an overgrown and seeping pond near the track and Robert observed the water breaching the adjacent drainage ditch to flow and then settle in the lane at some depth. The short ditch that should have ushered the over-flowing pond water away from the lane and into the nearby river had been blocked. There was a pile of large branches heaped across the ditch causing the obstruction and so Robert began lifting these out, one at a time. The sodden leaves made the branches heavier still and he wondered why yew branches should be heaped up in this way, unless someone was intentionally trying to block the ditch. After removing three branches, a larger one required dragging rather than lifting and he trailed it away to one side, to a clear space near the river bank. Returning to the diminishing pile of branches he stopped. A white hand and forearm had been revealed, a dead hand he was sure but he quickly pulled the remaining branches to one side. A young woman lay buckled in the ditch-water with a large stone placed upon her stomach to weigh her down. As he raised the stone, the body shifted slowly in the water. He positioned himself on the edge of the ditch, his boots sinking into the oozing mud and bending to lift her under her arms, he dragged her free of the ditch and kept dragging her towards dry land on the bank of the stream. Robert lay her down and straightened her up, placing her arms by her side and then cleared the long black hair from her face. She was dressed in simple clothes and Robert did not recognise her. She had once been beautiful, that much Robert could tell.

He returned home in haste and placed the bridle on Katy, his old horse that had belonged to his father. His son Samuel was out ploughing and preparing the land with the ox and Robert was relieved that no explanation was required. Robert then called upon Henry Dowty, the overseer of the poor, to borrow his cart, one of only two carts in the parish. The overseer was not at home but he explained to his wife that as the new waywarden, he was engaged upon parish highway business and required the cart. Dowty's wife's breasts were seeping milk through her smock and she looked at him blankly before indicating with her thumb that the cart was in the back yard and then closed the door. After harnessing the cart, he then set off to Edward Loper's house in The Street and in front of the parish constable's wife, Robert did not wish to say why her husband should now come with him. Even when they were on their way, Robert found that he could not tell the parish constable what he had found at Dudge Lane.

"You'll see for yourself," said Robert as they continued in silence.

There was some activity on the lanes but Robert urged the old horse on, their haste causing people to make way and then turn to peer after the cart. At the location of the previously obstructed ditch, Robert directed the horse to lurch out of the depression that was the lane and drew the cart alongside where the wet branches had now been heaped up, on the bank beside the

River Blackmere.

"Well," said the parish constable, "what be it then?"

Robert jumped down and began to pull away the dark branches from where he had piled them up in the early morning to conceal the body. As he slid the last branch away to the side, the young woman was revealed, laying as he had placed her but with the smeared mud from the wet yew across her white face.

"That's what were blocking thic ditch," said Robert, pointing towards the ditch and the large stone that he had earlier heaved to one side, "all weighted down n' covered over."

The parish constable peered down at the body from his seat at the front of the cart

"Who is she anyways?"

Robert shrugged.

"But we can't leave her 'ere," said Robert.

"That be true," said Edward Loper, slowly climbing down from the cart.

Robert had manoeuvred the cart so that between them they could lift the young woman onto the bed of the cart, he had even brought his own blanket to cover the body for the return journey.

"Right then," said Edward Loper, as he positioned himself at the head of the corpse, lifting her by the wrists. Robert quickly moved around to raise her ankles.

"Can thee count to three then Robert Penny?"

Robert nodded.

"On the count of three then," said the parish constable, raising the arms to begin the swinging motion, "one...two..."

Robert waited for the call of three but the momentum was now moving away from the cart bed and towards the flowing stream.

"Three," said Edward Loper, swinging and releasing his

grip.

Robert found himself letting go as the ankles were ripped from his hands with the force of a dead weight in motion. There was a loud splash as the body hit the water below and the young woman's long black hair wrapped around her face as the flow of the dark river guided her away downstream.

Robert stood on the river bank, open mouthed as the corpse turned sideways in the water, a white hand drifted and then reached out behind her.

"Thar," said the parish constable, climbing back up to his position in the cart, "she be somebody else's dead whore now."

Robert stood on the bank until he could see her no more and then, in a daze, climbed up to take the reins in the cart. He then stepped down to lay the wet yew branches across the back of the cart, securing them with a rope. Their return journey was as silent as before. As they neared the end of Watery Lane, before the slow climb up towards The Street and the church, the parish constable held up his hand.

"Stop 'ere," said Edward Loper, "Stimey the woodsman be harbouring a vagrant woman, so churchwarden Thigpen do say. Best 'ave a word. You go on Penny, thee'd better ready thyself before Sunday mind."

The parish constable climbed down from the cart and then held up a hand behind him in a gesture of goodbye. The rotting thatch of the woodsman's house could just be seen between the bare bones of the trees, the trodden path to the dwelling, a darker mush amongst the fallen leaves.

Robert's front door opened with a clatter.
"Father, father,"
"Steady boy, steady."

"Father, Mr Crouch is back."

"Be he now?"

"Yes, and the cart is filled."

"Well, now he be parson, he won't be doin' they... things."

"He says that there are new experiments."

"You spoke to he?"

"I did run alongside."

The boy waited at the open door as the father raised himself slowly from his chair.

"Well, we'll see," said Robert, moving to lean against the door jamb and resting his right hand on the boy's head.

Samuel was unable to keep still under his father's steady hand and kept peering down The Street.

"Go then," said Robert, "go and unload the carrier's cart as no other soul will help him."

The boy ran away, down The Street towards the parsonage.

"They'll not help 'im as they dun't think him worthy," muttered Robert to himself as he sat down in his chair, placing his head in his hands.

There was so much to do and he must eat but all he could think about was the young woman's long black hair swirling in the dark water and her white hand trailing behind in a gesture of farewell or an attempt to cling on to something, an alder root or life itself. But it was much too late for that now. She had slipped beyond the parish boundary and away into the Royal Forest. She had gone.

Robert had no time to think clearly about the details of his presentation on Sunday from the church pulpit directly after the service, but this did not prevent him from worrying about his new and unwelcome responsibilities. Firstly, there were the extensive surveys of all the highways and paths, bridges, ditches and encroaching hedges within the parish that he must perform at least three times a year. More threatening still was the organisation of the regular labour force that the unwilling parishioners were obliged to provide for the maintenance tasks which Robert must now stipulate; the how, where, when and who. Failure, on Robert's part was answerable to the Justices for which he could be fined. Failure on the part of those parishioners, those who did not fulfil their statutory responsibilities, then it was Robert's duty to extract fines from them. Any relief from these fears was only temporarily pushed aside by a hollow dread. How could he now stand up in church and face the parish after his participation in such an un-Christian act? Edward Loper, the parish constable, would be there, staring right back at him, knowing his secret and smiling, as he always smiled.

But today was Wednesday. He and Samuel had shared four boiled onions and parson Crouch had given Samuel some flat and dry fruitcake, which they now chewed slowly.

"How am I to deal with this...thing?" said Robert "you were here when Loper was at the door, you were listening?"

"I will help you father. When the preparing of the strips be done, we can start in the south and bring wood."

"No," said Robert quickly, "the north, Top Road first. The shitty land can wait."

They ate in silence for a moment.

"Parson Crouch will teach me Latin."

"Oh?"

"He said he would teach me Latin if I help him with his experiments."

"And will Latin bring food to our table?"

"He wants to move blood from one chicken to the other."

"He now be a servant of God, not a sorcerer, but if he be killing chickens then p'raps we'll have some food for the table after all?"

They talked about the tasks that must be undertaken the next day.

Robert picked up a final crumb of fruitcake from the table and placed it in his mouth.

"We shall walk Top Road tomorrow afternoon, parson Crouch's experiments can wait, and his Latin."

"Carpe diem," said Samuel.

"By the guts of God," said Robert, swiping an arm across the table at his son's ear, who leant back on his stool to avoid the blow, "come here now so that I may strike thee proper."

The recent storm had cleared the rain for a few days but the next day it rained until late in the afternoon and they were already wet when they set out to walk the Top Road, starting from the north western corner of the parish. This was the highest point on the ridge where a prominent long mound with its flanking ditches marked the parish boundary. As they climbed the long mound to look west beyond the parish, the sun suddenly burst through the ragged grey cloud, causing them to shield their eyes and it was as if by the climbing of the mound they had managed to rise above the prevailing weather. The sinuous wet scar of the chalk road on the ridge now shone gold in the low sun whilst the flocks of sheep on the broad grassland to either side of the track, began to shift and bleat as if something was about to happen. Robert and Samuel turned to the north. The horizon was crisp and there in the distance was the spire of St Mary's, seemingly rising above a forest but Robert knew that there were fields, villages, rivers and open land between here and the city. Beyond the horizon was the great plain that Robert had once crossed, fearful that he would become lost for ever in its endlessness. Their own long shadows were there to greet them as they turned east, to the task in hand, the Top Road with the exposed chalk swelling at the water splashes and narrowing on the gradients until it dipped and disappeared from view. Robert wondered why the parish boundaries lay as they did. Who determined that the Top Road should be in their parish when the parishioners themselves had little cause to use it and with him now responsible for its maintenance? Trade from elsewhere passed this way. Cattle, sheep, pigs and geese were driven along the Top Road, the trudging packhorse trains, the journeymen and salesmen. Also, the Justices travelling to the Quarter Sessions, those on church or legal business, even gentlemen and ladies in their finery. Few came down to the village and hamlets within the parish, apart from the recent arrival of parson Crouch from Oxford.

  On the track beside the long mound, a large and deep hollow had filled with water after the late summer rain. This was a natural pinch point as the ridge dipped away steeply to the north so each driven beast, packhorse train, rider and now with the steady increase in wheeled vehicles, every cart and carriage must pass through it. It would only get deeper and present more of an obstacle if it were not filled in some way but they were some distance from the nearest chalk pit. Robert tried to size up the volume of material that would be required to effectively repair the problem. There was no hazel bush nearby where a stick could be found to accurately measure the depth. Samuel picked up a fist sized flint from the edge of the hole and threw it into the centre where it plopped loudly.

  "Hmm," muttered Robert, "two feet deep, dun't you reckon? That be a main amount of chalk. It won't drain neither, it be too firm, tis a pond proper."

Samuel pointed back beyond the long mound where a rider was approaching from the west, cantering on the turf beside the chalky road.

The rider paused before the long hollow of water to glance across at Robert and Samuel, who were waiting expectantly for him to continue.

"What are you about?" said the man, "If you wish to rob me then I shall crack your heads and drown you both in that puddle, if you dare?"

"No, no sir," said Robert, "we are not robbers, I be the waywarden for the parish. We wants to see how deep the water do lay, when you passes."

The rider urged his large horse to enter the water and then stopped in the centre. He glanced across at them and nodded before continuing on his way, the animal hauling itself from the water, dripping as it stepped into a trot.

"We thank you, sir," Samuel called out after the rider.

"Then I were right, it be two feet," confirmed Robert, to his son, "and I would've cracked his head first. Perhaps we should become robbers Samuel? It would be easier work than the mending of the highways. Come on."

They continued eastwards along the Top Road, the worst sections were on the level ground where the water would sit and not drain away. There were sticky areas also where a smearing of reddish clay with angular flints seemed to lay above the chalk and here it sucked at their boots. Where the road became a mire, the traffic would move further to one side or the other to pass and so the openness of the broad ridge became its salvation with the used way getting wider as required and there was nothing to be done here to improve matters. Once they had reached the most north eastern point of the parish they walked directly homewards, back across the down.

"On Sunday I'll say that we fill the hollow next to Long Mound, come October," said Robert, "we'll need both they parish carts to haul enough chalk up to the ridge."

"We do not need to father," said Samuel.

"How so? To dig a new pit on the ridge?"

"No, not a new pit, Long Mound itself be chalk, you have seen the rabbit throws."

"No...Long Mound ...t'is a marker for the parish boundary, 'n travellers do keep their way by the passing of Long Mound? We cannot level it boy."

"Not to level, but to take enough?"

They returned home in silence.

In the night Robert awoke with a gripe in his belly. He felt that he must eat or shit but there was no food in the house and neither could he find any relief from squatting over the privy. Dawn came slowly and he got up to stand at the back door and watch the rain.

"We'll take the chalk from Long Mound," said Robert, after he had woken up his son, "you go and see parson Crouch this morning, see if he needs help with his experiments, but dun't come back here spouting Latin."

At least parson Crouch might feed Samuel, thought Robert.

The following evening there was a knock at Robert's door.

"Fish," said Edward Loper, thrusting a mackerel at Robert.

"Fish?" said Robert.

"Take 'un."

Robert took the fish.

"A train up from the coast came by, up Dudge lane and

then on up The Street, towards Top Road."

Ten or more packhorses would follow the leader, laden with panniers of mackerel, when the sea was thick with them, away to the towns or even to London. Occasionally they would take the Royal Forest route which brought them up through the parish.

"I could smell 'em coming," said the parish constable, cheerfully, "like a whore on a good night. I only got a dozen or so, t'was all I could hold."

"I ain't never cooked a fish."

"You needs a wife..I knows, I knows, you've had a wife, two wives, you dun't have to say..but you needs a new wife Robert Penny."

"I be thankful for this...for this fish," said Robert, who then paused before continuing, "does thee dwell on what did happen, down at Dudge Lane, you knows, when I took Dowty's cart? After I'd found her in the ditch?"

The parish constable grimaced and then looked thoughtful before smiling benignly.

"No, I dun't, not at all. Anyways, eat your fish and it be vestry Wednesday next."

When Samuel got back from the fields Robert was sitting at the table in the fading daylight, staring at the mackerel.

"Loper brought it."

"Look at its colours," said Samuel, taking the fish to study it by the open back door, "I'll get hot coals from Mother Goody. We've got a fish. We've got a fish."

Samuel ran to their neighbour's house whilst Robert continued to wonder why Loper had brought him a fish. This was largesse from a passing pack-horse train, perhaps he thought it legitimate to demand a dozen fish, he was the parish constable after all. And, when asked, Loper had given no consideration to what had occurred in Dudge Lane, near the parish boundary. Robert could not dispel the last sight of the young woman from his thoughts, her turning to reach back before she had slipped from view.

Samuel returned with some smoking wood-coal on a shovel.

"You've got to take the guts out," said Samuel, "I'll do it."

"You can take my guts out n'all, whilst thee be about it."

"Mother Goody says you needs a wife."

"That's what Loper did say."

Samuel got the fire going with the hot coals.

The fish was boiled over the fire, with two onions. When they had finished eating, Robert ran his fingers around his wooden bowl, licking them clean before he spent the next while picking bones from his teeth.

"If we did live by the sea," said Robert, "then we would be fishermen and eat well."

Samuel studied his father's face.

"Father, I am glad that we do now live here and you will build your windmill. Parson Crouch has said he will draw you a plan, he says that there is enough wind on the land and a miller is somebody who never goes hungry."

"You have talked of me?"

"He do remember you, when you was young, when you both lived here in the parish before."

"I s'pose we be of the same age, I remember that brother of 'is, Augustus. He did ram my head in a water trough and I feared I should die. We were just picking up fallen apples, behind the parsonage."

Robert had moved back to the parish after Easter, after

his father had died and then some weeks later his mother had died on Ash Wednesday. Robert had left the parish sixteen years before and four years later he had married Bess, Samuel's mother. She had died coughing blood and Robert had married again. His second wife April had died giving birth and he then lived with his elder sister Ann's family who ran an alehouse in Chauncy, the adjoining parish. With the death of his mother, Samuel and he had then returned to the tenanted smallholding where he had been born. Some years before he had seen a post-mill in a small village in the middle of the chalk plains when he had crossed to Edington to work with his uncle. Robert had been captivated by the small windmill and had spoken with the miller, looking inside at the workings. It had seemed an impossibility that the wind could spin the flimsy sails which in turn could drive the heavy millstones, with the whole thing turning on a post to face the wind. Here was a teetering and spinning toy that could turn grain to flour and ever since that day he had dreamed of building his own post-mill. What grain there was from the parish had to be taken to the neighbouring parish, where a large water-mill sat astride the river Adze. Everyone complained at the dishonesty of the miller who always took more than his sixteenth but there was no choice. Robert would be an honest miller and gain respect and then no one would need to travel out of the parish to the watermill. Now, being made a waywarden there was so much to do, so run down was the smallholding after his parents had been unable to work the land, having fallen on the parish for relief at the end and nearly losing the tenancy, but their death had spared that. He had borrowed money from his sister at the alehouse in Chauncy to pay the rent that was due, the parish rate and outstanding tithe monies. He would build his post-mill but in advance, he would now try to build his reputation as an honest man, through his duties as waywarden, as unpopular as his demands upon the requirements of others may become.

He belched a fishy belch.

"A bene placito," said Samuel.

"You have learned quickly."

"Parson Crouch do say Latin when I go to piss and then makes me say the words again, when I return."

"So, when you are pissing you keep saying it over?"

"Yes, he does not punish me when I say it wrong."

"I would. What do it mean?"

"It means..from one well pleased."

Robert belched again.

"Well, I still be pleased," he said.

"Parson Crouch says that you had two sisters?"

"Did he? Well, yes, Aunt Ann you do know, but there was an older sister, now I hardly remembers her name, how can that be? Her name was Catherine."

"Did she die?"

"She did leave, one night, when I was, I don't know how old I was, older than you. They say that she had a secret sweetheart and they ran away together. We did never hear of her again."

"Parson Crouch says that one sister was very beautiful?"

"Yes, Catherine, now I think on her, she were beautiful. She did'ave long black hair."

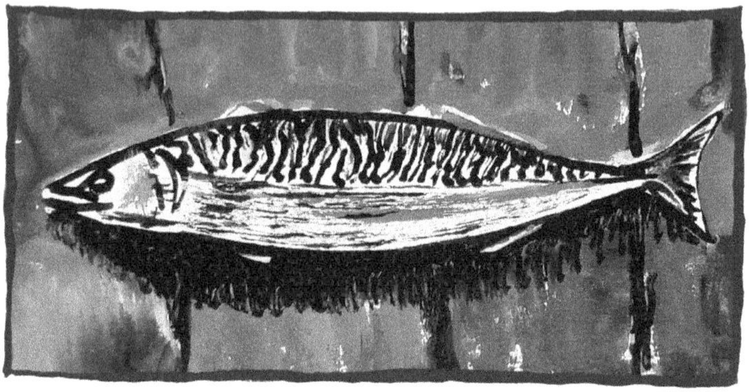

The harvest had been poor this year. This was Parson Crouch's first utterance from the pulpit. It was a fact and the congregation awaited the parable that would bring succour to the parish as to how they were to survive and how God would provide in other ways. But none came. It was just a cold and uncomforting fact, followed by a lengthy pause and then mutterings from the parish, coughing and a dog began to bark before John Jess, the beadle, took down the whip from its place upon the wall and cracked it at the cowering animal, making it yelp loudly and then silence.

It was the first time that Robert had encountered William Crouch since his return to the parish. He had not seen him for at least sixteen years, probably longer. They had both been away from the parish and returned but the new parson had been away to a different world, to Oxford where he had studied and also begun his mechanical experimentations in earnest. When they were boys in the parish, their world had been different then. Robert working on the land from an early age and William Crouch at the parsonage, before he was sent away to school. In The Street they very occasionally encountered one another, at an age when a child's curiosity about another child held no boundaries. A conversation would begin and end in the middle with William saying; "observe how the ladybird flies, it does not appear built to fly but fly it does." Or "if you suspend a small stone from a handkerchief by string it will not fall as a stone should." Robert could remember these occasions of practical demonstration, if not the fragment of the conversation itself. Robert would not contribute but just watch and listen and William would then drift away, his attention elsewhere. During the hiatus in the church, Robert observed the parson who now gripped the sides of the pulpit, staring ahead. He had grown tall and slender, his head bony but Robert imagined him as a child again, in pursuit of his curiosity, like a butterfly flitting from scent to scent. Those brief half conversations all those years ago had made their mark on Robert's imagination. In those moments it was as if his routines and labours were in suspension and a piece of magic or colour had been shared, he had been shown how to wonder, how there were other possibilities. Robert had not considered this until today, as he studied William Crouch who obviously had no wish to be standing up in the pulpit, confronted by the entire parish, waiting for him to behave like a parson. As if to give affirmation to Robert's thoughts, a butterfly then appeared, exploring the space above the congregation before settling on a damp patch on the wall, below a tall window.

Peter Thigpen, the churchwarden, coughed and stepped out with exaggerated importance from his box beneath the pulpit.

"The parson, he has not the time yet, since he do return to us, to gather his'self, for the sermon. Mr Butcher, would thee now read."

Having summoned the occasional afternoon preacher from his pew, parson Crouch had first to be extracted down from the pulpit, frozen and silent as he was. The preparations for this reorganisation then halted as the parson suddenly spoke out.

"You will well remember my father, parson Nathanial Crouch? He served this parish for thirty two years, the shepherd of all your souls betwixt birth and death and...I shall...endeavour to do so... as well as he...it will take...time...and God will... Amen."

"Amen," muttered the congregation, with no expression, followed by the churchwarden, who was supposed to lead the coda but had been taken by surprise by the sudden conclusion from the pulpit.

William Crouch then turned to step down cautiously from the pulpit, glancing to frown at the assembled parish as the butterfly left its position on the damp wall and ascended in seemingly chaotic motion to the roof of the nave. The parson paused to observe the flight of the butterfly, squinting upwards, before he turned to the anteroom and passed from view behind the musty curtains. He had been looking up to God for guidance, some said afterwards.

There was a sudden increase in volume from the assembled parish and a young child began to wail, causing the beadle to cross the floor and lay his hand on the whip handle, in its place upon the wall. The crying ceased and the congregation settled down again. The afternoon preacher climbed the pulpit and normality was restored to the service with a reading to which Robert did not listen. Since his return to the parish Robert had sat on a bench towards the rear of the church. When his father and mother were younger and more active in parish life there was the Penny family pew, to one side nearer the front. There would sit father and mother and the three children in order of age, Catherine, Ann and Robert with also two babies, on occasion, in mother's arms. Robert could not remember their names. Now it was as if he had to work his way back to this position in the church, in the parish, it all amounted to the same thing. There were faces that he did not recognise, now seeing the parish as one. From his bench near the back, he had grown familiar again with the renewed sight of those he had known since his youth, now older and with their own children. A church service was a time of wandering attention. Studying the blackheads on the neck of John Gale directly in front of him, and ahead, to the side, a distended earlobe, he wondered whether his ears would become the same, to the right a heavy eyelid resisting sleep and across the aisle there was always the swell of a young breast. Saints or the stories from the bible had not engaged Robert. A church was a building. Inside the building, this was bible enough. The parson would occupy this bible on Sundays and special days, some words would cause fear or wonder, but these would be quickly forgotten and replaced by the many distractions that a building containing the entire parish would endlessly provide. He could not keep turning his head very slightly to study the form of the young breast and as an alternative he found his own eyelids weighing down. From his bench he could not see who was behind him, or those standing at the back, the poorest folk, vagrants even, seeking shelter, with a toe in the parish by attending the Sunday church service. Their residence in the church porch would be brief with their pleas given short shrift by the overseer of the poor, to be whipped by the parish constable and sent on their way, back to be a burden on their own parish, wherever that was. Once the afternoon preacher had finished, Robert arose from the pew with a lump in his throat, to make his way to the pulpit.

"Coram deo," said Samuel softly, as his father shuffled passed him to reach the aisle.

Robert wanted to cuff his son but stayed his hand.

Looking out upon the collective parish, every man, woman, child and dog, Robert could well understand the parson's apprehension and reticence.

"I Robert Penny, now appointed as waywarden, do say this. On Thursday next and on Friday, there be highways work on Top Road."

There was an audible gasp at this news. The parish did not use Top Road. He caught Edward Loper's eye, in his pew near the front, nodding slowly in encouragement and not smiling for once, as if to lend gravitas to his support. What if Robert was to suddenly announce that he and the parish constable had cast the body of a young woman into the river Blackmere, at Loper's instigation? Robert did not wish to remain in the pulpit for any longer than was necessary and continued hastily.

"Next Sunday, I do say more about what be done, I dun't reckon that I can please all, but I shall do my duty, as best I can. Sir,"

Robert gave a deferential nod towards the sleeping squire in his family pew, a box at the front, opposite the pulpit. The elderly squire now lived in Chauncy parish and infrequently attended divine service at Saint Catherine's church. He had perhaps returned on this Sunday to observe the new parson but as he had slept soundly since his arrival, he would be none the wiser. Robert returned to his seat towards the rear of the church. Eyes and frowns followed him back down the aisle. There then followed more vestry business but Robert was relieved that he had said his piece.

His thoughts drifted from a trailing white hand in dark water towards blackheads, earlobes and then the swell of a young breast before forcing himself to look away. He looked down at his feet, at his old and worn boots that pained him to walk in. Both he and Samuel needed new boots but there was no money, nor the prospect of money to spend on new boots. He thought again about parson Crouch and how he had spoken truthfully, there had been a poor harvest this year.

Samuel had brought back some apples, carefully cradled in his arms from the parsonage and he gently rolled them out on to the table. After going out into the yard, he rushed back in.

"The ox has eaten yew. Father, you brought dead yew back to the yard?"

The yew branches from Dudge Lane had been covered over at the back of a woodpile of collected fallen branches but the ox had been loose in the yard and had tugged them free. Robert hurried to see as Samuel drove the beast away.

"Likely he'll die now," said Samuel, his anger flashing

towards his father, "why is there yew, where is it from?"

Robert walked up to his son and struck him hard across the face, knocking him backwards into the mud.

"You let he wander, tis your fault," said Robert.

Samuel wiped his mouth and got up to lead the ox to the trough, holding its head down to make it drink.

"Have you no Latin now boy?" said Robert, breathing heavily.

He looked again at the browning yew leaves and could not judge how much had been eaten. The ox stubbornly refused to drink any more water and Samuel ran to gather some hay for the beast. Robert felt a pounding in his head as though the ingested yew was a poison that he himself had consumed. He returned to the house to sit down and picked up an apple, carefully biting into it with the two firm teeth on one side of his mouth and then slowly crushed the sweet fruit between his gums. He tossed the core across the parlour and out into the yard and then picked up another apple before leaving the house by the front door. Down at the bottom of The Street, Robert entered the church yard, his parent's grave was marked by a simple wooden cross and he stood before the slightly raised grass mound, his mouth poised to speak but no words came. Instead, he cautiously bit into the second apple and began to chew slowly, the flesh of the remainder of the apple beginning to turn brown as he became lost in thought. He had not seen his parents since he had left the parish sixteen years ago and he now tried to summon up their faces. He remembered the fight with his father who had attempted to beat him again but this time he had been strong enough to defend himself. It was this event that caused Robert to leave the parish, his father attending church the next day with a broken nose, as if to shame his own son. But his father had retreated from parish duties even before this time. He had once been the waywarden himself and

Robert pondered upon the nature of the highway repairs that his father would have been proposed, although he was sure that few would have been undertaken, such was the feckless nature of his father.

"I be not like you," said Robert eventually, before taking another side-on bite of the browning apple.

His mother had kept the smallholding going, working in the fields, brewing the beer and butchering the pigs. They had not employed working men in the later years. She made some money as a seamstress and fought with her husband when he demanded to spend it in the alehouse.

Robert decided that he must tell his son about the body of the young woman and of his complicity in casting her into the flowing river. The yew had been concealed, or so he thought, until the wretched ox had found it. This was not Samuel's fault and Robert did not know what to do if the ox should die. He turned to leave but paused to observe the church whilst finishing his apple, a building with its roof desperately in need of repair but solid on its foundations. At each corner were very large and irregular heath-stone quoins, the reddish iron stone that could be found further south amidst the Royal Forest, but not here in the parish. It was the same stone that he had found weighing down the corpse in the ditch. Until now he had not puzzled about the practicalities of why heath stone or why yew branches, when neither could be found in Dudge Lane? Where had they come from? He wandered over to the large single yew tree in the churchyard and made a circuit of it. There had been no recent sawing of branches and the tree looked just as he remembered it from his youth, an intimidating but venerable presence, always dark when the seasons changed around it. Robert could remember climbing into it, amidst its tight mass of low branches, unable to see out or be seen. He placed his boot against the broad, rippled trunk and gripped the branches above him and began to heave himself up into the tree. By straining and gasping he elevated himself, clambering upwards, looking up for the next hand and foothold. He surprised himself that he could still climb a tree, albeit such an accessible tree as the churchyard yew. He felt the strain in his hips and knees but these were the effects of unfamiliar movement, the forgotten pleasure from boyhood was enough to keep him climbing. Breathlessly he reached a branch where there was room above to sit and he then dangled his legs. He did not wish to climb any further and began to think of the descent. Before he could heave himself back down, he heard voices.

"They are g...g...gone, f...f...from the p...p...porch."

It was the voice of Dowty, the overseer of the poor, calling out to another person approaching from the lych gate. Robert carefully tried to peer between the thick mass of branches and tightly clustered yew leaves. He could see down to the base of the trunk, where the stone-hard roots spread out beyond the girth of the trunk, where he had left his apple core on the ground beneath the tree. He could see nothing of Dowty or whoever it was he was talking to, but Robert felt reassured by this as neither could he be seen.

"Gone? Gone where?" it was Loper's voice in reply.

The two men met and stopped on the path, close enough under the boughs of the yew tree for Robert to clearly hear their conversation.

"G..g..gone is enough, no whipping to be had...th..this evening Ed..Ed..Edward."

"I'll call at the alehouse, beggars always tries the alehouse."

Loper's whip cracked making Robert start and the apple core, at the base of the trunk, span away into little pieces.

"It's your z..z..zeal that does s..s..sicken me Ed..Ed..

Edward," said Dowty.

"Thee not seed the badge 'pon my door that do say parish constable?" said Edward Loper, "I only be doin' my parish duty Dowty."

Robert had overheard talk in the church on Sunday how Loper had dragged the vagrant woman from Stimey the woodsman's house to the whipping post. The beggar's clothes had then been ripped from her back by the parish constable so that she could be whipped bare breasted before being turned out of the parish. Stimey the woodsman was fined three shillings for harbouring a vagrant and had been seen with a broken nose.

"I..I..I shall visit the porch again after s..s..sundown," said the overseer of the poor, "a...a...and if they should return then in the morning, I shall p..p..put her in the st..st..stocks. The two children shall wait by her and not stray."

"You're a weak man Dowty."

"W..w..weak, yes and w..w..weary."

"Then pass it on, thee've been overseer for two year now, name your successor. Tis vestry tomorrow night, think on it."

"And I do w..w..wish it, I thought P..P..Penny but now he is the way..way..waywarden. P..P..Penny took the cart the other day, I..I..I was not sure of his p..p..purpose, do you..?"

The two men had begun to walk towards the lych gate and Robert strained to listen after the hearing of his own name.

"Ah, for the highways," said Loper vaguely, "no needs really, 'twas a fool's errand. Penny's alright, he'll be as bad as his father at the highways. They Penny's starts well enough but tis all soon forgot."

One of the two broke wind loudly before Robert heard the click of the gate latch. Robert waited awhile before clambering and sliding back down from the tree. He returned home slowly, his right knee now painful after the exertions of climbing into the churchyard yew. Loper's opinion of Robert's father and of Robert's own ability to fulfil his waywarden obligations kept churning over in his mind. He would show them, he thought, he would do a better job than his father. At least by becoming waywarden he had avoided the even more thankless appointment of overseer, which had seemingly taken its toll on Dowty. And neither did Loper admit to their deed of casting the young dead woman into the river Blackmere. Robert was glad that even Loper could not brag about such a thing. Perhaps it weighed upon his conscience more than his ever-smiling countenance would admit.

When he arrived home, Samuel was cooking two rabbits in a pot.

"Coney?" said Robert.

"Yes."

"Where did you get they?" said Robert, inhaling deeply over the pot.

"From the parsonage garden."

"Trapped?"

"No."

"Oh?"

"With parson Crouch's crossbow."

"He has a crossbow?"

"He made it himself."

Robert shrugged and Samuel turned his back to his father as he stirred the pot.

"The ox?" said Robert, after he had sat down to rest his aching knee.

"Tis shittin' loose."

They ate in silence.

Robert awoke suddenly in the darkness and sat bolt upright in bed, sweating. He felt his stickiness after ejaculating in his sleep. Laying back down he could feel his heart pounding. He was alone but a woman had been astride him, urging him on with fingernails cutting into his chest. He strove to see her face and closed his eyes in an attempt to continue and savour the dream. She had reeled wildly above him, her long hair thrashing his face, the hair never clearing from her own face to enable him to see her properly. He had cupped her small breasts as she pressed down upon him, her thrustings creaking the old bed as Robert had groaned with pleasure but all the while striving to identify this young woman behind her mask of long black hair. At first, she had been the young dead woman from the ditch, the lifeless woman whose last gesture had been to trail a white hand behind her in the dark water? His hands had left her breasts and tried to clear the wild sweaty hair from her face, so much hair and then suddenly, a young face had appeared. It was not the young woman from the ditch but the face of his sister Catherine. He wiped his groin with the coarse blanket and lay back down again. He was going to get up but found himself being awoken at dawn by Samuel's voice.

"Father, the ox is dead."

Robert groaned, lifting his head for a moment.

Samuel disappeared back outside and Robert's head slumped down again. Through his own stupidity the ox was now dead. He could not think about the ox and instead held a vision of his sister's face, so close had it been to his own that he had felt her breath on his face. What did it mean? That he had not known a woman for a long time? But his sister? He had not seen her for at least twenty years and only a few days before he could barely remember her name.

Samuel was nowhere to be seen when Robert went out

to view the dead ox, a great lifeless lump with the flies clustered and unhindered around its eyes and mouth. Robert drank water from the well bucket and poured the remainder over his head. From the pantry he took a piece of barley bannock that Mother Goody had given to Samuel and an apple and left the house. His knee pained him and slowed him down whilst his boots crippled his feet. It was vestry tonight and he wanted to show that he had already taken his responsibilities seriously. Robert had not had cause to visit the east of the parish since his return and so he set out to survey paths and tracks that he had not walked for over sixteen years. Small dwellings threaded beside the broader tracks and pinched faces made silent acknowledgement of Robert's passing. A ram pulled at a hedgerow, the hedgerow had badly encroached upon the track, forcing a change to the course of the way, pushing it downhill towards a ditch when the higher ground was level, where the way should be. At one time the tenants were called Gigg but Robert was unsure whether this was still so. He stood for a moment to pick some of the higher ripe blackberries that were hard and now quite seedy. Carrying on and he entered the small hamlet of Roake, where there were no more than six small houses, chalk cob houses built on the claylands, each with a ragged roof of flat and sparse thatch, patched in places by fresh barley-straw. Robert followed footpaths across lush meadows. It had been Robert's father that had called the claylands the shitty land but it was land that could produce milk, cheese and butter. The sandy soils, in the middle of the parish, before the heavy clay was met, were good for growing and easier to plough than the chalk. He had not heard it said but perhaps those that lived in the south of the parish called the chalklands the bony, dry land where you had to dig a well for one hundred feet or more to meet water. The water would be untainted but was it worth the effort? The chalk grassland was overgrazed but the hooves did not rot.

Perhaps that was the way it was, each with their own prejudices and unspoken envy. Robert now began to envy the lush grass that covered his boots. At the south eastern corner of the parish the common was crossed by numerous tracks, the most easterly following the parish boundary and it now suffered from deep ruts in the clay surface where a cart had recently hauled either fallen timber or furze. In the drier months the clay would become hard and shrink and crack but after prolonged rain it just oozed and collected water. Robert emerged onto Dudge Lane and without pausing he followed the lane southwards until he reached the ditch where he had discovered the body. The water level in the ditch had lowered and no longer overflowed into Dudge Lane but a deep mire from the earlier inundation still obstructed the lane, certainly for those on foot. Robert looked about for the lump of heath stone and then felt in the dark water of the ditch as he thought it may have slid back down the bank. He rolled his sleeve up further but could still not locate the stone. He was certain of the position where he had found the body as there was an elbow in the course of the river Blackmere, bringing it close to Dudge Lane at this point. Robert searched for any stick to prod along the base of the ditch and found some twiggy birch but even then, he could not locate the lump of heath stone. He walked across to the bank of the woodland river, it was not flowing as vigorously now for there had been little rain over the last few days. He followed the winding river downstream for one hundred yards or more and in doing so, crossed the parish boundary to enter the Royal Forest. There was no sign of the body, Robert was not expecting there to be but he had to look, to dispel any thoughts that the body might have become tangled up amongst bankside roots further downstream. Could this be why he had walked out this morning, leaving behind the dead ox to survey the parish highways, knowing all the while that he would be drawn again to seek the stone in the ditch and inspect the dark river. The body had gone, the heath stone had disappeared and the yew had killed his ox, back in his own yard. He left the river and walked back through the wood to meet Dudge Lane again, now he was not sure whether he was inside or outside of the parish. He continued south, into the Royal Forest, along a straight section of the lane before it curved around, to reveal a glade in the woodland with a large pond at its centre. He had never been this far south before and he made a circuit of the pond, observing old fires where he imagined drovers or packhorse drivers had stopped overnight. At the far side of the pond there was a shallow area where animals could drink, where the clay was very pock marked and poached. The remainder of the pond was surrounded by an old oak fence that restricted access to what Robert imagined was the deeper water. He pondered about the origins of the pond. Clay must have been dug to form the pond in the first place but it was a strange place for a clay pit. He walked around the fringe of silver birch and then dipped into the woodland where he could see a number of raised mounds. He kicked away at the dried fern and bramble and then scuffed at the ground with his boot to see what these mounds were made of and amongst layers of a sandier soil he could see fragments of a broken pot. With a bit more scuffing he revealed more of these dull grey panshards and picked up some of the larger pieces that he took to be the rims and bases of small pots. He cast the pieces back into the undergrowth and walked back to look at the pond. At some time in the past pots had been made here, with clay dug from the pit, which was now a pond. There were small clusters of sedge near the wooden rail on the far side and walking around, Robert felt his boots sink in this wet ground. Here was a spring or a water seepage that would feed the pond and keep it filled with water. He felt pleased with his idle observations. Clay had been dug with pottery made and the old clay pit would always provide a place for beasts to drink, beside the track. He wondered how deep the pond was, away from the shallower area where the beasts took their water. The surface of the pond was still and dark and this stillness gave Robert a sense of foreboding. He wanted to disturb it, to break the layer where a water boatman skited about as if the surface was a solid thing. Looking about he could find no large stone or even smaller stones to cast into the water, to break this spell of stillness. He thought that he would retrieve some broken pottery to throw in but instead found a hazel bush and selecting a long rod he bent, stamped and twisted until he managed to detach it. He then ripped away the small branches and leaves and it must have been at least double his own height when he held it up straight. Carefully stepping over the wooden rail he prodded the narrower end of the hazel rod into the water, feeding the rod through his hands, expecting some resistance but none came and by holding the mangled thick end in his finger-tips, just above the water surface, he still did not sense the murky bottom of the pond. He withdrew the dripping hazel rod and cast it back into the fringes of the wood. There had been no resolution and if anything, the sense of foreboding and mystery had only been compounded by the unknown depth of the pond. He felt a strange shiver as he turned his back upon the still and solid water, returning to the track and within a short while, crossed back into the parish.

He walked back up Dudge Lane, avoiding the long mire from the previously overflowed ditch by diverting into the woodland for fifty paces or so. The more he thought about the circumstances regarding the body of the young woman, the more he believed that she had been brought into the parish, across the parish boundary from the Royal Forest and he and Loper had then returned her downstream, back to the Royal Forest. He could not account for the disappeared stone but the yew could have been cut from somewhere in the forest and Loper had not recognised the young woman, either from within the parish or as a recent vagrant entering the parish. Robert was trying to keep his mind from wandering back to the dead ox and how he was to replace it. How he wished that none of it had happened and he lamented that he was now the poorer for it. He soon met a horse and rider that he did not recognise and the two men nodded silently to one another, the rider must have been heading out of the parish as there was nowhere else to go. Robert turned to watch as the rider disappeared from view with the bend in the track. He joined Watery Lane and in time he passed Poll's house. The geese hissed as they always did and there was no sign of Poll. Robert continued and then stopped in the lane for a moment before returning to Poll's house. As he walked up to the door the geese flowed at him as one, hissing loudly. The door opened before he had a chance to knock. Poll hissed back at the geese and they retreated to the lane. He held open the door for Robert to enter. Before he could speak Poll handed Robert a goose egg. Robert shook it gently.

"Eat," said Poll.

Poll watched intently as Robert tapped the large white egg lightly on the edge of the table. The shell cracked and he carefully picked away to reveal the solid bright white of the egg. Poll nodded eagerly for Robert to continue and Robert half peeled the egg and took a tentative bite. The egg was hard boiled and delicious and he quickly peeled away the rest of the shell, throwing the pieces back out of the open door. He took large bites and then pressed the remainder into his mouth, closing his eyes to enjoy the sensation. He had not realised how hungry he was, he had eaten what little he had brought with him long ago. Poll poured some beer into a broken bowl and handed it to Robert who drank eagerly. The small beer tasted good and he accepted more from the jug until he had drained the bowl.

"Robert Penny," said Poll.

"Yes," said Robert, wiping his mouth on his sleeve.

Poll did not look any different from sixteen years before, when Robert had left the parish. As far as Robert could remember he had always been without hair and his large exposed head bulged out above the ears and Robert had always thought that this was why his name was Poll. He supported himself on a crutch under each arm, his crooked legs combined with the crutches to keep him upright, his feet dragging and bracing accordingly. Poll had lived in the house with his mother and when she died, with his younger cousin who had also died. Poll seemed to outlive everyone. He had not attended divine service sixteen years ago and Robert had not seen him at church since his return and it was though his crippled-ness had afforded him some kind of dispensation but there were other cripples who were chased out of the alehouse to drag themselves to church. An unspoken rule had developed over the years to let him be and there were some parishioners who were afraid of Poll. It was Poll the parish came to for guidance in all manner of ways; those who required guidance in the making of decisions, the treatment of pains in the head or sick cattle or to establish who had stolen someone's property, however small and even who was guilty of a person's murder. The judgement of the cunning man was as damning as any justice and so it was this fear that caused Poll to be left alone, unless his services were required and paid for. Robert did not know why he had turned back from returning home to now call at Poll's door. A crack of thunder was followed by a burst of very heavy rain and Robert was at least thankful for the shelter, the hard-boiled goose egg and the small beer.

"Thee brought home thic yew, with Loper," said Poll, "in Dowty's cart."

Robert was startled by this statement but tried not to show it. It was well known that whoever passed Poll's house along Watery Lane, night or day, would be observed.

"It blocked a ditch," said Robert hastily, "alongside Dudge Lane...I could not leave it to poison some beast..I am now the waywarden."

Poll laughed quietly and nodded to himself.

"Like thy father...before."

"Yes," said Robert, "you told Loper that the ditch was blocked, down Dudge Lane?"

"I had not seen, but I did hear."

"Who had said this?"

Poll snorted loudly at the asking of such an impudent question.

Robert wondered whether it was expected that he must pay for any further information but thought better of pursuing it. He carried no money anyway.

"I had two sisters," said Robert, instead, surprising himself, "Ann lives in Chauncy but the other, Catherine, I've not seen or 'eard of, now for twenty year. She went from the parish."

"As did thee," said Poll.

"But I come back."

"You wait for her return?"

"I wish...but I do not expect it. A long time has passed."

"Did she find a sweetheart?" said Poll.

Robert's eyes widened in the gloom of Poll's parlour. He could feel his heart beating faster. Before he could ask, Poll continued, the tip of his tongue darting across his top lip.

"Why else would a girl leave so?"

Poll had asked the question that Robert had been asking himself, these last few days since he had recalled her name and then her face had appeared before him in last night's unsettling dream as she had thrashed wildly astride him. Poll stared up at him, unblinking.

"I..I must go," said Robert.

It was still raining heavily as Robert left. Poll had told him nothing that he did not know already and yet for those that came to Poll's door, that was the way of it, for many already knew the answer that they sought, and Poll would give credence to those suspicions. For the guilty party, the fear of Poll's intervention would finish the job, when confronted, fingers would tremble and pale, clammy skin would rid any doubt in the mind of the accuser, emboldened by the judgement of the cunning man. As the rain ran down the inside of Robert's clothes, he realised that there was something that had been revealed by his visit to Poll's house. It was something unsaid or unseen that now confirmed his earlier thought that the young woman had been brought across the parish boundary, from the Royal Forest. Poll knew that Robert and Loper had returned with a cart load of yew and so would have observed any earlier south bound cart journey where the yew would have been conspicuously laden, concealing the body of the young woman on the cart bed. The sight of twice travelled yew would surely have been remarked upon. Poll had passed on information to Loper about the blocked ditch but that information could have been received from any person travelling up from the Royal Forest, although Poll would not say who, if indeed he knew their name at all.

Robert slopped in through his front door and immediately went out to the back yard. The dead ox was hanging outside the open barn doors and it had been butchered. Two magpies were pecking away at the meat and Robert waved his arms at them, making them fly to the roof of the house where they chattered noisily, waiting for their opportunity to return. Peering behind the carcass Robert could see that inside the old low barn, two stout ash poles had been placed to support the roof, taking the dead weight of the beast where it had been dragged up from behind the barn by the horse, with the ropes running over the ridge. The old barn might have collapsed without this bracing. Behind the barn, the ropes had been tied off at the foot of an old oak gate post and seemed secure enough. Samuel had worked out how to do all this and on his own with the horse providing the power. There was a large heap of skin and guts and the ox's head in one corner of the yard and the ground all around was stained and sticky with blood. There was no sign of Samuel. Robert went back inside and took off his sodden clothes, leaving them in a pool of rainwater on the floor and pulled the blanket from his bed to wrap around himself. This evening was the vestry meeting and he would have to wear his clothes again. He thought about lighting a fire but soon fell asleep, cradling his head on the table.

  He woke with a start, immediately feeling stiff across his neck and shoulders. It was the church bell that awoke him, calling the respective parish officers to the vestry. He looked down at the sodden clothes on the floor. Standing up he saw a pile of clothes on Samuel's stool and held them up. These were his father's clothes that must have been buried in the old trunk, there was even his father's old hat. He looked about and opened the back door but there was no sign of Samuel. Robert cursed the magpies but without his physical intervention they remained picking at the ox carcass. Samuel must have returned and viewed the sodden clothes on the floor and left his father sleeping whilst he sought out his grandfather's old clothes. Had Samuel realised that this evening was the vestry meeting? He dressed quickly, the breeches tight at his middle. Robert had no girth to speak of but his father was a smaller man than he. He shook out the water from his boots and pressed his cold feet inside. Stumbling out of the front door he was relieved that it had stopped raining but he wore his father's hat anyway.

The vestry meeting had already assembled around the table by the time that Robert reached the anteroom in the church and he had missed the prayer given by Peter Thigpen, the churchwarden.

"Ah, Robert," said Loper, beckoning Robert to sit beside him.

Two tall candles had been lit on the long table, complimenting for now the failing light of the day that seeped through the two clear glass latticed windows in the vestry. Across the table from Robert sat Henry Dowty and the churchwarden. Isaac Button, the vestry clerk, who was also the parish clerk sat at one end whilst John Jess, the beadle, sat upon a chair away from the table, near the wall, as if he were only partially entitled to be present at the meeting. The parson was entitled to participate at the parish vestry but of William Crouch, there was no sign.

"We welcome thee Robert," said the clerk, once Robert was seated and the small assembly nodded or grunted in acknowledgement. Robert had no idea about the order of proceedings or when he was expected to contribute and so remained silent. Evidently there had been some discussion going on before Robert's arrival, which now continued.

"So," said Loper, "I 'as to escort 'im to the constable in Chauncy and ee does the same and so on and so on 'til ee gets put on a boat aways over in the west somewhere, Minehead p'raps, I eard say?"

"And where be the Irishman now?" asked the clerk.

"He were a bit lively" said Loper, "he b'ain't so lively now and I put 'ee in the stocks."

"In the r..r..rain?" asked Dowty.

"Does you want 'im in your bed for the night, Mrs Dowty 'ud like that?"

"Well, n..n..no but...he can shelter in the church p..p..porch?"

"And be gone in the morn?" said Loper, "noo..they is used to rain in Ireland, they say it's as wet as a maiden's..."

"Edward," interrupted the churchwarden, "we be in the house of God, lest you forget."

"Anyways, I'll take 'im first light," said the parish constable, "n' John Jess will attend I."

At the mention of his name, the beadle straightened his back to sit upright in his chair.

There had been a surge in Irish vagrants over the last three or four years and in some cases they had banded together and were quite prepared to fight any who tried to incarcerate them or return them via the respective parish constables to a suitable port where they would be sent back whence they came.

"Might even give 'im a crust if 'ee promises to behave hisself," added Loper, turning to give Robert a wink.

"And Henry?" said the clerk, to Dowty the overseer, "you have a person in mind to nominate? Of late you've been made weary by your duties. It be a full two year now?"

Dowty glanced briefly across at Robert before speaking.

"I..I..wish it, it is a great burden, I..I..I had someone in mind, b..b..but I must think on it again. I..I..I do feel that I have done my b..b..best as a Christian, to others less fortunate and feel that k..k..kindness should not be forgot..in dealing with those who do th..th..throw themselves upon the m..m..mercy of the parish."

"No man would question thy time as overseer Henry," said the churchwarden, "and through persuasion rather than the whip, you have shown theeself to be a good Christian, and, in the main they have moved on quiet, p'raps returning to their own?"

"Yes, yes, and I..I..I th..th..thank you," said Dowty,

THE PARISH WAYWARDEN

lowering his head as if in silent and personal prayer.

The harbouring of a woman beggar by Stimey the woodsman was discussed, with Peter Thigpen thanking the parish constable for sending the vagrant woman on her way. The parish constable nodded gravely in acceptance of his duty in such matters.

Business turned to how many sparrows and hedgehogs Philip Martin had caught since last vestry and how much he was to be paid from parish funds whilst Robert found himself being distracted by the flickering candlelight, the candles shortening but brighter now as darkness fell outside. He had not seen a candle for some time, not entering the alehouse where rough candles would sputter wax, smoke badly and stink of animal fat. These were better candles, afforded by the parish, by which the parish officials could govern and administrate. Reluctant agreements were made to pay for this and that out of parish funds. Of the rates paid by the parishioners, it was the overseer that would extract a largest proportion, to facilitate for the labouring poor so that none may die of hunger. The justices were very insistent that the parish should look after their own. A coat for John Gale, a retired labourer, was agreed upon but an apprenticeship for Thomas Hole aged ten years with Joseph Creeper, a shoemaker, in Flower Lane was denied.

"Robert..." said the clerk, suddenly.

Robert sat up in his chair.

"...Thee has knowledge of your duties as waywarden?"

Robert had heard enough complaining about the onerous duties of the waywarden at his sister's alehouse in the neighbouring parish to know as much as he needed to. He had never spoken to his father about his term as waywarden, as that had occurred after Robert had left the parish.

"I reckon so," said Robert.

Loper reached down by his chair and produced an old pair of boots and dropped them on the table.

"Thar's the accounts from Hutchins, monies in ..that be in this one, the one that you do wear on this side," said Loper, gesturing with his right hand, "and thas t'other, the monies out and he do want they boots back."

Robert peered inside the boots at the coins, picking up one boot to shake it gently. The boots looked better than his own.

"Before we depart, I shall make a count," said the clerk, "there must be a record."

"I have been out on the highways." said Robert.

"Yes," said the clerk, "on Top Road, you did say, after the parson had.."

The church warden coughed gruffly, before interrupting.

"The parson? He were a disgrace," said Peter Thigpen, folding his arms and making two chins, "I shall be writing to his brother Augustus, he be the elder in the family now and he do know the Ordin'ry, the Bishop. Augustus, he best put his brother in order, parson or not."

"I think he was afeared...afeared by so many faces," said Robert.

"Afeared," scoffed Loper, "he should be afeared of God not we."

"Yes, but we must bide...and be patient," said the clerk.

"Patient?" said the churchwarden, "we dun't pay for a new hood for the parson, not til he do...be like a parson, n' til then he can wear his old father Nathaniel's hood, God rest 'is soul."

"So, um Robert..." said the clerk, "er...the highways?"

"Top Road first," said Robert, "but over towards Roake, where Gigg did once farm, sixteen year back? The hedge be across the highway, pushing all who do pass into the ditch.

THE PARISH WAYWARDEN

The hedge it must be cut, and the roots pared out."

The beadle jerked himself erect in his chair.

"That be my uncle," said John Jess, with some indignation, glowering at Robert, "Hutchins, 'ee never complained."

"Well, tis bad," said Robert, lifting up the boot nearest to him, on the table, "it'll be money in the boot, if he dun't cut it back."

"Well, ee'll be cursin' thee proper," said the beadle, "n' ee don't spect no fines."

The clerk frowned and glanced at the parish constable, who shrugged.

"Be there anything else...Robert?" said the clerk.

"No, but I'll be abroad agin," said Robert.

"You did send Samuel to borrow they meat knives from the farm?" said the churchwarden, nodding across the table at Robert, "said the ox had died at the plough, said your knives was all blunt?"

Robert was taken aback but kept silent.

"Tis only good neighbourly to lend," continued the churchwarden, "tis only good neighbourly to look where lookin' is needed."

"And blunt and ruined knives be useless," said Robert, "like my father's own knives, he made as bad a job of they as I 'spect he made of being waywarden. I be not my father."

The meeting continued until the candles had burned down, with the clerk hurriedly counting the monies from both boots as the candles guttered.

"Well," said Loper, by the dying of one candle, "the alehouse? John? Henry? Robert?"

"Not I," said the beadle crossly.

"N..n..not tonight Edward," said Dowty.

Neither the clerk or the churchwarden were included in Loper's invitation.

"Well, it looks like just me and thee then Robert?"

Robert left the vestry carrying the previous waywarden's boots but he carried no money of his own. Outside the church he tried to decline Loper's offer.

"I do have no money," said Robert, "bar the waywarden's accounts."

"I'll stand thee tonight Robert, always thirsty after vestry, n' best we looks at thit Irishman on the way."

The stocks were at one end of the parish green, next to the whipping post and in the gloom a figure could be seen slumped over the stocks, seated on the bench with one foot locked under the wooden bar. The man groaned as if in pain.

"'N good riddance to thee in the morning," said the parish constable, turning towards the alehouse.

Robert felt uneasy about entering the alehouse and had avoided it since his return to the parish. At his sister's alehouse in Chauncy there were times after his second wife had died when he had fought after too much beer and had been beaten badly on one occasion, too drunk to fight. His sister would then serve him no beer unless he changed his ways and with his return to the parish he did not wish for trouble or to gain the reputation as a fighting drunk and so he stayed away.

"I shall not stay for long Edward," said Robert.

"Nor I Robert," said Loper, as he pushed open the alehouse door, "but vestry, 'tis dry business."

They sat down and Loper reached across to a neighbouring table to take a lit candle in its holder, despite the protestations of the two drinkers who were sitting at the table.

"Shut thy faces, tis parish business," said the parish constable, who then slapped the table with the flat of his hand, "'ere Robert, put Hutchins boots where us can see they, don't trust none in 'ere."

Robert placed the previous waywarden's boots on the table.

The alehouse was owned by Tetty Bonner and she glanced across at Robert when she brought the beer.

"Tis Robert Penny, 'ee be the new waywarden," said Loper as he lifted the wooden pot to his lips.

"I know who 'tis," said Tetty Bonner, "looks like 'is father in that zunday suit. Ee would dress for church and then bide in 'ere."

"You does look like old man Penny in they clothes," said Loper, laughing, who then broadcast this observation to the room.

Robert looked down and took a sip of his beer. It was good strong ale and he finished his pot before the parish constable.

"Steady on, 'ee drinks like ol' man Penny un all," said Loper, gesturing for two more ales.

They were joined by William Toseland and Jacob Difford who Robert could remember from his youth in the parish and he nodded in acknowledgement.

"Robert's thy new waywarden," stated Loper again, "'n you best get yourn hedges cut or ee'll be onto thee like he was to Jess' uncle, old man Gigg. You should've seen thic beadle at vestry, his face t'were as red as a stiff cock."

"I did not know that it was John Jess' uncle, but it matters not," said Robert.

Loper looked across to Toseland and Difford.

"See, ee ain't afeared to call it out," said Loper, "even the churchwarden were agog, 'n 'ees got plenty 'o hedges that needs doin' and ditches 'n all. 'Ere, and Robert's got a slab 'o meat since the old ox died at the plough, best keep in with the waywarden boys."

That the beast had been poisoned by the yew, Robert did not wish it to be broadcast that he had an ox carcass hanging outside his barn. Could it even be eaten? Samuel had borrowed the butchery knives from the churchwarden without Robert's knowledge, as his own were beyond sharpening and with the handles all wormy. Samuel had lied that the ox had died at the plough, concealing his father's stupidity whilst also giving worth to the meat. In the time that Robert had been wandering the lanes and attempting to gauge the depth of the clay pond and then visiting Poll, his son had worked out how to elevate the ox without collapsing the old barn and had then butchered the beast on his own. Before Robert realised it, he was halfway through his third pot of strong ale and was on the way to becoming drunk. Robert listened to the conversation of the three men and occasionally contributed, he was feeling very hungry as the last thing that he had eaten was the hard-boiled goose egg at Poll's house.

"Ee needs a wife," said the parish constable, pointing at Robert as Tetty Bonner brought four more ales.

"Thee won't find a wife in the alehouse Robert Penny," said the landlady.

"Not even a good wench," said Loper, looking around him, into the darker corners of the room.

"Both my wives have died," said Robert, to Tetty Bonner.

"Reckon ee wore they out," said Loper, leering in the candlelight. The two other men at the table jeered in agreement.

The land lady cuffed Loper around the ear.

"E're, strike the constable would you?" said Loper, feigning injury, and as the landlady departed he muttered that he would still "give 'er one."

"Reckon she'd put up a sturdy fight though Edward," said Difford.

With another ale in his hand, the subject of conversation then returned to Robert being the spit of his father and an equally poor farmer, making Robert quietly seethe to the point where he was about to challenge the next insult. Jacob Difford was taking particular pleasure in Robert's discomfort and Robert could feel his fist clenching under the table when the alehouse door opened and a head peered into the room. Everyone turned to look as one, as the head quickly disappeared.

"It be thic Irishman," shouted Loper, lunging up from his chair, making his chair fall backwards and then staggering towards the door, vaguely hailing assistance as he went, "come, someone's let 'ee loose."

Robert did not feel inclined to chase escaped Irishmen about the parish and remained where he was, whilst Toseland and Difford followed reluctantly behind the parish constable. The candle had tipped over and Robert finished all the ale on the table and almost forgot to pick up Hutchin's old boots when he left. Outside in the fresh air he was sick in The Street. In the distance he could hear Loper shouting and he turned away, to head back up the hill towards home. There was little moon but he knew The Street and the roofs of the cottages were darker than the night sky and then the hill levelled out. The blackness of the old elm tree loomed above him and he could smell Dowty's dung heap. Samuel should not have gone to the churchwarden for the butchery knives, not without Robert knowing, he was made to look a fool. Samuel had found his father's old Sunday clothes and Robert had worn them in his haste to arrive on time for the parish vestry. He had done this on purpose to cause his father to be mocked, as Robert had been mocked in the alehouse. Robert's walking quickened. A dog barked from Chance's house, he could smell the woodsmoke from Mother Goody's chimney. Robert dropped one of Hutchin's boots as he struggled with the latch on his own front door. He groped for the boot, unsure whether any money had been lost on his doorstep. Retrieving the boot, he barged the door open wide, dropping both boots on the floor, just inside the door. Robert fumbled for the dog stick as he staggered into the room.

"Samuel," he screamed.

THE PARISH WAYWARDEN

There was a knock at the door, early the next morning. Robert was dressed, having put on his own damp clothes of yesterday. He opened the door and was surprised to see Isaac Button, the parish clerk, down on his haunches, picking up money from Robert's doorstep.

"Thar's money 'ere Robert," he said, looking up at the opened door.

"It be from the boot," said Robert, rubbing his eyes, "I did drop it, last night, comin' 'ome."

Robert picked up the right boot from inside the door, where he had left it and held it out to receive the collected coins.

"Dun't know which boot it was from," said Robert.

"I do have a record," said the clerk, pouring six or seven low denominational coins into the mouth of the boot.

"Er.. come," said Robert, walking across to close the back door to prevent the clerk from seeing the ox carcass that was suspended in front of the open barn doors, across the yard.

"Ah, bless you, tis early, I thought thee might be abroad in the field," said the clerk, "'n tis a loss, to lose thine ox?"

"He were old," said Robert, mumbling his response.

"And thee'll be wanting the borrow of an ox, 'til thee can get to market?"

Robert coughed and then opened the back door enough to be able to spit out into the yard, before closing it again.

"We do have our old ox," continued the parish clerk, "but first I needs speak... of the vestry Robert...'n the highways."

"You want that I should not be the waywarden?"

"Nay...thee must be waywarden, we do have a duty, we do have many duties.. as a parish. Peter Thigpen, he has been our churchwarden for ten years, near-on, he be a good man, he be the right man and his faith shall guide his actions, as a good Christian and a good farmer besides."

THE PARISH WAYWARDEN

Robert gestured to Samuel's stool.

"Yes, God bless you Robert," said the clerk accepting the seat, "and so...you see...and then there be John Jess.."

"What is your meaning?" said Robert, sitting down himself and beginning to understand the reason for the clerk's visit, but waiting for the clerk to spell it out.

"Well...and thee new to the parish.."

"I were born in the parish," said Robert, enjoying this game of cat and mouse, "I were born in this house... over there."

The clerk glanced across as Robert indicated his dishevelled bed.

"Yes..I did not mean..I did mean..thee have returned to the parish of your birth..now a man..and now with the office...of waywarden."

"Where I is to ensure that the highways be kept in good order?"

"As thee do say...in good order... with the vestry...all in accord...as good neighbours shall be unto each other..."

"What did happen to the Irishman, last night?" said Robert, skewing and prolonging the issue of the clerk's visit.

"Oh?" said the clerk, "he be still at large...the padlock, it were broken free, on the stocks."

"So, somebody let him out?"

"Edward, he be most...angry."

Just at that moment Samuel opened the back door and entered the room, pausing when he saw that his father had a visitor.

"Ah, ...Samuel," said the clerk, trying to peer out into the yard.

Robert got up and closed the back door.

"Good morning sir," said Samuel, addressing the clerk before taking an apple from the parlour and returning to the yard, closing the door behind him.

"So," said Robert, "on Sunday I shall say to all when the work on Top Road next be done, if I is to stay as waywarden, as you do say?"

"Yes, yes and not to be...too watchful of each and every highway Robert."

"And you do have an ox...that we may borrow...when we needs plough? The strips they have been left and wants for manure, we do hope to yield barley, oats and wheat next harvest."

"Ah, yes..the ox.." said the clerk.

"And you have a record of the waywarden's accounts?" said Robert, getting up from his chair and in doing so, drawing the clerk to his feet, in preparation to leave, "and I shall, with Samuel's help, make sure that all be correctly kept and not be thrown about the doorstep."

"Yes..I thank you and I shall send a reckoning..of the monies that were passed to you," said the clerk, placing his hat back on his head.

Robert opened the front door.

"On Sunday then," said Robert.

"Er..Sunday, good morning Robert..and you knows your vestry duty...how it must be done...as a good neighbour," said Isaac Button, glancing towards the back door, before ducking out into the street.

Robert closed the front door and then crossed to the parlour where he picked up the last of the apples from the parson's orchard. Opening the back door, he surveyed the dark mess across the yard from the ox butchery. He could not see or hear Samuel and ate the apple slowly as he looked down at his father's clothes, where he had ripped them off last night and thrown them out of the back door. Two magpies swooped down to begin feeding on the ox carcass and Robert crossed the yard, shouting and waving his arms to deter the birds who hastily flew away in noisy protest, towards the elm trees. Robert had once seen a hay-man in a field of corn and wondered whether a hay-man would keep the magpies from the carcass in the yard. He collected up the strewn clothes, tying knots at the sleeves and ankles and he then stuffed them with hay, from inside the barn. On the hay was Samuel's blanket, indicating where Samuel had slept last night. He recalled his own sense as a child, of knowing when not to be in the house. He needed a head for the hay-man, and screwing up an armful of straw into a ball, he tied it around the top of the wooden post, in front of the barn. He then placed his father's hat on the figure and stepped back to admire this lumpy image of his father. He gave the figure a kick between the legs and left the back door open to observe whether old Judd Penny could even do this job properly. His head ached badly but he felt a little better after the clerk's visit, amused even.

"Will it kill us?" said Robert when Samuel appeared again.

"No father, I do not think so."

"Everyone do know that we have ox meat, are we to poison us both and our neighbours?"

"I will eat it first," said Samuel, "you cannot bleed a dead ox, the innards cannot be ate, nor the tongue."

"So little yew to kill a great beast, it be some poison. Am I to sit and watch you eat when I could eat the whole ox now, to myself? We shall die together. We light the fire this afternoon."

They went out together onto the land, deciding where to plough the strips. Even with the sheep sometimes folded across the great patchwork of parish strips, the yields were poor this harvest. Robert had so few sheep in the collective flock that he could not command more folding and the sheep were always moved on by the shepherd, before they fully voided in the early morning. More manure was needed, more substance to the soil, the soil that his father had neglected over the last few years. They decided that when the ox could be borrowed, they would plough down the broad rigs and build them up where the drainage furrow was now. There was a ditch to one edge of their main strip which Robert and Samuel then set to dig out, after cutting back the scrappy hedge. They accumulated the dug spoil alongside the ditch and then Samuel went to borrow Chant's wheelbarrow so that they could move and pile up the spoil, in preparation to working it into the drainage furrow, after the first ploughing. On top of this pile, they dumped the contents of the privy mixed with used straw and any vegetable scraps, of which there were very few, the ashes from the fire and then the contents of the sheepcote. The heaped pile steamed in the afternoon sun. They then dug a hole, behind the barn, out of sight of the strips and the fields and wheelbarrowed the ox's innards, skin and head to bury them. The wet mass threequarters filled the hole with the ox's head pressed down on top. They filled it in and heaped up the displaced chalk and soil, carefully pressing it down afterwards, so as not to force up the more liquid remnants to the surface.

  Samuel then went in to prepare the fire with a shovel of hot coals from Mother Goody's. Robert hacked off some meat from the carcass with his own knife that he had sharpened as best he could, Samuel having already returned the butchery knives to the churchwarden. There were enough chunks to stew, along with two onions and the meat flavours soon filled the house. They both stood, staring into the pot, as if by looking they could tell whether they were about to poisoned or not but an overriding hunger determined that they would eat the meat, come what may. In near darkness, the stew was slopped out onto the wooden platters and then, remembering something from the night before, Robert retrieved half a candle from one of Hutchins' boots, that was still beside the front door. He lit it in the embers of the fire and dripped some wax onto the table to set the candle upright.

"There, half a candle from Tetty Bonner's. Half a candle and a bad head the day long," said Robert.

For a moment, they looked at each other across the table, poised with steaming meat on their spoons. They ate the first spoonful in unison and then in silence until they had dished out the remainder from the pot and licked their platters. A pile of gristle had accumulated between them on the table and Samuel scooped it up and threw it on the embers where it flared up and sizzled.

"Go on, sing," said Robert.

"I do not wish to."

"Sing."

The candle spat and extinguished itself. In the darkness Samuel's clear young voice began, softly, a song that he had overheard on many occasions in his aunt Ann's alehouse in Chauncy.

> "There were three ravens sat on a tree,
> down a down, hay down, hay down,
> There were three ravens sat on a tree,
> With a down, derrie, derrie, derrie, down, down.
> There were three ravens sat on a tree,
> They were as black as they might be.
> With a down, derrie, derrie, derrie, down, down.
> The one of them said to his fellow,
> Where shall we our breakfast take?
> Down in yonder green field,
> There lies a knight slain under his shield,
> His hounds they lie down at his feet,
> So well they can their master keep,

His hawks they fly so eagerly,
There's no fowl dare him come near
Down there comes a fallow doe,
As great with young as she might go,
She lifted up his bloody head,
And kissed his wounds that were so red,
She got him up upon her back,
And carried him to an earthen pit,
She buried him before the prime,
She was dead herself ere even-song time.
God send every gentleman,
Such hawks, such hounds, and such a mistress.
With a down, derrie, derrie, derrie, down, down."

They went to bed and Robert snored loudly.

"Are you still alive?" said Robert, in the darkness, at the cock's crow.

"Mors certa, hora incerta," said Samuel, sleepily, from across the room.

Robert lay and farted loudly.

"There be meat in the house," he said.

Later in the morning the parish constable knocked loudly upon the door.

"'N where were thee when we were seeking out the Irishman?" said Edward Loper, unsmiling.

"I was drunk," said Robert, "I'd not drunk strong beer since I were in Chauncy and I were sick in The Street, I could not walk straight."

"Pish," said Loper, dismissively, "you'm a vestry man now, drunk or no, I come by yesterday."

"We were out in the fields. What happened to the

Irishman, who let him go?"

"I've a notion who, come on, we're goin' to Poll's. Bring some meat for he, n' some meat for I n'all."

Robert did not want to visit Poll's again but felt that he had no choice. He hacked off some fatty ox meat for both Loper and Poll. He did not know what to do with the meat and so he squeezed it into his coat pocket.

When they got to Poll's, the geese must have been around the back of the house, in the yard and all was quiet.

"And don't eat no hard eggs, Poll do boil they in his own piss," said the parish constable, knocking firmly on the door.

Robert thought about this. Poll opened the door and looked sleepy. He ushered them in with a nod of his prominent head.

"Give 'ee the meat," said the parish constable.

"Ox," said Robert, drawing the dark stretch of meat from his pocket and wiping it with his hand. It pleased him that he could offer the cunning man meat from a poisoned beast, after unknowingly eating Poll's piss boiled goose egg, "it did die at the plough."

Poll accepted the meat and placed it on the table.

"We 'as a question," said Loper, "the Irishman was let go, at the stocks..."

"The lock," said Poll slowly, speaking for the first time, "t'was broke,"

"Ah, by some... they did break the lock, as you say, so, t'were they a vestry man?"

Poll shuffled across the floor on his crutches and took down the shears and sieve from a nail on the wall. Propping himself up whilst pushing the round wooden sided sieve into the open mouth of the pointed shears, the sieve moving freely as it was dangled above the floor. Robert looked on as the parish constable placed the tips of two fingers under the top of the handle, lightly balancing the shears, together with Poll's two fingers. Poll then uttered some strange words that Robert thought might be Latin and nothing happened.

"A vestry man?" said Poll, breaking the silence and drawling his words.

The sieve moved slightly in one direction and then back again.

"It be Dowty," said Loper, "I knew it were Dowty."

"One who may be vestry, or their kin?" said Poll, broadening the enquiry.

The suspended sieve turned a quarter way around in response.

"I still reckon it be Dowty," said the parish constable.

Poll lowered the shears and released the sieve and then looked up at the two men in turn, without expression.

"Come Penny, let's get to Dowty's," said Loper, hastily opening Poll's front door and striding out towards the lane. Robert smiled weakly at the cunning man as he closed the door behind him and hurried to catch up with the parish constable.

They walked back to The Street in silence.

"W..w..why would I d..d..do such a thing?" said Dowty, standing at his open front door after Loper had accused him of releasing the Irishman.

"Because you is weak."

"I..I..I am weak, weak of spirit, b..b..but I b..b..broke no lock."

Robert sensed that the overseer of the poor had the look of a man who was not being wholly truthful.

"We 'as bin to see Poll," said Loper.

Dowty averted his eyes and looked down.

"I..I gave him bread, on my w..w..way to the church,"

THE PARISH WAYWARDEN

said Dowty.

"Bread?" said Loper, "I 'as to stand before the justice n' say what went on. They will fine I for losing 'ee, whilst you was givin' 'ee bread? God will shit thee Dowty.."

Robert grabbed the parish constable's arm to prevent him from striking the overseer of the poor.

"You were going to the church Henry?" said Robert, as he wrestled with the parish constable, thinking that asking questions was a better way between vestrymen.

"I w..w..went to p..p..pray," said Dowty.

"Pray?" scoffed Loper, trying to shrug himself free from Robert's grip.

"Y..y..you were in the alehouse, whilst I..I..I were in the church."

"You would swear to it..on the holy book?" said Loper.

"Come, Edward, we must believe a man who do say that he was at prayer in church," said Robert, now letting go of the parish constable.

"Who saw thee at church?" said Loper

"The p..p..parson, he p..p..prayed also, by my side, he.. he..he p..p..prayed that he might find strength."

"Lord, give I strength," said Loper, "when we did search the church, not you nor the parson were there."

"We..we..we had left, he to the p..p..parsonage and I to home. The Irishman was at the stocks, when I p..p..passed."

The parish constable puffed out his cheeks.

"Well," he said, "givin' vitals to the rogue, you is guilty of somemut."

Robert ushered the parish constable away from Dowty's doorstep.

"Good day," said Robert.

The overseer for the poor withdrew back inside his house

and closed the door and before Loper could say or do anything, Robert reminded him of Poll's actual words.

"Poll, he did say "one who may be vestry, or their kin,""

"One who may be vestry, or their kin," repeated Loper, slowly.

"Edward, we must think on it," said Robert, turning to walk back up The Street.

"'Aint you forgot somemut'?" said Loper, grabbing Robert by the shoulder, "give I the meat Penny, like we did say."

Robert pushed away the parish constable's arm before drawing out the second cut of ox meat from his coat pocket and handing it over.

"I 'opes it dun't kill thee," said Robert under his breath as he walked away.

In the afternoon Robert prepared another stew which he and Samuel ate before darkness came. Robert pushed his wooden plate away and belched.

"Where were thee when it was vestry and then after, when I was at the alehouse?"

Samuel frowned.

"At the parsonage."

"But the parson, he was at the church, praying for strength," said Robert, "do not lie."

Samuel's eyes darted about.

"I was looking for you father."

"And you did know that I were in the alehouse?"

"Yes. I went to the back door and spoke with Mary Bonner."

"You did, did you? And why did you needs know I be in the alehouse?"

Samuel looked down and Robert reached across the table to lift up his son's chin, forcing him to look his father in the face.

"I was afeared."

"And so you slept in the barn?"

Robert let go of his chin and Samuel nodded.

"Do not lie to me Samuel, drunk or not, I will punish you if you lie to me. Did you see the Irishman?"

"He were in the stocks."

"You went and looked?"

"I went with Mary Bonner. She give him bread."

"God's teeth, he must be the best fed Irishman in Christendom, we dun't 'ave bread boy."

"I saw..someone, they come to the stocks."

"Who did you see?"

Samuel stayed silent.

"Who did you see?" repeated his father.

"I saw...Simon Gigg."

"And did he break the lock?"

"I do not know, I had walked back to The Street with Mary Bonner."

Robert thought about this and after a silence, Samuel spoke again, looking across the table at his father.

"Father, what did happen when you took Dowty's cart?"

"What do you know?" said his father, surprised that Samuel knew about his borrowing Dowty's cart, but then there were many eyes in the parish. Surprise then turned to anger as Robert raised his voice, "and do not turn it about so."

Samuel did not break his gaze and it was Robert who looked away. Robert's anger subsided.

"It was as I did say, the yew, it blocked the ditch, down in Dudge Lane, I could not leave the yew...and you'll talk no more about it boy."

Samuel got up from the table and went out into the yard, taking some hot coals from the fire and in time Robert could smell a bonfire. Robert followed outside and the flames from a fire behind the barn were crackling and glaring brightly in the fading light. Samuel was burning the yew, the finer branches with the leaf still on, making the fire on top of the buried ox's head and innards.

Robert stood with the fire between himself and his son. Robert thought that he could see a likeness to Samuel's mother Bess as Samuel screwed up his face at the closeness of the fire, as he pressed down on the springy yew branches with the singeing wooden pitch fork, to keep the fire raging.

"I will tell you Samuel, when..when I be..able," said Robert across the fire, "and you'll think the less of me."

Robert returned to the house whilst Samuel stayed with the fire, ensuring that all traces of the yew leaf that poisoned the ox had been burnt.

The following morning neither Samuel or Robert felt ill from the ox meat and they hauled the carcass up inside the barn, now more protective of the meat that was not going to kill them, or any other members of the parish. The hay-man had done his job in keeping away the magpies and Robert thought that he would use old Judd Penny in the field, when the green shoots were up. His father finally doing something useful. Robert and Samuel worked again on the strips but they now needed to borrow the ox from the vestry clerk to plough in the accumulated manure on the broad rig. As he worked Robert had also been pondering about Simon Gigg and whether he should inform the parish constable that Samuel had seen him in The Street on the night of the vestry. Robert did not know Simon Gigg but John Jess, the beadle, had said that the overgrown hedge was at his uncle's farm, Gigg's farm. Robert thought again about Poll's words. Simon Gigg would be the son of old man Gigg and therefore John Jess' cousin. They were kin. John Jess must have visited the Gigg's, to tell them what had been discussed at vestry, with Robert's mentioning of their hedge encroaching upon the highway and the prospect of a fine. Had the Irishman been let go as a way to hurt the vestry and did it really matter about one escaped Irishman? Loper was furious as it was a blemish on his standing as parish constable, a failure before the justices and also a cause to be ridiculed by the neighbouring parish constable in Chauncy who was due to receive, detain and escort the Irishman across to the next parish constable. The chain of detention had been broken. Robert decided not to tell Loper about Simon Gigg as it would only make matters worse. Tomorrow was Sunday and he would not mention Gigg's hedge in church either. He would concentrate on the repairs to Top Road, heeding Isaac Button, the parish clerk's, advice and he would hint as much when he went to borrow the ox. It was how things seemed to work in the parish.

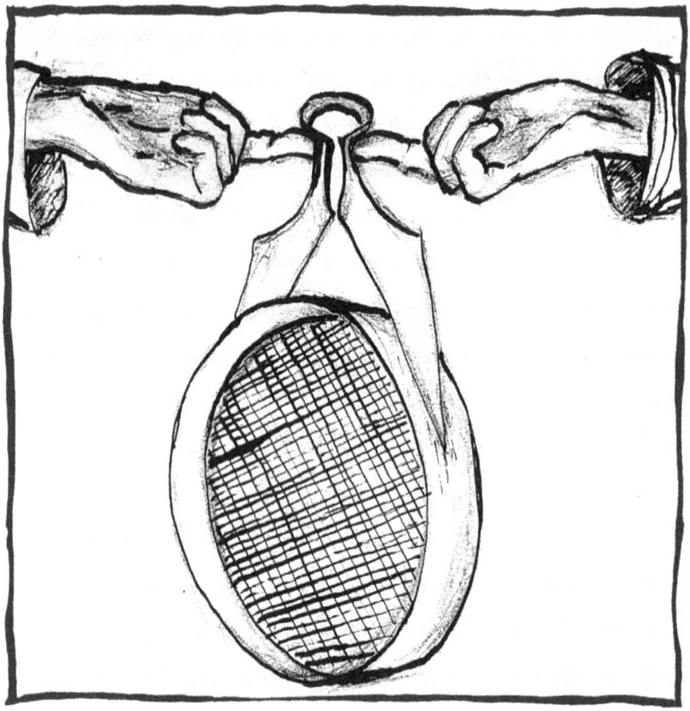

THE PARISH WAYWARDEN

Parson Crouch acquitted himself better from the pulpit and word had got around that he had sought strength through prayer in the church, on the night that the Irishman was let go. Robert addressed the parish after the sermon with the distraction of wondering which was Simon Gigg, of the three brothers in the Gigg family pew. One of the brothers had red hair and had kept his head bowed and Robert also thought that John Jess, the beagle, looked notably ashen faced. Edward Loper was scowling throughout and Robert kept his address brief. The parish knew what was required of them, for every householder, cottager and labourer who was still able to labour, to work six days upon the repairs to the parish highways, as instructed by the parish waywarden. The waywarden's most onerous duty, more so than surveying all the parish highways himself, was to ensure that the parishioners turned out, as and when required, to participate in this unwelcome and thankless activity. The congregation groaned as one when Robert repeated his intention from the previous Sunday that repairs would be made to Top Road, predictably followed by individual protests that none in the parish ever used Top Road anyway. Robert waited for the voices to settle. He had not specified that Long Mound would provide the chalk to fill the hollow on Top Road but said that only spades with metal blades would serve and to bring sturdy buckets also. There were two carts, Dowty's and John Arnold's in Asseley and then there were two wheelbarrows that Robert knew of, Chant's and Hutchins also, the previous waywarden. He could not think of anything else other than the setting of two dates for the end of the week, avoiding the market days in the city and at Wayborough in the next county, which was Samuel's idea. Robert did not mention Gigg's encroaching hedge and he sensed the vestry clerk, Isaac Button, listening intently as Robert concluded his presentation. Robert required the clerk's ox as soon as it was available and tried to catch Isaac Button's eye on his way back to his seat at the rear of the church. More parish business was discussed and then the parish constable climbed the steps to the pulpit to state what everyone already knew, that an Irishman, bound for Ireland, had been released from the parish stocks. Any embarrassment on Loper's part was overshadowed by a barely repressible rage as he scoured the congregation, his white knuckles gripping the dark lip of the pulpit. The parish constable growled that any who knew the name of the one who had broken the lock, then they should declare it now. In that awful silence within the church, Robert wished that he could see the faces of Simon Gigg or John Jess. No-one spoke out and the parish constable returned seething to his pew, whilst Robert and Samuel resisted exchanging glances.

It was the next day that the identity of the person who had broken the lock to set the Irishman free became known. Mary Bonner had confided in her elder brother Will that she had seen Simon Gigg approach the parish stocks. Will Bonner had in turn told the Difford boys and one had then told their father and Jacob Difford wasted no time in relaying this information to the parish constable. By the next morning the red headed Simon Gigg was in the parish stocks and John Jess, the beadle, had a black eye. A temporary padlock, borrowed from the parish chest, had been used to secure the youngest Gigg brother in the stocks and the parish constable had visited each vestry member in turn to state that they should be present when the whipping took place in the afternoon, when the church bell would be rung to summon the parish.

"Well," said Robert, after the parish constable's brief visit, "that din't take long. At least thy name has been kept out of it Samuel. If Loper had known that I did already know about

Simon Gigg and said nothing, t'would be bad for the both of us."

"I shall not go," said Samuel.

"You will come," said Robert.

The church bell tolled on many occasions but this afternoon Robert thought that it sounded mournful as they drew the parishioners from the fields and strips, the dairies and the kitchens and the alehouse, which would close for the duration of the punishment, but open again soon afterwards. It was not raining but the low cloud added to the solemnity of the threaded parish procession from all quarters, to the Green, to the whipping post where the red-haired boy of perhaps sixteen years of age had been moved from the stocks and now awaited his punishment.

For the parish, gathering not in the church but under the grey afternoon sky, this was a break from daily life and toil. Groups talked, whilst a few laughed and joked. The Gigg family stood together, facing the tethered brother whilst the majority crowded around the opposite side of the whipping post, where they could clearly see the act of whipping. The boy's shirt had been removed by the family to prevent the parish constable from ripping it away, as he had done on many occasions before, to both men and women at the post. Parson Crouch stood to one side, his head bowed and hands cupped together but not pointed in prayer. Robert sensed that Samuel wished to stand beside the parson for when Robert took up his position with the vestry members, Samuel twice turned his head towards the parson but Robert kept a hand on his shoulder. Edward Loper stood to the front of the assembled vestry members, with the whip under his arm and the two long and twisted leather cords dangling down behind him. Robert saw that knots had been tied at intervals along the two cords which he thought was no longer practised at public whippings.

Jackdaws noisily circled the church tower across the Green

whilst the collective parish fell silent. With no pronouncement, the parish constable drew back his shoulder, twisting his body before forcefully throwing forward the whip hand, the trailing knotted leather cords suddenly a blur, cutting the air and slapping into white skin. The red-haired boy's tethered body convulsed and he gasped out in pain and Robert watched the unchanging expressions of the Gigg family, as they faced their brother. The first few lashes drew the same jerk and gasp from the boy, red wheals were showing now, especially across the buttocks and the parish constable shrugged off his coat, tossing it to the black-eyed beadle, John Jess. As he got into his work, it was the one wielding the whip who now gasped at each exertion whilst the red-haired boy made little sound, nor barely moved at the whipping post with each blow delivered. Robert looked about at the encircling crowd, those grim faced and those seemingly enjoying the spectacle, justice being delivered but able to take some pleasure in another's suffering. Robert was suddenly startled by a face, set back behind the crowding circle and staring directly at him. It was a girl, a girl with the palest countenance and long black hair. Robert looked away but quickly looked back. He sought her again and swayed slightly to change his view, lest the girl was now obscured behind another. He had been unmoved by the whipping but now felt a surge of excitement but also fear. He looked again for the blackness of her hair but saw only muted shades amongst the crowd. He tried to concentrate on the events before him, with Loper now grunting at each exertion.

"Thar's blood," said a voice from the crowd, drawing murmurs of agreement but quickly drowned out by louder urges for the punishment to continue.

Robert glanced across again to where he had seen the girl, there was now movement amongst the crowd, craning necks, edging ever forward, tightening the circle, but still he could not glimpse her pale face and the blackest of black hair.

"Thar's blood, 'tis enough," said the voice again, prompting more jeering.

It was John Arnold from Asseley who had spoken. Loper paused and then spat before delivering a final brutal flurry, the leather cords wrapping around the sides of the blotchy white and red torso, with blood now beading and running freely but smearing as the retreating knotted leather drew back across the body.

"Now, thar's blood," said the parish constable, as he threw down the whip, bending forward with his hands on his knees, breathing heavily.

At the casting down of the whip, the parson turned and walked away. Robert had been tightly gripping Samuel's shoulder throughout and his son freed himself, to disappear back through the crowd. Robert quickly moved around the disbanding circle, to where he had seen the black-haired girl at the rear of the gathering. Who else would have noticed the girl's presence when everyone's attention would have been on the whipping of Simon Gigg? As others criss-crossed the green, he walked amongst those that had remained, but of the girl there was no sign. Simon Gigg was given strong beer to drink by his family and his wounds were swabbed using water from a leaking bucket, the boy jerking at each touch. Unable to support himself, he was transferred to the stocks by the beadle and two brothers, taking care not to touch his wounds. A blanket was placed across his back, causing him to scream out and so his back was left bare. The back and buttocks that had presented so bony and white before punishment, now blotchy pink, bloody red and criss-crossed by raised wheals. The boy would remain in the stocks until dusk, for all to see. For the next three Sundays, he would serve penance in the church porch, before, during and after divine service and parish business. He would also pay for a new padlock for the stocks and some said that he had got off lightly, as he could have been handed to the justices to be charged as a felon but mercy had been shown by the parish.

Collecting his coat from the grass, where it had been discarded by the beadle, the parish constable gestured for Robert and the other vestry members to join him at the alehouse and Robert nodded but instead he wandered away, passing through the lych gate to look inside the church porch. He did not the follow on behind the other vestry members to the alehouse and returned home, to hack away at the ox carcass and prepare another stew. With the fire lit and the smell of boiling meat filling the house, Samuel came in through the back door. They did not speak until after they had eaten, as the failing light outside drew the room towards darkness.

"I saw her, my sister, Catherine." said Robert, waiting for Samuel's reaction across the table.

"Where? Today?" said Samuel, after a long pause.

"At the back of the crowd, she was as young as when I last saw her," said Robert.

Samuel stared at the dark shape of his father, realising what had been said.

"Then she is dead?"

"She did stare at me, her hair was as black as night, her face so white. Then she were gone."

Robert began to sob and hid his face behind his hands but immediately he was crying without control, gasping for air, snotting and dribbling and then with a sound coming from deep within, from his throat, his chest, his stomach, from his whole body, he lowered his hands, his face contorted, breathlessly imploring but no words came, just the sound that shook his whole body and screamed inside his head. He wanted to say "help me".

Samuel got up from the table and guided his father across to the bed where Robert slumped down and curled up, sniffing loudly. Samuel covered him with the blanket and left the house.

Robert opened his eyes as light flickered in the room, moving shadows and whispers. Samuel's voice and another, an older voice. Robert raised his head and blinked into the candlelight.

"Who is there?" said Robert.

"It is I, the parson..William Crouch."

Robert could not understand why parson Crouch should be in his house.

"Am I to die?" said Robert, rubbing his eyes.

"No, no, do not be afraid..Samuel, he did ask me..to call."

Samuel dripped wax upon the table to stand the candle upright, keeping the shadows in place.

"You brought a candle?"

"Yes, a candle."

"I did see the ghost of my sister Catherine, is that why you've come?"

"I remember Catherine Penny," said the parson, "she was.."

"She was beautiful," said Robert.

"She was kindly," said the parson, "kindly to me, when others were not."

Robert felt exhausted.

"She was here, this very day," said Robert, looking up at the parson from where he lay, "she was on the Green, and then...I looked for her again, where did she go? All the years that have passed, where did she go?"

"Where? Oh dear, I had heard that she..she had met another and they.."

"But she has not grown old, not...gone, she is here still. I saw her with my own eyes."

"She..the apparition, the ghost..did she convey..was she troubled?"

"Is not a ghost always troubled?" said Robert, heaving himself up from the bed to place his feet upon the floor, "she were deathly pale, looking at me, at her brother who was once younger than she."

"May I sit?" said the parson.

"Yes, sit," said Robert, gesturing towards his chair.

The parson lifted up the back of his garment and sat down, making the chair creak and then Samuel sat upon his own stool.

"Samuel is...a most welcome visitor...at the parsonage," said the parson.

"Yes, and I be thankful," said Robert, "we have little here."

"Catherine, she too visited the parsonage, my father and my mother wished for her to enter service there, it was agreed with your father."

"Then...why?"

"Even her clothing was got. She was born on St Catherine's day, the twenty fifth of November, and she was named so."

"Catherine is the blessed saint for our church also?" said Samuel.

"Yes," said the parson, "it was a great loss to my father when Catherine did leave the parish, so suddenly, as ..um..I am sure it was likewise for Mr and Mrs Penny, and to give no word."

Robert had not known that his sister was due to enter

into service at the parsonage. With her position secure, why would she then wish to leave the parish? He had also made no association, or not remembered, about the date of his sister's birth and why she had been named Catherine. Then there was the significance of St Catherine's church that he had known all his life. How could he not remember? Last week he could barely remember his sister's name but today he had seen her ghost upon the Green.

A silence filled the room before the parson spoke again.

"Ghosts are known to visit us sometimes, in our dreams whilst we.."

"No," said Robert firmly, gesturing with his hands, "no, she must never."

"But, perhaps..you have been troubled..of late?" said the parson.

"What has Samuel told you?"

"That you are now the waywarden, that you have much to do here, upon the farm, that has not been kept...these are burdensome matters. I too am finding my way, back here in the parish, the parish of our birth. We have both grown to do what our father's once did."

"I am not my father," said Robert, raising his voice.

"Nor I," said the parson quietly, "nor I, and we shall never become our fathers, but we must find a way, a way to do what is right, by our family, also the parish...and before the ultimate judge, God himself."

"But..but..what of the ghost, what of Catherine?"

"I cannot say. If she should happen, then pray, pray that she might rest peacefully...if indeed she is...Let us pray now."

The three knelt upon Robert's floor and the parson spoke for them all, before God, ending with the Lord's prayer which they spoke together;

Our father which art in heaven,
hallowed be thy name
Thy kingdom come.
Thy will be done,
in earth, as it is in heaven.
Give us this day our daily bread.
And forgive us our debts,
as we forgive our debtors.
And lead us not into temptation,
but deliver us from evil:
For thine is the kingdom, and the power,
and the glory, for ever,

"Amen," said the parson.

"Amen," said Robert and Samuel together.

The parson stayed upon his knees with head bowed and Robert looked at Samuel who also bowed his head. Robert bowed his head but then the parson arose.

"I welcome you...here.." said Robert, climbing from the floor and gesturing to the room, "here, into our home."

"Thank you, Robert," said the parson, nodding in deference, "it is the first occasion that I have visited, members of my flock, in the parish, since I was made parson. I shall visit each and every house in time."

Samuel opened the front door.

"You do not have a wife?" said Robert.

"No," said William Crouch, pausing by the door, "I was to marry, in Oxford, but the one that I was to marry, she died, there was a visitation of the plague, to her parish. Samuel tells me that his mother died and then your second wife died also. You will marry again?"

"I..think..I wish..yes," said Robert, "but I have not.."

"Nor I, it is a subject upon which my brother Augustus is always prompt to remind me. I have many challenges ahead... and many distractions."

"Goodbye sir," said Samuel, closing the front door, after the parson had stooped below the threshold, out into The Street.

Robert lay back down on his bed and Samuel snuffed out the candle.

When Robert opened his eyes, a pale light showed between the front door and the door frame. Looking around the room, the half candle listed on its waxy footing upon the table. He thought about the parson's visit and then about Catherine, on the verge of entering into service at the parsonage. Suddenly he realised that today was the first day for the repair of the deep hole on Top Road, by Long Mound.

"Samuel?" he shouted out, arising hastily, but Samuel was already out in the yard, organising the tools and harnessing the horse.

"I shall fetch Dowty's cart and come back," called out Samuel, as he left the yard.

Robert dressed quickly and picked at some cold meat left in the pot, chewing slowly as he visited the privy. He then splashed water into his face, spitting out gristle as he did so and wiping his mouth. He gulped down the remainder of a flagon of sour small beer and replaced it with water from the well, bunging the top with a rag. This morning it was not raining.

As Robert and Samuel arrived with Dowty's cart at the water filled hollow beside Long Mound they disturbed a flock of lapwing. Robert was silently relieved that there was no impatient gaggle of parishioners, awaiting his direction as this gave them time to make a start. His initial relief was then overtaken by a fear that no one would appear at all and that his first planned work on the highways as waywarden would end in failure and mockery. From the limited tools that they had mustered and brought with them in the back of the cart, they took a spade each and clambered up the eastern end of Long Mound. Samuel gestured towards the sloping downland where two figures were approaching, small under the wide sky. They remained small as they drew nearer.

"It's Chant's and Hutchins' daughter, the younger ones," said Samuel.

Robert was busy trying to make an impression on the heavy bulk of Long Mound. Having scraped away the thin turf he then struck solid chalk with the metal blade. He scraped away more turf and tried again but with the same result. The chalk was displaying all the properties that he had considered when comparing chalk to the shitty land, it was hard, dry, solid and here, on Long Mound, impossible to break into. The two young girls stopped beside the cart and watched as Robert clashed his metal spade against the dense whiteness of the interior of Long Mound.

"Christ's own piss," cursed Robert loudly.

Samuel climbed down the slope and took a bucket from the back of the cart and handed it to the taller of the two girls.

"Here, give the horse water," he said, pointing to the water filled hollow.

The taller girl dipped the wooden bucket in the opaque brown water and put it down before the horse. The horse sucked at it for a moment and then remained with its head over the bucket whilst the taller girl returned to stand beside the other girl.

"It be Mary and Elizabeth?" said Samuel, for his father's benefit.

The two girls nodded whilst Robert chiselled away and cursed the ungiving chalk.

"Father wants 'is boots," said Elizabeth Hutchins, the shorter of the two girls.

"Do he now?" said Robert, stopping his scraping with the spade and looking across at the girls, "well, as he 'aint come himself to ask me, you can tell him.."

"We needs a fold bar," said Samuel, interrupting, "to break into the chalk."

Robert paused.

"We dun't have a fold bar," he said.

A fold bar was an iron spike that could be driven into hard ground so that the pointed foot of the hazel sheep hurdle could be secured upright. The shepherd would have a fold bar but the parish flock was grazing elsewhere on the down.

Robert then saw a straggling line of advancing parishioners appearing over the near horizon, having set off from their various homesteads on the lower ground they were now converging as they drew closer across the down. Even from this distance Robert could see that one third of the new arrivals were children of various ages and there were a number of labourers and cottagers carrying no tools and some other men besides, who he could not yet identify. John Arnold was in advance of the others aboard his cart and arrived first.

"Robert, n' Samuel," he said, looking about him from his seat in the cart, at the water filled hollow and the small area of exposed chalk at the eastern end of Long Mound.

"Mornin' John," said Robert.

"Good morning Mr Arnold," said Samuel.

John Arnold was a farmer and had in the past served on the vestry as parish constable, overseer and waywarden. It was he that had called out at the punishment of Simon Gigg, saying that blood had been drawn and enough was enough. He had whipped many a vagrant and miscreant but had done so fairly, fulfilling a requirement but with no pleasure or personal settlement of dues. He was a good parish man and it did not surprise Robert that he would be present himself today and not send a child as a representative.

"What thee doing here Robert?" he asked, after climbing down slowly from his cart and then limped over to peer at the water filled hollow, "where's thy chalk? where's thy flint?"

Robert lifted up his spade and clattered it on the solid whiteness under his feet.

"Long Mound?" said John Arnold.

"Have you a fold bar?" said Robert.

John Arnold frowned in disapproval.

"But thit's Long Mound, the parish marker, we do stand on thit mound to beat the bounds."

"But it be big John, and we only takes what we do need."

"Who do say that it needs be done? Fillin' in thit hollow on Top Road? Parish dun't use Top Road, you do know that Robert?"

"The Justices say," said Robert, "it's the main way, the way to market in Wayborough, the Justices themselves, they do use it, and folk going long ways, it's in the parish John."

John Arnold frowned again and then looked towards the arriving parishioners.

"Best do it then, but I ain't got no fold bar, Shep do have 'un. Francis'll make up a bar."

Francis Skutt was the blacksmith, and Robert could see that his youngest son James was amongst the new arrivals, now all standing around, muttering and surveying the scene. Robert knew most of them by sight and some by name. Amongst them was Tetty Bonner's husband Mark and Jacob Difford, who Robert had taken a dislike to recently at the alehouse.

THE PARISH WAYWARDEN

"There's the hole to fill and here's the chalk," said Robert, gesturing to the water filled hollow and then jabbing his spade down onto the square of exposed chalk on Long Mound.

"Where's thy beer warden?" said one of the labourers.

"Where be your tools?" said Robert.

This initial knot of amassed labour soon dispersed into smaller groups, some muttering and complaining whilst a group of labourers drifted away to sit at the far end of Long Mound to enjoy a break from their daily toil. Robert continued to battle with the stubborn chalk at the higher eastern end of Long Mound and these few bucketfuls of loose white chalk were then tossed into the hollow to make ghostly swirls in the murky brown water. Samuel suggested dipping the buckets into the hollow to bail out some of the water and the younger children then hauled away these slopping buckets to empty them in all directions. A herd of horned cattle were being driven across the downland from the west by a man and boy and two dogs. The beasts were soon splashing down into the water hollow to stand until they were forced to clamber out again at the far end, making way for the cattle at the rear, being urged on through this narrow gap by the two dogs. Robert was keen that the herd moved on but the drover was content to rest a while whilst the cattle soaked and drank and shit. Once it was established that he was taking the cattle to the coast, passing on down through the parish, John Arnold stated that there was water down at Clay Pond, just over the parish boundary in the Royal Forest to which the drover nodded amiably whilst he shared some food with his boy. The man then lay back on the turf and pulled his hat down over his eyes and was soon snoring gently. A horse-rider approached at a canter, to which all the labourers scampered down from Long Mound to form an addition blockage to the highway.

"Get thee gone you rogues," shouted the horseman, "I

shall not pay you a penny to pass. Get these accursed cows out of my way."

Robert called out that he would be glad for the cattle to pass but the drover was sleeping.

"Then I shall drive the cattle out myself, I shall not wait for a drover to wake and scratch his arse."

The horseman raised his crop whilst blaspheming and making violent noises at the cows, urging his horse onwards. The cattle twisted and turned and blundered from the water, the cattle dogs snapping before them to hold them back but the herd was on the move, the cattle dogs spinning, kicked to the sides by the flurry of splashing hooves. The trumpeting herd bucked onwards, the rider, now free of the water took a wider line out onto the green sward and had soon overtaken the cattle who now slowed to a walk and then stopped to graze, enabling the pursuing drover and his boy to catch up with his herd. One of the dogs had been killed under the hooves of the cattle and the drover returned to make a plea for the cost of his dog, holding up the lifeless shape by the back legs.

"Ask im on the 'orse, not we," said Mark Bonner, "I fancy he were a churchman, 'im with a tongue like the devil."

"Shame he dunt end up in thic shit," said Jacob Difford.

"Thee should've moved on," said John Arnold, to the drover, "to Clay Pond, like we did say."

The drover remonstrated that he always stopped to rest at Long Mound, where the herd would drink.

"Well, we be filling in the hole and thee can take it up with the justices," said Robert.

The drover tossed the dead cattle dog into the water and glowered at the assembled parish highway workers, as his herd drifted on down the grass slopes and away from Top Road.

"Now 'ere do come Shep," said John Arnold, pointing

to the east where the sheep flock drifted closer across the down, a broad, slowly shifting whiteness under lowering cloud.

Robert cursed under his breath and went back to chipping away at Long Mound beside Samuel, leaving John Arnold to talk with the complaining shepherd, who then kept pointing at the water hollow, now a shitty brown where even the massing sheep seemed reluctant to drink. A sudden ruffling breath of cold wind caused Robert and Samuel to turn as one to the south west where a distant shrouding of the hills confirmed the approach of rain. The labourers, themselves alerted by this vanguard of cold wind, hastily descended from the mound, calling out and pointing across to the south west.

"Tes rain snaw, ere warden, tes rain a coom."

The younger children clustered under the two carts as the rain swept in whilst the boys and men turned their backs to the weather, standing as still as the sheep flock, as all beasts do under heavy rain. The shower was hard but the slanting rain told that it would be short lived.

"Look there," said Elizabeth Hutchins, pointing, after she had emerged from beneath the cart.

To the north, a perfectly defined rainbow spanned the horizon but with its termini rising amongst the fields at one end whilst entering the forest at the other.

"I do set my bow in the cloud," called out John Arnold, raising an arm to the sky, "and God said unto Noah, this be a token of the cov'nant."

"Amen," said the men, boys and children as they looked to the north, each with their own unvoiced questions or simple wonder at this perfection in the sky.

The labourers were now reluctant to sit about on the wet ground and began to drift away with the children following on behind until only Mark Bonner, Jacob Difford and John Arnold remained with Robert and Samuel.

"Jes like 'is father when he were warden," said Jacob Difford, loudly to Mark Bonner, "they Penny's do stir it up 'n to no end."

Robert continued to chip away at the chalk

"They'm poor farmers 'n poor wardens both," continued Jacob Difford, "they'm never make good n' young Sam'll go the same, you mark my word."

Robert dropped his spade as he clambered down from Long Mound, to stand before Jacob Difford, staring him directly in the face.

"Now Jacob," said John Arnold, "dun't you.."

"Dun't I what? It was thee John Arnold that wanted to stop the whipping of the Gigg boy, punishment that was due, Loper did it proper, not like thee when thee were constable."

It happened so quickly that neither Robert or Jacob Difford could see it coming. For a moment John Arnold's brow furrowed and his dark eyebrows drew together and then with a blur of a seasoned forearm, Jacob Difford was now flat on the wet ground, his eyes rolling back into his head.

"Loper was cruel, he wunt too far," said John Arnold, "now get up and I'll strike thee agin."

"'E ain't getting up," said Mark Bonner, with a laugh.

John Arnold grabbed a wooden bucket and dipped it into the water hollow, before returning to throw it down into Jacob Difford's face, who then spluttered and coughed himself up into a sitting position.

"Get thee up," said John Arnold, taking off his coat and handing it to Robert.

Jacob Difford scrambled on his hands and knees, out of the reach of John Arnold and then rose unsteadily to his feet, holding his jaw and spitting out fetid water before stumbling

THE PARISH WAYWARDEN 87

and sliding away, passed the grazing horses and the carts and on across the down, back towards the parish.

"Well, tis the best that's happened today," said Robert, handing John Arnold his coat.

"Nay, thic rainbow were God's own work," said John Arnold, massaging the knuckles on his right hand.

Together they looked around at the scene, at the thick brown water in the hollow, at the barely floating cattle dog and the shit slime spread all about the turf, the small exposure of white chalk at the eastern end of Long Mound and the building rain clouds in the south west. Mark Bonner sat with John Arnold aboard his cart whilst Robert and Samuel returned Dowty's cart. They would be borrowing it again in the morning for the second day of highways work.

Before dusk Robert went to see Francis Skutt the blacksmith at his forge in Flower Lane, a short lane off The Street and Robert explained that he needed a pointed iron to break out the chalk from Long Mound, to then fill the hollow. The blacksmith told Robert to come back in the morning and he would get his son James to beat a chisel end onto two iron bars at first light.

"And thy'll need a sled to beat thic iron," said Francis Skutt, "'n praps thee'll all get some work done, plenty of sittin' I hears, up on Top Road."

Robert confessed that he had not realised that the chalk from Long Mound could not be easily won with spades alone but with the right tools, then tomorrow would be a better day and a full day of work.

When Robert arrived home, Samuel had lit a fire and ox meat was being boiled. They ate in silence, in near darkness. Once in bed Robert thought back through the events of the day.

"How can a rainbow be?" he said eventually, but Samuel

was already asleep.

Robert turned over but then remembered the pond, just beyond the parish boundary in the Royal Forest, it now had a name, it was called Clay Pond but he did not wish to stir the bottomless pond and thought instead of Jacob Difford, laying on the shitty wet grass. John Arnold had spared him that trouble.

The next morning there were less parishioners up on Top Road, but with the chisel ended iron bars and a heavy iron hammer that the blacksmith had lent them, a deal more chalk was released from Long Mound. By the end of the day one third of the hollow was chalk filled and a lot of the remaining water had been bailed out by the bucketful. There had been no rain and a number of travellers on horseback had passed through the hollow, initially sinking in the fresh chalk but dragging themselves through without mishap. Robert hoped for dry weather throughout the following week when they would all return for two more days and perhaps the hollow might then be filled and the justices satisfied. The labourers, who had been better employed, now with a substantial amount of chalk to shift, still found time to muster before the arriving travellers to seek largesse. One family, a man and wife and three children, looked on warily at the parish activity from a distance before John Arnold approached them to see what they were about. He reported back that the family were vagrants and had asked the name of the parish and whether they could seek sanctuary in the church porch. John Arnold, well versed in vestry matters, could be seen shaking his head but whether he had given them any small money from his purse, or his bread, Robert could not be certain. The family silently edged around the slippery lip of the water hollow and continued on their way westward.

On Sunday, the whipped boy Simon Gigg was already

standing in the church porch when the parish shuffled through, to take up their pews and positions on the benches. Robert thought that he looked as pale as the old whitewash on the walls of the porch. After divine service and parish business was concluded, when everyone shuffled back out again, Simon Gigg was laying on the floor, by the heavy church door. He was taken back to Gigg's farm in Dowty's cart but early the next morning the church bell tolled and everyone knew it to be the death knell for Simon Gigg.

On Monday evening there was a heavy knock on the door and Robert found William Toseland and the parish constable on his doorstep. Toseland was holding up Edward Loper.

"Penny," said Edward Loper.

"Edward?" said Robert.

"I'll leave 'un 'ere," said Toseland, unhitching his arm from supporting the parish constable and pushing him towards Robert and the open door.

Toseland set off back down The Street whilst Loper belched as he staggered into the room and then clutched the table.

"Whoa, tis dark in 'ere Penny."

Samuel entered through the back door and Loper lifted up his head, looking at the boy.

"Is that thee Samuel?" said Loper.

"Sir," said Samuel, looking across at Robert in the faint light of the dying day.

"What does you want?" said Robert, "we are soon to bed."

"Talk of more..Irishhh.." said the parish constable, belching again, "hidin' in the forest."

"Not in the parish?" said Robert.

"Dunno... but they is comin'. Talk that they is comin' for I, that I did maim the Irishman... afore that Gigg boy did let un go."

"You want the vestry men to look? Who has seen them, who says?"

"Tis Poll, 'ee sees all...dun't go no place, but sees all...'n hears all."

"You've come from Tetty Bonner's?"

Loper was making retching noises, low down, but then pointed at Robert and Samuel, now vague shapes in near darkness.

"Parish...'n you...you all seed... justish...justish done...on the Green," the parish constable then spluttered a short laugh, "'n 'e wun't do it agin, will'un?"

"Samuel, take him home and see he don't fall in a ditch."

Robert helped Samuel manhandle Loper back out into The Street and then left Samuel to support the parish constable's weight as they staggered away. Robert was already in bed, nearing sleep, when Samuel returned, finding his own bed in the dark.

"Father?"

"Uh? What boy?"

"Father, when I walked Mr Loper back, I thought that I heard something."

"All this talk of ghosts," said Robert, sleepily.

"Not a ghost but...in the dark, I did hear whispers ...and quiet steps."

Robert said nothing but now could not easily find his path back to sleep. He thought of a band of Irishmen on the fringes of the Royal Forest, or in the parish, or in The Street.

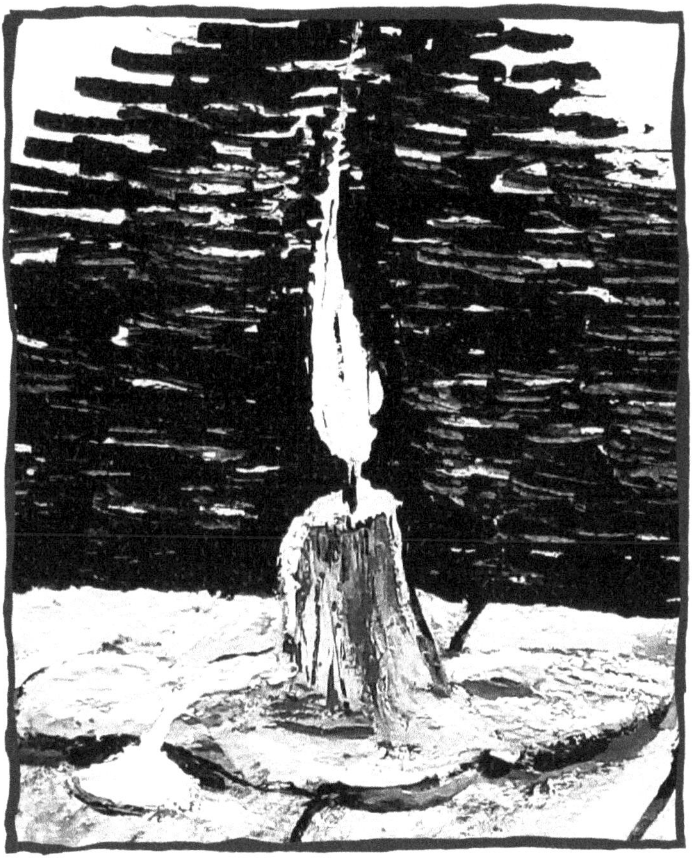

At daybreak Samuel went to bring back the ox for the ploughing of the strips, now that the various collected manures had been spread about. Robert knew that he must now visit Poll and he hacked away some more ox meat, stuffing it into his coat pocket. The chill air clouded before his face as he walked down The Street. The geese were out in Watery Lane, seemingly waiting to hiss at Robert as he approached. Poll's door was open and Robert leant in to knock.

"Robert Penny," said Poll's voice and Robert peered around the open door, into the parlour.

Poll was sitting before his table where a goose egg rolled about on its own, stopping and then moving again, in an arc and wobbling slowly back and forth.

"Eat," said Poll.

Robert took the meat from his pocket and placed it up against the goose egg, preventing any further movement.

"Ox meat," said Poll.

"I'll not eat the egg," said Robert, "who told thee about the Irishmen at the edge of the Forest, coming to the parish, coming for Loper?"

Poll's domed forehead wrinkled as he frowned.

"I hear," he said.

"You hears a lot, but who did say?"

Poll snorted, but not dismissively enough to deter Robert.

"Who have you seen, who has visited?"

Poll reached out and picked up the meat between his thumb and forefinger, dangling it above the worn grain of the table, setting the goose egg in motion once more.

"Who tells all?" said Poll, dropping the meat, "nobody do tell all."

"Was it the Giggs? Their boy has died, they will be

vengeful."

"Dead boy."

"Yes, dead, after the punishment...for which he was deserving."

"Deserving to die?"

"Not to die, no, Loper was severe I grant, but the parish called him on, only one voice spoke against it. I ask thee agin, were it the Giggs, saying about the Irish coming to the parish?"

"Vestry man, now Robert Penny."

"Yes, now a vestry man, who dun't wish for things to grow worse in the parish, a vestry man who do know the smell of shit under his nose."

"Take the egg."

The egg rolled towards the edge of the table.

"I will not," said Robert, they both watched the egg fall to the floor and break open, the yolk and clear fluid seeping together on the dirt.

Robert passed again the hissing geese and walked back to The Street, intending to return home and help Samuel plough the strips but instead, he turned eastwards, away from the church. He was hungry but could not have accepted another of Poll's hard eggs, that had turned out to be a fresh goose egg anyway. Poll was suspicious about the ox meat and there was now a curious understanding, now that Robert was not in the enthral of the cunning man.

As he approached Gigg's farm, he could feel his empty stomach knotting up. A big dog started barking from behind the house, in the back yard and Robert took a deep breath before knocking loudly on the door. A young woman answered with a baby on her hip. Robert had seen her with the rest of the Gigg family at the whipping post, standing and facing their own whilst the rest of the parish clustered to witness the punishment.

"Who is there?" said a man's voice, from inside the house.

"It is I, Robert Penny," Robert called out, "the waywarden."

A tall man, a brother, came to the door as the young woman and baby retreated. His eyes were wide, his mouth small and gathered as if he were about to spit.

"I come to talk," said Robert.

The tall man looked Robert up and down and then peered beyond Robert, as if checking that Robert was on his own.

"What does you want?" he said, eventually.

"You have an overgrown hedge, that blocks the way."

"And you is to fine we, be that it?"

"Well, not if it be cleared."

The tall man shrugged.

"I din't call it out in church, as I should," said Robert, "but I do come, to say it now..and.."

Another brother appeared at the door, not as tall but broader of shoulder.

"..And the punishment to Simon.." Robert tried to continue, knowing that inside the house the corpse of the boy would be laying, awaiting tomorrow's funeral.

"Dun't talk of Simon, dun't say 'is name," said the broader brother.

"It be a just punishment, for a wrong that was done.." said Robert.

"Loper did kill'ee," said the taller brother.

"Edward Loper be the parish constable," said Robert, "it is for he to punish any wrongdoing. He be a vestry man, it is for all the parish that we do act. Thee'll be vestry men both, in time, tis a duty not asked for, nor wanted by any, tis a burden that must be shared."

The two brothers glared but said nothing.

"I did begin this..." continued Robert, "by speaking at vestry, as the waywarden and now it do bring me to your door. When will the hedge be cleared and they roots grubbed out? It is I that must answer to the justices, if it not be done. I will come..I will help.."

"No," said the brothers together.

"We dun't want your help," said the taller brother.

The two brothers were swaying slightly, back and forth, as if they both wished to grab Robert and beat him on their very doorstep.

"I speak for the vestry," said Robert, looking in turn into the faces of both men, "none wished for your brother to die. His is to be prayed for, that he might rest in peace..and the parson, he has spoken of his sorrow."

The two brothers stared at Robert.

"I have to plough," said Robert, turning to leave and then pausing, "and...there be talk of a band of Irishmen, on the edge of the forest and that they may yet come to the parish, but there be no grievance here, for they seek only bread and strong beer. But if they should come, then the men of the parish must gather, so that there might not be trouble or injury. The beadle will come for thee both, if this be so. It is Poll that has told the parish constable of these Irishman and I did speak with Poll this very morning."

He could sense the eyes of the two brothers, watching him until he turned the corner and disappeared behind the encroaching hedge.

Robert did not at first tell Samuel where he had been. He felt strangely relieved. He had acted on his own, hopefully to avert further injury and so that the parish might heal and mend itself. He would not tell Loper either, who would still be intent on seeking out rogue Irishmen. Robert wondered why he had acted to protect him, he who had shown no remorse at the death of Simon Gigg and would always be brutal with his punishment? Edward Loper should not be parish constable and Robert would speak with the parish clerk, once they had finished the ploughing of the strips by the borrowing of the clerk's ox. He also knew that a spiteful Loper could tell of their casting of the young dead woman into the River Blackmere, rather than ensuring a Christian burial. Robert lamented that day when he and the parish constable had become forever shackled by this deed, certainly in the eyes of God, if not yet the parish. Robert had also lied to the Gigg brothers about the parson speaking of his sorrow.

After they had eaten some more of the ox that evening, in the darkness, Robert told Samuel about his visit to Poll's and then to Gigg's farm.

Samuel said nothing, but Robert knew that across the table his son was thinking, even if he could not see his face, the thoughtful, brow knitted face that was perhaps how he would look when he was older, when his childish ways were behind him.

"You think it were the Gigg brothers that I did hear, when I took Mr Loper home?"

Robert nodded in the darkness.

"Yes...and Poll has played his part."

"And done so knowingly?" asked Samuel.

"A cunning man do know more than his neighbour," said Robert, "and that is why he be a cunning man. I may yet end up dead in a ditch, let us hope that it will not be so. But, I have told the brothers that the parson has spoken of his sorrow, at the death of Simon Gigg and I did speak an untruth about

THE PARISH WAYWARDEN

this. The parson never called out at the punishment, as did John Arnold?"

"His eyes, they were closed," said Samuel.

"You have spoken of this?"

"No, I did see his face."

"I must talk with parson Crouch at first light, tomorrow is the funeral. The grave is dug and all grievance must be buried also."

Robert climbed into his creaking bed and after tossing and turning his breathing settled. On the threshold of sleep, he thought he heard, or perhaps dreamt of, a wind that rattled the door.

"T'was the wind, not a ghost," he muttered into his blanket, but Samuel did not respond.

Robert was already awake at the cock's crow, he had slept fully clothed. He stumbled across the parlour to find Hutchins' boots as they were better than his own and then sat in his chair, pushing his foot into a boot that had been shaped by a larger and heavier man than he. Samuel stirred.

"Father, where are you going?" said Samuel, sleepily.

"I must see Crouch, before the funeral."

"But the parson, he will be already out in the parish,"

"How do you know this?" said Robert

Samuel yawned and stretched.

"I did visit the parsonage yesterday. I spoke with the parson, he wishes to do more experiments."

"Yesterday?" Robert paused with one boot on and the other on his lap.

"When he came to us, did not the parson say that he wished to visit each and every house in the parish?" said Samuel.

"Yes...but we spoke last evening...and you did not say

this?"

"I am sorry father, I have remembered, now that it is morning."

"And is he to visit Gigg's farm before the funeral?"

"Yes, he did say, to pray with the family."

Robert studied his son, who looked away.

"Samuel."

"Yes father."

"No matter. Saddle the horse. I shall instead call upon Loper to seek out the rogue Irish. It will keep the parish constable busy in the parish until the funeral is done."

"Si vis pacem, para bellum."

"Samuel."

"Yes father?"

Robert threw a boot across the room at Samuel's head, who easily fended it away.

Robert spent the day in the mounted company of the parish constable and a subdued Jacob Difford, who was still nursing his bruised jaw. Robert took the opportunity to inspect some of the highways in the south west of the parish, although he kept this purpose to himself as he guided the search, suggesting possibilities. With no sign of the rogue Irish, Edward Loper took out his frustrations upon a squatter's family on the edge of the parish, tearing down a flimsy hovel and chasing the occupants away into the Royal Forest. Jacob Difford had no appetite to join the parish constable's eviction and Robert wished that the squatter's house had remained undiscovered but felt sure that the squatters would return and rebuild. For Robert, as waywarden, it had been a fruitful day and in the palling afternoon light, as they passed the church, he could see that Simon Gigg's grave had been filled and there were no persons in the graveyard.

Samuel was not in the house and Robert was staring at the hanging ox carcass in the barn. It had a rotten smell about it and he wished that there was something different to eat.

"Look father," said Samuel, entering the barn, holding up a dead chicken by its legs.

"A chicken?"

"Yes, after the funeral the parson wished to experiment with the moving of blood between two chickens but there is more to learn."

"It is a welcome experiment that brings chicken to our table."

"For the chicken to receive the blood it must be placed lower than the other and there needs be a pump within the joining pipe, to make the blood flow, only a simple pump, a small bag that may be pressed..."

"And the fire needs be lit and the bird plucked?"

"Yes father."

"Boiled chicken with onion," said Robert, rubbing his hands together.

On the Thursday, the parish again sent representatives for the work on Top Road. They were fewer in number but Robert had already realised from the previous work days that more work could be achieved with less parishioners in attendance. He had not kept an account of who had attended or sent representatives but he was heartened that progress had been made and surely the justices would be satisfied, when he attended his first session at the start of the new year. It had not rained since the previous week and Robert was keen to make an early start. He and Samuel were busily heaving out more chalk from the eastern end of Long Mound, using the two iron spikes to good effect, when they struck a depth of large flint nodules. John

Arnold looked on approvingly as these could bolster the infill of the hollow and he lifted out the larger flints individually and placed them on the growing level of chalk, treading them down with his boot. Sparks flew and a strong sulphurous smell came from the flint when it was shattered by the driven irons. A line of boys, girls and men then formed to pass the flints directly from Long Mound to the hollow where they were either thrown or placed in position and trodden down.

A number of travellers, passing in both directions, found their way across the chalk and flint infill, with a commendation from one horseman regarding the work to which he distributed a handful of small coins to the younger members of the parish, much to the grumblings of the labourers.

With nearly a full covering of flint nodules across the hollow, Samuel prised a huge animal skull from amongst the flints within the mound and held it up for all to see.

"'Tes bigger than any ox head I've seen avore," proclaimed John Arnold, as work stopped to observe the giant horned skull.

Mark Bonner took the heavy object from Samuel and lifting it up before his own head, then chased the children around the carts and the grazing horses whilst they screamed for him to stop. The skull was very heavy to hold up and he dropped it in the hollow to add to the fill, before sitting down to catch his breath. Shortly after work had resumed, further bones were uncovered amongst the flint in Long Mound and Samuel pulled out these brittle long bones and laid them together to which were added three large ox feet. More longer bones followed with rounded ball ends and what looked like a dozen broken ribs. Work stopped again to view these oddities.

"Thas a man's bone," said David Crust, a labourer, who had joined in the flint line, "I dug they up with the sexton,

THE PARISH WAYWARDEN

digging father's grave. Leg or arm or summat."

Samuel carried on levering with the iron bar as everyone looked on and the seam of flint gave way to a much darker depth of soft and dampish soil that could be dug with a spade.

"Seed that n'all, that be 'n old grave," said David Crust, "same as in the churchyard."

There was no mistaking the object that Samuel then brought to the surface, the eye sockets filled with the dark, moist soil. There was a drawing of breath and looks were exchanged as Samuel held up a skull.

"Tis a man's grave," said John Arnold.

"Tis a big grave then," said Robert, "and with oxen bones?"

One by one they climbed down from the end slope of Long Mound and stood back to observe the mound, as if for the first time.

"T'wud be a grave for a giant," said Mark Bonner.

"And this end, it be higher," said Samuel.

"They bones should be buried proper, not up 'ere, on the 'ill." said David Crust.

"How old do it be?" said Mark Bonner, after holding up a brittle long bone that crumbled in his hand.

"I ain't never seen beasts and man, all cast in together with no sense." said John Arnold, scratching his head.

There was now a reluctance to resume work with David Crust broadcasting that bad luck would come. They had dug into a man's grave, a man who had been buried alongside a beast.

"Tes the devil's own grave," said the labourer.

"Father wants 'is boots," said Elizabeth Hutchins, the previous waywarden's youngest daughter, pointing at Robert's boots.

Everyone looked at Robert's boots, that were not his

own.

"We cannot leave the hollow unfilled," said Robert, ignoring Elizabeth Hutchins, "one more day and it will be done."

"Perhaps parson Crouch will come to bless the work?" said Samuel, "so that we may finish, in good heart and for it to bring no bad luck?"

There were murmurings of approval at this suggestion.

"Let us leave Long Mound be, 'til it be blessed," said John Arnold.

With the parish elder having spoken, everyone then withdrew, to amble back across the down, with Mark Bonner aboard John Arnold's cart and Robert and Samuel following on behind. Samuel returned Dowty's cart and then went to see the parson.

Robert was downcast at the discovery of the bones and skulls in Long Mound and also the child's demand to return the boots that were much better than his own. He boiled up the chicken carcass from the previous evening, adding an onion and some soaked barley from Mother Goody and in time he and Samuel were sitting down in dusky light to eat bowls of pottage. Parson Crouch had agreed to visit Long Mound in the morning but Robert suspected that there would be less parishioners now that the bones had been discovered, now that there was a reason to stay away. If anyone was to blame for digging into Long Mound in the first place then it was Samuel and he glowered across the table at his son, who was avoiding his father's eye. Robert took off his boots and threw them forcefully towards the front door.

"Shall I take them back to Mr Hutchins?" said Samuel.

"It will keep that child quiet, if nothing else," said Robert, who then mimicked the previous waywarden's youngest daughter, "father wants 'is boots, father wants 'is boots. I should've booted 'er all down the hill."

Samuel picked up the boots and hurriedly left the house. By the time that he returned, his father was in bed, muttering to himself.

At dawn there was a cold wind from the north that whistled between the rafters.

"Light the fire," Robert called out from his bed, "heat the pot. Will the parson come early?"

"He will know when to come," said Samuel, pulling back his blanket, "he looks out of the window and can just see Dowty's yard."

The fire soon crackled and Robert searched for his old boots, swearing as he pulled them on. They ate the steaming pottage in last night's bowls and then Samuel harnessed the horse. Robert thought that his shit in the privy smelled like badger shit and then he put on all the clothes he could find and an old hat, that must have once been his father's but seemed to fit Robert's head.

They were facing the wind as they climbed the down aboard the cart, making slow and cold progress towards Long Mound. Only John Arnold and Mark Bonner had arrived and they were sheltering beside the cart from a forceful north wind as it blew across the narrow ridge. Today John Arnold had a pair of horses before the cart, both eating from their nosebags. The parson arrived on horseback as Robert and Samuel finally reached Top Road and they all held on to their hats as they greeted one another. Samuel then showed the parson the retrieved long bones and the skull and then the ox feet and also the ox skull that was lain amongst the flints in the hollow. The parson delved himself with a spade, into the dark moist soil that existed below the mound of flints, to produce more broken long bones and also a shaped flint, as long and slender as an axe and with a rounded and smoothed cutting edge. This object was passed between them, the familiarity of the shape was recognised by all who had handled and hafted an iron axe, but none could account as to how a piece of flint should appear so. There was also a shard of broken pot, thick and crumbly and covered on one side by simple marks that could have been made by a thumbnail. The parson gathered the three men and the boy to cluster together but his words were blown away so that none could hear. They turned about so that the parson now stood with his back to the wind and then linked arms to hold themselves steady, before the exposed chalk from the mound.

"From what I see, I believe Long Mound to be sepulchral," shouted the parson, "a burial and a place of great antiquity and visible to all, up here on the ridge. Perhaps of a time, even before our churches were raised, down in the valleys."

Robert was impatient that the blessing should be made, so that work could commence and the hollow be filled, he was cold and shuffled uncomfortably in his old boots.

"I shall now make the blessing," the parson's voice straining in the strong wind and he unlinked arms to take from his pockets a glass phial, a small leather bag and a simple wooden cross. Everyone removed their hats, tucking them under their armpits for safe keeping from the wind

He gave the phial and bag to Samuel to hold whilst he turned and raised the cross aloft, towards Long Mound.

"At the bounds to our parish we bless the works to Top Road and banish all that be unholy amongst the soils of Long Mound. Our Father, protect all who did come together and let there be no evil spirits or bad luck that shall persist here. Blessed too are the travellers who pass this place, both night and day, that they might not be troubled," the parson handed the wooden cross to Samuel, exchanging it for the phial and small leather bag, "I hereby bless Long Mound with water and soil, holy water and sacred soil from St Catherine's churchyard."

The parson broke away to climb further the slope at the eastern end of Long Mound and crouching down, so that the soil and water did not get blown away to the side, he emptied both onto the dark soils from whence the bones and skull had emerged. He then took back the cross from Samuel and held it up once more.

"I charge thee our Lord, by the holy and blessed trinity, for any souls disturbed by these works to rest in everlasting peace. Amen."

"Amen," said the gathering, together.

The group dispersed and with no more parishioners appearing, John Arnold stated that he would return to rouse the parish, with the news that a blessing had been made and all should again attend to finish the work. He also said that there had been flints piled beside his strips and last evening he and Mark Bonner had loaded them aboard the cart and these should now be tipped into the hollow before he departed. The cart was brought about by the team of two and the flints were tumbled out by hand, nearly making level the eastern end of the hollow. Mark Bonner accompanied John Arnold back in the cart, so that he might turn any souls from the alehouse, who should be working up on the hill. It was well known that Tetty Bonner would not let her own husband abide in the alehouse during the light of day and so he would take some pleasure in the task. Parson Crouch and Samuel were in discussion about Long Mound and its content and parson Crouch paced out the length of the mound, declaring it to be four perches long. Robert continued to prise out the flints around the dark mound of soil and when the parson and Samuel were distracted elsewhere, he would throw any revealed bones or broken skulls, away into the hollow. He found a pure white flint disc, chipped all around at one end and with a curled underside, he studied it for a moment, drawing the curled underside across his open palm. Fat could be scraped from a fresh hide with such a tool and not cut the animal skin. He cast the circular stone into the fill the hollow. The parson and Samuel were now just below his position, observing the long flanking ditches, that ran along both sides of Long Mound.

"And here is where the spoil for the building of the mound would be won," shouted the parson, across to Samuel who nodded in agreement.

How was it that the parson could interest his son more than he, the boy's own father? Robert could not call his son back to him, back to work beside him whilst the parson was present. He even began to feel jealous at the spark in his son's eye after Samuel had been in the parson's company. He had seen it when Samuel had returned from the parsonage after assisting with the experiments and he could see it here today upon Long Mound. Robert stood up with his back to the wind, looking across the down to see if any were yet coming from the parish, but the near horizon was empty. To the west a horseman approached, a black cloaked figure upon a black horse. Parson Crouch and Samuel had now moved to the far western end of Long Mound as the rider drew closer, stopping just before the hollow. He called out but Robert could not hear above the wind and so Robert climbed down from the excavation to stand beside the rider. The rider pointed ahead of him.

"Wayborough?" he shouted.

"Yes," called back Robert, nodding as he did so to be sure that he was understood.

"I have come far," said the stranger, straining to lean forward so that he could be heard, "from Bath and to Salisbury."

Robert nodded.

"I seek one who is lost," said the stranger, "it is my sister who is lost. She is young and troubled. She has black hair...I say, long black hair. I have sought her this last month and now I go to Wayborough. There is a market there?"

"Tomorrow," shouted Robert.

"Good, and this parish?"

Robert shook his head.

The stranger turned his horse so that he could lean closer to Robert.

"What is the name of the parish?"

The stranger pointed down into the valley, where the squat tower of the church could just be seen above the trees. Robert screwed up his face against the wind and again shook his head, demonstrating that he had not heard. The horseman frowned.

"And the name of the one you look for?" shouted Robert, the wind whistling into his open mouth as he formed the words.

"I seek my sister Alice Brigg...a reward of five guineas..."

The stranger studied Robert's face for a moment before turning away. He then ensured that his sleek black horse stepped carefully through the fill of the hollow and spurred it on, once they were clear of the loose flint and chalk. Robert watched the black figure grow smaller, with his cloak trailing behind him in the wind.

"What did he want?" shouted Samuel, making Robert jump as he did not know that Samuel had come up behind him, to make himself heard.

"Wayborough," said Robert, "he wanted to know of the way to Wayborough."

"Parson Crouch will go now," shouted Samuel.

Robert walked across to thank the parson for coming to

make the blessing.

"And here is the parish come," said the parson, smiling and pointing towards the line of approaching figures and John Arnold aboard his cart.

The parson departed and Samuel returned to prising out more flints with the iron bar whilst Robert stood with his back to the wind, his heart pounding. The stranger's quick, dark eyes, like a jackdaw or a magpie, had pierced his very soul. Robert had not heard all of what was said but he had heard enough to chill him beyond the coldness of the northern wind. He had heard enough to know that the young woman that he had found in the ditch now had a name and her name was Alice Brigg.

John Arnold drew alongside Robert in his cart with Mark Bonner aboard.

"They are come," shouted John Arnold.

"John did bang on doors,'n said thee would fine all that stayed away," called out Mark Bonner who then gestured to the back of the cart, where Mary Bonner clung on to a beer barrel to stop it rolling around, "or p'raps it be the beer."

The parish representatives were soon put to work with spades, shovels, buckets and two wheelbarrows. The loosened chalk and flint from Long Mound was scooped away and trodden down in the hollow that would soon be level ground. After the barrel had been given an inadequate time to settle, it was tapped by Mark Bonner and wooden cups of strong beer were shared and drunk by all and all wished to be busy, to finish the work, as none could sit idle in the cutting wind. The chalk beneath the dark soils within the mound was not so firm and more could now stand upon the sloping eastern end to heave it down to where it could be shovelled and bucketed away. Some sang as they worked and all would gather to jump up and down upon the chalk and flint filling of the hollow. In time John Arnold got the team of two to haul the cart back and forth, riding through and then turning to repeat the pass. The wheels and hooves would sink and these depressions would be filled with fresh chalk. As the daylight faded, the marks left by the passing of the cart grew less and the filled hollow had become raised above the surrounding ground.

John Arnold looked down at Robert from the cart and then called out.

"We are done?"

"Yes," shouted Robert, "we are done. I thank you John, for seeing it done. And the beer?"

"Thirsty work," shouted Mark Bonner and then giving Robert a wink, "Tetty said vestry'll pay."

The parishioners cheered and turned their backs to the wind that now hurried them homewards, leaving a trail of white boot prints across the turf. John Arnold and Mark Bonner followed on behind whilst Samuel and Robert remained, standing on the mass of chalk and flint that had been a deep hollow in the highway and a source of complaint. Long Mound gaped open beside them but the turf would grow, in time, to dullen the deep scar. The perfect shape of Long Mound was now spoiled but there was ample left to mark the bounds of the parish. As he leant back against the wind, Robert told himself that he should be gladdened by the work done but the passing of the stranger had opened up a fear, a fear that he thought lost to the dark flow of the river Blackmere.

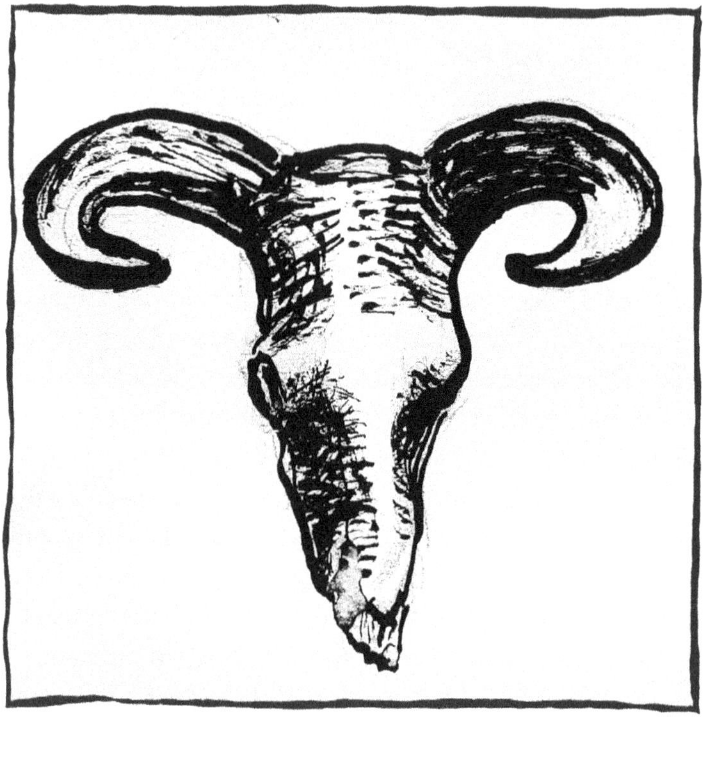

THE PARISH WAYWARDEN

Samuel had asked the parson to help with the writing down of the survey of the highways within the parish, so far undertaken by Robert and also the work completed and any costs incurred. The barrel of strong beer from Tetty's had helped to draw the parishioners up onto cold and windy Top Road to finish the job and Robert would pay for the beer with the money that came from Hutchins' old boots, that Robert now kept in a box left by Mary, his mother. There were two days remaining of parish labour on the highways that Robert had yet to organise. More pressingly there was still much to do and repair on the smallholding that had been long neglected by his father. The roof needed patching and also required new timber joists. The barn was held up by the two ash tree poles that Samuel had wedged under the main beam when the ox was hung up. On the land there had been no crops this year other than the onions and cabbages that Robert had planted, when he and Samuel had first arrived. The strips had been ploughed twice with the various manures now ploughed in. They had an aged horse, twenty or more sheep in the parish flock, a carcass of ox meat, a heap of old damp sheep's wool and no income. There were rates, rent and some tithes to pay, the shepherd must be paid and Robert could not borrow again from his sister Anne. He needed to buy a dairy cow as it would be a hard winter without their own milk, butter and cheese. There was some barley and smutty wheat seed to sow but very little for milling. Over the summer Robert and Samuel had collected a supply of gorse from the common in the south of the parish and a good stack of brushwood that may last the winter. The neighbours and parishioners had been generous to the returning son of Judd Penny, knowing that Robert and Samuel had arrived with little whilst the Penny smallholding had offered little, as it was. Latterly, Isaac Button, the parish clerk, had lent the ox and they would need to borrow it again when the time came before sowing. Mother Goody, their neighbour, had given morsels of food, bread and small beer but she herself was now ailing. He could sell the remaining sheep but they would forfeit their stake in the folding of the strips. Robert was faced with having to find work as well as undertake his own repairs and also survey the remaining highways in the parish. Samuel too, would have to stop his visits to the parsonage and instead go out and earn money. It was back in August after the old parson Nathaniel Crouch had died, when William Crouch had returned from Oxford for the funeral that William and Samuel had first met. It was then that Samuel had shown an interest in assisting with the experiments. This was necessarily after William's elder brother Augustus had returned to London after his father's funeral, for he was opposed to the trifling of his younger brother. Samuel had told Robert that an enraged Augustus had before broken up experiments, saying that they were un-Godly and not befitting of one who was soon to become the parson of the parish. That Samuel was learning Latin by spending time at the parsonage was of little consolation when the household had no money. Things would have to change.

There was also the passing stranger up on the Top Road and what if he were to return, to visit the parish? If the stranger were to approach the parish constable to ask about his sister then Loper may talk, especially with the reward of five guineas at stake. Robert even found himself imagining the weight of five guineas in the hand. Who would believe him that he had not meant to cast the young woman into the river Blackmere and that it was the parish constable's doing, when they should have returned her to the parish for a Christian burial? Worse still, if he confessed to his part played then could he not also be accused of Alice Brigg's murder? It was only his word against that of Edward Loper, the parish constable. Robert wished that he had never been made the

THE PARISH WAYWARDEN

parish waywarden and that he had never sought Loper's help on that first day of surveying the highways. Why after all this, did Robert not let events take their course, when it seemed like the Gigg brothers had made their plan to seek revenge on the parish constable? Robert felt confused about what he should and should not do, but do something he must. Robert had eavesdropped on Loper and Dowty's conversation when Robert had climbed the churchyard yew and Dowty did challenge then the parish constable's zeal at the whipping post, even before Simon Gigg had died after the punishment. Robert would speak with Dowty and see also whether he required any carpentry work on the farm buildings. He had to start somewhere. Amidst all this, there was the sighting of his sister Catherine at the whipping of Simon Gigg. Her ghost had appeared before him, so briefly, but she and the young woman in the ditch had now become one unsettling entanglement in Robert's head, the same pale and deathly face, either stark on the parish green or slipping away in black water. The previous night he had lay in his bed, in the darkness, fearful to close his eyes to sleep but by listening to the steady breathing of Samuel from across the room, sleep did come.

In the morning Robert finally caught up with Henry Dowty, in the open fields. After wincing and sucking air through his pursed mouth, the overseer of the poor took off his hat to scratch his scalp that looked red raw in patches. By these actions Robert knew, when the answer eventually came, that it would be no.

"W..w..well n..n..no," said Henry Dowty.

"I be a better carpenter than my father ever were," said Robert.

"I..I..I..c..c..could not say."

Robert learned that Henry Dowty's son Henry now

undertook the repairs and there were also two labourers employed on the farm who could assist. There were no other suggestions as to how Robert or Samuel could be engaged. Robert thanked Henry Dowty but then asked whether, as a vestry member, the overseer thought that Edward Loper should continue as the parish constable. Dowty looked surprised, his eyes darted from side to side as if he might be overheard in the open field and as he tried to form the words Robert interrupted.

"Is he not too zealous with the whip?" said Robert, using the overseer's own words, that Robert had overheard in the churchyard.

Robert continued, prompting a response

"Did not the Gigg boy die after the punishment?"

"L..L..Loper d..d..do say that the b..b..boy was sick, that it w..w..was n..n..not the..p..p.."

"We all saw," said Robert, impatiently, "the parish saw. Blood had run but Loper kept on and John Arnold did call out."

"B..b..but.."

"And Loper did use knots in the whip."

"Y..y..yes.."

"And we said nought. The vestry said nought."

Dowty's shoulders dropped, his head then bowed. The silence was broken by a large dog barking in the distance.

"S..s..speak t..t..to I..I..Isaac," said Dowty, eventually.

"But.." began Robert.

The overseer of the poor held up his palm to silence Robert and then turned and walked away, changing his direction twice along the baulks between the strips before he settled on a course that took him towards a small copse at the foot of the down.

Isaac Button was inspecting the diggings at the clay and sand pits in wet ground beside Watery Lane, where a new brickworks was to be established. A number of labourers were digging sandy brickearth and clays and making separate heaps, to weather this material in preparation for the brickmaking next spring. Robert had heard that a large new house was to be built in Chauncy by a wealthy merchant from the city who had already bought a large parcel of land from the squire just across the parish boundary, at the far end of Sun Lane. The Button family owned the rough land that would become a brickworks and which would, in time, be a profitable concern. An itinerant brickmaker had been appointed to confirm the suitability of the brickearth and clays and was now engaged to visit monthly to oversee the works and he and the parish clerk were discussing the position of the clamps for the eventual firing of the bricks, when Robert arrived. Robert hung back and waited for the clerk to acknowledge his presence and observed the labourers in the misty rain, sliding and slipping as they cut back into the pits. This was shitty land, as his father would call it, but here it offered yet another opportunity.

"Robert," said the clerk.

"Isaac,"

"What brings you?"

"I wanted to thank thee for the borrowing of the ox. We are now prepared. We have seed already, seed I bought when we came, when I had money, and, when it be time to sow, we shall pray that the harvest will be good."

"Let us pray indeed. I'm best glad that you are making good the holding and the strips, Samuel is a good boy."

"He's a...yes," said Robert, "Isaac, we needs to find work, to buy a cow."

"Ah, but, first there be a vestry matter."

"Oh?" Robert was surprised.

"Tetty's beer," said the parish clerk, "parish is to do their duty on the highways and we dun't spend on strong beer, they be wanting it all times now. No."

"I didn't ask for it, it just...came."

"Well, they was clever, they knew you dun't know better and John do know, he just wanted a drink and that Mark ain't allowed none dayswise, so he's plenty keen."

"But, the barrel, it will be paid for? The work it were done."

"And Shep do complain to I about it, says thee took the water from the down."

"But tis a highway and the justices did say," said Robert, his shoulders dropping.

"Sun Lane," said the parish clerk, after a pause, "it be bad, bad in spots."

Sun Lane ran west from midway along Watery Lane, towards the parish of Chauncy, towards the site of the new large brick house just across the parish boundary. Sun Lane would be the route taken to transport the thousands of new bricks, once they had been made and fired next year. Sun Lane was also the way that Robert had returned to the parish in the spring, from Chauncy. At the time he did not know of his forthcoming responsibility for the highways in the parish of his birth and had paid little attention to its condition.

"I have not yet visited the highways in the west," said Robert, "there be two days of parish work left this month."

The two men stood in silence, observing the muted earth colours of bespattered labourers heaving the soils and clays into large piles, as the rain fell harder.

"I did say about finding work, to buy a cow?" said Robert.

"Well, there be work here, p'raps 'til November?"

"What do it pay?"

"Eightpunce, a day's labour."
"Samuel?"
"Sixpunce."
"And the beer drunk on Top Road?"
"You'll be surveying Sun Lane I 'spect?"
"Well...I will."
"And say in church?"
"Yes."
"You best pay Tetty from the fund...but no more, no more barrels."
"I will see Tetty."
"Then I do bid you good morning Robert," said Isaac Button, as he turned to walk away, back towards his farm beyond the brickearth pit.

Robert suddenly remembered about Loper. Robert was to speak to the clerk about Loper not being the parish constable. What could he say anyway to the clerk about the officers of the vestry? The clerk was at the punishment of Simon Gigg and had raised no objection. A parish constable who vigorously undertook his responsibilities was surely to be welcomed as the same sturdy beggars who had appeared with regularity were now wary of the severe punishment meted out at the whipping post and so stayed away. Vagrant families at the church porch also were soon travelling on their way and not becoming a burden upon the parish. Although Henry Dowty appeared to have been made weary by his duties as the overseer of the poor, the zealous Loper was quick to step in and suppress any charitable hand. Passports issued to vagrants who must then return to the parish of their birth was a burdensome administrative responsibility and one which the vestry had circumvented by swift and brutal punishment, ensuring that the parish was not a place for a vagrant to knowingly return. Why would the parish clerk now wish to disrupt things as they were?

Robert still needed to find work, if he were not to dig clay for eightpence a day. He should return home and begin repairs to the house as he had told Samuel to visit Chant's smallholding in The Street and exchange ox meat for wheat-straw, to enable the roof to be mended and not to leak when it rained. Instead, upon entering Watery Lane, he turned left towards Asseley. He wanted to ask John Arnold whether he needed a carpenter to make repairs at his farm and also why he and Mark Bonner had brought the barrel of beer up to Top Road when John knew that the vestry should not pay. John and Mark had been very helpful but he felt let down that they should have led him on so. The blisters on Robert's feet were raw from his old boots where the hard wrinkled leather had become misshapen and ungiving. He desperately needed some new boots, as did Samuel whose feet had now grown beyond his own boots. The only money Robert had was vestry monies. If he were to survey the remaining highways in the parish and again thrice yearly then he needed boots that he could walk in. Perhaps he should visit the cobbler and purchase new boots and then, when he had some money, pay what he had borrowed, back to the fund. For now, he walked in slow discomfort. Turning down towards Asseley onto Timothy Lane, a large puddle spanned the lane where water and mud had drained from Watery Lane to form in a dip. The only way to pass was to cling to the hedgerow and clamber along the bank but the banks were now oozing mud where many feet had done the same. As he gripped the various small branches of the hedge, Robert lost his footing and one boot slid down into the brown puddle, instantly filling it with water.

Robert cursed as he squelched onward, beyond the puddle. The puddle needed filling and the ditches digging out to ensure that parishioners could pass on foot, without having to struggle around the obstruction that the puddle now presented. There were two days of parish labour remaining and here was a highway that could be repaired for the benefit of the parish and the comings and goings from the hamlet of Asseley.

John Arnold had just returned in his cart from the Common and was unloading furze, tossing them down to his son John who then hauled the prickly bundles to stack them in the barn. John's son worked on the farm and, as the eldest son, he would one day run the farm himself.

They greeted each other and once the cart was empty, younger John, led the horse away to unhitch the cart.

"You have fuel enough for winter Robert?" said John Arnold.

"Perhaps we have enough furze and brushwood. But if it be a hard winter, then we may not," said Robert, "and I have to patch the roof, there is work to be done."

"And it is a blessing that you have Samuel," said John, "but you must look for a wife Robert, 'tis bitter toil without a wife."

There was a moment when the two men fell silent. John Arnold uncertain whether there was business to discuss and Robert, unsure how to begin.

"John, the barrel from Tetty's, up on Top Road..."

"Ah," said John Arnold, with a half smile.

"Isaac has said that the vestry will not pay for strong beer, on parish days. He said that you knew this to be so?"

"Well, it happened to I, when I was first waywarden, it did happen to my father when he was such...and it happened to your father Judd Penny, when he first was waywarden. It do happen to all Robert."

"But I have no money to pay for it," said Robert, not indicating that the parish clerk had consented to it being paid for from highway monies, on the condition that Sun Lane be surveyed and repaired to enable the transportation of many bricks for the new house.

"Well, Isaac knows how it do run, it be the way, 'tis customary for the parish labour to play the new waywarden. 'Tis in the ledger, from years gone by, which he do hold. Now you be the waywarden proper Robert and the parish shall accept thee."

"This lane?" said Robert.

"Timothy Lane?" said John Arnold.

"Yes, Timothy Lane, where it do meet Watery Lane, there be a hollow of water and no passage round, save holding the hedge. There are two days of parish labour for this year and I shall now call for its repair."

"Very well," said John Arnold, "it has been done afore but never stayed done. There are ditches to dig."

"And the hole, it needs to be filled?"

"There is gravel, not a long ways off. Then, let it be so."

They both nodded in agreement, but there was still a question hanging in the air.

"John, I need to work, just for now, to buy a cow. We shall need a dairy cow to get us to the other side of winter."

"Judd Penny din't leave thee much, I grant."

"Have you need of a carpenter, I have the tools and can make repairs? I am a better carpenter than my father?"

"We does our repairs, John and his brother Luke, they both can do this work. Have you asked Peter Thigpen, he do run a bigger farm?"

Robert nodded.

"I shall ask the churchwarden," said Robert, turning to leave, "I thank you John."

"Robert," said John Arnold, pausing to rub his chin, as if unsure whether to speak, "Robert, does thee know why the

Penny pew was lost in church?"

Robert frowned at this question. He had never known why, after his absence from the parish and when he and Samuel had returned, the pew where the Penny family had always sat, for which they once had a key, was no longer an entitlement. The pews had been rearranged since his childhood and now Robert and Samuel sat upon a bench towards the rear of the church. The rain began to fall heavily now and John Arnold indicated that they should enter the barn for cover.

They stood and watched the rain fall from inside the open door of the barn. It was straight rain with no following wind to usher it along.

"Twas after you left for Chauncy, Judd did get to be waywarden and things did start well enough. I were the parish constable..." John Arnold thought for a moment, "yeay, and it were the clerk's brother Matthew Button, God rest his soul, who were the overseer. Judd were more and more at the alehouse and the beadle did have to tip him out, often as not, before church. There'd bin a poor harvest previous, followed on by another poor harvest and we did have but little. Parson Crouch wanted his portion regardless and Judd did stand in church and say that you canst take nothing from nothing. Then the surveys of the highways was not made and the justices did fine Judd at the sessions. Penny's they had no money and so Judd paid his fine with the highways money and then he did pay the landlady at the alehouse the same, till there were no funds. Judd would fine they in the parish that did not look after their highways or did not come to work on the highways and all the parish did know where that money were to go."

John Arnold paused, as if he wished that he had never begun the account of how the Penny family pew was lost and sighed before continuing.

"The clerk did call the vestry together and Judd were asked to show the money. Corse, there were no money and the clerk wished to take it on to the justices. I and the other vestry members did say to the clerk that Judd should be punished in the parish and then pay back the monies, in time. They were poor times for all and Penny's had long been in the parish. It were agreed, Judd were to be put in the stocks but after, some did say that it weren't punishment enough and so it was that Judd were whipped and...I did whip Judd Penny."

"He deserved it, by your telling," said Robert.

"He d'in't deserve what he got," said John Arnold, shaking his head, "it were my first time at the whipping post and I were afeared by what I had to do, to whip a parish man, a man I had knowed all my life. They took I to the alehouse before and gave I strong beer by the jug, said I must do it proper and got I riled up."

"Who was there? Who riled thee?"

"T'was Edward's father, Thomas Loper, he and Christopher Toseland, Toseland did get murdered, not long after, on the way to market. Killed for cheese he were, nobody did know who killed him, Toseland's never did make good cheese neither."

"So, you was drunk and riled, when you took up the whip? Was it knotted?"

John Arnold nodded slowly. The rain outside slowed, as if it would clear but then burst heavily again.

"The parish goaded I, they did want blood Robert, blood that ran. The whip, it was took from my hand."

"Who stopped you? Who took the whip from you?"

"Old Hutchins, he did stop I."

"And my father?"

"He were bad."

"And did the parish get all the highway monies back?"

"Some, not all. Judd did then get...troubled...and would stay in the house. Your mother Mary Penny, God rest her soul, did all she could do, she worked the land, she did weave and sew but still after two year, all the monies did not come. Judd would bark like a dog if he were asked, t'was worthy of pity. The churchwarden, then it were Joseph Thigpen, made changes in the church and pews were moved about to suit. When it came to it there were no Penny pew."

"Who did get the pew, after?"

"T'was the Lopers that did get the pew, Edward's father were the parish constable after I. I was twice more after and were the overseer and waywarden besides. They did say I was to be churchwarden but I never were. The Thigpen's have a mighty hold there, they do run the glebe farm."

"You did whip again? As constable?"

"Never like that day, I did always hold back, nor drink afore punishment."

"That's what Difford did say, up on Top Road, before you lay him on the ground."

"He did say the wrong thing, he din't know what had passed but I ain't ne'er forgot."

Robert wanted to leave but the rain fell heavier still, splashing up the mud from the puddles into a dirty blur.

"Truth be that your father was hurt bad when your sister Catherine did ...go. Parson Crouch were hurt as bad, Catherine were to go into service at the parsonage, your mother wanted her to stay and weave but Judd did agree it without her say so. Catherine was tall and, may God strike me down, she were a good shaped woman Robert, when not yet sixteen, many did say so. Then she did go, London they say, nobody knew who was her sweetheart. She was saintly, saintly to all as if she were an angel. She were allus making marks with chalk, from a young girl and it would get on her face, a white face with black hair and some would say...."

"Say what John?"

"Well, some did say...that she were a witch."

John Arnold walked to the back of the barn and pointed to a large circle drawn in chalk upon a beam above one of the byres.

"Your Catherine did make that mark, to settle the cattle here on the farm and the beasts have allus settled and no horse has been hag-ridden since. She said where it were to go and I did hold the ladder."

"Catherine did that?" said Robert, moving to inspect the mark and he then reached up to touch the bottom of the drawn chalk ring.

"Dun't break the circle Robert," said John Arnold, laying a hand on Robert's shoulder.

"But, if she were a witch, why did old Parson Crouch wish her to enter into service at the parsonage?"

"Robert, there were a light that did come from her, from all about, many did see it."

Robert rubbed his face with both hands.

"I saw her John."

"When were this?"

"At the whipping of Simon Gigg, I did see her."

"She has come back, to the parish?"

"It were her ghost, she were young, perhaps sixteen, John, she never did leave."

John Arnold swayed unsteadily, searching for somewhere to sit and lowered himself down onto an upturned barrel.

"She never did leave?" said John Arnold slowly, repeating the words back to Robert, "she din't go to London and she be...?"

He looked up to study Robert's face, as if he might find an answer amongst the bristles and unsmiling brown eyes, the buckled lines in the skin.

"She must be dead John, a long time's back," said Robert, causing John Arnold to look away, "I had long forgot her, even a month ago I din't remember her name. Parson Crouch did say about her to Samuel first off and then to I. I was a boy, a boy of Samuel's age when she.."

"And her ghost?"

"Only once have I seen her," Robert avoided mentioning the dream, "I saw her there on the Green and I looked for her after but she was gone. I have told Parson Crouch that I see'd her ghost ...to see her ghost John, it do mean that she did die here, in the parish, there can be no other way of it."

An urge now welled up inside Robert, to say about the body of the young woman and how Loper had made it happen that she was cast into the river Blackmere instead of being brought back for a Christian burial.

"I wish to tell thee..." began Robert.

"And I be...struck feign hard by what you do say. Robert, we all do know that some do live and some do die before their good time but...none have I met like your sister Catherine, she did adorn the church, St Catherine's church. Tis now a dark day."

"But how did she pass? How did she come to die?" said Robert.

"I cannot think on that Robert."

Unnoticed, the rain had stopped.

"John, I must return to patch the roof, I shall talk with Peter Thigpen, in time."

John Arnold remained seated upon the barrel and barely acknowledged Robert's departure. As Robert walked homewards, he thought about his elder sister, moving about the parish, her face all covered in chalk and with some saying that she was a witch. The chalk mark inside the barn, drawn by her own hand all those years ago and it was there still to this very day. He then considered John Arnold's words about the losing of the Penny pew and also the whipping of his father, a tale that the parish elder had found difficult in the telling. Both feet were now made wet and squelching through the large puddle in Timothy Lane. He now realised that John's words were a warning to Robert. His father had been in the same situation, with no money other than the parish highway funds, parish monies that his father had then spent. Was the son to repeat the same mistakes as the father or would Robert learn from the lesson dealt to Judd Penny? It would not be John Arnold with the whip but instead Edward Loper and a cheated parish baying for blood.

Samuel had already stacked the long straw in the barn and had now returned with Chant's ladder, leaning it up against the damp and thinning thatch at the back of the house. The grey clouds had cleared and the old shaggy wet roof now steamed in the late morning sun.

"I have cut spars also," said Samuel.

At the foot of the ladder there was a pile of freshly split and pointed strips of hazel. The curls of white hazel trimmings lay scattered all about the yard.

"Catherine, she did make signs with chalk, in the parish," said Robert, "I have seen one, in John Arnold's barn. John said that she was like an angel and a light shone about her. I knew none of these things...about my own sister."

"We have a chalk mark in our own barn father."

"Show me."

Robert followed Samuel into the barn and looked to where his son was pointing.

"I saw it when I did wedge the ash poles, before Katy did drag the ox up and over."

A small chalk circle had been drawn on the far side of one of the thicker cross beams. The circle was incomplete, with a smudged interruption at the base.

"The circle, it is broken, a finger has touched it," said Robert, "t'was you?"

Samuel frowned.

"Then you must make it full again, once we have mended the roof."

"Mr Chant says that the straw should have been put on in the summer, when the roof be dry."

"How much ox did you give? For the straw and his good advice."

"Enough, it now be maggoty, in part."

"Tomorrow we do portion it, some to sell."

Together they dragged the straw from the barn and yealmed it into bundles, the sharpened harvester's scythe cut forming the flat base of the wheat straw at one end with the empty ears curling over at the top of the bunches. Robert climbed the ladder with an armful of hazel spars whilst Samuel clamped a number of bunches of long straw under one arm and followed up the ladder. The existing thatch was thin and mossy and Robert now covered this over with blocks of the new straw bundles, pulled tight together, twisting in the spars to pin it all down. There were areas at the front of the cottage that required the same covering and the light was failing as the last bundles of long straw were secured. Samuel took the ladder back to Chant's and Robert peered at the meat carcass in the half light, disturbing two rats that clambered up the rope and scurried away along the beam. He tried to avoid the maggots as he cut enough decent meat for a stew. When Samuel returned, he gathered hazel shavings and loose straw from the floor of the yard with which to start the fire and then collected hot coals from Mother Goody. He returned with a shovelful of embers and told his father that Mother Goody was still ailing.

"We will give her some stew, cut some more meat," said Robert.

Once the stew was cooked, Samuel took a bowlful around to Mother Goody before he and his father then sat down to eat in near darkness.

"It be good that the roof is repaired," said Robert, pushing away his wooden bowl, "knowing that the rain will not drown you in your bed, or to have the snow falling through. Perhaps now my mother's weaving room can be used also, where the rain did rot her loom?"

"Yes father," said Samuel

"Samuel?"

"Yes father?"

"You begin work at Isaac Button's brickworks after Sunday, digging clay, for a good month, so that we may save for a dairy cow. I will buy you boots from Joseph Creeper, the shoemaker. He will take ox meat."

Robert could not see the expression on Samuel's face across the table and his son remained silent.

Once they had gone to bed, the rain and wind had gathered force with doors rattling and rain thrashing at the windows. Robert pulled his blanket tighter around himself, again thankful that the roof would no longer leak.

He awoke with a severe griping in his guts, his knees buckled up to his stomach.

"Samuel," said Robert, and then louder, "Samuel?"

Robert got up quickly, staggering bent double out into the back yard, where he puked violently.

"Samuel," he spluttered, between wretches.

The wind and rain had died down from the night before and through a gap in the clouds, a half moon illuminated the yard. Robert could see the pool of lumpy vomit before him, its wetness shinning in green luminescence.

"Father."

Robert could hear Samuel's weak voice close by.

"Samuel?"

Robert wretched again.

"I am here father, in the privy, the meat, it is bad, I have puked but I'm shitting water."

"Get out, I need to shit."

Robert could not move from his crouched position on the floor of the yard and could feel his bowels flow.

Neither spoke and a cloud passed before the moon. Robert toppled over to lie on his side, alternately puking and shitting. The crowing of the cockerel made Robert open his eyes but still he could not move. Samuel was first to his feet.

"Father... you will die of cold."

Robert groaned.

"I wish to die."

"Come," said Samuel, heaving his father's arm towards the back door and once inside he stripped him of his breeches and pulled the blanket from the bed to place over him, "I will boil some water."

Robert could hear Samuel's slow shuffled movements. The cold fire could not be rekindled.

"I have to go to Mother Goody's," said Samuel quietly.

Robert did not move. It seemed a long while before Samuel returned with a glowing shovel.

"Chant's have lit their fire, Mother Goody's fire is cold, I think she may be dead."

"We have killed her," said Robert, in a whisper, "I have told Mr Chant not to eat the meat."

The fire soon crackled and in time the water could be heard to swell in the pan.

"Can you stand?" said Samuel.

"I cannot ...I will...help me."

Once he was upright, Samuel pulled him to the back door and dowsed him with warm water, rubbing his father all over with a cloth, wringing and rinsing it out with cold water as his father shivered.

"Come," said Samuel, guiding his father back indoors where he collapsed upon the bed.

Samuel took the blanket from his own bed to cover him.

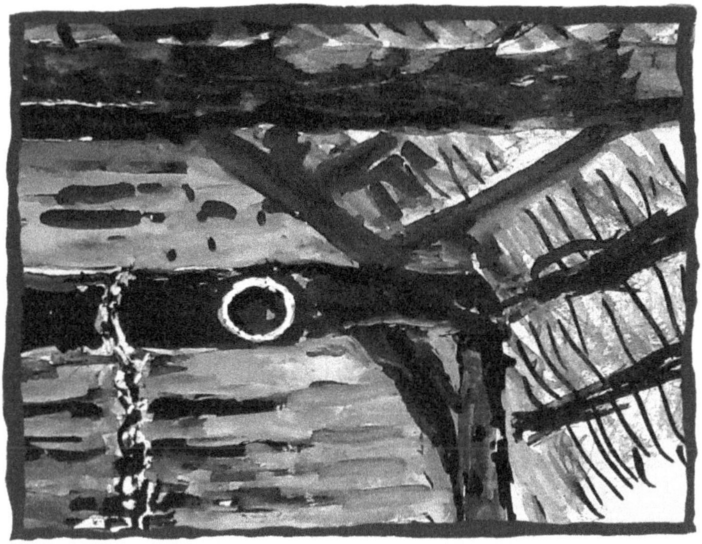

The sun was blazing through the gap under the front door when Robert opened his eyes and he quickly closed them again at this assault of blinding light. He could not open his mouth where his lips had become sealed together in their dryness. He tried to call out but made only a low moaning sound. He raised his head slowly, opening his eyes again, only slightly, to peer around the room at the blurred brightness. His head dropped back down and he slept again, awoken by the opening of the front door.

"Father?"

Robert groaned.

"Drink water," said Samuel, gently lifting his father's head to present a cup to his mouth and then dipping his fingers into the water to wet his father's lips, "drink father."

Robert drank and dribbled water and then demanded more until his head dropped back down.

"Mother Goody is not dead," said Samuel, "she did not eat the meat, the bowl was left cold, she is about and her fire is lit."

Robert tried to remember what had happened.

"The meat?" he whispered, "it is all bad?"

Samuel nodded.

"I cannot lay here," said Robert, "how long...?"

"Two days, today it is Friday."

"Give me water."

Robert could now move his tongue, raking it across his cracked lips. Very slowly he arose, pulling the blanket around him and at first cradling his head before standing unsteadily and then shuffling towards his chair to sit down.

"Can you eat," said Samuel, "there is pottage, there are eggs, bread and cheese and milk. There is honey also."

"How?"

"Parson Crouch has given food."

Robert drank some milk from a bowl and then tore up bread and dipped it into the milk, chewing slowly.

"I should have sold the meat," said Robert, after draining the milk from the bowl, "it be not cold enough in the barn, to keep from going bad and now...we do have nothing."

He dipped his finger into the small bowl of honey and placed the slow dripping blob into his mouth, sucking and licking his finger, savouring the rich sweetness.

Samuel brought his father's clothes and Robert turned his head away.

"I cannot wear those."

"I have scrubbed them. I have borrowed scissors also, from the parson."

Samuel trimmed his father's whiskers and hair whilst Robert sat motionless, his son brushing away the cut clumps to the floor. Samuel then helped his father to get dressed. After standing for a moment in the middle of the room, Robert hunted for his boots and then heaved himself upright to wander out into the yard, which had been swept clean since he had lain there. Entering the barn, he could now smell the meat which made his stomach turn and he covered his mouth and nose with his hand. He left the barn and walked slowly into the sunshine to where the horse was feeding from a pile of fresh hay. Robert stood with his hand upon the lowered neck of the beast and began to stroke it gently.

"Old Katy," he said, "look at the day."

The horse lifted its head and stood still as Robert continued to rub its neck. Robert turned around to face the sun and leant against the shoulder of the horse, the horse adjusting its stance, leaning in slightly to offer firm support.

"Well, Katy, how are we to live? I am a fool not a farmer

nor even a true carpenter, I have no trade, sometimes I be a cooper and do know how to make a barrel. I do empty a barrel well enough. I have poisoned our ox and the meat did rot in the barn. I have no wife, two have I already lost. There is Samuel and all do say he be a good boy but he do wish he were the parson's son."

The horse dipped its head again to eat, forcing Robert to stand, with no support. Robert turned to observe the horse, realising something for the first time.

"Katy? Judd did name you after my sister? Her ghost is on the Green, she is there in the chalk marks within the barns… and…you be Catherine also."

"Father?" Samuel called from the back door.

Robert shuffled slowly back through the yard.

"Mary Bonner has been to say that the barrel of strong beer must be paid for," said Samuel, "she is now gone."

"Yes," said Robert, "I had meant to. I will go, but not to drink. Take down the ox, drag it out into the field where I cannot smell it and let the rooks and the rats feast on it. Then make good the chalk mark on the beam, before we be visited by more ill fortune. I do not blame you Samuel."

Robert took enough money from his mother's box to pay for the barrel and left the house by the front door. He felt unsteady on his feet, thankful that the way to the alehouse was downhill. He passed Chant's door, hoping not to be seen as the long straw would now have to be paid for, with the rotten meat of no value. He entered the alehouse and peered around the dark interior, his eyes not yet adjusted from the brightness out in The Street. There was a figure seated on a bench to one side and Tetty Bonner looked out from the inner parlour, having heard the latch on the door.

"Ah," said Tetty.

"Mary has been, I come to pay for the barrel," said

Robert, releasing the coins from his hand onto the nearest table, "how much?"

"Thee didn't know about the waywarden's barrel then?" said Tetty, with a smile.

"No, but John Arnold has said. It was welcome, t'was bitter cold up on Top Road, filling the hollow."

"We did tap it to a fresh barrel, to keep it clear," said Tetty, pushing around the coins on the table until the correct amount was taken, "there, tis two shillin' 'n six pence. You'll have a drop?"

"I have no money, this be highways money."

"Here, have a splash," said Tetty, returning from the inner parlour with a small wooden tankard, "'un dun't tell Mark that I gave thee beer."

Robert was not sure that he had the stomach for beer and took small sips.

"Still no wife?" said Tetty, standing back to look Robert up and down, "Robert Penny, waywarden."

Robert shook his head. He was not sure that he could drink the beer which tasted very sour, the slops Robert thought.

"Tetty, does thee need new barrels?" said Robert, "I can make barrels, I need work."

"Well, p'raps we shall, have you the tools?"

"I have most what I need, I should have to get oak from Stimey and the iron hoops from Francis Skutt, I can fit them myself."

"Old Will Feather did make our barrels, even though he were near blind but now his fingers is all gnarly. He were the only one in the parish to make a good wet barrel and all our barrels be getting old now. Make we a firkin, Robert Penny and if it dun't leak then, we'll see."

Robert nodded in agreement as he tried to finish his beer.

"I will," he said.

"Robert Penny, waywarden," said the voice of a man, approaching from the shadows, "pray excuse me for I have listened to your talk. We have met, upon the way that you call Top Road."

Robert looked at the man as he drew nearer. It was the eyes that he recognised, quick, dark eyes, like a magpie.

"Landlady, ale for the waywarden," said the man who was the brother of Alice Brigg, "come, sit Mr Penny."

"I..I have things that I must attend to," said Robert, quickly, his mind racing.

Tetty placed a full tankard on the table as the stranger gestured for Robert to sit. Robert's tender stomach was already churning from drinking the sour slops and the sudden appearance of the stranger in the alehouse caused the bile to rise in his throat. Robert blinked and gulped to prevent himself from retching.

"I grant that the wind was harsh, when we spoke up on Top Road, as you call it," said the stranger quietly, seating himself across the table from Robert.

"I could not hear," said Robert, "the wind, it was harsh, as you say. I have not seen your sister sir."

"Then you heard that much of what was said? She does need me to find her for she is troubled and I fear for her. You say you have no money?"

The stranger produced a large silver coin and glancing towards the parlour, to ensure that they were not being overlooked by the landlady, he then pushed the coin across the table towards Robert.

"You will help me to find her Mr Penny? What is the name of the parish constable, for he should know of any comings and goings, the overseer also?"

Robert blinked.

THE PARISH WAYWARDEN

"Yes, speak with Henry Dowty, he be the overseer," said Robert.

"And the parish constable?"

"He is...not to be...he is..."

The alehouse door rattled open and Edward Loper strode in, slamming the door shut behind him.

"Ah, Penny," said the parish constable.

The stranger cupped his hand over the coin on the table and drew it back towards himself.

"Here is ...the parish constable," said Robert, looking down at the table and then taking up the tankard to sip the beer.

"And you'm be the stranger on the black horse?" said Edward Loper.

"Yes, I seek one who is lost."

"And you'm be passing on?"

"Join us," said the stranger, gesturing to a place on the bench beside Robert, "landlady, a tankard for the parish constable."

"I'll drink if you're payin'" said Edward Loper, with a broad smile, squeezing up against Robert on the bench, "'n your name sir?"

"My name? My name it is Jonathon Brigg, I am from Bath and I seek my sister Alice Brigg."

"I said to John Jess," said Edward Loper, nudging Robert, "'ee wun't be no sturdy beggar, not with a fine 'orse. This sister of you'rn, what do she look like? We do send them that's vagrants on their way 'n dun't care where to, in the main."

"My sister is no vagrant sir," said Jonathon Brigg, drawing himself up straight in his chair, "she is of good family, as am I, she is troubled is all."

"This beer do taste good but we dun't know no more than that," said the parish constable, smiling, "'tis Sunday tomorrow and p'raps thee'll see in church that there ain't nobody of that name here in the parish."

"I intend to sir, I shall find a bed. You did ask of my sister and how she looked?"

"D'es she 'ave one leg or a gurt nose?"

"She is beautiful, she is pale of skin and her black hair it is long, amongst the crones in the parish you would see her well enough."

The parish constable scratched his head under his hat and then gave Robert a sideways glance.

"Robert, did we ever see one, as he do say?"

"There is a reward of five guineas, for when she is found," said Jonathon Brigg.

Edward Loper spluttered into his beer.

"Five guineas you say? Robert, five guineas be a handsome sum?"

"But... we do not know of her Edward," said Robert, trying to remain calm, "come to our church tomorrow, as the parish constable do say and you shall see for yourself."

"I must be gone," said Edward Loper, finishing his beer, "and I shall see thee in church sir, n' p'raps we shall talk again?"

"Yes," said Jonathon Brigg, "we shall talk again."

The parish constable purposefully trod on Robert's foot as he rose to leave and Robert stifled a yelp of pain from this aggravation to the blisters on his toes.

After ensuring that Loper had departed, Robert then finished his own beer and rose to leave.

"The overseer?" said Jonathon Brigg, "I must speak with him, Mr Dowty? My sister may have been mistaken for one who is of no abode. Will you help me in my search Mr Penny?"

The coin was slid back across the table and left in front of Robert.

Robert was glad to leave the alehouse, glad for once that he should have to drink no more beer. He felt weak and his stomach was churning. He wanted to return home to eat the eggs that Samuel had brought from the parsonage. They walked to Dowty's farm but Henry Dowty's wife only shrugged when they asked of his whereabouts and then closed the door. Before going out onto the strips, Robert said that they would visit the church where the overseer may be at prayer or if there were beggars then he might be found in the church porch, undertaking his vestry duties.

Jonathon Brigg halted on their approach to the church.

"See there," said Jonathon Brigg, pointing to the roof at the eastern end of the building, "the cross upon the church be broken."

Robert squinted at the apex of the chancel roof. There was a small stone cross but one of the two cross bars had been broken off. Robert had not noticed this before and gave the man a blank look.

"And you, a man of the parish Mr Penny?" said Jonathon Brigg, shaking his head, "the shepherd on the downs did know the name of your church and he spoke of the broken cross, perhaps he is the more Godly man, or just the more watchful?"

On passing through the lych gate, they could hear sounds coming from the church porch, a woman's voice and as they passed the churchyard yew, the unmistakable, laboured speech of the overseer of the poor.

"W..w..w.."

"I do not know what you are about sir? Please, my daughter is afeared."

"W..w..w.."

"Sir, do not come near."

"W..w..d..d..?"

With the appearance of Robert and Jonathon Brigg, the overseer stepped back out of the porch whilst a woman and her daughter clutched each other against the closed door of the church.

"I do not know what he says," said the woman.

"Henry," said Robert, acknowledging the overseer.

Henry Dowty rubbed his forehead and shook his head in frustration.

"Do not be afeared," said Robert to the woman, "Mr Dowty is a good man but his words are not made so easily. Where are you bound?"

"We are...not bound, we have no place."

The woman choked back her tears whilst comforting her daughter, who was younger than Samuel's age.

Henry Dowty, waved his arm at the woman and then pointed towards the downs and beyond to the Top Road.

"He is the overseer," said Robert, "he shows that there is nothing for you here. You must leave the parish. Where is it that you were born?"

"But...we have nothing there...the parish did cast us out."

"And it be the same here. The parish constable, he will not spare the whip. You must not stay."

Jonathon Brigg leant against the outer wall of the porch, looking away as if the activities within the porch were a tiresome delay to his own business.

"Am I to understand that you are near mute sir?" said the stranger, directing his question at Henry Dowty, who all the while was slowly backing away from the scene in the church porch, "sir, will you not settle? I have need to ask, you have news of my sister?"

The overseer stopped his backwards motion and shook

his head.

"You shake your head but I have not yet told you of her. Over the last weeks or indeed a month, she has been lost to me. I have sought her in many places, perhaps you have encountered her, here in this very porch?"

"B..b..b.."

"She is troubled, some would say forespoken and did say things strange. I fear for her and she did leave the city of Bath, to walk the highways, she would have little money about her person, perhaps none by the time that she came to this place. She is beautiful, she had fine clothes but none would appear fine after such a journey."

The woman and the girl talked quietly together in the porch, the mother stroking her daughter's hair.

Robert's hollow stomach gripped tighter as Jonathon Brigg, continued to describe his sister and her plight. It was only Robert, and of course the parish constable, that knew of her demise and yet he could say nothing.

"She has long black hair Mr Dowty, clothes that were once fine and long black hair?"

"Henry, do you know of such a woman," said Robert, "here in the parish, or one who has moved on?"

The overseer began to back further away, his eyes darting, his mouth opening and closing in silence.

"Come on man, speak," said Jonathon Brigg, advancing towards Henry Dowty, as if he were to cuff his head, "say whether you know of her."

Robert moved quickly to stand before the overseer.

"Do not make to strike him sir," said Robert, "he be a vestry man, as am I. His words, they do not come, he cannot say. Henry, will you nod if you have word of Alice Brigg, for that is her name?"

Henry Dowty shook his head vigorously before scurrying away, encircling the church to reach the lych gate rather than pass close to Jonathon Brigg.

Jonathon Brigg let out a long sigh, taking off his hat and looking about him, displaying the weariness of his quest in seeking his sister throughout these last weeks. It gave Robert an opportunity to study the stranger who he had first seen briefly in strong winds up on the ridge and then across the table in the dim light of the alehouse. He had a blockish head and a square face, quite unlike the heart shaped face of his sister and in the sunlight his hair carried a reddish hue. Robert felt a coldness to the man before him, a dislike in his manner, in the way that he had reared at Henry Dowty.

"I am not done," said Jonathon Brigg, replacing his hat and turning back to face Robert, his black eyes pierced like a magpie at too close quarter, "and I shall stay as long as it takes until my sister is found and do not forget our bond Mr Penny. There is a bed for me at the tailor's house and you shall find me there. Tomorrow, I shall attend divine service and pray amongst you all in this miserable parish, that my sister is safe and that we shall soon be reunited."

"You can pray all you like," muttered Robert, under his breath, as Jonathon Brigg strode away towards the lych gate.

"Sir, what are we to do? My daughter has poison in her foot and cannot walk more."

The vagrant woman was reluctant to emerge into the sunlight, from the fragile sanctuary of the church porch. Robert felt weak, consumed by his own hunger.

"I do not know," he said, not wanting the burden of another's hardship but he found that he was unable to turn and walk away.

"Come," said Robert, eventually, and then with some

urgency, encouraging the mother and daughter to follow him, "come as quickly as you are able."

Robert hoped not to encounter the parish constable in the alehouse, as he peered inside. There were three drinkers upon a bench but none paid them any attention as they argued amongst themselves.

"Come," he said, gesturing for the couple to sit down upon the bench just inside the door that he had vacated earlier, "sit."

Robert sought out Tetty Bonner, calling softly until she appeared in the inner parlour.

"Robert? Back again?"

The landlady, sensing something other than a request for beer, then looked out into the room to see the mother and daughter huddled together on the bench.

"Feed they, give they something and then get them gone out of the parish," said Robert, "here be a coin."

"Vestry money?" said Tetty with a frown, "or you bin sellin' barrels already?"

"No, not barrels, nor vestry money neither, but 'tis money that I have not fairly earned, I grant."

"I dun't want to know Robert Penny," said Tetty, taking the coin, "but they canst stay here longer than it takes I to feed 'em."

"And don't let Loper know, Dowty has seen them in the porch."

"Dowty's 'ad 'is go then?," said Tetty Bonner, and then under her breath, "lucky for they it weren't the night."

Robert left the alehouse as Tetty ushered the couple to sit out of sight around the corner, in the inner parlour. Robert then struggled back up The Street, hoping that Samuel could cook the eggs whilst he lay on his bed.

"Samuel?" Robert called out, as he entered the house, but there was no answer. His voice had sounded weak, like somebody else's voice and he sat down in his chair, trying to summon the strength to gather hot coals and then cook the eggs himself. Instead, he broke away a piece of hard bread, chewing it slowly, his eyelids growing heavy.

"Father?" said Samuel, entering through the back door.

Robert drew himself upright in his chair to blink at his son.

"Uh," said Robert, the bread he had placed in his mouth was now stuck to the roof of his mouth and he tried to prise it away with a dry tongue

"There is a man who seeks a sister that is lost," said Samuel, "Mary Bonner has told me."

"How should I know of her?" muttered Robert.

"He gave you a coin with which you have fed two beggars, father, we have no money ourselves."

"You know too much boy," said Robert trying to wake up to confront his son, "what should I do, leave them to Loper? They must go on their way, but they were starved."

Samuel sat down on his stool on the opposite side of the table and stared at his father.

"You have seen the stranger?" said Robert.

"Yes."

"I do not believe that he is the brother of the one he seeks," said Robert.

Samuel frowned, whilst Robert battled to think about what he could admit to, before his son.

"He, he...said that she is of good family, as was he. He said this to me ...but as brother and sister, would you not say... we be of good family both? I...I... do not know, I...I...and he said that her hair was long and black and that she was beautiful, yet he has a head like a block of wood and his hair, it be red in the sun. Samuel, I am weary...and hungry, do not say more."

Samuel got up and taking the small shovel from beside the fire, he left the house to return with hot coals.

"And the meat?" said Robert, as the fire crackled.

"It is gone from the barn. Katy did drag it to the elms," said Samuel, stirring the pottage and then cracking two eggs into the steaming pot, "and I made good the chalk circle, in the barn. Chant's did not eat their meat, so we do owe for the long straw."

They ate in silence.

Robert's stomach had begun to settle, now that he had eaten a good meal.

"Today we eat like kings." said Robert, after belching loudly, "no matter what tomorrow shall bring. So, have you no Latin for me?"

Samuel shook his head.

"He will be at divine service tomorrow?" said Samuel, after a long pause.

"Who?"

"The stranger?"

"He said so."

"What is his name."

"His name is Jonathon Brigg, it is the name he do give. His sister's name was Alice Brigg."

"She is dead?"

"Why do you say so?"

"You said her name was Alice Brigg, as if she were dead."

"I do not know whether she lives or not, or...or... whether she be even in the parish or...has passed this way...but he will not leave without news of her. I do not like he. Why do you speak of him?"

Samuel shrugged.

"Father, I wish to go to the parsonage?"

"You dun't always ask? Go, but will not parson Crouch be busy at his sermon?"

Samuel shook his head.

"He looks at bees, with his microscope, until it grows dark. He thinks the largest bee a queen and not a king."

Robert opened his mouth to speak but then closed it again.

It was near to darkness when there was a faint knock on the front door. Samuel had not yet returned from the parsonage and Robert was sitting in his chair, thinking about the stranger, Jonathon Brigg.

Robert opened the door and Tetty's daughter, Mary Bonner, having knocked upon the door, then backed away.

"What are you about?" said Robert, squinting into the darkness.

Two figures emerged, to stand upon the threshold, it was the mother and daughter from the church porch. Mary Bonner now retreated, to hurry back down The Street.

"Why are you here?" said Robert, "why have you not gone from the parish?"

"My daughter cannot walk sir, her foot is poisoned, she do need a potion."

"I know nothing of such things," said Robert.

"The landlady said that your neighbour would know of it, I do know some."

"Mother Goody?"

Chant's dog began to bark, as if it were at large in The Street and the daughter drew herself closer to her mother's skirts.

"Get in, come," said Robert, standing to one side, "there be no candle here."

Robert closed the door and they stood in the dark room in silence.

"Sit down," said Robert, "there be a chair and a stool, next the table, can you see? I will speak with Mother Goody and then you must go on your way."

At that moment the front door opened, with Samuel shouting and kicking out at the loose dog outside, before slamming the door shut.

"Father?" said Samuel.

"Go to Mother Goody's," said Robert, "there is a potion to be made. The girl here has a poisoned foot."

"Who is here?" said Samuel.

"There be a mother and daughter here, the girl, she cannot walk. Go, take the stick."

Samuel paused before opening the front door again and picking up the heavy stick, then slammed it shut, shouting at the dog out in The Street.

Robert did not wish to know their names nor tell his own. Once the potion was taken, then they would leave.

"Do not return to the church porch, once you go from here," said Robert, breaking the silence, "you must find charity in another parish."

The woman did not reply and it seemed an age before Samuel returned. The dog could be heard barking but Samuel entered through the back door.

"Here, Mother Goody has made a potion, she said to stir in the parson's honey, if it be not yet been eaten?"

"I have dipped my finger in," said Robert, "it is there, upon the table, I wished to eat more."

Samuel went to the parlour and clattered until he found a spoon and then sought the honey on the table, before scraping it into the steaming cup and stirring it.

"Take this, here is my hand," said Samuel, holding the wooden cup until the mother felt for it and then guided the cup to her daughter's mouth. The girl spluttered at the taste but her mother then encouraged her to finish the potion.

"It is done?" said Robert.

"Yes," said Samuel, moving away into the parlour and lowering his voice, "but the girl, she must rest,"

"Rest? Where must she rest?" said Robert, following his son and speaking in whispers.

"Mother Goody has lent blankets, let them sleep in the barn father?"

"By Christ, they will not..." said Robert.

"Sssh," said Samuel.

"They must be gone at first light, no person must see them here."

With the mother carrying her daughter over her shoulder, Samuel guided them to the barn, to where they could sleep amongst the dry hay.

Robert was nearly asleep by the time that Samuel returned to his own bed.

"Mother Goody's potion did make her puke," said Samuel, "she could not keep it down. We must look at her foot, at first light."

"And then they do leave," said Robert, turning over in his bed and pulling the blanket around him.

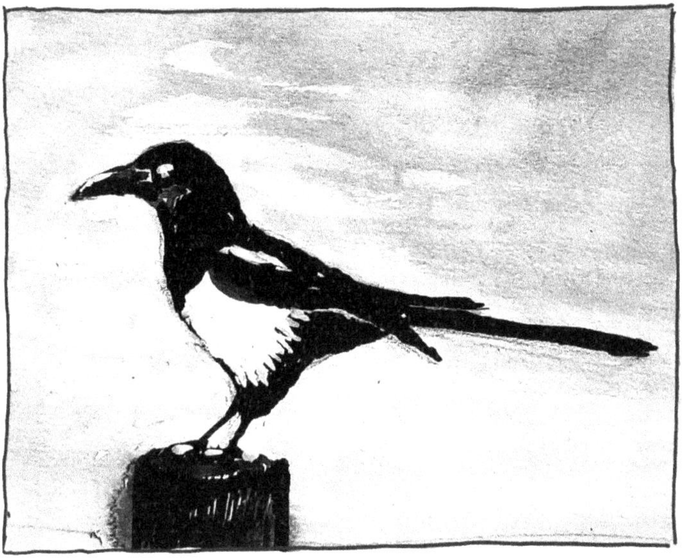

In the morning Robert was awoken by Samuel lighting the fire.

"Why do you light the fire, there is nothing to eat? Are they gone from the barn?"

"No, they are still here, the foot it is bad, I have looked. We have not a clean cloth to wrap around it. Mother Goody has given some milk and gruel for them and for us."

"They cannot stay, they shall be evicted and we fined."

"Get dressed father," said Samuel.

Samuel brought the woman and girl in from the barn and they sat at the table. After they had eaten, they stood and then moved towards the front door, the girl hobbling.

"Where are you going?" said Robert.

"To the church, it is Sunday, we may be given alms in the porch, before divine service."

"You will be punished is all, the parish constable, he is a cruel man," said Robert, "go from the parish, when all are at church, then you will not be seen."

The girl fell against her mother and then slid to the floor.

"She has a fever," said the woman, laying her hand upon her daughter's brow.

"Lay her on the bed," said Robert, "on Samuel's bed."

"I am afeared for her," said her mother, "she be all I have."

The girl closed her eyes whilst the mother sat on the edge of the bed, stroking her daughter's hair.

"What is her name?" said Robert, afraid that the girl would die in his house and he would not even know her name.

"She is my Rose," said the woman, "I am Joan."

"I am Robert, Robert Penny and Samuel is my son."

"The landlady did say sir,"

"We go to church now, Joan, but you must stay."

"It is wrong that we do not go to church."

"What would be wrong is to suffer punishment, here in this parish. Do not stray from the house. We have nothing to steal either, if that is your thinking?"

"Sir, I do not steal."

Before they left for church, Robert hid the vestry monies on a high beam, above the privy.

"The water, it is from our well, it can be drunk," said Samuel, to Joan, as he and Robert left by the front door, "and there is hot water on the fire and hay in the privy."

Robert and Samuel walked down The Street in silence. Many parishioners were also leaving their houses in the Street, closing doors behind them and greeting their neighbours whilst others had already mustered before the church with a growing hum of conversation. Once the church was entered the talk became a murmur, with heads together, whispering or monotonic acknowledgements accompanying the touching of a hat, the sudden yap of a dog and then the yelp of swift retribution. Still Robert and Samuel had not spoken, Robert preferring a silent nod where required. As they gathered on their bench, the stranger, Jonathon Brigg was the last to enter the church and proceeded up the aisle, towards the front of the church. He walked slowly, taking his time to observe the seated women on the opposite side of the nave.

"Mr Brigg sir," called out a young voice, Robert then realising that it was Samuel who had tried to catch the attention of Jonathon Brigg.

"Mr Brigg," called Samuel again, his voice clear above the congregational whispering.

Robert nudged his son hard with the point of his elbow.

"Sssh," said Robert, in an urgent whisper, "I do not wish to sit with him."

"Mr Brigg sir," called Samuel again, this time gaining

the attention of the stranger, "Mr Brigg sir, you may sit with us."

Jonathon Brigg returned a short distance back up the aisle towards them.

"I thank you boy, but Mr Loper has found space in his pew," said Jonathon Brigg, at which the parish constable hailed for him to join him.

"Why did you do that?" hissed Robert, to his son.

"If his name be Brigg," said Samuel quietly, "then he would have turned sooner. Everybody does know their own name."

As the service got underway Robert thought about this, realising that Samuel was right, the man had not answered to his own name when clearly spoken. He gave his son an approving look but it went unnoticed, with Samuel looking ahead. Robert did not like the fact that the parish constable had befriended the man, inviting him to the family pew. The pew that had once been the right of the Penny family. Loper was surely attempting to secure the five guinea reward for news of Alice Brigg but what news could he give, other than to say she was found dead and had then been tossed into the river? Robert could not even recall the subject of parson Crouch's sermon, his mind wandering to all parts and then wondering what a microscope was and why would the parson wish to study bees? He hoped that the woman and child would quickly be gone from the parish, as a vestry member he could not be seen to take in beggars, especially a woman, into his house. His distraction was sufficient for Robert to be unprepared for his turn to climb the pulpit and declare which work was next required on the highways, with two days of parish labour yet to be fulfilled. From a pew at the front, the parish clerk nodded when Robert caught his eye, a reminder of their conversation about the survey and subsequent work to Sun Lane, to facilitate the transportation of bricks in the new year, for the building of the large house. Robert, not having thought about the details then declared that the following Thursday and Friday would be spent repairing the hollow in Timothy Lane, in Asseley. There was a general murmur of approval to this statement, given that many had struggled to pass the broad and deep stretch of water whilst clinging to the hedge but filling their boots with brown water nevertheless. This would then fulfil the parish labour obligation for the year. Robert spoke that he must complete his surveys as soon as he was able and certainly before he met with the justices in the city, in the new year. The parish clerk scowled at him as Robert returned to his bench.

With the service and parish business over, Robert lingered outside the church porch. He wanted to speak with the clerk about Samuel working at the brickworks tomorrow and whether he would pay more than sixpence a day. The clerk would have passed him by, if Robert had not then blocked his way. After listening to Robert's request, he shook his head.

"You be mistook Robert, there be no work. Nor the ox to borrow."

Despite Robert's questioning, the clerk again shook his head and then turned to speak with the churchwarden, Peter Thigpen. Edward Loper emerged from the church, with Jonathon Brigg still inside, where he remained behind to speak with the parson.

"Robert," said the parish constable.

"Edward," said Robert, "you are now friendly with Mr Brigg then?"

"Ah, well, dun't hurt to see if one man canst help another."

Robert drew closer and then looked about him before lowering his voice.

"Edward, you know as do I that the woman be dead

and she will not be found."

"But there be five guineas Robert."

"So he do say, but he also do say that his name is Brigg."

"'Tis Brigg," said Edward Loper, "tis his sister that he seeks."

"His name is not Brigg and the dead woman not his sister."

"How durst thee know such a thing?" said the parish constable, louder than Robert would wish.

"Do not say you know this Edward," said Robert, quietly, "keep as you were and we shall ask him, together. It should be where none can see or hear, behind the church after evening prayers be a quiet place. We talk is all."

The parish constable frowned briefly but then smiled as Jonathon Brigg approached.

"Ah Mr Brigg," said Edward Loper, "oftentimes we go to the alehouse, after the sermon?"

"I may join you, for a short while," said Jonathon Brigg, giving Robert a predatory stare, "and Mr Penny, you have word of my sister?"

"No sir," said Robert, "but I shall say, when there is something to tell. Perhaps soon, this very evening, if I do know more."

The stranger nodded and then turned to walk with the parish constable, towards the alehouse.

Samuel had left the church already and Robert walked home on his own. The sky had cleared of all sketchy cloud and there was a still and settled coldness in the air and Robert thought that tonight would bring the first frost of the season. He wondered what was to be done now that the parish clerk had said that there was to be no work at the brickearth pit. It was up to the waywarden to determine which highway was to be repaired, not the parish clerk and Robert would not bend to improve Sun Lane for the clerk's own gain. Timothy Lane was bad and there had been acknowledgement in church that many in the parish would be helped by this work. But now, with the clerk displaying his pettiness, how were they to save and buy a dairy cow? They had no money nor food, with the ox meat having turned bad. Then there was the woman and daughter in his house, that he wished were gone. More mouths to feed and with nothing on the table. Chant's dog was barking again and Robert kept his head down lest Chant asked after payment for the long straw, with the offered meat now rotten. He paused at the threshold of his house, hoping that the young girl was not dead but sufficiently healed to move on, in the morning. They could sleep in the barn tonight and set off at first light.

Joan was busy in the parlour, whilst the girl Rose still lay upon Samuel's bed.

"Is Samuel here?" asked Robert.

"He has been," said Joan, "he did look at Rose's foot and then he has gone again."

"Is she still bad?" said Robert.

"I fear for her."

"Is the fire lit? It will be cold tonight, it is cold now."

"There are embers."

"Let us keep the fire going, even if we have nothing to eat. You have come to a house where there be nothing."

"But I am thankful sir."

"Do not say sir, Robert is my name."

"I am thankful...Robert."

"What are you about, in the parlour?"

"I am cleaning."

"This house it is poorly kept. How long... how long have you been...from where you live?"

"We have no house, since my husband passed. He passed in the spring."

"You have travelled since?"

"From place to place, there was some harvest work."

Robert went out into the barn and brought in an armful of dry branches, cracking some in half across his knee before rebuilding the fire.

"Samuel and I have lived here since after Easter. I was born here but did move away. When my mother died, we did come back, too late to plant corn. We grew onions and cabbages and took hay and we shall sow for next harvest, the strips are ready. I am to fetch my tools from where we did live with my sister, for I learned to make barrels there but I have not yet the craft of one who is a cooper."

"I have been a wife and kept a house and worked in the dairy. I have lost two children to the pox and if Rose shall... then I do not wish to live more, my heart it cannot break further."

Robert expected Joan to cry as she spoke of her sadness but she did not. Her face was set but then she met Robert's look with a faint smile.

"I was once quick to laugh," said Joan.

After a long silence, Robert went out into the yard and then wandered across to the strips, returning in the fading light with the coldness of the night ahead now beginning to bite.

"It is I, Robert Penny," said Robert, as he entered through the back door, into the darkness of his own house.

Joan answered quietly, adding that her daughter was sleeping but feverish. The front door soon rattled open and Samuel entered but then lingered at the door.

"Parson Crouch, he is here," said Samuel, "father, the parson knows of Joan and Rose, that they are here and that Rose is poorly."

THE PARISH WAYWARDEN

"Parson," said Robert, "come, but our house, it be dark."

"Good eve Robert and a good eve to you also, Joan and young Rose," said parson Crouch, "I have brought candles, Samuel?"

Samuel lit a candle from the fire.

"Samuel says that you have an onion?" said the parson.

"It is all that we do have," said Robert

"Then place an onion, as it is, in amongst the embers and the ashes. It needs be hot, the outer will burn, the inside it will grow soft. There is hot water?"

Samuel found an onion and pushed it in at the base of the fire, he then swung the steaming water kettle over the flames.

"I will place a poultice on the child, but first her foot must be bathed and clean," said the parson, who then moved to sit at the end of the bed, to attend to the bathing with a clean bright white cloth that he tore in half, "the candle please?"

Samuel held the candle close by, so that the parson was not working in his own shadow. An old grey cloth had been wrapped around the foot and was now stained with pus and blood and the parson peeled it free, wrapping it up to toss it into the fire, where it sizzled and then flamed. Rose's left foot was dirty and on the outer edge a blistering had turned angry, with red lines snaking upwards, away from the soreness and rising up the girl's lower leg. A pot was filled with hot water and the parson then carefully washed both of Rose's feet with a torn half of the clean cloth. Rose stirred and opened her eyes to see the parson at the end of the bed attending to her feet.

"Tis like Jesus washing the feet of the disciples, my dearest," said Joan.

"The foot needs be clean," said Parson Crouch, smiling at the girl, "there, now the poultice can be applied. Is the onion hot?"

Samuel hooked out the onion from the base of the fire and juggled with it.

"It is hot," said Samuel, blowing on his fingers as he passed the onion back and forth between his hands.

"In the basket, there is honey also, once the cloth is soaked in the boiling water and the honey covers the blister, then squeeze out the middle of the onion and place it on the honey and I shall wrap the cloth around. The poultice, it must be hot, to do its work. Be not afraid my child, for it will draw the poison."

The preparations were made and Rose drew back her foot at the sudden heat.

"There my Rose," said Joan, holding down her leg, "it is soon done."

Rose moaned but her eyes closed again.

"I had thought to bleed her," said Parson Crouch, "but we shall see how this does draw the poison back down the leg. There are apples and eggs in the basket and some bread. Keep the honey for the next poultice, there is more white cloth also. Samuel, you can do tomorrow as I have done?"

"Yes sir," said Samuel.

"When you look beneath the poultice, you will know if the poison is drawing out as it should."

"Bless you parson," said Joan.

The parson smiled.

"I shall speak to no one that you are here, the girl is weak, not only from the poison, she does need nourishment," said the parson, rising to leave.

Robert spoke quietly to the parson at the front door before he left.

"We thank you, let us hope that the girl will soon be well enough..."

"Well enough to walk from parish to parish?" said the parson, in a whisper, "Robert, she will not live the winter, if she is to sleep in church porches, whilst she does also starve."

"But she cannot stay, the parish will not allow and that is the way of it," said Robert.

"Little by little, let her be made well first and pray that the poultice will do its work. Samuel can say to me how it is, in the morning," said the parson, as he ducked outside, under the door frame, "goodnight Robert."

"Father, I am to start at the brickworks at first light," said Samuel, after the parson had gone, "how shall I then change the poultice?"

"You were listening? You are not to be working at the brickworks," said Robert, "the clerk has turned against me for not doing his bidding on the highways. He wants that the parish should attend to Sun Lane, so that his bricks may make a better journey to where the big house is to be built. I have not yet surveyed Sun Lane but Timothy Lane is bad and that can be made better in the two days that we have left, better for the parish and the parish clerk can..."

Robert suddenly remembered his conversation with the parish constable, about confronting the stranger, to ask of his true name, if it not be Brigg and the dead woman not his sister. It was already dark and evening prayers would be over, with the afternoon reader Mr Butcher, leading the prayers, rather than the parson.

"I have...business to attend to," said Robert, looking around for his coat which he had not taken off, since returning from divine service, "boil some of the parson's eggs Samuel, for us all."

The night was cold with the moon low in the sky, but at least Robert could see his way down The Street. Would Loper and the stranger be already at the churchyard, behind the church, as Robert suggested? How were they to say to the stranger that they do not believe what he says? Robert wanted him gone from the parish, so that he no longer had to think about the dead woman. There was too much else besides to consider without those magpie eyes of the stranger, piercing into Robert every time that they met. There were a few parishioners walking back from evening prayers and Robert quickened his pace. The churchyard was quiet as he entered through the lych gate and he could see no persons in the church porch as he passed by. He continued around the end of the building and saw in the moonlight, two figures wrestling upon the glass. One then pulled themselves up, to sit upon the other and they were now beating down with their fists as Robert ran across to grip the shoulders of the figure on top.

"Edward, stop, we said to talk is all, not this," shouted Robert.

The figure turned and in the moonlight Robert could see the blockish head of the man who called himself Jonathon Brigg. The stranger then swung his arm back fiercely, striking Robert in the face, knocking him back onto the soft cold ground.

"Talk is it?" said the stranger, who turned back to force the parish constable's head down with one hand before delivering a final heavy punch with the other, "we've talked Mr Penny, the parish constable has talked a great deal."

The stranger then stood up, leaving the prone body of the parish constable laying still upon the grass and advanced towards Robert.

"We wanted to know the truth, is all," said Robert, scurrying on his hands and backside until he backed into the wall of the church and could retreat no further.

"The truth?" said the stranger, "you have lied since our

THE PARISH WAYWARDEN

first encounter. Even up on the ridge when I asked you to name the parish in the valley."

"I..I could not hear."

"Your eyes did give it away then. You have the eyes of a liar, Mr Penny."

The stranger took something from his pocket and Robert could see a glint of metal in his hand.

"Now, you tell me the truth," said the stranger, "I have heard the parish constable's words. Now you tell me what did happen."

Robert's heart was racing, his breath clouding in the air before him. What had Loper said? Had Loper had the truth beaten out of him? If Robert lied further then the stranger could fly at him, with a knife in his hand. Loper would have said what did occur, he would not care anyway. It was a thoughtless act to get rid of an unwanted body. Robert was staring hard at the hand with the knife in it. He then told the stranger exactly what happened, on his first day of inspecting the highways as the parish waywarden.

"It is the shame of it that does make me lie," said Robert, "that there be no Christian burial."

Once Robert had concluded his account, the stranger remained silent. A barn owl screeched from its perch upon the church roof.

"I will fight," said Robert, "but not when thee holds a knife."

"Get Mr Loper up from the ground," said the stranger, returning the metal object to his pocket.

Robert walked around the man, keeping his distance and squatted down to revive the parish constable, all the while keeping the stranger in view.

"Edward, Edward," said Robert, shaking him.

"Hwuh?"

"Get up., be quick."

"Wh...where's ...what...?" said the parish constable, raising himself up and then standing unsteadily.

"I am here Mr Loper, calm yourself," said the stranger, "now I know what did happen."

"And you are not her sister," said Robert, "I do know that much."

"No, Mr Penny, you are right, she is not my sister, but her name is Alice Brigg, whom I was to marry."

The parish constable spat beside Robert.

"Lost a tooth," said Loper.

"I apologise Mr Loper."

"We had a go at each other," said Loper, "then I dun told ee what did 'appen and after, he did punch I."

"I lost my temper, I did not want to believe what you said...but then Mr Penny did say the same and so...I must believe it. But there shall always be doubt that the one you found was Alice Brigg."

"She did have long black hair," said Robert, "she were dead but..that she were once beautiful, twas plain to see."

"Not that you would know but she had a mark," said the stranger, "a small black mark that could not be seen by... any."

In the bright moonlight, Robert involuntarily raised a finger to point centrally below his chest.

It was then as if the stranger had been stabbed himself, buckling up almost double and letting out a cry of anguish.

"Aaaah, no, then it is true," said the stranger, turning to pound the wall of the church with the flat of his hand.

"How durst you know about thic mark then Penny?" said the parish constable, managing a pained laugh, "thee took a peep at a dead whore's tits? What else thee go for Robert?"

"It was as I found her," said Robert, quickly, "I did straighten her hair...and her clothes."

The stranger turned away from the wall.

"Then it is over. I am ruined."

"Her clothes were not fine as you did say, earlier," said Robert, trying to brush aside Loper's accusation, "they were simple clothes, that a maid might wear. Her clothes, when I found her, they were awry."

"She may have required clothes, she must have lived as a beggar, for those weeks, whilst she walked from parish to parish."

"Why did she leave her home? For what reason?" said Robert.

"Does it matter now? She is dead is all, how or where she died is of no interest to me. I was to gain two thousand pounds a year and the guardianship of a further one thousand pounds by her marriage. Her father and mother, they did entrust me to find their daughter but I am not deserving of their trust and nor shall I return to tell of the death of their daughter and only child, Alice Brigg. The stone that you speak of, when she was found, was not the only great weight that did sit heavily upon her belly. That she was...forespoken and with not a clear understanding of the world, did most likely get her murdered, but they...whoever they were, they were not to gain by her death, as I have lost."

"That were the bad tooth that I did lose," said the parish constable, rubbing his jaw, "thee did save I the bother of pullin' 'ee. Now, what to do with thee Mr...whatever your name be."

"What is your meaning sir?" said the stranger.

"By rights I should put thee in the stocks, jumpin' on I, like you did 'n me the parish constable.."

"You started it by putting your hands around my neck."

"Enough, Edward, let it pass, none in the parish need know of it," said Robert, who then turned to the stranger, "and you go on your way, leave the parish by first light and I shall forget that you pulled a knife."

"It was a pair of scissors," said the stranger, "I had to put the fear in you, Mr Penny, to prise from you the truth. I am a tailor and a very good tailor, unlike your own in the parish, with whom I have lodged and would not trust to piss straight, let alone cut a line of cloth. But no matter, I shall be gone and I will leave you to your...blessed parish and this accursed country. My luck is not here, my luck is in France or even to Rome, there is a way down through the forest, to the port?"

Robert pointed.

"Down Watery Lane, below the church here and keep straight, first there be Dudge Lane, then away into the Forest. Two days walk, they say."

"Then I shall sail tomorrow night, if there be a ship and the horse I will sell on the quay. Sirs, I enjoyed the fight, and now this fighting tailor bids you both goodnight."

The stranger then bowed in the moonlight and strolled away, across the churchyard.

"If I ever sees him agin, I shall kill 'un, as cold and cruel as you like," said the parish constable, after the lych gate had clicked,

"We don't even know his name?" said Robert, "who killed her then Edward, who from this parish killed Alice Brigg and put her in the ditch with a great lump of heathstone to weigh her down?"

"I dun't know 'n I dun't care," said the parish constable, "I hope's the alehouse be open as I got the taste 'o blood in my mouth. Thirsty Penny?"

Robert now realised that he could not see out of one of

THE PARISH WAYWARDEN 165

his eyes and it was tender to the touch.

"Best not be seen together," said Robert, "lest they think we've been at each other."

"I shall say that I did hit my own face with a hammer, if any do ask."

"I will walk with you to the alehouse, but I'll not go in," said Robert, as they both walked slowly from the churchyard.

Outside the alehouse, Robert again refused the parish constable's offer to join him.

"No, not tonight. Edward, do not say to anyone about the woman in the ditch and I will not say about you losing a fight in the churchyard."

"I din't lose no fight, the man dun't fight fair, 'n I ain't finished with 'un Robert, thee hear my words," said the parish constable, feeling behind his head with the flat of his hand and then inspecting his fingers, "my hair be wet, 'ee did bang my head upon summat hard, anyroads, dun't thee go peakin' at no more dead whore's tits, Robert Penny."

Edward Loper then pushed Robert aside, to enter the alehouse. Robert was cold and would have dearly liked to sit and drink as much beer as he could, but not with Loper and not without his own money. He walked on slowly, back up The Street.

It was dark in his house, as Robert entered through the front door.

"Father," said Samuel, quietly, "I shall light a candle. Both Rose and Joan are sleeping."

Samuel lit a half candle, after blowing on the embers of the fire, to make a flame.

Robert slumped down onto his chair.

"Father, what has happened to your eye?"

"Loper and I met with the stranger, who calls himself

Jonathon Brigg."

"And you fought?"

"There was a fight, but I did not wish it. He is to leave the parish at first light."

"Then he is not who he says, Jonathon Brigg?"

"No, he did lie."

"And the one he seeks, Alice Brigg? She is not here?"

"No, she is not," said Robert, looking about with his one good eye, "our beds, they are taken?"

"Yes, I said to Mrs Young…Joan…that she must sleep, she did not wish to take your bed but..she was straight away to sleep, after she had eaten."

"Did the girl eat?"

"No, she did not wake to eat but she did drink water, she is still hot with the fever. There are two hard eggs?"

Robert nodded and Samuel brought two hard boiled eggs from the parlour. Robert slowly peeled and ate the eggs and then carefully ate an apple, leaving the egg shell on the table but eating the apple core and chewing on the stalk.

"I am going to Chauncy in the morning," said Robert, "I'll take Katy and borrow Dowty's cart, if I am able, to fetch the barrel making tools from my sister Ann. I may stay over but when I am back, they…Joan…Mrs Young… and her Rose, they must be gone. We still have Mother Goody's blankets?"

Samuel nodded.

Robert picked up the candle and opened the back door, Samuel followed with the blankets, closing the back door quietly behind him.

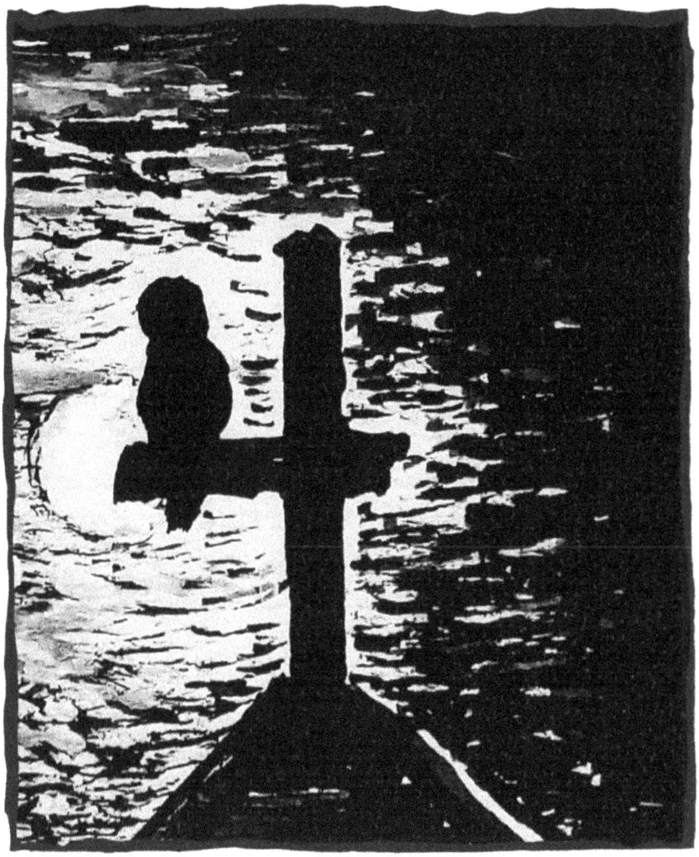

Robert awoke at first light, sneezing and waking Samuel, who stirred in the hay and then got to his feet. When Robert entered the house, Joan was standing with her head down, beside her daughter.

"I..I..am sorry," said Joan, not looking up, "I took thy bed sir, I didn't mean to.."

"We did sleep," said Samuel, "and father snored louder than he does in the house. Rose, has she waked?"

"She has drunk water, she is not so hot."

"Samuel," said Robert, "go to Dowty's with Katy to borrow the cart, say 'tis vestry business."

"But I am to change the poultice father."

Robert scowled at Samuel and then took an apple to eat in the privy. He then gave fresh hay to the horse, preferring to stay and watch the horse eat rather than go back inside the house. When he returned, the fire was crackling and water had been put on to boil. Robert clattered noisily around the parlour before going back out into the yard, slamming the back door behind him. He led Katy to Dowty's house but Dowty was already out with his cart.

Robert cursed under his breath as Mrs Dowty closed the front door.

Robert then mounted the horse from the block in The Street and rode slowly, without a saddle, to Asseley, holding on to Katy's mane.

John Arnold agreed to let Robert borrow the cart and harness and Robert then added that he may return from Chauncy the following day.

"Well, I shall need 'un afore the work day, in Timothy Lane. Keep thic harness safe Robert, we do know what they Chauncy boys be like. Father did get robbed in Sun Lane but he did see they men again at market and made they wish they never set to thieving. What thee done to thine eye Robert?"

"I weren't fighting at market," said Robert, trying to raise a smile, "Loper did need some help last night."

"Loper," said John Arnold, shaking his head. "no parish man ever did wish to be constable, not like Loper do."

Robert thanked him and harnessed the horse, sloshing back with the cart in tow, through the water splash at the start of Timothy Lane. He stopped in the water to look down from his elevated position at where the ditch needed to be dug out. There was even need for a new ditch to be dug, to lead the water away on the downside, to the south of the lane.

Turning onto Sun Lane from Watery Lane, Robert kept an eye on the condition of the highway, as this was to form part of his obligatory inspection of all the highways in the parish. He thought that it must have been called Sun Lane because the sun would be seen either rising or setting, depending on whether you were arriving or departing, at the beginning or end of the day. He was later than he hoped, but it was still dark and cold in the deeply sunken lane. The empty cart lurched heavily in the pot holes in the track on the level sections but as the horse's straps tightened, with the slight rise ahead, the going was better. Robert had observed before how fallen water sits on level ground and the passing hooves and wheels then splash out the old natural surface to make the holes deepen. Some tracks will help themselves, if there is enough wind and sun to dry them out in the warmer, drier months but Sun Lane would only get worse. There was a lot of work to be done here, with many cart loads of good gravel to crown the lane on these level passages, to then encourage water to drain to the sides and not sit in puddles in the track itself. Robert smiled to himself at the thought of the parish clerk's bricks jiggling and breaking, on their way to the new house. In time, the banks began to drop down and the elms became more spread out along the straight lane, the sun even announcing itself by casting faint shadows. Robert noted an upright stone that was likely to be the parish boundary marker, positioned at the top of the low bank. As he crossed into Chauncy parish there was no marked improvement to the surface of the lane, with the banks again rising up and the highway holding water on the level ground. He had lived in Chauncy, where he had married twice and where Samuel was born, but Robert had never thought much about how it compared to other parishes. Having returning to where he was born, he now thought his parish the poorer of the two. His was a sprawling parish, not wool rich nor fine dairy land and with the ragged forest edge to the south and the darkness of the Royal Forest beyond. Robert would shiver inside when he thought of Dudge Lane and the forest. Chauncy parish was all chalk and no shitty land, with a broad river flowing through lush meadows before turning the paddles of a large mill. There was a row of fine cottages on both sides of the street and two alehouses where well-dressed men smoked tobacco whilst discussing money and business. The flint of the parish was packed upright and proud, chequered into the walls and tower of the church. Here even the church bell sounded tuneful and not mournful, like his own church, where the bell would solemnly toll, a death knell regardless of the occasion.

 Robert left the horse and cart at the side of his sister Ann's alehouse, tethering Katy to a wooden post, but so that she could drink from the trough.

 "Come for the tools," said Robert, to his sister Ann, after she had taken beer to a table of men who were sat before the window, overlooking the street.

 "You bin' fightin'?" said Ann, looking up at his eye that was still partially closed.

 "Not drunk, I were helping the parish constable. He did

lose a tooth."

"Di'nt go well then?"

Robert shrugged.

"The tools is gone," said Ann.

"Gone? Gone where?"

"The family of old George, they came."

"Din't know he had family. He left they tools to I. Said that one day I might make a barrel that do hold beer. Our sister, I needs to earn some money."

"Rob, we needs money too."

"Did thee sell the tools?"

"Yes, we had to."

"So, there were no family?"

Ann shook her head.

"Then I will go," said Robert, making no move to leave.

Ann went to the parlour and came back with a tankard of beer.

"Here," said Ann, handing it to her brother, "let me see thine eye."

"There's nothing to be done," said Robert, taking the tankard and turning his face away from his sister, "it will heal."

His sister stood for a moment, observing her younger brother.

"How is young Sam?"

Robert shrugged and then took a sip of beer.

"He thinks me a fool," said Robert, "doesn't say so, he just looks. I am doing what I can my sister, but tis hard. There was nothing done nor planted. We've took enough hay and have fuel for the winter. Some of the strips, they have been made good, the roof is repaired, the ox did die but Katy still goes on. Do you remember Catherine?"

More men entered the alehouse and Ann called out to

her husband Richard to come out front.

"Rob," said Richard, as he walked by.

"Richard," replied Robert, with a nod of the head.

"I did call her Katy," said Ann, gesturing for Robert to move into a corner of the parlour, to continue their conversation.

"I could not remember her name, not even a month ago," said Robert.

"You were younger."

"She was to go into service, at the parsonage?"

"But she left, just before then, her clothes, they were bought. Then she were gone, they say she did leave the parish."

"But with who? A sweetheart?"

"No one did ever know Rob."

"And she made signs, in chalk?"

"She always did play with chalk and then she made signs in barns and houses. She made her face white with chalk, like a ghost."

Robert took a gulp of his beer.

"There was a punishment, on the Green," said Robert quietly, "and there I saw our Catherine."

"She has come back?"

"No, she was young, as she once was...it were her ghost. I looked and she were there, she did look to me, her white young face and her hair was blacker than black. I looked again and she were gone, I have not seen her again."

Ann put her hand on her brother's arm.

"Oh, Rob."

Ann let out a sigh and they stood in silence for a moment.

"She were born on St Catherine's day and so she were called Catherine," said Ann, "mother did want her to stay and weave."

"So John Arnold did said to me."

"John Arnold? I have not heard that name for many a year. He did want to marry Katy, when she were too young. He would watch her, he came to ask father if he could be promised her, when she were old enough. He were plenty older than she. Father took against him and said she must go to the parsonage. She would earn there and p'raps he thought the tithes be forgot, some chance with old Crouch."

"John Arnold didn't say that he wished to marry Catherine, he just said about the chalk marks, he showed me one in his barn, we have the same."

"Tis mortal sad, if her ghost be in the parish, that she never did leave?" said Ann, with sorrow in her voice, "Poll, is he still there, still watching? What do he know?"

Robert shrugged as he emptied his tankard.

"He has said to me already about Catherine...and her sweetheart," said Robert, "what we all do know, do you think he do know more?"

"Who knows what Poll do know?" said Ann,

Robert had not considered that Poll would know more than he had already told but perhaps if Robert had paid money rather than pulling a stringy piece of ox meat from his pocket, then Poll would say all that he knew.

"Does thee remember young William Crouch, the parson's son?" said Robert.

Ann smiled.

"He was a funny boy, always out in the lanes, standing and looking at...something."

"He now be our parson, since old Crouch died, back in the summer."

"And not the other brother?"

"Augustus?"

"He were the more Godly, always following old parson

Crouch about the church. Some did say that his father did beat him bad, that the son did wish it, to cleanse him of his sins. He did scare I."

"He near drowned me in a trough for scrumping in the parson's garden, that weren't so Godly."

"P'raps he were baptising thee?"

"Big hands," said Robert, "but William, he dun't like standing in the pulpit, he'd rather be out in the lanes, watching the ladybirds. He be a good man though, by his deeds better than what he do say in church. He and Samuel, they gets on and Samuel helps with the experiments, but dun't ask me what they be and then he comes home spouting Latin."

His sister smiled and shook her head.

"Christ's teeth," said Robert, as three men entered the alehouse and he heard a familiar voice.

He quickly moved further around the corner into the parlour, to keep from being seen.

"Thee still do curse bad then our Rob?" said his sister, looking puzzled.

"Tis our churchwarden, Peter Thigpen."

"His brother Roger do live in the parish, he be the vestry clerk. Dun't thee get on?"

"I want to ask him about work, but not like this, with my face all beat. They all think me like our father, good for nothing but drinking and a bad farmer with it, but I dun't even go to the alehouse, my sister. T'is like old Judd Penny's ghost is just sat there in the corner, wherever I goes. And they've made me waywarden and tis a burdensome task I tell you, when there's not even a crust on our table."

His sister sighed and laid a hand upon his shoulder.

"Well, stay round the corner here and I'll get thee more beer," said Ann, "you'll eat with us? I must get to work or else

Richard'll soon be cursin' with the best of thee."

"He did give I a look when he passed by," said Robert, "I will make good the money that I do owe."

"We knows you will Rob, when you are able," said Ann, answering a call for more beer.

He could hear Peter Thigpen's voice clearly from where he stood, not that he wished to listen.

"St Catherine's be humble, I grant, the roof, it do let in the rain but with old Nathaniel now gone, God rest his soul, there be changes talked about," said Peter Thigpen, loading his pipe, "Augustus, he be mighty keen on the repairs, after the desecrations. Old parson Crouch were not so bold but his eldest son do say that the cross be now mended and that the parish will pay."

"And no parish do gladly pay," said Roger Thigpen, Peter's brother, "not before a main amount of grumbling. Augustus don't live in the parish, so he won't hear no grumbling."

"He'll be returning for St Catherine's day and do every year. We have been in correspondence," Peter Thigpen lowered his voice and Robert craned his neck to hear, as close as he dared, without being seen, "I've written of my concerns, about his brother, William. Tis my hope that the elder brother will be able to knock some sense into our new parson. Roger, let me tell thee, his sermons, they be poor, nobody do listen and he'd rather be anywhere but in the pulpit but he be the....damned parson, excuse my tongue. Augustus, he says he do know the bishop, then we shall see what do come about, when the bishop learns how it be."

Peter Thigpen lit his pipe from a spill and puffed busily. With the low ceiling, the expelled tobacco cloud soon rolled about to all corners and Robert inhaled deeply.

Robert was expecting more beer, but instead Ann's husband Richard appeared.

"Best make use of thic cart then, at least thee'll earn thy beer," Richard then beckoned for Robert to follow him, through the alehouse,

Robert reluctantly left his position, being hidden from view around the corner and he looked down as he passed Peter Thigpen, hoping not to be seen.

"It be Robert Penny," said Peter Thigpen, "Robert be our waywarden."

The two brothers sat comfortably together, well dressed in heavy woollen coats, both ruddy and rounded. Roger Thigpen declared that he had met Robert before, here in the alehouse.

"Waywarden be a main task then Robert?" said Roger, the older of the two brothers.

"Top Road's bin repaired," said Peter, "justices'll be glad, next session. What thee done to your eye then Robert?"

Robert muttered about helping the parish Constable, the previous night.

"Proper vestry man," said Roger, nodding approvingly.

"Is John Arnold with thee?" said Peter, "I did see his cart."

Robert explained that he had borrowed John's cart to carry home some tools. He did not mention that the tools that he thought were his, had now been sold. He suspected that Richard had arranged this, given that Robert already owed a sum of money to his sister Ann.

"John be a good man n' a good farmer," said Peter.

"Have you work for a carpenter?" said Robert hastily, wary that Richard was waiting for him to follow, "I can do repairs, I be a better carpenter than my father ever were?"

Richard whistled from the open door of the alehouse.

"Looks loike thee be wanted," said Roger.

"Carpenter?" said Peter Thigpen, slowly, before sending

more tobacco smoke out into the room, "well, we do have men, but let I think on it Robert."

Robert touched his hat and followed Richard outside. The two men said little throughout the afternoon as they loaded and hauled various manures out to the strips, concluding with the contents of the alehouse privy, just as the setting sun blazed across the broad patchwork of baulks and cultivated strips.

When they got back to the alehouse it was dark and Ann stated that Robert should stay and return in the morning. Katy was fed with a nosebag of oats and John Arnold's cart, which now stank of shit, was kept at the back of the alehouse. They ate pottage together and Robert drank more beer, on his own in the alehouse and then slept in the loft, where he and Samuel had slept before they had returned to the parish.

In the morning Robert walked up and down the street, passing the small house where he had lived with Samuel's mother, before she had died. Bess was a good dressmaker who was always busy. Robert had worked as repair carpenter and general labourer, with small jobs here and there. It was later on after his second wife had died that he had worked with old George, the cooper, not as a true apprentice but providing an able pair of hands. Old George had been a cooper at sea and by noon he was too drunk to hold his tools. Robert would do what he could whilst the old man slept but he had never made a barrel from start to finish. Now that his cooper's tools had been sold, he would have to go back and tell Tetty Bonner that he could no longer make her a barrel, with the hope of making more, if it did not leak.

"I'm sorry our Robert, that the tools been sold," said Ann, as Robert was about to return home.

Robert shrugged. He was going to tell his sister about the mother and daughter that had stayed in his house whilst the child's poisoned foot was cared for, but as he now expected them to be gone, he said nothing.

    Ann looked about to see where her husband was before she pressed some coins into Robert's hand, closing her hands around her brother's fist, to ensure that they were concealed.

    "Go on, my brother, and say hello to young Sam. I do miss he, he were like the child I never could have. I have thought plenty about our Katy, since you did say about her."

    Ann wiped a tear from her cheek and then smiled at her brother.

    Robert nodded and then left. On the way back to the parish, he stopped to throw some fallen dead elm branches into the cart, after scouring around the trunks of these huge trees on the high banks of Sun Lane. After a number of stops the cart was piled high, making Robert feel that it had not been a completely wasted journey. He had also surveyed Sun Lane and could now approach the parish clerk, explaining the scale of the task, which could certainly not be achieved by the two days of parish labour still available. Isaac Button, the parish clerk, had been quick to turn against Robert when he had stated in church that Timothy Lane was to be the next task and not Sun Lane. Ever since the parish clerk had turned up at Robert's door, picking up the coins dropped on his doorstep, Robert had realised that Isaac Button liked to get his own way, even dictating parish affairs to his own end.

    With the cart now full of broken elm brushwood, Robert gave a lift to a labourer who was walking back to the parish. They did not speak. Robert thought instead about the stranger. Would he be in France by now, seeking his luck, tailoring and fighting? Robert had never wished it before, but the thought of travelling down through the forest, looking upon the sea for the first time in his life and then setting sail to new lands excited him but also scared him. Was it the uncertainty of what lay ahead or the leaving behind of an old life that made him feel this way? The stranger was carefree. Once he knew for certain that Alice Brigg was no more and gone were two thousand pounds a year and whatever else came with her marriage, he quickly turned to new horizons and prospects, without a thought for the beautiful young woman that Robert had dragged lifeless from the ditch. The young woman that only he and Loper knew the fate of, now that the stranger had departed. Robert then realised that this may not be true. If she had died in the parish, then the murderer would certainly know, and he, Robert, would know this person in the parish. They would be present in the church, every Sunday at divine service. Robert gave a shudder and grunted out loud at the passage of these thoughts and then glanced at the labourer beside him, to see whether he had noticed. The labourer's eyes were closed, his head lolling forward with the motion of the cart. He then swayed over to the far side and was about to fall from the cart before Robert clamped a hand on the man's shoulder, hauling him back upright.

"Uhh...what?" spluttered the labourer, looking about him and then frowning at Robert.

They continued in silence. Robert paused at the junction with Watery Lane. What if he were to turn down Watery Lane to Dudge Lane and then out of the parish, into the Royal Forest and to the sea beyond, what would happen? Katy slowed tugged the cart forwards, turning towards home and Robert stopped to let the labourer down at the bottom of The Street. At the top of The Street, he took the cart around to the back yard and stepped down, calling out for Samuel to help him unload the brushwood. The house was empty. Robert returned to unload and stack the dead wood in a corner of the barn. He then threw the saddle and reins into the cart and set off for Asseley, to return the cart to John Arnold. As he sloshed through the long puddle at the start of Timothy Lane, Robert thought that the first of the two remaining parish highway days would be spent digging ditches which should at least prevent the hollow from holding water. The second day could then be used to fetch and tip gravel, to build up the surface of the lane. John Arnold was not at home but Robert left the cart in John's yard and hung up the harness in the barn. He then saddled up Katy as he wanted to check whether the Gigg's had cut back their hedge that had been encroaching upon the highway, as Robert had requested when he visited the farm, shortly after the younger brother Simon Gigg had died. Taking Katy on the lanes through the hamlet of Roake, to the east of the parish, Robert approached Gigg's farm. A line of blue woodsmoke from a chimney showed how windless the day was and Robert could hear a cockerel crowing in the distance, spurring a loud and shrill response from close by, somewhere behind the farm. He could hear voices in the cold stillness but these came from the fields and strips beyond and he saw no one as they slowly passed the farm. The hedge still had not been cut back and Robert would now have to call this out in church on Sunday, after divine service. He wondered whether the Giggs would send a representative for the parish labour days at the end of the week. Robert considered climbing the downs to see how the repairs to Top Road, beside Long Mound were holding up but he felt that Katy was labouring and moving more slowly now. He let the horse travel home at her own pace, Katy stopping to eat some longer grass beneath a hedge before moving on again. Back in his yard, Robert took off the bridle and saddle and pulled out some fresh hay from the barn and raised a couple of buckets from the well to fill the water trough.

"Old Katy," said Robert, rubbing the horse's neck as she fed.

There was nothing to eat in the house and the fire was

cold. Robert sat at the table and made a small pile with the coins that his sister Ann had given him, without her husband Richard noticing. He felt his eyes closing and leant forward, placing his elbows on the table and resting his head on his hands. Before drifting into a deeper sleep, he heard footsteps outside, approaching, the fast steps of someone running. Robert jolted and sat upright as the front door latch rattled hard and the door was thrust open. Samuel, breathless, burst into the room.

"Father, you must come."

"Come? Come where? I've only just..."

"Now, father, come," said Samuel, gesturing with his hand for Robert to follow him.

Samuel was back out in The Street, running down the hill, before Robert slowly raised himself, blinking sleepily as he left the house, closing the door behind him.

"To the Green," shouted back Samuel, "come."

Robert was not about to run, his knee had never fully recovered from climbing the churchyard yew and walking was painful enough.

"I'll not run," said Robert, walking stiffly, with Samuel pausing for his father to catch him up.

"Father, hurry, it is Joan...Mrs Young, Loper has put her in the stocks."

"What?" said Robert, lengthening his stride, "but she was to leave the parish? Where is the girl?"

Samuel did not wait to reply but carried on, running down The Street with Robert hobbling behind as fast as he was able.

When Robert turned the corner to the Green, Samuel was already by the stocks and he could see the woman, seated on the stock bench, her foot locked under the wooden bar, with the girl huddled next to her. Robert was puffing as he approached.

"Why is this?" said Robert, "why did you not leave the parish?"

"Rose, she still cannot walk," said Samuel, "her fever has lessened and the poultice did draw the poison, but she is weak father."

"And the parish constable did this?" said Robert, moving around to stand before the mother.

Joan nodded.

"Did you go back to the church porch?" said Robert.

"Where could I go?" said Joan, looking up with anger in her voice, "first the overseer came and then the constable, who did twist my arm."

Robert looked about him and then set off in a limping run, back across the Green.

"Where are you going father?" said Samuel, calling after Robert.

Without turning around, Robert cursed and then raised an arm in response, flapping it in the air as he turned the corner, back into The Street.

"Steady on, steady on," said the parish constable, as he opened his front door, "oh, tis you Robert?"

"The woman who be in the stocks," said Robert, "you must let her go."

"Whoa there Penny," said Edward Loper, "what be this, is you become weak, like old Dowty?"

"No, but come now, bring the key."

Robert moved away from the front door and began to walk back down The Street. The parish constable remained unmoved, at his front door.

"Penny, I ain't unlockin' thic beggar woman, not fer thee and not for nobody."

Robert paced back up The Street to confront the parish

constable.

"Do this thing Edward, do it for me, as I have helped you."

"What 'ave thee done to help me Penny? Do say as I've forgot?"

Robert stepped up to the open front door, his face now close to Loper's.

"I have saved your life, not that thee did know about it."

"When? When did this go on?"

"After the boy died.."

"He were weak, 'afore the punishment."

"Not him being dead, but the Gigg brothers, they did come for you after. When you was drunk and Samuel took you home from our door. They were there, wanting to kill the man that did kill their own. There was talk of Irishman, coming to the parish. There were no Irishman, t'was a story so that the Irishmen could be blamed when you was murdered. It were the Giggs, they did tell Poll about the Irishmen coming for thee. I went to speak with the Giggs and let them know that there were no Irishman. I told them that I knew what they were about, what they did plan."

The parish constable frowned as he tried to follow what Robert was saying.

"Why din't thee say about this?"

"What, to make matter's worse?" said Robert, "tis a parish, tis our parish, folk do have to get on and for there not to be bad blood."

The parish constable grunted and taking his coat from the peg he shuffled slowly behind Robert, down The Street, towards to the Green. As they turned the corner the sexton beckoned them from the church yard. The parish constable stopped to wait for the sexton and the labourer David Crust to pass through the lych gate and walk across towards them. David Crust was holding something small in his hand and held it out as he approached. It was a leather purse, drawn together but heavy with coins.

"Thas my purse," said Edward Loper, "where'd thee find it?"

"David found 'un on the grass, round the back o' the church, where we is digging old Joyce's grave," said the sexton, "din't knows whose it be, but it be yourn? Were goin' to take it to the churchwarden. When was thee behind the church Edward?"

"Jess gimme the purse," said the parish constable, snatching it from the labourer's hand.

The sexton shrugged and set off, back towards the churchyard. David Crust, the finder of the purse, loitered for a moment in hopeful expectation.

The parish constable raised a hand as if to strike the labourer, until he drifted away, to catch up with the sexton.

"That was when you were fighting with the stranger," said Robert, "thee must have dropped it."

The parish constable weighed the purse in his hand, not to estimate its content Robert thought, as he did not count the money but he appeared puzzled by the return of his purse, before stuffing it into his coat pocket.

"Come," said Robert, encouraging Edward Loper to hasten across the Green, "where be the key?"

"T'aint right," said the parish constable, shaking his head with his hands firmly in his pockets, "it be the law, like everyone do know, beggars be put in the stocks, whipped and sent on. Nobody do want beggars."

"Let her go," said Robert, quietly and firmly.

The parish constable's eyes narrowed, his lips drawing together in ugly anger.

"I dun't believe thee, what you did say, about the

THE PARISH WAYWARDEN

Irishman, Poll and the Gigg boys, reckon you be a liar Penny."

As Edward Loper turned to walk away, Robert caught him by the arm.

"Edward, I am to marry...I am to marry...Mrs.."

"Mrs Joan Young," said Samuel, quickly.

"You what Penny?" said the parish constable, shrugging Robert's hand away, "you're be goin' to marry thic beggar?"

"Yes, I do know her, she did come here, to the parish, so that we may marry."

Joan Young raised her head slowly, to look up at Robert but said nothing.

The parish constable rubbed the back of his head and grimaced.

"Let her go Edward," said Robert, "let her go now and I will look after her and the girl."

"Rose," said Samuel.

"And Rose," said Robert.

"But thee'd be harbouring vagrants Penny?"

"She'll be my wife and not a beggar. Parson Crouch will marry us, he has said so."

"By God's guts Penny, you'd best know what you is about," said the parish constable, puffing out his cheeks and blinking, he then put out a hand onto the stock post to steady himself, his hand shaking as he aimed the key.

The padlock clicked and parted and Samuel raised the bar to enable Joan's foot to be lifted out from the holes in the stocks and with Samuel's help she then raised herself up, unsteadily. The stocks bar was lowered and relocked, the parish constable pocketing the key, before turning and walking away unsteadily, muttering to himself.

"Come," said Robert.

They walked together, slowly, with Rose then stopping

and looking up at her mother.

"Here," said Robert, lifting up the girl and carrying her over his shoulder.

They walked back in silence to the house.

"Light the fire," said Robert, to Samuel as the front door was pushed open, and Rose was lowered to the floor, "there be coins, on the table, get bread, get eggs and cheese. Sit...Joan and Rose, sit there on the bed."

Samuel ran around to Mother Goody's to gather embers and once the fire was lit, he took coins from the table and ran back down The Street. Nothing was said, with Joan and Rose both huddled together on Samuel's bed. Robert went to the barn and collected an armful of the elm branches from Sun Lane, snapping the thinner ones and smashing the thicker branches to fracture them on the rim of a large iron pot. He poked furze into the fire to encourage the elm to burn and the fire was soon blazing.

"Warm thyselves," said Robert, "come, near the fire."

Mother and daughter slipped from the bed and stood before the fire, warming their hands. Robert then went back and forth to the barn to collect armfuls of fresh hay and packed it down upon the floor in his mother's small weaving room, where the roof had recently been repatched with long straw. Samuel returned with bread and eggs but no cheese.

"Mother Goody has pottage on the fire and we can have some," said Samuel, going back out of the door.

Robert dragged the table over towards Samuel's bed so that when they ate, Joan and Rose could sit on the bed and he brought over his chair and Samuel's stool. Samuel came back with an old iron pot and hung it over the fire, stirring as it heated. There were two wooden platters and two wooden bowls but only two spoons which were given to Joan and Rose. When the pottage was shared out, Robert and Samuel used bread to mop up the pottage. Rose was looking less pale and she ate hurriedly.

Samuel asked his father about the barrel making tools. Robert stated that when he arrived at his sister's, he was told that all the tools had been sold.

"It were Richard that did sell them," said Robert, and then for Joan's benefit he added, "my sister Ann's husband. I do owe them, when Samuel and I moved back here, I did need money. I still do owe them money."

Samuel then asked his father about the parish work days that were coming up.

"Timothy Lane," said Robert, mopping up the pottage, "ditches must be dug first. A ditch is needed to take the water away onto land below, where there be no ditch. I dun't know whose land that be but it needs be done and they must put up with it."

"It's going to be another cold night," said Samuel, keen to keep the conversation going and avoid silence, with such big questions hanging in the air.

"I've put fresh hay in mother's weaving room, Joan and Rose can sleep there."

Joan nodded and smiled, but looked worried.

"I had to say..." said Robert, looking down at the table and then putting his head in his hands, "I had to say... to make Loper unlock the stocks. I...I din't know what to say...and now I've said..."

Robert looked up and puffed out his cheeks. Samuel smiled at his father. Rose looked up at her mother, who then started to sob. The light in the room was fading. Robert got up and went out into the back yard, closing the door behind him. He stood still in the yard, looking up at the sketchy high cloud, coloured by the sun setting behind the elms. The back door opened and closed and Joan stood beside him.

"What is to happen...Robert?"

"I do not know...I just... I have lied...again."

"Lied about what?"

"Lied that...we are to marry...lied that Parson Crouch will marry us. It is what I does, best of all, is to lie."

"You are kind."

"Kind? I do not think so."

"You took us in, when Rose was bad."

"You came, it was not my doing."

"But we did stay, we had no place to go...and my Rose.. she might have..."

"I be glad that she...that she has ate."

"Tomorrow, we will go, we will walk to the next village."

"To Chauncy? You'll fare no better there."

They stood in silence as the colour drained from the darkening sky. A skein of geese flew high above, in a straggled line.

"Oh, to be a bird," said Joan, "they do always know where they are bound."

"This morning, at the bottom of Sun Lane, I had a thought to turn the cart away, towards the forest and the sea, but old Katy did bring me home."

"I'm glad she did bring you home."

"Did Loper hurt you?"

"He did twist my arm. Said he would strip me before he took up the whip. He be a brute, but the overseer, he did fright us both, the way he do come close...and touch thee."

"Dowty did?"

"I've 'ad worse, but he do come at you with his words all funny. Like an owl he did come...Wuh...Wuh...Wuh, flappin' 'is arms...and then, with his hands and fingers..."

"Do not get cold, you must both settle to sleep, before you cannot see in the house," said Robert, "piss here, I will go inside."

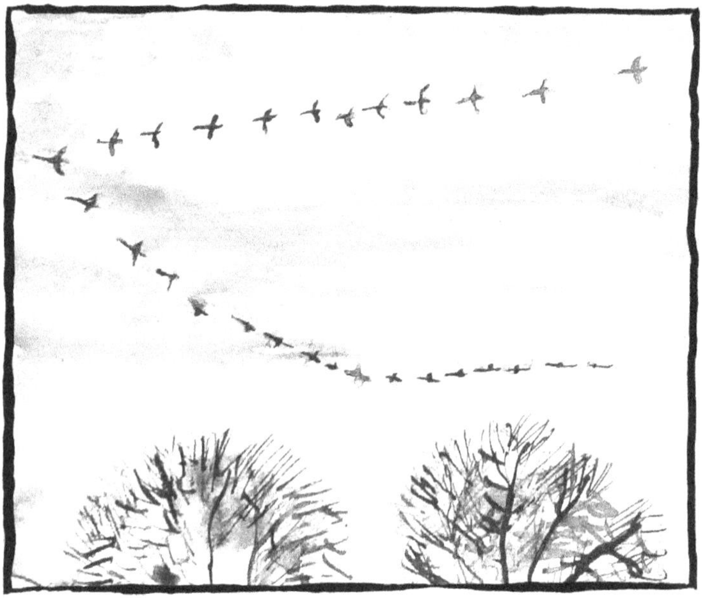

THE PARISH WAYWARDEN

Robert awoke before dawn and listened to the others breathing in their sleep. He sat up quietly, forcing his feet into his ungiving boots and then taking one of the larger coins that his sister Ann had given him, that were now on a shelf in the parlour, he quietly lifted the back door latch and went outside. In the grey half-light he visited the privy and then raised a bucket of water from the well from which to drink and splash into his face. He took fresh hay for Katy and drew another bucket to fill the trough. He could not think what to do next about Joan and Rose. There was no open path to take, Loper knew of his actions, the vestry would soon know and the law would be exercised. He had lied in saying that Parson Crouch would marry them. Robert left the yard and walked down The Street. There were early comings and goings and he met a packhorse train coming up the hill. There was a briskness in their passing, causing the bell on the leading pony to jangle, an urgency to make progress with the day barely begun. It was a short train with the attendant striding behind with a boy beside him, not burdening the laden bell pony with his own weight in the saddle, as they climbed the hill, on towards the downs and Top Road. Robert breathed in deeply, smelling the cargo of fish from the coast, from a world beyond the parish. He was tempted to demand a fish, as Loper had done some weeks before but instead he nodded at the driver as they passed and found himself asking where they were bound.

"Hell, if I dun't make haste," said the driver, calling back and then belching loudly.

Robert had noticed before how the packhorse drivers would often call briefly in the early morning to drink a pot of ale at the alehouse, whilst the train would stand and make dung in The Street.

Robert carried on downhill, passing the church and then on down, into Watery lane. There was a sickliness that Robert felt in his belly, when he was to visit Poll. It was early and Robert wanted to get it done. He had spoken to Ann about Catherine, about seeing her ghost and how their elder sister had never left the parish. When Ann had pressed coins into his hand, he knew that she wished him to see Poll, to ask him what he knew. Before, Poll had confirmed what they all did know, but Robert had not told of seeing her ghost, at the punishment of Simon Gigg. The geese were out in the lane, hissing and then lunging towards Robert as he approached Poll's house. Robert kept his hands in the air to stop them from snapping at his fingers and then swore at them as they gathered about him. The door to Poll's house was open. Robert kicked behind him to fend off the last of the geese that had followed him to the door. After all the noise of his approach, it seemed unnecessary to knock but Robert did so and then peered around the door, into the gloomy parlour. Poll was standing in the middle of the room, propped up on his crutches. Robert placed the coin upon the table.

"Robert Penny," said Poll, hoarsely.

In the grey early morning light Robert thought that Poll looked more wizen and hollow-faced than before. The cunning man opened and closed his mouth, making a sticky, sucking sound, his tongue protruding to try to moisten this dryness. He then twisted about and using his supporting crutches, he dragged his feet across the room and took down the sieve and the shears from their place upon the wall.

"Catherine, Catherine Penny," said Robert, "be she alive or dead?"

Robert noticed Poll's eyes widening, at the mention of Catherine's name. The sieve and the shears were placed upon the table but Poll made no move to set the sieve into the mouth of the shears, as he had done before when he and Loper had consulted Poll as to the identity of the one who had let the Irishman free from the parish stocks.

"She were a witch," said Poll, with sudden venom and he then hawked and spat upon the earthen floor, "they wanted her drowned, drowned in Clay Pond, down in the forest, out of the parish."

"Who wanted her drowned?" said Robert.

"T'was a bad harvest, after she did go making they chalk marks. Said she did curse the seed, for it not to grow and for they to starve and so they was to take her. But thic old parson, and his boy, did want her for theyselves, said she were saintly and no witch. Said the church would fall if she were drowned."

"Who? Who was to drown her?"

Poll shook his head slowly and gave a sickly smile, smiling at Robert's discomfort. Poll's hand slid across the table, towards the coin that Robert had placed there.

"No," said Robert, grabbing Poll's skinny wrist, "I did ask thee, Catherine Penny, be she alive or dead?"

"Why's thee come back from Chauncy Robert Penny?" said Poll, pulling his wrist away, "To find a beggar and make they a wife?"

Robert drew his fist back, as if to strike Poll, but then asked again whether his elder sister was alive or dead.

"Do it," said Robert, pushing the sieve and shears, across the table towards the cunning man.

Poll scowled and then picked up the shears, opening them as wide as they would go before forcing the sieve between the blades. He held up the shears with the sieve dangling below and Robert positioned himself so that he could place his two fingers opposite Poll's, to balance the shears.

"Catherine Penny," said Poll, spitting her name, "the witch, be she alive or dead?"

The sieve remained motionless.

"Did she go from the parish, as some do say?" said Robert, "with her sweetheart?"

Poll said nothing.

"Was she drowned for a witch?" said Robert.

The sieve dropped to the floor from the jaws of the shears and rolled slowly across towards the open door, before toppling over.

Poll made a dry cackling sound, at the back of his throat. Robert turned to leave, kicking the sieve across the floor as he went, leaving the door wide open. Reaching the lane, he then returned and stuck his head back around the door.

"She were no witch, just as thee has no cunning, just... big ears. If she were here, in the parish, then none would come to your door...for your pissy eggs...they would seek her. Tis you, in the parish, that would wish her dead, more than any."

"You Robert Penny, you do have blood on your hands," spat Poll.

Robert burst into the parlour, his hands were around Poll's neck before he knew what he was doing. He crashed the crippled man up against the wall, the crutches falling away to the floor.

"You keep thy mouth shut," shouted Robert, letting go of the cunning man who then slumped to floor, "or t'will be your blood that do flow."

Poll looked up, speaking weakly but with spite in his eyes.

"The stranger, he did pass early, but where be he now? T'was a fine black horse that did then come back all wild, up from the forest, but where be the mount? Did he fall Robert Penny?"

Robert stared down at the crumpled man upon floor. He knew nothing of this, about the returning horse. The stranger, he had gone, never to return.

Robert left the house as a woman appeared at the gate, coming to Poll's door, a woman from the parish that Robert vaguely recognised but did not know her name.

"Poll dun't feel well," said Robert, above the noise of the geese, "best come back, come later."

The woman did not speak but turned and walked hurriedly away, as if she did not wish to been seen and turned back to look at Robert as he followed behind her, up the lane.

Robert cursed the idea of going to see Poll, and wished he had not done so. The stranger's horse had returned to the parish? He must see Loper, to find out what had taken place. Did all the parish know that he and Loper were fighting with the stranger, behind the church? Where the parish constable's purse had been found.

Tetty Bonner was outside the alehouse talking to Mrs Chant but she caught Robert's eye as he approached. As Robert loitered Mrs Chant soon continued on, up The Street.

"Robert?" said Tetty, sensing that Robert wished to speak.

"Is Loper there?" asked Robert, gesturing towards the alehouse door.

Tetty shook her head.

"Not since he came in, with his face all swollen, from striking a tooth, so he did say. He din't have his purse and do still owe for his beer, so you can tell him to come and pay when you do find he."

"Why did you send the woman to me, and the daughter, Rose?"

"Come Robert, you do know why, she be a good woman."

"I lied, to get her from the stocks."

"Not if you do as you say. She do need a home and you

needs a wife. Not many gets asked to wed, when they be in the stocks."

"She says Loper were a brute but Dowty, he were worse."

"Robert, everyone knows how the overseer do keep the beggars away, they dun't return when he has had 'is turn in the church porch. Loper, he's worse than a brute to vagrants, we all do know that. The parish clerk knows how it be done these last two years and it dun't trouble he to stop it, keepin' the beggars from the parish, is all. Talk to parson Crouch, he will marry thee, it'll be the churchwarden, where the trouble do lie, dun't expect he to agree."

Robert turned to walk on up The Street but then paused and looked back.

"The cooper's tools in Chauncy, they all be sold. I did not know."

Tetty shrugged.

"Go to old Will Feather, he do have the tools and bad hands and bad eyes. He'll lend thee tools and learn thee p'raps?"

Robert nodded and continued on up The Street, to the parish constable's house.

"Married yet Penny?" said Edward Loper, opening the door slowly, his words slurred like a drunk.

"The stranger's horse has come back," said Robert, ignoring the question, "the man, he has returned?"

The parish constable shrugged, his eyes wincing in the light.

"I ain't seen 'un. The clerk do 'ave the horse, says he be looking after it, sayin' t'wud wander if left in the pound."

"He did leave? As he said, the morning after the fight?"

"Sssh Penny, dun't say about that," said the parish constable, looking up and down The Street.

"Poll did just say to me about it, as if I were to be blamed."

"Get in 'ere Penny, off The Street, then we shall talk."

Robert had not been inside Edward Loper's house and he was offered a chair in the parlour whilst the parish constable moved slowly to his own chair, puffing as he sat down. Mrs Loper could be heard in the back yard, calling out as she fed the chickens. The church bell tolled at ponderous but regular intervals.

"That'll be for old Joyce," said the parish constable,

"What did happen Edward? What did you do?" said Robert.

The parish constable was not smiling for once and looked about vaguely to ensure that his wife was still out in the yard.

"The horse, it came back, din't mean for it to come back, meant it to run on."

"Where was this? Not Dudge Lane again? And you thought he'd stolen your purse, in the churchyard?"

"He were a bad 'un Robert. We did do right by it."

"We?"

"You n' I, he did torment us both."

"No, no, do not say me, do not make me part of this Edward."

The parish constable turned slowly in his chair to glance towards the back door, before pulling a soft leather bag from inside his coat and thrusting it into Robert's hands.

"Here, take this, hide it and dun't tell anyone, 'specially not thit son of yourn. It can't stay here, not if someone do ask Poll about thic stranger, now that the 'orse did come back. You hide it Penny."

Mrs Loper came in through the back door with a basket

of eggs and greeted Robert. Robert stood up, unable to say what he wanted to say and left without speaking.

Robert's head was reeling as he walked back up The Street, towards his house. He had clamped the small but weighty leather bag under his arm, inside his coat. What was in the tied bag and now he was as guilty as any, if something bad had been done to the stranger? Loper had said on the night of the fight that he wanted to kill the stranger. Then his own purse was gone, giving him cause to think it stolen and he had lain in wait in the early morning, where he knew the stranger would pass, on his way to the forest and on down to the sea and then to France. How was it done? Robert did not want to know. And then, Loper's purse was found in the churchyard by David Crust, and returned. Robert had seen the parish constable's face, when he had weighed the purse in his hand, knowing then that it had not been stolen but dropped. Robert thought that he should now tell the vestry and the justices, what has taken place and give them the stranger's tied leather bag. He would tell the clerk and the churchwarden the whole story from when he first found the body in the ditch. He should speak out about Dowty also, how he did go for women in the church porch.

When he arrived back at the house, Robert went around to the back yard and then stuffed the small but weighty leather bag on the high beam above the privy, where the parish money was also kept.

"Father, parson Crouch's older brother is come back," said Samuel, as Robert entered the house through the back door.

"So?" said Robert.

"He has already said about Long Mound," said Samuel, "and how it now be spoiled...that it be an ancient parish boundary mark. Said it should be made good."

"And he knows what he can do. So, he come down from

Top Road?" said Robert, "and the first thing he do see in the parish displeases him. He may have drowned in the water splash, if the highway work not be done, that wouldn't have pleased him none either."

"He has come for the saint's day, St Catherine's day. 'Tis on Tuesday, and parson Crouch hopes that he will be gone soon after."

"I did see the churchwarden in the alehouse in Chauncy, sayin' that Augustus do always come to St Catherine's day. Thigpen do think high of the brother and they do write, saying how bad parson Crouch be in the pulpit."

"He be a good man," said Joan, who was listening from the parlour, "a good parson, to my mind."

"And I must speak with him," said Robert, rubbing his face hard with both hands, before sitting down in his chair, beside the table.

Robert's head ached and he felt like getting drunk. There were still some coins left from his sister Ann. Joan placed a boiled egg on the table in front of him.

"You have not eaten, I heard you go this early morning," she said.

Robert stood up wearily. Taking the egg, he went out of the back door, into the yard. He walked across to where Katy was standing, peeling the egg as he went. What was in the bag that Loper had thrust at him, not wishing for it to remain in the parish constable's own house? If consulted, Poll would certainly point a finger at Robert, after his visit this morning and then he would be the guilty one, if it were indeed stolen property and he were accused. Robert dared not look in the bag. He would get rid of it tonight, bury it where it would never be found. And how did Poll not see Loper pass his door on that morning, Poll only mentioned the stranger and then his horse returning? Loper must have gone to the east, across the Common and then down into Dudge Lane. Loper knew that Poll would see all and how did Poll know about he and Loper's involvement with the stranger anyway, perhaps even their fighting behind the church? The parish had eyes and ears and Poll had many visitors. Then there was the talk of Catherine, being a witch. Robert wondered who it was in the parish that did wish for her drowned in Clay Pond, or was it just words and Poll's own poison stirred into it all. Poll did say that it was old parson Crouch and his son that protected her, so that the church might be saved from falling down. Was she a witch or a saint, his eldest sister Catherine? He stroked the old horse's neck. Robert went back into the house and took half of his sister's coins that remained and left without speaking.

Old Will Feather lived in Flower Lane, near the blacksmith. Robert had seen him at church but they had never spoken. Robert knocked on the door of a house that was badly in need of repair.

"I b'aint risin' from me chair, zo go or coom 'n I dun't mind which it be."

Robert lifted the latch on the front door and looked inside. The sunlight from the clear morning sent a blazing shaft into the room.

"It is I, Robert Penny. I wish to talk, about making barrels."

Will Feather had a shock of white hair that stood up on top of his head. It was this hair that Robert had noticed in church. The old cooper never seemed to wear a hat, proudly displaying his pure white hair as proof of his years.

"Penny?" said Will Feather, who then coughed to clear his throat, "Judd's boy?"

"Yes, I did come back to the parish. I lived in Chauncy."

"Now Judd be in the ground, you coom back. I did

know Judd Penny. Knew he afore and then after."

"After?"

"Is thee coomin' or standin' at the door, lettin' in the divel?"

Robert entered the room and closed the door slowly behind him, the light retreating and then banished altogether, as the latch clicked. At first, he could not see the position of the old man in the parlour.

"The wife be dead but the daughter do come," said Will Feather.

"Tis dark," said Robert, stumbling into a chair or a table.

"Tis allus dark, when yourn eyes do die, afore the rest of ye. If yea be wantin' a barrel then Robert Penny..?"

"I want to make a barrel. Many barrels. Tetty said that she still has your barrels but they are old now. I did make barrels in Chauncy. Not as an apprentice but a man did show me how. I thought that his tools were left me, but they was sold."

"Coom, give me thy hand, rise me up."

Robert shuffled slowly towards the voice. The darkness was pricked by pinpoints of sunlight, entering through small holes and gaps as the sun struck the outside wall. In these lines of light, dust hung in the air. Robert, seeing better, helped Will Feather to his feet. Robert held his gnarled fingers until they reached the back door and then he could see where he was going. A barn door was swung open and inside was the cooper's workshop; the cooper's block, the two handled knives hung up with the axes and the adze, the irons, the planes, a long plane and the shaving horse, the augers and round shaves.

"Worm," said Will Feather, "thy needs to make handle's afore you makes a barrel. Planes is not so bad. What thee pay?"

"Can you walk," said Robert, "to the alehouse?"

"Tis a path trod, Robert Penny," said the cooper, closing the barn door.

He smiled in the sunlight, his hair stiff white, his pale blue eyes glinting but unseeing and he led the way to the alehouse.

"Robert," said Tetty Bonner, "and Will Feather. That didn't take thee long? New barrels is it then Will? Got thee a young 'prentice?"

"Not so young," said Robert, "not an apprentice neither."

"Can't talk barrels wi' a dry mouth," said the old cooper, "hope thy ale's not all leaked away vrum thic old wood and thee've zum left vor us?"

The two men sat down by the door and Tetty brought over two full tankards. Robert pushed the coins that he had brought across the table, towards the landlady.

"If thee is talking new barrels, then I give you these," said Tetty, "after that, I do take your money."

"Take it while I have it," said Robert, sipping his beer.

Tetty left the money on the table and retreated to the inner parlour. The cooper raised his tankard slowly between two twisted hands and took a large gulp before lowering it back down again but kept his hold before repeating the action

"Ahhh," said Will Feather, gently placing the half full tankard back on the table, slowly releasing his grip and then wiping his mouth with his sleeve.

"I've got no money," said Robert, "not 'til I've made and sold barrels. I could do work, carpentry work?"

"House, tis bad, but it do need more thin carp'ntry. When I be gone thems can pull 'un down, for all I do care."

"What about the tools, will your daughter not sell them?"

The cooper lifted the tankard again, taking two gulps to

drain the remaining ale.

"She do 'ave money, married a puritan, he do say that strong drink, it do the divel's work. 'Ere Tet, thirsty sinners do want more ale."

Robert tipped back his tankard and Tetty slid a coin from the table, when she returned with the beer.

"Thee dun't drink as vast as ole Judd," said Will Feather, "after he got bad."

"What made him bad? Was it Catherine...?"

"Whoa Robert, dun't say 'er name."

"But she be my sister."

"She'm no more, Judd did cast her out."

The old man's hands shook as he raised the tankard to drink.

"But, I thought she was to go into service, at the parsonage? Poll does say she were a witch."

"Huh, Poll do say a lot. T'was the 'arvest, back then, all did have the chalk marks, in the barns but the corn, it dun't grow. Say t'was...er fault, say she did curse the ground, did curse the seed."

"Catherine?"

"Sssh, Robert. Come harvest, there were none, none in Thigpen's strips, nor Button's, nor Arnold's, nor Gigg's, Loper's, Dowty's, Chant's, none in Judd's neither. Some did come to Judd, not all, saying that...she had cursed the very ground. Judd did get beat one night and after, t'were late, some came to the house, sayin' that...she... were a witch, Poll did say, all did say. Said that she must be thrown in Clay Pond, the Witches Pond they did call it. They did come for her Robert, but she was gone to the church, said they'd 'ave God to answer to, if she were taken. But Augustus did come, he did strike one of they and then she did run from thic church. Zunday afore, old parson Crouch did say from the pulpit, that…she were no witch and said she would be goin' into service, at thic parson's 'ouse. Then, she were gone. D'int start in zervice, none did know where she were. They chalk marks, they still be in the barns, none did rub they out, they daren'st. 'Arvest were better thit next year."

The old man gulped at his beer and then drained it.

"I thought that I saw her ghost," said Robert, "on the Green, at the whipping of Simon Gigg, I saw her, I saw Cather…"

"Ssssh. I dun't know, about no ghost. All I knows is, Judd did go bad after."

"Did he mean to give her up, on that night?"

"He let they in, but she were gone, gone out the back, she did know. Yourn mother, she did beat at they men with the dog stick."

"I do not remember that night, Ann, my sister, she were older, but she did not say about it when we spoke."

"Prap's thee were sent to Goody's, knowin' they would come. Zo, Robert Penny…"

"Who were they, that did come?"

"Vools they wus, drunk. Zo, Robert Penny, canst thee make a hogshead stave, all proper done?"

"I have before," said Robert.

"Coom, make we a stave, in the shop."

"What, now?"

"Noo, more ale vurst," said the cooper, throwing his head of white hair back and laughing as he banged his empty tankard down on the table.

It was bright, out of the alehouse. The walk back to the cooper's was slower. The barn door was thrown open, letting in good light but it was cold in the shadows. Will Feather moved about the shop, muttering and then selecting a short plank of dusty oak, he held it out for Robert.

"Twill do thee," said the cooper, who then rolled a small barrel outside, on its rim and placed it in the sun, "you get on, I'll get we zum zider in thic old 'arvest bottle."

Robert looked around, at all the tools, many more than he had used in Chauncy. He felt the edges of the blades on the planes and the shaves. The was a bubbling rustiness on some of the metal and the ash handles on many of the tools had worm, the wood flaking away in his hands. He tried the shaving horse and hoped that it would take his weight. Will Feather returned with a large round flagon of cider and sat down upon the small barrel.

"'Ave a pull on thic zider, Judd Penny."

Robert smiled to himself as he looked upon the old man, at the shock of stiff white hair, shining brightly in the sun. There must have been many occasions when his father would have drunk with Will Feather and Robert drank deeply, needing two hands to lift the heavy clay vessel to his mouth. The ringing sounds from the blacksmith's anvil could be heard from the shop next door and Robert began to feel part of something, here he was, charged with showing that he had the craft to make a barrel. As Robert prepared to get to work, the cooper drank again, cleared his throat and then spat upon the dry earth before starting to sing.

"Young men give ear to me awhile
If to yea merriment are inclined
I'll tell thee a story to make 'ee smile
Of late done by a woman kind
An' as she went musing all alone
I 'eard she to sigh, to sob and make moan..."

It was a good year since he had last made a stave and Robert set to work, at first clamping the plank in a hook on the cooper's block, but the oak still moved about and so he moved on to the shaving horse, which despite its old and splaying legs, did not collapse under him. With the side axe he started to shape the clamped stave so that it was broader in the middle and thinner at the end and then he cursed, remembering that the stave needed to be sawn to the exact length before the shaping. He talked to himself, cajoling himself on, he did not want to ask questions of the old cooper, he just wanted to present the finished stave for his approval. He looked about and found an old rule with markings on it and then guessed at the right mark, to give the length for a hogshead stave. Robert was warming up in the shadows of the shop and took off his coat and then accepted another deep pull on the cider flagon, as the old man continued to sing.

"For 'un dildoul, a dildoul a dil dil doul.
Coom thee Judd, ajoin with we…"

Robert knew the song and joined in as he worked.

"Quoth she, I be undone if I han't a dildoul
For I'm a maid 'n a very good maid
And sixteen years of age am I
And fain would I part with my maidenhood
If any good fellow would with me lie
But none to me ever proffered such love
To lie by my side and give me a shove…"

Robert could hear a third voice. The ringing of the bouncing hammers upon the blacksmith's anvil had stopped as Francis Skutt's deeper voice joined the song.

"With his dil doul, a dil doul , a dil dil doul
O happy were I
With his dil doul, a dil doul , a dil dil doul
At night when I do go to bed
Thinking for to take my rest
Strange fancies comes in my head
I pray for what I love best

For it be a comfort and pleasure doth bring
To women that hath such a pretty fine thing
Call'd a dil doul a dil doul , a dil dil doul
 O happy were I
With his dil doul, a dil doul , a dil dil doul".

A woman voice could be heard, shouting out, and the ring of the blacksmith's anvil started up once again. The old cooper laughed and called out.

"Is thee b'aint allowed to sing then Francis? Ere Judd, Mizzus Skutt dunt like thic song we do sing, p'raps she do like ol' Diddle Diddle?"

Robert stopped to take another drink. The old man rocked back and forth on the small barrel, the sun still trapped in this corner of the yard. He looked up at Robert with smiling, unseeing pale blue eyes. Robert now had to plane the sides of the stave, judging the correct bevel according to the size of the finished cask. He moved to the long jointer plane and drew the stave back and forth on the fixed, upside-down plane. The blade should be sharpened anew but Robert hoped that for this one stave it would cut cleanly enough. Will Feather had begun to sing again, raising his voice over the sounds of the planing of the hard oak stave. Robert did not join in with the song as he concentrated on the task at hand, fuelled by the beer and now the strong cider.

"Lavenders green, lavenders blue
You must love me, cause I do love you
A brisk young man
Met with a maid
And laid her down
All in the shade
Oft have I lain
With him in the dark
But he has ne'er

Shot at the mark
But now my dear
Have at thy bum
For I do swear
Now I am come
Lavenders green......"

Mrs Skutt, having prevented her husband from joining in with the singing, now appeared in the yard with hands on hips.

"You keep thy filth, Will Feather, tis not for my ears, nor my young Sally."

"Dun't thee loike a bit 'o diddle diddle then Mrs?"

"I'll throw a pail o water over thee, if thee starts up."

The old cooper slapped his thigh and threw his head back in laughter.

"Ere Judd Penny, she dun't like our songs."

Mrs Skutt peered into the cooper's shop at Robert, squatting over the long jointer plane.

"Tisn't Judd Penny, thee old fool, 'tis Robert Penny, praps he be as bad?"

Will Feather stopped rocking on the barrel, his brow puckering in confusion.

"Tis Robert Penny," said Robert, "Judd be in the churchyard. There I have made thee a stave, a stave for a hogshead."

Mrs Skutt shook her head and returned next door.

The sun had now withdrawn from the corner of the yard, the shadows cast by the roof of the house consuming the old man who then visibly shivered.

"Robert Penny?" said the old man, quietly, doubtfully.

Robert held out the stave, touching the cooper's arm with the end, so that it might be taken. Will Feather took the stave, the pleasure of the day now gone from his face. He handled the piece of wood, one of the many staves that would be required to make the barrel, the bevelled edges angled to join tightly together.

"Tis a quart too big," said Will Feather, casting the stave onto the ground, "tis good fer the fire but nought else."

"I will make another," said Robert.

The old man got up unsteadily and turned to shuffle back towards the house. Robert puffed out his cheeks and lifted the cider flagon to take a deep swig. He had done the best he could and yet this was deemed not good enough. The cooper, feeling the stave, absently measuring its tapered width between his finger and gauging that it was very slightly too big, when joined with the other staves to make the barrel it would be a quart over the measure for a hogshead. Robert began again, finding another old oak plank. It was now cold in the shop and after the first shaping of the new stave, Robert threw it down and cursed before picking up the cider flask to drain it in one lift. He pushed the door to and walked around behind the blacksmith's, rather than go back into the old cooper's dark house.

"Thought it were ol' Judd back," said Francis Skutt, pausing at the anvil and wiping the sweat away from his face, as Robert passed the open doors to the forge, "they were some good drinkin' days. Are thee now makin' barrels then Robert? They do say it be the hardest of all, to make a wet barrel."

"I shan't be making no barrels," said Robert, without explanation.

He wanted to drink more but needed to return home for the remaining money, before visiting the alehouse. Robert stumbled into the house, through the front door. He went straight to the shelf in the parlour but the remaining coins had gone.

"Samuel has bought milk, eggs, barley and bread," said Joan, with Rose close to her side.

"Where is he?" said Robert, holding himself steady on one corner of the table.

"He is...I do not know."

"And you thinks it a good notion? To spend my money?"

Joan edged around towards the opposite side of the table, Rose wide eyed looking up at Robert. Robert lurched forwards and then continued towards the back door, opening it and slamming it shut behind him.

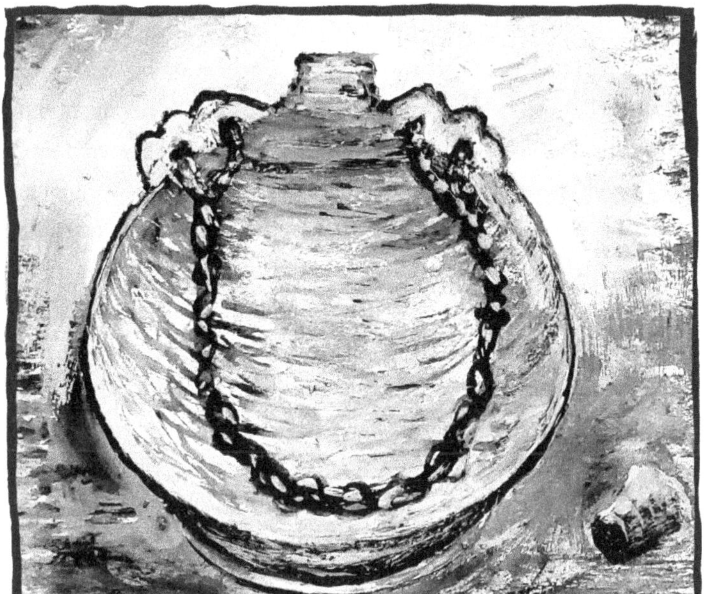

He could remember nothing more until he awoke in the morning, his eyes sticky and his mouth dry. Samuel had lit the fire and Joan and Rose came in through the back door, Joan holding their folded blankets.

"Why do you sleep in the barn?" said Robert, croakily, sitting up in bed.

Joan went through to the parlour and stood with Rose beside the fire.

Robert had slept fully dressed and he got up to stand blinking beside the bed. He forced his feet into his boots and went out to the well, drawing a bucket of water before tipping it over his head. His hands felt slimy and stank of rotten animal fat. He scraped and rubbed at his palms before smearing them on an old wooden gatepost and then, drawing more water, he tried to rinse away the stench. What had happened last night? Robert shuffled to the privy and then stood in the yard, his hair still dripping water. Joan came out into the yard, her blanket now wrapped around her.

"What did I do?" said Robert, quietly, "did I beat Samuel?"

Joan shook her head.

They stood in the yard as the sparrows squabbled amongst the ivy, that covered one wall of the barn.

"Robert, I cannot marry thee, we cannot marry, not like that."

"I was drunk, I grant, but I cannot say...How did I do bad? Why did you go to the barn...I didn't...not with thee?"

"No," said Joan, raising her voice in protest.

"Tell me?" said Robert.

"It were the songs," said Joan.

"The songs?"

"So loud they were, I did cover Rose's ears but.."

"Songs?" said Robert again, "I were singing?"

"Such bad songs Robert, not for a girl to hear, nor a woman. I do know thee better now, you are kind, but I cannot stay. We cannot be man and wife. We shall go, we leave today."

Joan turned to walk back to the house.

"No, do not go, you cannot. I wish to marry. I will not drink and I will not sing. Do not go, I pray, do not leave. Say you will marry?"

Joan paused but said nothing. Robert spoke about his visit to the cooper's, that he wished to make barrels, to earn money, so that they might eat and live. The old barrel maker had asked Robert to prove his worth, to make a stave. They had drunk and Will Feather had sung, the old blind man had thought that Robert's father was returned from the grave, to drink and to sing as they had many times before. When it came to him that it was not old Judd Penny in the cooper's shop, but his son Robert, then he said that the stave was only fit to burn, that it was a quart over size.

"He did not need his eyes to know that I had made wrong," said Robert.

"P'raps he were being spiteful?" said Joan.

They stood in silence, with the space still between them.

"God's blood..." said Robert, loudly, turning quickly towards the back door

"Robert," said Joan, in reprimand.

"Tis a parish work day, I must be in Timothy Lane, I needs go."

"Then take an egg, take bread, you have not ate?"

"Samuel," shouted Robert, as he barged back into the house.

John Arnold and Mark Bonner were waiting in Timothy Lane. John had the cart whilst Robert had arrived with nothing, shouting to Samuel, before he left, to bring two spades.

"Robert," said John Arnold and Mark Bonner, together.

Robert acknowledged the two men with a nod of his head and then rubbed his face with both hands. It was another clear and cold morning. The water had gone down a bit more in the big puddle as there had been no rain for two weeks now.

"Let us get to work," said John Arnold, "to warm thyselves up. Shall us see where the ditches needs be dug?"

The three men walked around to the lower land, behind the hedge where the ditch was full of leaves and sloppy mud that ran for some distance along the underside of the hedge.

"It needs a new ditch, to run the water downhill," said Robert, "once this ditch be full then the water does sit. Whose land be this?"

"Dun't know, to be fair," said John Arnold.

Samuel arrived on the track with two spades and a basket. He pushed the basket into the hedge on the higher side of the track and then brought the spades around, to the lower ground. Robert took one of the spades and stuck it in the moist ground, midway along the long and broad ditch. He then began to dig, not intending to connect with the full ditch until the new ditch had been formed. The water could then be released later on, by digging out the remaining spit of soil that had been left and once that had been breached, the water could then flow away downhill. More parishioners arrived, both from Asseley and from Watery Lane. Robert showed what was to be done and they split into groups, some dragging out the leaves and twigs from the full ditch whilst others with spades began upon the length of the new ditch, digging sections that would then join up. The spoil was all raised upon one side of the new ditch. By midday, the new ditch was dug and it only remained to remove the final spit from the top, to release the water from the old ditch. This task

Robert gave to the youngest member of the parish workgang, Mary Chant after he had chopped at the remaining tussock of grass with his spade, the young girl then took hold of the rough grass with both hands to drag and lift it out, tossing it to one side. The still, dark water laying on the underside of the hedge was then ushered into the mouth of the new ditch, its downward passage cheered on by the parishioners, at first a trickle and then a gush, the head of the flow nosing on downhill, along the base of the freshly dug soil. Once the level of water in the old ditch began to fall, those with spades paddled the water along to speed it away, downhill. Across the base of the track a depth of sloppy clay was now revealed and Robert said that it would have to be dug out or scraped away before any gravel could be laid. This was very messy work and many were soon covered in the light brown of liquid mud. John Arnold turned the horse around from where it was grazing and brought the cart into the revealed mud of the long puddle, where sloppy spadefuls were cast into the back gate of the cart. Once the sitting mud had been reduced and the cart full and leaking, John took it around to the lower side of the track and using spades, the mud was then flopped out across the open grass slope by David Crust and another labourer.

Robert then stopped to eat an egg and bread that Joan had packed in the basket. He drank deeply from the flagon of well water, realising how thirsty he was. John Arnold ushered Robert to one side, as he was eating, and spoke to him in quiet tones.

"Robert, tis it true that you wish to marry a vagrant? A woman with a child?"

Robert frowned, his mouth full with bread.

"The parish, they will not hold with it," said John Arnold, shaking his head, "the churchwarden, he will not let it be so, even if the parson do agree. Thee now be harbouring the vagrant at thy house Robert? Tis not how it should be, the parish they won't pay, when there be poor enough of our own?"

"The hedge needs be cut right back," said Robert, ignoring the question and wiping his mouth on his sleeve, "it will let the wind and sun do its work, for the highway to grow better of itself."

John Arnold shrugged.

"T'will cause trouble Robert, thee mark my word."

Robert set those with billhooks to cut the rough hedge on the lower side, now that the deep puddle had been drained. The branches and cuttings were either lifted into the cart or tossed over the hedge, beyond the old ditch, to be gathered up into a heap.

"There be dug gravel," said John Arnold, thinking again of the task in hand and pointing back towards Watery Lane, "not far."

"On whose land?"

"Thigpen's, but gravel be gravel."

This was true, already dug stone or gravel could be used for highways work, taken from anywhere within the parish. For Top Road it was too far to haul gravel and so chalk from Long Mound was used for the fill. Here, in Timothy Lane, there was gravel available and so for the remainder of the day and the following day then gravel would be loaded, hauled and tipped to make level the deep depression where the water would sit. If done well, the raised surface would hang to the lower side and help guide the fallen water through the gaps in the hedge and away to the ditches beyond. John took four men to help load the gravel, whilst the hedges, on both sides of the track, were cut back.

Before the end of the day, Robert found himself again listening to John Arnold's concerns.

"Thee needs a wife Robert, but t'ain't done this way."

"She is a good woman John," said Robert, "better than I do deserve."

Robert did not wish to talk. If he had, he would have asked John Arnold about his sister Catherine and how John Arnold wished to marry her, even when she was so young. Then there was the visit to the house, just before she had disappeared, after the crops had failed, when a gang of drunken men came to the house, to demand that Catherine be thrown into Clay Pond, to see if she were a true witch. As it was, they worked in silence until the second cartload of gravel had been put down and spread about, under Robert's direction, on Timothy Lane. The gravel had a good amount of clay amongst it and would compact well, in time and with use. Some declared that the job had been completed but there was still a depth to be made up, to ensure that the water would be tilted towards the downside, towards the ditches.

"Tis done," said Mark Bonner, "tis done in a day."

"And would you be back next year, doing the same?" said Robert, "tomorrow we bring gravel, all the day, and then it shall be done."

John Arnold nodded in approval. He knew that to stay done and passable then more work and more gravel was required.

"Robert Penny be our waywarden and we be thankful."

There was a general murmur of approval to this statement. Many would benefit from this work, unlike the repairs to Top Lane, where few parishioners did pass and others from elsewhere would benefit. With light still left in the day, the parishioners drifted away and Robert nodded to John Arnold as he turned his cart around, returning to Asseley. Robert and Samuel collected their spades and basket and walked back up Watery Lane. Robert felt hungry and weary and neither spoke, he did not wish to enter an empty house.

As he opened the front door, Robert could smell cooking, he could smell meat. Joan and Rose were near the fire and a pot was steaming.

"But, you said you would be gone?" said Robert, "I feared you would be gone?"

"And I thought you would be hungry," said Joan, "it is rabbit, Mother Goody did bring it, still warm."

Robert crossed the room and found himself taking both of Joan's hands, but he could not speak. His eyes had filled with tears. Joan smiled and then drew one hand away to wipe a tear from her own eye.

"So, here we be," she said.

"And I am glad," said Robert.

"I'm hungry," said Rose.

Samuel brought the table across to his bed, as before and then the chair and stool.

"We shall need more chairs," said Robert, "at least a stool and a chair."

They sat down to eat and Robert inhaled deeply through his nose, savouring the smell of the meat.

"Ubi bene, ibi patria," said Samuel.

"He does this," said Robert, to Joan, "pay no heed."

"He is a good boy, a clever boy," said Joan, as there was a knock at the front door.

Robert spooned in another mouthful of rabbit before he drew away from the table, to answer the door. Issac Button, the parish clerk, John Jess the beadle and the parish constable, stood, bunched together on the doorstep. Robert chewed his meat, unable to speak as he looked at all three.

"Robert," said the parish clerk.

John Jess nodded and Edward Loper shifted about uneasily.

"What?" said Robert, pushing the meat to the side of his mouth, with his tongue.

"You did meet with the stranger?" said the parish clerk, "the one who sought his sister?"

Robert nodded.

"His horse, it did return but of him there were no sign," continued the clerk, "Edward do say that you and he did meet with the stranger in the churchyard, after evening prayer, Sunday last, when you asked questions of the stranger?"

Robert swallowed his mouthful and looked at Loper, who looked down at the floor.

"We did meet," said Robert, "we did not think him truthful. He was not as he did say, the brother of the woman he sought, but instead he wished to marry her, he wished for her money. He was to leave early the next morning, for the sea, to France."

Robert moved forward, stepping out of his door, making the three men move backwards and Robert then pulled the door half closed behind him.

"Yea, he was not as he did say," agreed the parish clerk, "but he were a thief who did steal from my house. Before divine service, when all were walking to church, he did sneak to steal and then rushed to the church on his horse, where he joined with Edward, in the pew."

Robert eyes widened but he said nothing. Isaac Button continued.

"When the horse did return, there were no sign of that which was stolen. Robert, we have spoke with Poll, so that he may guide us."

"Is that why thee have come to my door? Because of what Poll do say?"

"We think that the thief was met, in the early morning,

down in Dudge Lane, near the forest. Of the stranger there be no sign, whether he be...alive or not?"

Robert glanced at Edward Loper, who remained with his head bowed.

"And you think it was I?" said Robert, "that jumped out at the stranger, to kill and rob him?"

"The sieve and shears did say," said John Jess, "we needs search for that which was stolen. Poll did say to look in the privy, where things oftentimes be hid."

Robert's stomach sank like a stone.

"The privy?" said Robert, "heed me Isaac Button, I have done no such thing. Ask John Arnold when I did borrow his cart in the early morning that you talk of, ask the churchwarden who I did meet in Chauncy on that same morning? Do not accuse one who was elsewhere. The stranger, he did return back to his lodging after we...after we did speak in the churchyard. Ask the tailor.."

John Jess eased his way past Robert, to enter the room.

"Samuel Penny," said the beadle, producing a half candle from his pocket, "light this candle and show me the privy."

Samuel frowned but took the candle to the fire and lit it. He gestured for the beadle to follow out of the back door. Joan looked down whilst Rose huddled up close to her mother.

"The harbouring of vagrants, tis a crime," said the parish clerk, peering in to see who was at the table, whilst the beadle conducted the search, "Edward, you be the constable?"

The parish constable voice wavered as he spoke for the first time.

"Ah, but Isaac...it be not that way," said Loper, his voice weak.

"We are to marry," said Robert, "she did come to the parish, so that we may marry."

"The churchwarden, he will not let it be so," said the clerk.

The back door opened and candlelight lit the parlour. Robert felt sick. How could he have accepted the leather bag from Loper, that he knew came from the stranger but knew not what it contained?

"There be this," said John Jess, holding out his mother's old box that contained the parish highway monies, that Robert had hidden on the shelf.

The box was opened and the contents tipped out into the beadle's hand. The clerk peered at the coins.

"Tis the highway money," said Robert, with confusion and relief, taking the coins and holding them up in the clerk's face, "as Poll do say, it be kept safe in the privy, but there be nothing else here. Search if you will?"

"No, no," said the parish constable, turning and wanting to leave, supporting himself on the doorframe, "Robert, he be saying the truth...see, his hand, it do not shake, like that of a guilty man, Robert Penny be not your man. The murderer, p'raps he be not a parish man at all, but a stranger hisself?"

Standing around the lit candle, the parish clerk looked from one to the other and then peered at Joan and Rose. Robert leant forward and blew out the candle.

"Goodnight to thee," said Robert, ushering the three men out of the door and closing it behind him.

Nobody spoke and the meal was finished in near darkness. Joan and Rose returned to sleeping on hay in Robert's mother's weaving room. Robert lay in bed, in the darkness, with his eyes open. He was sure that he had hidden the bag that Loper had given him, in the privy, and yet the beadle had not found it, finding only the parish monies that had been concealed in the same place, on the same beam. How could Loper appear at his door, knowing that he had given Robert the bag to conceal? The stranger had now been accused of the theft from the house of Isaac Button, before church on the Sunday. Robert recalled how the stranger had appeared late in church, when most were already seated. What had been stolen? Robert thought money but the parish clerk had not stated what had been taken. The theft and then the stranger's horse returning with no sign of the rider had caused an enquiry of Poll, the cunning man quick to raise the name of Robert Penny. Robert was not surprised by this. After his last visit, Robert had left Poll lying on the floor. Joan had not spoken, after the interruption to their meal. Did she now think Robert a dishonourable man, as well as a bawdy drunk?

The weather had changed overnight and it was raining when Robert awoke. He was quick to visit the privy to establish for himself that the leather bag was no longer where he had placed it, up behind the highest rafter. Was it really so commonplace for all to conceal their valuables in the privy, as Poll had determined? It was the place where no person wished to loiter and none would speak to others of the whereabouts of their own valuables. It was only the cunning man, hearing over and again the ways and secrets and guilty confessions of the parish that he would learn of such a thing. Not cunning, thought Robert, just a festering sore at the very heart of parish affairs. He thought of Joan, stealing his possessions and quickly dismissed the idea. She would not, nor could she even think of doing such a thing, of that Robert was certain. Samuel knew nothing of the bag and had never stolen anything, to Robert's knowledge. If such a hiding place was so readily used throughout the parish, then any person who knew of this most obvious place of concealment, could steal from all, not just from Robert. He would have surely heard of such a thing, from amongst his neighbours, but it had not been so.

In the misty rain, he and Samuel left the house for Timothy Lane, to complete the final day of parish highways work, for that year.

"Why did they come?" said Samuel, quietly, as they walked down The Street, looking up at Robert with fear in his eyes.

Samuel's enquiry only confirmed to Robert what he already believed of his son.

"It is Poll," said Robert, "he wishes to cause me harm. He has been spiteful and he has been against our family, since Catherine was...here. The parish, they believed in her ways. Poll, he did not like it."

They walked on in silence.

"Joan, she will think that I am a bad man now? A dishonest man?" said Robert, turning to his son, "she will not leave?"

Samuel did not answer.

The day was spent loading and hauling gravel from land off Sun Lane that belonged to Peter Thigpen, the churchwarden. It was scrappy land with spoil heaps from previous diggings and gravel already dug and piled up.

"It is yours to take Robert, as waywarden," said John Arnold, "the churchwarden, he do as he wishes and dun't send labour as he should."

"I shall say so in church and he shall pay," said Robert, "tis only right."

"Hmm," said John Arnold, doubtfully.

Whilst John Arnold and Robert went to collect the second load of gravel, the parish labourers were set to gather faggots from the cut hedge, to lay in the deepest hollow in the track, before the rest of the gravel was put down. Twists of honeysuckle were used to tightly bind the blackthorn and it was then placed crossways, across the hollow, to build up the base of the depression and to prevent sinkage of the whole repair, into the underlying clay. Robert did not speak of the visit to his house on the previous evening as he himself was still churning over in his head what had happened to the tied leather bag, that Loper had thrust at him for safekeeping. Robert asked John Arnold instead about the night when the drunken men came to take Catherine, to cast her into Clay Pond, to see whether she truly was a witch. John Arnold gave a pained look and shook his head and by the lengthy pause, Robert thought that the parish elder would refuse to speak of it.

"Oh, Robert, tis a time ago," John Arnold said eventually as the laden cart jogged back towards the work party in Timothy Lane, "and they all be dead and lain in the sacred ground. Save one."

"Who?" said Robert, quickly, turning towards John Arnold, "who still lives?"

"Twas a son, of one of they, he were of Catherine's own age and he had drunk with the men, but tis best left be Robert, for none can bring her back now. You did see her ghost yourself, upon the village Green? Surely tis testament enough that she be dead?"

"But I do still wish to know..."

"Who be that?" said John Arnold, pointing at a horserider on a large black horse that had stopped in Timothy Lane, to observe the work party.

"That's Button," said Robert, not elaborating as to why the parish clerk was mounted upon the stranger's fine black horse.

"Isaac," said John Arnold, as they approached, "tis a fine horse?"

Robert left the parish clerk to explain the circumstances

of the sleek black horse to John Arnold, whilst he jumped down to trample on the bulging faggots that had been lain so far. Robert did not wish to speak to Isaac Button. John Arnold and the parish clerk remained in conversation whilst the gravel was thrown out of the cart, onto the thorny bundles. Robert, Mark Bonner and David Crust then returned to the gravel pit as many more loads were required. Samuel was sent to take Katy to Dowty's yard to borrow the other cart, so that efforts could be doubled to complete the repair before the end of the day. When Robert returned, the parish clerk had gone. As the gravel was flung down, John Arnold told Robert that the clerk had stated that the hedge and the land below Timothy Lane was his and no permission had been given for a new ditch to be dug, to take the fallen water away downhill. Robert wondered if the clerk had also asked John Arnold about Robert borrowing the cart in the early morning of the stranger's disappearance. Did he not wish to establish whether Robert was telling the truth about his actions, the proof that it was not he that had pursued the stranger, causing his horse to return to the parish?

"I told ee' that you had every right to dig a ditch and to take Thigpen's gravel. He did concede and say that he would keep the hedge cut back and get the ditch dug, when his other ditches be dug."

Robert nodded.

"Then I should rightly fine he as well as the churchwarden," said Robert.

"It don't pay to take against the clerk Robert, he did say he would do his duty, when time came. Tis pecu'lar about thic horse and thic stranger mind, but Isaac, he do look mighty fine, jes like a knave, up high on the king's own horse."

Robert smiled at this. The clerk evidently had not questioned John Arnold about the borrowing of the cart to go

Chauncy, to visit his sister. Perhaps the clerk now believed that it was not he, after the fruitless search of Robert's privy by the beadle, despite Poll's accusations?

"Neither do it pay to rile the churchwarden," said John Arnold, giving Robert a cautionary stare, "not when thee wants to marry, as you say. Robert you must learn not to bring it on thyself, I shall speak plain."

"You shall John and I thank you for it," said Robert.

The work continued until all the faggots had been buried under a thick layer of gravel, with a crossfall on the new surface to send the water to the lower side. The carts had been taken back and forth to roll and trample down the gravel and the ditches were ready to accept the water, when next it rained hard. A little rain would help to draw the gravel down and make firm the repair. When most of the labour had disbanded Robert observed the work. John Arnold was about to take the cart home and Samuel turned Dowty's cart about.

"Tis something I can do," said Robert, "repairing the highway. More's the pity that I cannot earn by it. John, I am grateful for your help."

"Robert, thee shall earn by it," said John Arnold, his cart rolling forward, "you shall earn the respect of the parish, for they all did work today. Good eve, Robert and Samuel."

Robert and Samuel returned the cart to Dowty's yard. Samuel then led Katy home with Robert trailing behind, wary that Joan and Rose would have now gone from the house, after the unexplained visit the previous night by the parish officials. He followed Samuel and Katy around to the back of the house and drew water from the well for the trough. The setting sun gave everything a wash of ruby light, a short-lived beauty before the muted tones of dusk enveloped the yard and buildings. The back door opened and Rose appeared, now walking without hobbling, her foot fully repaired.

"Rose," said Robert, smiling at the girl.

The girl skipped across the yard.

"Can I give Katy her hay, Mr Penny?" said Rose.

"Yes, she has worked hard today," said Robert.

Joan appeared at the open back door.

"Robert," said Joan.

Robert nodded and smiled.

"Every day, I wonder that you will still be here, when I do come home," said Robert.

"I have been at Mother Goody's," said Joan, "she is good to thee and Samuel. We have made her beer and butter and I have stitched up old clothes that she has given. Rose did clean the parlour. I cannot just sit Robert, I needs be doing something. On Sunday, Rose and I shall attend church, do not say that we cannot."

"I shall not say so," said Robert.

"There is still the rabbit stew, come, before we cannot see."

They ate hungrily, without speaking. Robert licked his plater clean.

"The parish labour is now done, for this year," said Robert, "I have still to survey the rest of the parish. I shall do so tomorrow and then speak in church, on Sunday, about that which must be attended to. On Sunday, we shall all walk to church together."

"You have not spoken...to the parson?" said Joan.

"No, I have not," said Robert, pausing before replying, "but I shall, I must."

"If we are to marry," said Joan, "Mother Goody has said that we may sleep on her floor, until that time...so that we are not..."

"Not to give cause for tongues to wag?" said Robert, "she is kind but neither must she be found guilty of harbouring vagrants. Loper, for now, he is not making that charge against us, you heard him say so upon our own doorstep. If we had money and had land then none would say against our union, 'tis the way of it."

They sat in darkness, each with their own thoughts until Joan broke the silence to say goodnight and that she and Rose must now sleep.

Robert spent a restless night and almost got up again in the darkness but then woke up after dawn, when all were now awake in the house. Samuel came in quickly through the back door, slamming the door behind him, against the wind and rain. It was Robert's wish to be up early, to survey the remaining highways in the parish. Last evening, seeing the red sky, he felt certain that today would be clear, as yesterday had been.

Robert stopped himself from cursing the rain as Rose sang softly to herself as she twisted a length of twine and the fire crackled. Joan collected up the loose hay of their beds, piling it up into one corner of the weaving room. Samuel frowned as he watched the wisps of steam, curling up from a pot of water on the fire. The water could soon be heard to seethe. Robert studied Samuel's face. He had thought before that the boy looked like his mother. It was the frown, often it would be short lived, a lone cloud before the brightness of the sun, once the smile returned.

"Samuel," said Robert, still lying on his bed.

"Yes father?"

Samuel did not smile, his brow still furrowed.

"Tis the brother? Tis Augustus?" said Robert.

Samuel appeared surprised but the frown lingered.

"Parson Crouch is afeared of his brother," said Robert,

"he always were so. Now he be back, thee are not welcome at the parsonage?"

Samuel nodded.

"But he will soon be gone?" said Robert.

"After St Catherine's day," said Samuel, "he has broken up some experiments, saying that it is the devil's work. Father, no person wishes for St Catherine's day, it is only he. Many will not even speak her name."

"But she were never a witch," said Robert, defensively, raising himself up on the bed, "she were not yet a full woman. T'was one bad harvest and the parish, they did blame her. Poll has stirred in his poison, it is he that has tainted her name so long. Catherine, she did not gain from her foolishness, making those chalk marks, she were too young to know what she did. Would that we were born in the shitty land, where there be no chalk..the devil do piss on we Pennys.."

"Father," said Samuel, abruptly.

"My mouth," said Robert, cupping his face in his hands and mumbling an apology.

They ate eggs and drank buttermilk and then Robert peered up at the sky, from the back door. Joan joined Robert, in looking up at the sky.

"Today, the rain, it will come in fast and go just the same," said Joan.

"Are you now a farmer? Knowing when to reap or sow?" said Robert.

"Do not mock me," said Joan, gently elbowing Robert in the ribs "when you must walk from parish to parish, you learns how the rain will be. When there be no roof that shelters thee and no roof to which you return."

Robert nodded, accepting Joan's words. He then turned to kiss her upon the forehead, before knowing what he was about to do. They both glanced back into the parlour, to see who had seen.

The rain, it did come and go all day. Robert sheltered against the trunk of a huge elm tree for the worst of it, but the slicing rain soon passed and the sky again briefly cleared. The lanes and paths on Button's and Thigpen's land were in part neglected but hedges had been cut and ditches dug where it was of benefit to the comings and goings on the land. A culvert on Thigpen's land had collapsed, causing a lane to be flooded. On Button's land, a well-used path nearly sucked Robert's boots from his feet but it was the shitty land and was to be expected. There could be bound faggots put down, upon which to tread and he would remember this for next year. That there was only six days in the year, given to the repair of the highways, then there would never be fair passage within the parish. There were encroaching hedges on both Button's and Thigpen's land, for which they should be fined if they did not clear and as waywarden it was Robert's responsibility to call this out in church, after divine service.

Robert dropped down into Sun Lane, to return home and again found himself at the junction with Watery Lane, where he had sat upon John Arnold's cart, after returning from Chauncy. He had thought then about the life he might lead if he turned towards the Royal Forest and the sea but old Katy had made that decision for him and then plodded on home. Robert's house did now feel like home and it was with a happy heart that he turned back towards The Street. As Robert approached the church, he stood to one side to let a pack horse train go by on its way to the coast with Robert nodding to the driver as they drew level. The pack horse driver nodded in return. Robert wished to call at the parsonage but not with Augustus there. He would have to wait until the elder brother departed, after St Catherine's day. He wished that his elder sister had not been born on that blessed day. It was her ghost that Robert had seen briefly on the village green, but how did she die, if not drowned by drunken fools? Surely, if she had a sweetheart, as some did say, then he would not be a stranger to the parish?

Passing the alehouse, Robert avoided a mass of fresh droppings, where the pack ponies had waited for the driver to quench his thirst. He thought of borrowing Chant's wheelbarrow to collect the heaps but he knew that they would be gone by the time he returned. A tall figure dressed in black approached, walking down The Street as Robert walked up. Robert knew it to be the parson's brother, but felt sure that Augustus Crouch would not recognise him, as it was years since they had last met, since he had plunged Robert's head into a water trough, when Robert had been caught picking up fallen apples from the parsonage garden. Augustus was tall, like his brother, but he was broader of build, his face fuller and ruddy, his eyes piercing. Robert recalled the fierce expression but today the parson's elder brother smiled as they drew closer. Robert sensed that he meant to stop to talk but he avoided the tall man's eye as they passed. What did he have to say to Augustus Crouch?

"Yours is a face that I do know...," said Augustus Crouch, stopping and turning in The Street.

Robert halted and looked back, nodding in acknowledgement.

"...But...I do not recall your name?" continued the parson's elder brother.

Robert shrugged, reluctant to give his family name.

"I am Robert," said Robert.

"Robert?"

"And you are Augustus,"

"I am indeed."

Henry Dowty's cart came down The Street and Robert managed to step back, causing the cart to come between himself and the parson's elder brother, thereby pausing their exchange.

"Dowty? It is you that I wished to see," called out Augustus Crouch, but the cart continued on down The Street.

Robert withdrew further up the hill as the parson's elder brother remained distracted by the passing of Henry Dowty's cart. Robert did not look back and continued on towards his house. Joan had been making buttermilk and Samuel and Rose had gone to buy bread.

"The first survey, it is done," said Robert, sitting down in his chair.

"Robert, that is good," said Joan, pouring Robert a bowl of small beer, "tis from mother Goody, we shall make beer next week and give some back."

Robert took a sip and then emptied the bowl, wiping his mouth afterwards. Joan half filled the bowl again from the jug.

"She do make good beer," said Robert, after drinking the second pouring of beer in one go.

"And I can make beer just as good," said Joan, "and you do drink too fast."

There was a knock at the door and Robert frowned towards Joan, before getting up from his chair to see who it was. The last time it had been the vestry members, come to search for stolen property. Robert opened the door and the tall blackness of Augustus Crouch's clothes and hat, filled the doorway.

"Robert Penny," said Augustus Crouch, peering into the parlour and catching sight of Joan, "Robert Penny, I now remember your name. You are Catherine Penny's young brother, now returned to the parish."

"Yes," said Robert, "mother and father died."

"I asked for directions to your door."

Robert nodded.

"Your sister Catherine was born on saint Catherine's day, my father parson Nathaniel Crouch did name her so."

"Be that good or bad?" said Robert, stepping forward and pulling the door closed behind him, "being that she is not here to speak for herself."

"Catherine was saintly, our own Saint Catherine, of the parish," said Augustus Crouch, unhearing of Robert's question, "she did seek sanctuary in our blessed church, when men came for her, drunken men, with blame that she did curse the seed. I myself beat them away and cracked their heads, I did save her, save her from this...wickedness ..."

Robert waited for the brother to continue but instead the man's eyes widened, staring at Robert, staring beyond Robert, then swaying as if he were about to topple forward. Robert edged back into his own doorway, bracing himself, to catch the huge dark figure, to break his fall. The parson's brother began to mutter fast words that made no sense to Robert and then twitched his great head before continuing to speak, as if nothing had occurred.

"...My blessed father, my blessed father, parson Nathaniel Crouch, did begin again the saint's day, the parish day, for it is this next Tuesday when we shall gather to give our thanks, to our beloved saint. Let cattern cakes be ate and beer and cider be drunk. Let them gather to forget their foolishness on that day. Catherine Penny, your elder sister, she did then leave the parish and no person saw the going. My father and I searched and asked amongst the parish and in Chauncy also, but none would say of her, none did know. We shall pray for Catherine Penny, on our saint's day, as we do each and every year. We shall pray that by the beneficence of the parish, Saint Catherine's church shall be restored and that new vestments may be got, then my brother shall at least look a parson. Your wife, tell her she must bake for St Catherine's day Robert Penny."

Augustus Crouch then turned and walked away. Robert watched him go, puzzling at the sudden stopping of his words, at the blank stare that seemed to take an age to pass. He went back inside and closed the door.

"Well, did you not hear the parson's brother?" said Robert, not mentioning the strangeness at the door, "he already thinks you my wife and that you must bake for St Catherine's day. Tis the job half done."

Joan then chased Robert around the table with a wooden spoon until he let himself be caught and he held her wrists, drawing her close to him. Just at the moment the back door rattled open and Robert pushed Joan away. Rose entered first, carrying a warm loaf and then Samuel followed behind cradling six eggs.

"We shall bake our own bread next week," said Joan.

They ate bread and hard eggs and Robert then sent Samuel to the alehouse with a jug for strong beer with the last of the coins from his sister. Joan settled Rose upon the hay in the weaving room and then sat at the table, upon Samuel's stool. In near darkness Robert asked Joan about her husband.

"Walter were a good man," said Joan, after a long pause, "he did treat me and Rose well, he did save our lives," Joan sniffed, holding back tears, "he were a chapman and went from market to market. He would be gone, sometimes for one week but would always return, in good cheer, he did not drink like some men do drink. He did make I laugh and brought I clothes to wear. We had a pig and a cow, even a place in church…"

"What did happen?" said Robert, once Joan's words in the darkness faltered.

"…A man come to our house, he brought back our pony,

but did not enter...he said that he did bury our Walter beside the High Road. As he travelled home, Walter, he had the fire of distemper upon him but then the botch and the swelling, he knew that he had the plague and was to die. He di'nt want to bring the plague to our house nor the parish. The kindly stranger, he did stop...to attend to Walter and Walter said to bury him there, beside the road so...that none may perish. The man, he did stay beside him until morn when Walter...he were cold. The man, I do not know his name, he did walk to a near farm, to lend a spade and the farmer, he came, and the parson also. Words were said...but there be no cross, where he do lay."

Joan cried openly as Robert cupped Joan's hands, upon the table before them. She then pulled her hands free to wipe her eyes and felt again for Robert's hands, to entwine their fingers.

"Then he were a good man," said Robert, "tis brave to do as he did, not to come home. To spare thee and Rose the sickness and 'twas a good man who came to tell thee what had been."

"Yes, I be thankful, to the stranger, to know what did happen."

"But then you took to...be a beggar?"

"Not one week after the stranger came, to say about Walter, our house burned down, the houses all in the row did burn. We had nothing but a pig and a cow and our pony, that we did sell. T'was not my home parish and the constable and the overseer made me go back to where I were born, said I had no right to charity. I went on, but my parish did then send me away, t'were bad of they, for I were born there, but none would help. I have no kin living and went on from town to town, parish to parish."

In the following silence, they could hear footsteps approaching and Samuel entered through the front door.

"Did you go to Chauncy for my beer?" said Robert.

Samuel passed the jug towards Robert who searched for it with his hands, before taking it. Without speaking, Samuel found his way to his bed and the bed creaked as he sat down.

Robert drank deeply from the jug before offering it to Joan.

"I will, tonight," said Joan, accepting the jug and taking sips.

The silence built, in the room, until Robert spoke.

"Samuel, we did have the parson's brother knock upon our door."

"What did he want?" said Samuel after a pause, with little interest in his voice.

"I could not say, he has not yet blamed me for digging out Long Mound, p'raps he does not yet know who be parish waywarden. He spoke of Catherine and the saint's day, coming. Said that my wife should bake cattern cakes. I did not say we were not married, not yet. Seems he be the only one who do want the saint's day, so that it not be forgot. Tis a day of rest for the parish, for which they be thankful and they shall be most thankful for Joan's cakes."

"Other's shall bake cakes, not just I," said Joan, reproaching Robert.

"Father?" said Samuel, quietly.

"Yes,"

"Can we speak?"

"Yes, speak."

"Speak... just we..."

"Say what you want to say."

"Robert, I shall sleep now, speak to Samuel," said Joan.

"Outside father," said Samuel, getting up from sitting upon his bed and opening the back door.

Robert picked up the jug and followed Samuel out into the yard.

"What be this?" said Robert.

It was cold with little wind and few stars. The moon was still low in the sky.

"Father?"

"Yes, say it."

"I know not what I have done."

"What does thy mean? What have you done?" said Robert, before drinking from the jug.

"I cannot say ...but it cannot now be undone."

"We cannot stand here all the night, shall I beat it out of you?"

"I am sworn, not to say."

"Sworn? Sworn to who?"

Samuel turned to go back inside the house.

"Whoa," said Robert, reaching back and grabbing Samuel by the shoulder and then holding on to his clothes when Samuel tried to wriggle free, "you say what you have to say, say it now."

Samuel's voice trembled as he spoke.

"There are things...that you did not say...when I did ask you."

Robert thought on this, letting go of Samuel's clothes.

"I said that I would tell you...when, it was right to say. I did wrong, not as a Christian should do. I...I felt shame, that you would think bad of me. It was not all my own fault, that which did happen."

"I do know father."

"How do you know?"

"Mr Loper did say."

"When did he say? What did he say?"

"I did ask him, when he came drunk to our house and I did walk him home, when I heard noises in the dark."

"And he told you, when he were too drunk to walk?"

"Yes."

"Loper told you...about...?"

"The dead woman, that you threw into the river."

"God spare us Samuel..."

"I wanted to know... and you would not say."

They stood in silence, side by side, in the yard.

"I could not say," said Robert.

"And now...I cannot say," said Samuel.

"You have known, for all of these days? Do not judge me for what I did, for what Loper did make happen? I wished to bring her back, to the parish, so that she might be buried. He.. he.. You do not say to Joan about this," said Robert, turning and crossing the yard to make sure that the back door was firmly closed.

"I will not," said Samuel.

"She was murdered," said Robert, "Alice Brigg, the young woman that the stranger sought, saying she were his brother, she was murdered and left in a ditch."

Robert then told Samuel the whole story, about the lump of heathstone that had weighed the body down, but had gone from the ditch when Robert returned to Dudge Lane. The branches of yew that had covered the body, the yew that Robert had brought back to the yard in Dowty's cart, which poisoned the ox.

"If I wished to throw her into the river, I would not have borrowed Dowty's cart," said Robert.

"Father, then who did murder Alice Brigg?" said Samuel.

"I do not know, I do not know even if the murderer be from the parish. Whether she came to the church porch, as a wandering vagrant. She were from a wealthy family, yet her clothes were that of a maid. That she were troubled, forespoken, I hold no doubt. She was with child Samuel, the stranger, he did say that the heathstone, it were not the only great weight that did sit heavily upon her belly."

"And did Mr Loper...kill the stranger? Mr Button now has his horse? And why did the clerk and the beadle come to our house, to search the privy?"

"Sssshh, you know too much Samuel, you say too much."

Robert did not wish to lie again, to his son.

"What Loper has done," said Robert, quietly and slowly, "I do not know. But I have not wronged and I would swear so upon the bible. I know not either what they sought, when they came to our door, in all honesty, I do not know. It was Poll that did send them to our door."

Robert thought again about the leather bag that Loper had thrust upon him, when Robert had visited the parish constable. He neither knew what was in the bag or even where it was, now that it was not where he thought he had hidden it, above the privy. Then there was Loper himself, as parish constable, who came to seek the thing that he himself had bestowed upon Robert. At the door, Loper had not once looked Robert in the eye, but neither had he acted upon the harbouring of vagrants. Gone was Loper's smile and Robert thought that he had the face of a guilty man, also a weakness or frailty that had happened since the fight in the churchyard.

"Samuel, it was you that wished to speak?" said Robert, "and now I have spoken of a thing which has weighed upon me...like a great stone...but it is a thing that you already knew of. Now you do not say what troubles you?"

"I cannot father, but...I do know that none may be

blamed, other than myself. I have made a pledge, not speak of it... until..."

"A pledge with who? Until when?"

"Until...tomorrow, I can say no more father."

"Then...we shall wait," said Robert, draining the remaining beer from the jug.

Robert lay in bed, wondering what it was that Samuel could not say. The boy was restless in his bed but Robert felt as though he had been freed from something, from a prison of his own making. For the first time, he thought clearly, about the young woman and her misfortune to visit his parish, her shame at being with child when not yet married. Her death by the hands of another. He wanted to know more, now that he was not trying to forget or conceal, now that Samuel knew.

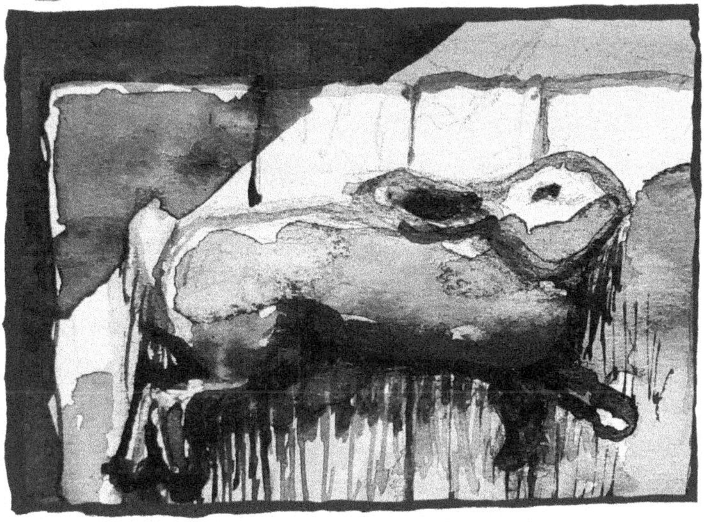

In the morning, Joan and Rose wore clothes that Mother Goody had given, clothes that Joan had mended. Silently, they all gathered before the front door.

"We shall walk together," said Robert, opening the door and leading the way.

A weak sun made weak shadows out in The Street. Samuel was pale and looked down at the ground whilst Rose began to skip, before her mother took her hand, encouraging her to walk. Robert thought of what he must be sure to say when it was his turn to climb up to the pulpit, to speak about the highways. They greeted fellow parishioners and wished them a good morning, as if it were any other Sunday. Any mutterings or questioning looks went unheeded. This was how it was going to be, thought Robert, this was his family. They did not stand outside the church, to join the mustering there and once inside, Robert encouraged Joan and Rose to sit upon a bench at the rear of the church, on the left-hand side of the nave. Robert crossed the aisle, to the bench where he and Samuel sat. Joan looked about her, at the interior of the church, at the high ceiling, at the cold light through the clear glass windows. They glanced across to each other, as the benches and pews became filled with the assembled parish. From his position near the rear of the church, Robert watched Edward Loper walk on towards his pew. The parish constable now looked weary, gone was the swagger and the smile, he now shuffled and then slumped down into his seat. Henry Dowty, the overseer walked slowly to his pew, his hands already locked together, as if in permanent prayer. Isaac Button unlocked his pew gate and then tried to conceal a yawn before sitting down. Augustus Crouch swept by and greeted Peter Thigpen, the churchwarden, warmly and they stood together in earnest conversation beneath the pulpit, both nodding and then looking back up the aisle and pointing. Robert sensed that they were talking about him and he shrank down in his seat. Had the churchwarden informed Augustus about Joan and Rose now living in Robert's house, with Robert harbouring vagrants? The parish constable had not acted but the churchwarden would not let such impropriety pass within the parish and now the parson's brother had been made aware. The churchwarden had said to Robert, in his sister's alehouse in Chauncy, that the parson's elder brother was friendly with the bishop and Robert had not yet even broached the subject of his marriage to Joan with the parson. With the churchwarden and now Augustus Crouch taking against him then surely the parson had not the command to permit such a marriage. Samuel continued to look down and Robert was relieved when the churchwarden and Augustus Crouch ended their discussion and seated themselves. He turned again to look at Joan and Rose and then saw a figure amongst the seated women and girls that made him start. His sudden movement causing Samuel to look up and frown at his father.

"Who is that?" hissed Robert, to his son, "over there, in front of Joan, with the long black hair and pale face?"

Samuel leant over to peer across the aisle.

"Tis...Sarah Crust, they say that she will soon die. She is weak and is now carried and cannot walk. I have not seen her in church before, she does stay in her bed."

Robert turned and looked ahead of him, blinking and unseeing. How certain he had been, at the whipping of Simon Gigg, that the ghost of his eldest sister had appeared before him. There had been no ghost. It had been a sick girl from the parish, carried from her bed to witness the punishment. Robert had told about seeing the ghost to the parson and to others, his thoughts now tumbling in his head. He knew no more than before, whether his elder sister be alive or dead. Was she living, married to her sweetheart, with children of her own or did the deep stillness of Clay Pond hold the secret of her fate? Robert shuddered and a baby cried as parson Crouch emerged from the vestry room and walked slowly towards the pulpit. The crying grew louder and the beadle stepped from his pew, to look about and scowl in the direction of the mother and baby. The crying continued, making the beadle scurry up the aisle to confront the source of the disturbance. The baby cried louder despite the mother's comforting and then a mastiff growled, emerging from between the benches, causing the parish official to back away, his whip out of reach on its hook upon the opposite wall. The dog snapped at the beadle's hand, drawing blood and then advanced, snarling and salivating. The enormous black clothed figure of Augustus Crouch quickly swooped from his pew, snatching the whip from its position upon the wall and cracking it across the aisle, the tip caught the hind legs of the mastiff, causing it to yelp and leap away, whimpering. The censured dog then growled from under the legs of its owner whilst the baby settled and the parson's brother frowned at the congregation before recoiling the whip and hanging it back up upon its hook. Parson Crouch looked on from the pulpit as his brother and the beadle returned to their seats, the beadle grimacing and clutching the fleshy part of his right hand.

As with his first visit to the pulpit as parson, William Crouch gripped firmly the wooden surround but, on this occasion, he did not utter one word. In recent weeks the parson had spoken well, growing into the task, but today, with his brother Augustus glowering up at him, he remained silent and then began to shake. As before, the churchwarden coughed and stepped out from his box beneath the pulpit. The parson required no prising from the pulpit and descended the steps on his own and, as if by some predetermined arrangement, Augustus Crouch rose up from his pew whilst the parson retraced his steps back to the vestry.

THE PARISH WAYWARDEN

"We be fortunate that Mr Augustus Crouch be amongst our number today," said Peter Thigpen, "sir, would thee take the pulpit...for otherwise..."

A mighty silence fell upon the assembled congregation, with no baby or dog daring to make a sound as the parson's brother slowly ascended the creaking pulpit steps. This huge figure in black, elevated above the parish, now appeared to savour this moment, his features softening as he looked around at the building itself, at the walls and windows, finally lifting his gaze up towards the roof. He closed his eyes to breath in deeply through his nose, as if to take in the very essence of the church itself, the hard fabric of stone, plaster, glass, lead and timber, his benign expression then confused and corrupted by the living flavours of the parishioners themselves, seated below. As he opened his eyes, he placed his enormous hands on the sill of the pulpit.

"Our church, our beloved church, dedicated to our saint, saint Catherine of Alexandria. Not in my father, parson Nathaniel Crouch's time, nor in parson Willett's time before he, or parson Samwell's time before he, or the unfortunate parson Tomily ...but parson Thrake it was, in his tenure, who oversaw the great...changes to our beloved church, for so long a bright and beauteous house of God, the gilded crucifix, the rood screen, the painted glass, the candlelit shrines ...all banished, the walls washed white, the old stone altar, dragged by oxen out into The Street, where it lays askew to this day across a filthy ditch..."

Robert then suddenly realised why, as a child, he had followed the older children by the making of a sign, if ever he passed over the short stone bridge, to one side of The Street, when the ditch flowed and it could not be stepped over. He knew not what sign was being made, only that it was bad luck not to do so and he would just circle his finger upon his breast bone, following the older children. He thought about an ox in the church, dragging out the heavy slab, did it crash to the floor from its pedestal, why did it not break? Robert could not understand what had happened so long ago in the parish, so many parsons ago. Why would a stone slab be raised in a church anyway? It certainly served well as a small bridge and required no maintenance on his part. He tried to imagine painted glass, pouring colours into the building when the sun shone brightly.

"How do we know of these...changes?" asked Augustus Crouch, pausing to survey the rows of unresponsive faces, "we do know because parson Thrake did keep record and it was I who found this dutiful account when I was but sixteen years old, kept as dusty papers in a wormy box in the parsonage. Ever since that day, when I did read the words of parson Thrake, his guarded words, not critical of the reasons why but an account of the great undoing of centuries and generations, the dismantling of our sacred church which is today but a shell, its glory stripped. The church bells were silenced across the land, their clappers taken should they be used to call the parish to rebellion, as did happen at the introduction of the English prayer book. Many died at this protest, but not here, not in our parish, there was no fight made here. Your ancestors did not rise but did submit. Once there was a golden shrine to our beloved saint, our patron saint, saint Catherine. It is no more, nor any image to demonstrate her suffering, her saintliness. Today, here in Saint Catherine's church... it is the royal arms, there upon the wall, that does make the only colour. Today our good king, King Charles faces the same tide that washed the colour from our beloved church. Parliament is suspended and seethes like a pot of boiling oil. Archbishop Laud is now made the Archbishop of Canterbury and I shall soon be writing to his worship, for I believe that even in our small parish, we are in accord and some goodly traditions may yet be restored, with the altar, or rather I should say, communion table, placed back in the sacred chancel. Our holy days are to be encouraged and games shall be played..."

Robert cast a look back towards Joan and received a smile in return. His eyelids began to feel heavy as the parson's brother continued.

Somebody farted loudly at the end of Robert's bench, waking him up and Robert's neck was stiff, where he had been slumped forward. Augustus Crouch was still expounding the glory of St Catherine's church and how can a church display a broken cross upon its roof?

"Twas lightnin' did strike the cross," said a voice from the congregation, that Robert did not recognise.

"Yea, twas God and not the hand o' man," said another voice.

Augustus Crouch scowled down from the pulpit, choosing to ignore the interruption. Instead, he went on to say how his own father, Parson Nathaniel Crouch did procrastinate in these matters, but monies shall now be got, through the benevolence of the parish. There was a collective groan from the rear of the building, causing the slap of a great hand upon the old timber of the pulpit, causing a small wooden panel to fall to the floor.

"You would see our church crumble into the dust?" accused Augustus Crouch, angrily, before staring ahead, staring above the heads of the congregation and then silence. The same had occurred at Robert's door, when the huge dark figure had faltered in his speech, his eyes unseeing, like that of a blind man. From his position at the back of the church, Robert could not see or hear whether the same fast mutterings now followed this repeated strangeness. The parson's brother then made a low growling sound before speaking again, as if there had been no interruption to his flow.

"It is our earthly duty, as a parish, to provide the house in which to praise our Lord, so that he may fill it with his magnificence."

Robert blinked and stretched in his seat, he wished that Augustus Crouch would be gone from the parish, as Samuel also wished. The parson could then be left alone, to grow to be the shepherd of all their souls, in his own quiet way. Samuel still looked down at the floor. What had Samuel done, that he was so afraid of, a thing that could not now be undone? Robert tried to gather his own thoughts, as he was soon to speak about the parish highways. He looked again to catch Joan's eye and she gave him a small smile. His neck was stiff from where he had slumped forward, seated upon the long bench. The door of the church began opening and closing with the shuffling back and forth of those amongst the congregation that must piss. Once the parson's brother had stepped down slowly from the pulpit, the churchwarden then summoned Robert to speak. As he approached the steps to the pulpit, Augustus Crouch rose from his pew to turn and broadcast his views to the congregation, on the harbouring of vagrants, within the parish. Since his appearance at Robert's door, he would have been informed, most likely by the churchwarden, that Joan was not Robert's wife but instead a vagrant in the parish.

"And I understand that the transgressor is Robert Penny, a vestry man? With a beggar woman and child? A woman called Joan Young."

"Aye sir," said the churchwarden, "'tis matters that will be dealt with, tis ungodly and it be aginst the interests of the parish."

With a heavy tred, Robert climbed the steps to the pulpit and then sought Joan's face at the back of the congregation, but his eyes were not so strong as they once were.

THE PARISH WAYWARDEN

"Waywarden?" said Augustus Crouch, before Robert had spoken, "there is damage to Long Mound, undertaken under your auspice, for the so called repairs to Top Road, where our great parish marker has been dug...like some common chalk pit."

"Timothy Lane be free of water, after many a year," called out John Arnold, from his place in the Arnold pew.

"But the ditches be dug, on Button land, without my say so," said the parish clerk, stirring in his pew.

"And gravel be taken from our diggings," said Peter Thigpen, the churchwarden.

"But these be things that the waywarden must do by right," said Robert, "if thy doesn't want I as waywarden for the parish..?"

There was a call of support towards Robert from the congregation, which surprised him but then he thought that this task would only fall to another and so all were keen for Robert to continue.

"Robert Penny be doing a main good job," said John Arnold, to which there were more nods and grunts of approval.

"There be no more highways beer," said Robert, causing laughter beyond the austere faces of the front pews.

Robert paused to take a deep breath and then stated that he had now undertaken a survey of all the highways that he knew of, within the parish and he would attend the justices at the next session, at the start of the new year. He then called out the overgrown hedge on Gigg's land that had not been cut back and for which they would now be fined five shillings. The Gigg brother's shuffled in their pew seats, exchanging angry looks and then they both scowled at the parish constable. Robert did not wish to stir the resentment caused after the brutal whipping of young Simon Gigg, but neither could he ignore his duty. He now meant to continue, to call out Thigpen and Button, for the many highway problems on their lands. He squinted again towards the back, where he knew Joan to be but could not see her amongst blurred dun colours and vague faces. How were they to be married when the churchwarden and now the parson's brother were against such a union? Isaac Button would also relish this denial. What was a waywarden anyway? A reluctant parishioner given a thankless task for no money. He would not be the first waywarden to hold his tongue and not speak out about the highway encroachments of the other vestry members. Memories for ill deeds done were long, but for his own failings as waywarden, then they would soon be forgot and at worst, he would be compared again to his father. It was the wishing of his marriage to Joan that would cause him not to speak out, not to make this a harder thing than it already was. Robert found himself descending from the pulpit, having left unsaid the highway issues upon both Button's and Thigpen's land and he returned to his bench with a sense that he had not fulfilled his duty. On his way down the aisle, John Arnold caught Robert's eye and nodded gently, confirming that Robert had done right by his reticence.

The churchwarden then spoke about the saint's day on the Tuesday, St Catherine's day, for which there was some preparation required. Augustus Crouch had already asked for cattern cakes, when he called at Robert's house, thinking that Robert had a wife. Robert wondered whether they would now stick in the man's throat if a beggar and her daughter did bake cakes for the saint's day? The churchwarden spoke again about the church repairs and that new vestments were required. He then declared that there was a letter to be read.

"It be sealed, from a friend of St Catherine's church, and we be 'opeful that they be generous. Tetty Bonner do 'ave the 'spondence."

Tetty Bonner rose from her seat in the pew, to the left of the aisle, and walked to the pulpit.

"Can Tetty even read?" whispered Robert to his son, who looked up for a moment.

"She does read and she does write," said Samuel, quietly, and he then looked back down at his feet, wringing his hands so that his knuckles grew white.

"Tis a letter, as yet unread," said Tetty, "there be a note to say that it be written by a friend of St Catherine's church and a friend of the parish."

The churchwarden in his own pew, beneath the pulpit, rubbed his hands together in anticipation. Tetty Bonner then broke the wax seal on the folded letter and unfolded the page. She took a deep breath before beginning to read.

"I Margaret Coxe, once of this parish, do wish to give alms to the poor but to mainly begin the schooling of children in St Catherine's church, on Sundays, before divine service. If there needs be provision of a teacher or books, then of this cost, I shall pay for as long as I am alive and then hereafter it shall be paid by terms, within my will."

The churchwarden frowned and formed a second rounded chin as he listened to the content of the letter. Tetty cleared her throat.

"None shall know me by my name Margaret Coxe, but you shall remember Catherine Penny..."

There was quickly a growing hum of surprise from the parish. Individual voices rose up, questioning the words that were being read. Tetty spoke out loudly, so that she could be heard.

"I, who was Catherine Penny, did not wish to be named after the church, nor meant harm by childish games. I were never a witch, as some did say. I did leave the parish after a call to throw a silly girl into Clay Pond, for her silly ways. I did hide in the church and Augustus Crouch beat the men that came for me, I did then run from the church."

Augustus Crouch, stood up at the mention of his name, looking about in surprise at those about him, but also raising his chin in acceptance of any praise for his actions, all those years ago. Tetty raised the palm of her hand in a gesture for all to be patient and to let her speak.

"In the morning light, a young man did find me, in Watery Lane...he did abuse me so and beat me. If he still be alive, he be there now, amongst you all."

Tetty read the following sentence before speaking it aloud and then frowned as she looked about her, uncertain whether she should continue.

"Read on," said a voice and it was the parson, approaching from where he had been listening, at the vestry door and he stood before the pulpit, "I say read on."

Tetty's voice quavered as she read.

"I did leave the parish with the train from the coast. The young man, the driver, Abel Coxe, I did speak with before, when he passed, with the fish. He said to ride the lead pony and he covered me with a blanket, so none may see my going. I did marry the driver, Abel Coxe. The bastard it did die and I were never blessed with a child after."

Tetty stopped reading and Robert wondered whether the letter had ended. He peered ahead of him, looking for those that were then young men in the parish, one of whom had abused his sister in Watery Lane. Robert's eyes at this distance could not scrutinise guilty faces. He could see Isaac Button, with no neck looking back and forth, like a bird, Edward Loper, a hunched figure in his pew, unmoved by these new disclosures, John Arnold was on his feet, leaning forward against the pew rail, Robert could sense anger in the shapes that he made, Henry Dowty, putting a hand to his head whilst Augustus Crouch remonstrated with the churchwarden, Peter Thigpen who then shouted, as loud as he was able.

"Silence."

Augustus Crouch joined in, until the congregation paid some heed and quiet was restored.

"Enough," said the churchwarden, gesturing for Tetty Bonner to come down from the pulpit, "this...thing, it shall end now."

"But I ain't done, there be a name," said Tetty Bonner.

"Come thee down woman, tis enough," said the churchwarden, forcefully.

"It be your name in this letter Peter Thigpen, our own churchwarden," said the landlady.

The churchwarden steeped back, his legs faltering. He reached out for a pew end to steady himself, blinking and open mouthed. The parish burst into voice as one and it was some moments before the parson attempted to be heard. Robert grabbed Samuel by the wrist and hauled him up the crowding aisle, where the parish were now leaving their seats but reluctant to depart, least they missed something. Robert wanted to witness the face of the churchwarden for himself and he drew close to see. The churchwarden's eyes began roving about, fruitlessly seeking something to settle upon, his breath short and gasping.

"Mrs Bonner, is the letter now read?" called out the parson.

"It is parson," said Tetty, folding up the correspondence and turning to descend from the pulpit.

"But...but," began Augustus Crouch, in protest, "this is just the word of...someone who wishes to do harm to our parish, a woman of no bearing."

"She did say about you, my brother?" said the parson,

"how you did protect her, when others wished her harm, that you did act as a true Christian."

The noise within the church and the clustering and pushing of the parish to look upon the face of a guilty man, the churchwarden, was too much for the parson's brother. Augustus Crouch rushed at the congregation with his arms raised, as if moving a clutch of stubborn beasts through a narrow gateway.

"Get out, be gone all of you, go, be gone."

The bewildered parishioners turned and trampled towards the church porch, Robert maintaining his grip on Samuel's wrist, dragging him back down the aisle amongst the herded egress from the church as they spilled out into the churchyard. Tetty was already outside and being surrounded by questioners, Robert pushed them aside and hauled Samuel to stand between he and the landlady.

"What is this?" shouted Robert, his anger causing him to spit, "how has this...thing...happened?"

"Do not blame your son," said Tetty, firmly, "you can blame me, if any. Samuel did wish to do good...to heal..."

"Heal? By Christ," said Robert, striking his own forehead in frustration, "how will this thing heal now?"

"Your sister, she be alive Robert Penny. Talk of ghosts and witches and drownings, she went with the fish ponies, to London, she did marry, she did learn to read and write there and to teach. She has money."

"But...how did the letter...who did say to her?"

"Weeks ago it were, Samuel did listen to the driver talking and heard him say about a relation that once come from the parish, by name of Margaret Coxe. Samuel went to the register in the parish chest, the parson did help. They found that your sister's name was Catherine Margaret Penny. Sam came to me, to write to Margaret Coxe, to ask if she were once called

Penny, daughter of Judd and Mary. The letter I gave to the driver. He stopped for ale yesterday, on his way to the sea and he did bring her letter in return, along with her note. I did not know what were in the sealed letter, honest I did not. In her note she did ask that none would say about who the letter be from, before I did read it in church."

"That is why I could not say father," said Samuel, looking up.

Robert suddenly remembered about Joan and Rose, in the church and then spoke with venom towards his son.

"Get thee home, so help me I shall deal with you."

Robert let go of Samuel's wrist and pushed his way back into the church, through the glut of parishioners still filling the porch. Inside, the churchwarden was now seated in his pew beneath the pulpit with his head in his hands whilst Augustus Crouch loudly berated his brother as the other vestry members stood by. Of Joan and Rose there was no sign. Robert walked hurriedly amongst those still lingering in the churchyard and then made a circuit of the church. The black haired girl, that Robert had mistaken for Catherine's ghost on the village Green was being carried to the lych gate on David Crust's back, a girl as tall as her father but barely strong enough to hold on around his neck. Robert thought that Joan must have gone straight back to the house, rather than stand about after the service and he made his way up The Street, as fast as he was able. As he reached the large elm near Chant's house, Samuel came running back down the hill, towards him.

"Boy, I did say to thee..." shouted Robert, breathlessly.

"Father, they are gone, Joan and Rose are gone from the house."

"Where? Where have they gone?" said Robert, halting.

"I do not know, they are not with Mother Goody, she is

not yet back from church."

"They have left, they will go to Top Road...or to Chauncy. You go to Chauncy, I will take Katy to Top Road. Go now."

Samuel ran on down the hill whilst Robert hobbled back to the house and then fumbled with anxious fingers at the saddle and bridle as he prepared the old horse.

"Come, we will find them Katy, to bring them home."

Robert did not wish to urge the old horse on in his panic but kept a steady pace that would in time catch up with a woman and child on foot. At the bottom of the Downs, Robert could see that there were no figures walking ahead of him, ascending the long climb up to Top Road and Long Mound. The parish sheep flock was shifting eastwards, along the crest of the ridge and Robert rode across to speak to the shepherd's boy, who tended the flock when his father was at church. The boy had seen no woman and child walking up from the parish but listed the passer's by on the Top Road, keen to talk as any shepherd might, when encountering another on their long vigil, the boy practising the ways of his father. Robert grunted and rode on, drawn towards Long Mound where the white chalk from the highways work gaped open. The shepherd's boy called after him.

"Sheep do shy from Long Mound, now it be dug, where they once did take their water from the highdown. Tis bad."

Robert ignored him. Katy stopped just before the repaired water splash and would go no further, despite Robert's encouragement. From his position, he could see that the depth of chalk and flint in the repaired hole had held firm but the surface was sticky white, where the passage of many hooves had trampled in times of rain. In time it would fail. Perhaps after a hard winter when the frost would weaken the chalk and heave up the infill. He looked about him, following the scar of Top Road

THE PARISH WAYWARDEN

in both directions and then looked north, towards the city. Today there was a pale winter light and Robert felt a great emptiness. He turned Katy around, to return home.

Samuel would not yet have returned from Chauncy and Robert thought that Joan and Rose might have taken the path to the coast, down Watery Lane and then Dudge Lane and into the Royal Forest. Joan may have heard Robert talk about this way. Poll would know, thought Robert. Poll sees all who pass his house. Robert passed back down The Street, beyond the church and into Watery Lane, where his sister Catherine was ravished by Peter Thigpen, all those years ago. Robert would confront the churchwarden and he could feel his fists clenching at the thought but first he must find Joan and Rose. Robert stopped and turned Katy in the lane outside Poll's house and remained in the saddle, the geese stretching low necks to hiss but wary of a kick from a hoof.

"Poll?" shouted Robert, "it is I, Robert Penny."

The front door of the house was open. Robert waited a moment before calling again.

"Poll, it is I Robert Penny. I knows thee can see and hear me."

Slowly, Poll dragged himself to the doorway and then leant against the doorframe.

"Did a woman and child pass this way? When all but you were at divine service?"

"'Ave thee lost thy wife, Robert Penny?" said Poll, slowly and mocking.

"A woman and child, a girl," said Robert, repeating his question.

Poll starred at him but eventually shook his domed and hairless head.

"Catherine Penny," said Robert, "she is alive, she were

never drowned nor was she ever a witch, like you have said to all. Peter Thigpen did ravish her, here in Watery Lane, did you watch then? Did you not see? Then she did leave the parish, by the fish train up from the coast. She married and be a teacher. Perhaps, one day, she will come back to the parish of her birth, perhaps she will come to your door?"

Robert took pleasure in watching Poll's eyes widen and he coaxed Katy as close to Poll's fence as she was able, Robert leaning forward in his saddle, to threaten the cunning man.

"If you send men to my door ever again, then I shall kill you. If you speak ill of Samuel and me, then I shall kill you. If you do ever meddle in my business or speak ill of Joan Young or her daughter Rose, then I shall kill you."

Robert rode home and gave Katy hay and water before sitting at his table, whilst the light slowly died in the room. Much later, Samuel entered quietly through the front door. By Samuel's quietness, Robert knew that Joan and Rose had not been found. Samuel sat down on the stool, opposite his father.

"None have seen her," said Samuel, eventually breaking the silence.

"Did you say to Ann about Catherine?" said Robert, "that she is alive?"

"Yes father. She be glad. She says that she will come, to speak with you."

"You knows more about it boy," said Robert, "why does she wish to speak with me? Did you not say what thee have done? What you did behind my back?"

Robert lunged across the table towards his son, knocking Samuel backwards from his stool, the boy quickly scrambling in the darkness, towards the back door, opening and slamming it behind him. Robert fumbled to his bed and slumped down.

At first light Robert woke up cold and wrapping his blanket around himself, he then took the blanket from Samuel's empty bed and wrapped that around himself also. There was nothing to eat. He shuffled to the well, his boots untied and drew a bucket of water for Katy and another that he poured over his head. He gave Katy some hay and returned to the house to sit at the table with his head dripping water. He tied his laces and put on his coat, picking up the thick dog stick by the front door before leaving the house. He walked down The Street, beyond the church to Sun Lane where there was a track to Thigpen's farm. A horse and rider approached and Robert recognised it as the figure of the churchwarden, coming from his farm. Robert stood in the middle of the track as the rider began to trot faster. As he drew closer Peter Thigpen called out.

"Robert, I am to Chauncy, be it about the carp'ntry work?"

"Carpentry?" Robert shouted back, "I would not work for thee."

The churchwarden spurred his horse on, passing to the side of the track as Robert tried to grab a rein or a stirrup but he was then knocked off balance by the force of the passing horse, onto the dewy grass.

"You do know what you have done," Robert shouted as he climbed to his feet and then, aiming the dog stick, he threw it after the horse but it missed and became lost in the hedge, "God do know what you have done and you cannot hide from him or say what is a lie...and your honour...it be gone. And if you believe that you can drink in my sister's alehouse then I shall tell her what you have done."

Robert watched the horse and rider turn into Sun Lane and he cradled his right arm after hurling the dog stick as far as he was able. He walked back home slowly, the day's purpose now lost. Robert passed the alehouse, where he thought Samuel had spent the night but he did not call in. He paused at the parish constable's house, Robert had not spoken to Loper since he had arrived at Robert's door with the clerk and the beadle. He knocked and Mrs Loper opened the door.

"Robert, Edward be poor in his chair, come see."

Robert entered the dark front parlour and the parish constable was sitting in his chair, staring ahead, a lit candle on the table next to him.

"He dun't eat or say nothin', he did stay there all night, he wun't raise for bed. You talk to 'ee Robert."

"I have private business, Mrs Loper, I needs speak with Edward."

"Spec he dun't hear private business any more than my prattle."

Mrs Loper went out into the back garden where she called the chickens.

"Edward," said Robert, placing his face before the parish constable, "you were in church, you heard all, Thigpen, he did ravish my sister Catherine. He needs be punished."

Edward Loper did not respond. Robert leaned forward and shook his shoulder gently.

"Edward, when I came to you, came here to your house, after the stranger's horse came back. You gave me a bag and then you came to my door with the beadle, on Poll's say so. Why such a thing? What if it were found, would you then say that you knew nothing of the bag?"

Robert nudged the silent figure again and then held up the candle, before the parish constable's face. The eyes were unseeing, in one eye the black centre did not shrink in the light but kept like a black hole that went beyond the face and into the head. The skin on his face had the greyness of wet cloth. Mrs

Loper could be heard coming back into the house and Robert placed the candle back upon the table.

"He does not speak," said Robert.

"Needs must I shall visit Poll," said Mrs Loper, "Robert, I do be worried about my Edward, but Poll, he will make him as he was?"

Robert backed away, towards the front door and then left the house, the question unanswered. Robert returned home and lay down upon the hay that was Joan and Rose's bed, pulling the loose hay around himself. A loud knock upon the front door woke Robert and he struggled to his feet.

"Robert?" said the parson.

Looking beyond the tall and thin figure of the parson, Robert could see that it was dusk and he must have slept all day.

"Parson," said Robert, brushing some of the loose hay from his coat and picking more from his hair. He then opened the door wider, "come, sit, it is cold. It will soon be dark."

The parson entered and Robert positioned his own chair for the parson to sit down at the table, whilst Robert sat upon Samuel's stool.

"There is much, of late that will concern you Robert?" said the parson, "the letter that was read and the...accusations?"

Robert blinked at the parson.

"Robert, I will speak plain. I cannot marry you and Joan Young. My brother will say against it and he will enlist the bishop, to do so also."

"I have not yet asked thee to marry us," said Robert.

"No...no...Robert, but was this not...what you wished to happen?"

"Samuel did say?"

"Yes...Samuel, he..."

"Samuel do say too much, he do too much when I do

not know. The son rules the father, that should not be so?"

"Or a brother ruling a brother? Samuel, he does for the best, he sees more than most, he sees ahead, what others do not see. Ingenious youths, as rose buds, imbibe the morning dew."

"I shall beat him, when I do catch him."

"Then, you may forever be chasing him, but I am not a father, I have not a wife nor children and would find it a distraction from my work. For the parson's life, then it would be the better way, I grant. Robert, I am saddened that Joan and Rose are gone, I hope and pray that they do find a position..."

"And go from parish to parish, from porch to porch, when winter do bite? No parson, I shall find them and bring them back and we shall be married, and you parson shall marry us and bishops and brothers can...go rot...and Thigpen, he cannot show his face, to tell me right from wrong."

The parson stood up to leave and placed a basket on the table.

"I understand you Robert, goodnight. I have brought eggs and apples, the basket Samuel can return."

Robert made himself go to Mother Goody's for hot coals and then lit the fire, huddling before it, sitting upon Samuel's stool as the eggs boiled. He shelled the eggs where he sat, sucking them hot and whole into his mouth and then squashing them with his eyes closed. He ate an apple and went to bed.

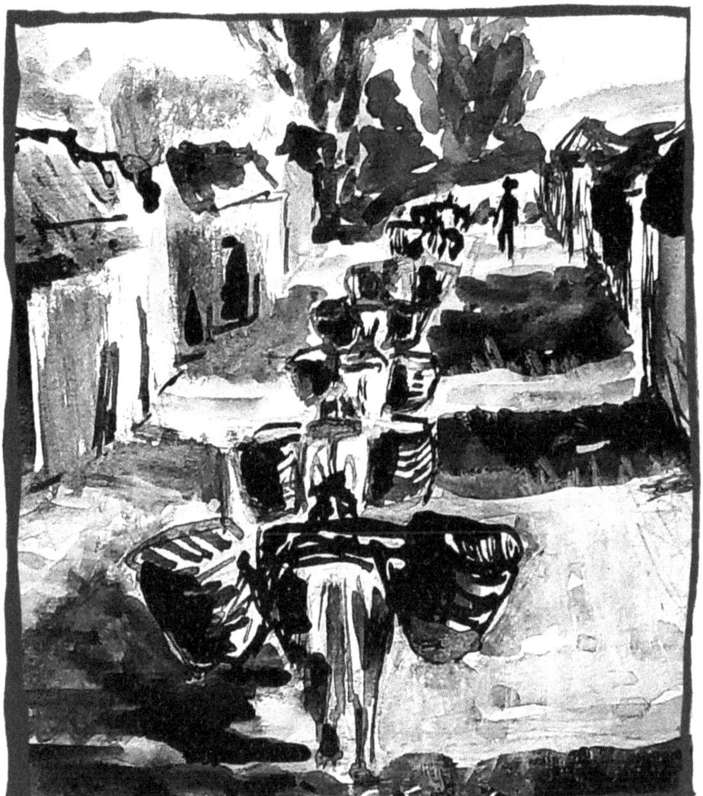

Robert lay in bed and listened to the rain. He thought of Joan and gripped his cock and then let go, withdrawing his hands and placing them on the outside of the blankets. Joan and Rose would be out there somewhere, out in the rain, between places. It had been Augustus Crouch, speaking out in church, when Robert had walked to the pulpit, that had caused Joan to leave the church and the parish. The parson's brother had said that he, Robert Penny, had been harbouring vagrants and named Joan as the beggar woman, with the churchwarden confirming that the matter would be dealt with. Joan had left the church before the letter was read. The rain was falling harder now and Robert felt no inclination to get up and went back into fitful sleep. He awoke suddenly, hearing children's voices outside in The Street, singing.

"Saint Catherine's feast do come year by year
Some of your apples, some of your beer
Some for Peter, some for Paul
Some for him who made us all."

Robert hauled himself out of bed and opened the front door. Ten or so children of various ages stood in the steady rain. He knew Mary Bonner and one or two others but Rose was not amongst them, nor Samuel. Robert went back in and picked up the apple from the table.

"Take my last apple," he said, offering it, "or have an onion and I'll keep the apple?"

Mary Bonner reached out and took the apple and the sodden children moved on up The Street to Hutchins' house, the youngest skipping whilst the rest shuffled behind. The church bell rang to tell the parish that it was St Catherine's Day and Robert closed the front door and went out to the privy. He gave Katy fresh hay and water and then came back inside to stare at the growing puddles on the weaving room floor, despite he and

Samuel having recently patched the roof with fresh longstraw. Robert cursed when he remembered that he had not yet paid Chant for the longstraw.

He was going to light the fire and stay at home but he was hungry and there would at least be cakes at the festivities and strong ale and cider. It was raining harder than ever and Robert hurried down The Street, as fast as his old boots would permit. The surface of The Street had become milky white by the rain scoured chalk, the flow gathering in force as it snaked on down the hill, tailing away towards Watery Lane and passing under the stone altar bridge that Augustus Crouch had spoken of in church. Robert involuntarily touched his breast bone as he passed over the short culvert, knowing now that it was the making of the cross that he had misconstrued since childhood. The top of the church tower was shrouded in misty rain and the parishioners sought any shelter they could find, packing the church porch, huddling under the yew tree in the churchyard and pressed up ineffectively against the church walls. The church was open but there was to be no drinking in the body of the church itself. The barrels of ale and cider had been set up under the spreading yew tree, when they were meant to be out on the Green. Robert knew that there would be looks and mutterings from the parish about the letter in church, the churchwarden's rape and deflowering of his sister Catherine, also the disappearance of Joan Young and her daughter Rose, with whom he had walked so brazenly to church on Sunday morning, as if they were already married, already a family. Robert forced his way amongst the steaming wool of wet men to receive a cup of strong ale from Mark Bonner and drank it down in one before demanding another.

"Winter do now coom," said Colly Francis, an old labourer, now solely dependent on parish charity, "zo canst 'spec much, there be rain, 'n cold, 'n thic vrost 'n snow."

"T'were rain last year," said Richard Beck, a labourer still working, "and the yer avore. Do allus rain on saint's day."

"Then dun't let thic yew drip into thy ale mind," said Colly Francis, "or be the last saint's day thee'll see, Richard Beck."

There was cake in the church porch, where most of the women were gathering, whilst the children played and sang in the church. Robert finished his second cup of ale and moved to the bustle outside the porch.

"Cake?" shouted Robert, to nobody in particular.

Robert was about to push his way into the porch when Tetty Bonner, dressed as a man, emerged from the church, holding aloft two small cakes and a hunk of bread and offered them to Robert.

"Take 'un," said Tetty, "Samuel be at ours last night."

Robert took the cakes and bread.

"Why is you dressed like Mark, with his clothes and hat?" said Robert, before stuffing the cake into his mouth.

"Tis the day when a woman can dress like a man. Others have done so"

"Joan, she be gone," said Robert, spitting crumbs, "and Rose."

Tetty nodded.

"I know, Sam did say, twern't Sam's fault mind, t'were Augustus Crouch that spoke out."

"I shall find her and bring her back," said Robert, tearing the bread before putting it in his mouth, "and we shall find a way to marry. You should have told me what you were about, you and Samuel?"

"I know's Robert, but in her note, Catherine, she wished us to swear that none would say, before the letter were read or it mayn'st get read at all. She did want all the parish to know, what

THE PARISH WAYWARDEN

did happen, why she did leave the parish. The churchwarden, he dun't show 'is face, on this day, on our saint's day."

"And I would put my fist into his fat face, if he do show. I needs more ale," said Robert, wiping his mouth on his coat sleeve.

Will Feather, the blind cooper, had found his way to the cider and lay his hand upon the barrel, like an affectionate father greeting his returning progeny.

"Thee be good to I my deary and dun't be runnin' dry."

Robert kept silent whilst the old man talked, not wishing him to think that Judd Penny was back amongst the living, from his place on the far side of the yew tree. Robert nodded to Mark Bonner to refill his cup with ale and then wandered away from the dripping tree to stand out in the rain. He had still not caught sight of Samuel and presumed that he was inside the church, with the other children. Archery targets were to be set up on the Green but none gathered there and most still clung to whatever shelter was on offer. Augustus Crouch squeezed his way through the throng in the church porch to inspect the sky.

"The rain, it will soon cease," he called out, clapping his hands loudly and then turning to force his way back into the church.

"What do 'ee know?" muttered Richard Beck, the labourer, as he passed by Robert, in search of cake.

Robert returned again to stand beneath the yew tree, as the last dregs were being tipped from the barrels. Parishioners clustered together in their collective dampness, some leaving now that the beer and cider had gone. Mark Bonner then joined Robert in looking out at the rain, as thunder growled in the distance.

"I did not know what they were about Robert, not the letter...to Catherine, Tetty did not say to I..."

"I know not what my own son is about and I be the last

one that do know," said Robert.

"Robert, you are blessed with a sister that you thought were dead... she will come back?"

"I do wish it, but I do not know her Mark, only the stories I do know, I had forgot her, even her name I had forgot."

"Tis hard to do when our church be named the same?"

"Do not be so harsh on I Mark, I lived away, I did lose two wives. I weren't sure to ever come back here, to the parish. Our name be bad amongst some, we did lose the Penny pew."

"Sam do say that Joan and Rose are gone from the parish?"

"I will find them," said Robert, "in the morning, I shall go."

"Will you find them in the city?"

"I reckon, I'll will look there, then to her parish, north, across the plain."

"But will our parson marry thee, even when you does find her, finds Joan and brings her back?"

"Thigpen, he'd put against it, but he is not to be the churchwarden, not now, not after the letter be read in church, it can't be so. And Loper, just sits and dun't speak, when Thigpen, he should be in the stocks on this day of all days and then put before the justices."

"I didst hear that Loper be sat in a chair all the day," said Mark Bonner, "tis a thing for he to keep his mouth shut."

"The parson's brother, he is thick with the bishop. Parson Crouch, he would marry us but he is weak against his brother."

"T'would be hard to see it done, when she be a vagrant Robert?"

"I shall leave in the morning," said Robert, confirming his intentions, "but I'll say this Mark Bonner, Tetty do make a fairer man than thee."

"She do, I grant," said Mark, laughing, as the thunder moved closer, "and she do read and write, says she wishes to be the teacher, on Sunday mornings, if your sister Catherine Penny do agree."

"Catherine, she is to be good to the parish, after what the parish did do to her."

Lightning flashed and the thunder rolled across soon after.

"Reckon it be over Chauncy way," said Mark Bonner, peering out from under the yew tree.

"I needs words with Dowty," said Robert, ignoring the thunder and lightning, "how he did come at Joan, when she be in the church porch. Has thee seen Dowty today?"

Mark Bonner shook his head.

"Nor've I seen Button nor John Arnold. I reckon some do stay away, after the letter be read. We all do know that it be Augustus who makes us all stand in the rain on our saint's day and tis only the beer and the cake that do make the parish show."

Samuel emerged from the church and seeing Robert, he ran to the shelter of the yew tree.

"Samuel?" said Robert.

"Father," said Samuel, placing himself the other side of Mark Bonner.

"There be another flash," said Mark Bonner, making room for Samuel to then squeeze between he and Robert, the crash of thunder following soon after, "it be coming our way."

Robert was aware that Samuel was very afraid of thunder and lightning. His second wife, April, was the same, after her own father died under an ash tree that had been struck. Robert felt Samuel leaning into him, unafraid now of any beating that his father could summon up.

"The ash do court a flash," said Robert, knowing that Samuel had heard this over and again when he was young,

"Father," protested Samuel, trying to bury his head in Robert's coat.

"But p'raps the yew be a lucky tree?" said Robert, putting his hand on his son's head.

"Thic gurt yew did get struck at the parsonage and a whole bough did fall, only weeks back, after harvest," said Mark Bonner.

"Then it be not a lucky tree," said Samuel, pulling his father by the hand with some urgency towards the church.

"P'raps tis best to bide in the church, until it do pass," said Mark Bonner, following behind Robert and Samuel.

There was a sudden flash of lightning and a deafening bang above their heads, causing the three of them to break into a run and then force their way into the church porch.

Robert picked up some more bread as they squeezed their way through to enter the main building. There were many already seeking sanctuary from the rain and now the thunder and lightning had driven more parishioners in from the churchyard. Inside the body of the church, water spouted down through the leaking roof to spatter upon the floor, floating the dead rushes from Easters past. The parish stood in dripping huddles, their collective breath clouding amongst them. Augustus Crouch was beginning to tell the children the story of Saint Catherine and Robert and Samuel found themselves close enough to listen. There was a passion, a joy in the eyes of the parson's brother as he retold the story of the young woman, Catherine of Alexandria. How Catherine, when she was very young, experienced a vision of the virgin Mary and Jesus and embraced Christianity. When the young Roman Emperor Maxentius embarked upon the persecution of Christians, she challenged his cruelty. The

Roman Emperor summoned fifty philosophers to dispute her stance and to change her mind but through the strength of her arguments and debate she succeeded in converting these pagans to Christianity, whereupon the Emperor had them all put to death. Robert thought that there were many bloody stories told in church and the children's eyes widened as Augustus went on to describe Catherine's own imprisonment and torture, her body covered in wounds and how the blood flowed from her. How she was then starved only to be fed by a dove from Heaven. Robert tried to imagine being fed by a dove. Sudden light flashed through the clear windows, blinding in the dark interior of the church, making an image of faces, fixed in fright, the thunder crashing directly above the old stone building. Some cried that the church would fall down upon their heads as Augustus Crouch rose from his seat, lifting a long arm to settle his audience, so that he may not be disturbed from concluding the story of Saint Catherine. Samuel gripped Robert's sleeve and the children huddled tighter together, looking about them, awaiting the next blinding crash. Robert's own sister did not wish to be named Catherine, thinking it a misfortune and not a blessing to be born on the saint's day? Perhaps it was the memory of the night when the drunken men came for her that she now called herself by her middle name, Margaret? It was her name and her saintliness, however, that saved her, when Augustus beat the drunken men away, as Catherine sought sanctuary in the church. She then fled the church to spend the night in the open, to be raped in the cold morning by young Peter Thigpen amongst the hedges and verges of Watery Lane. She left the parish with the driver, riding upon the laden fish ponies, away to London, to be married. She had gone with a sweetheart after all. Another flash of light within the church caused more disturbance but the thunder was slow to follow and some declared that the storm was now passed whilst Augustus Crouch clapped his hands together impatiently, to gather again the attention of the parish children. Robert then thought of Alice Brigg. There was to be no such story told of her rescue, as had happened to Catherine, his sister. If she came to the parish to seek charity in the church porch, her life ended here. A young woman of uncertain mind, forespoken as the stranger had said. By the dealings of man, she had been cast into a ditch with a lump of heathstone to hold her down and covered over with branches of yew. The yew that had poisoned his ox.

  Parson Crouch entered the church and a place was made for him to sit upon the end of a damp bench, to listen to his brother talk. Robert thought that it had got lighter within the church, as though the cloud was lifting outside. He leant forward to speak to Samuel, to tell him that he was going to piss and he then threaded his way back through the clustered parishioners, towards the porch. Once outside he pulled his coat around himself, the thunderstorm seemed to have passed over and the rain was misty now with a chill in the air. He walked around on the grass to the small wicket gate in the churchyard fence that led to the parsonage, across the Green. He needed to piss but he had been thinking about Mark Bonner's words, from when they were sheltering beneath the churchyard yew. Mark had spoken about the yew tree in the parsonage garden that had been struck by lightning and how a large yew bough had fallen during the great storm. Only days after the storm, Robert had found the body of Alice Brigg in Dudge Lane. Now, there would be no person in the parsonage, Samuel had said before that the old maid was deaf but today she would be in the church. Robert went around to the side of the old parsonage, where he had walked through the same broad entrance, all those years ago, to pick up fallen apples, when Augustus had caught him and forced his head into a trough of water. Autumn had stripped the colour from the garden, making the severe darkness of the yew tree all the more imposing. Here was a taller tree, with not the low crowded branches of the churchyard yew, but with a deep and fresh gouge down the far side of the main trunk where a portion of the main trunk had ripped away. There were no remnants of yew branches on the ground from that night of the storm. The same storm when Samuel had awoken Robert in the night, frightened and seeking comfort and he had lain beside Robert, covered by his own blanket until morning. The yew bough had missed the parsonage and had fallen instead upon open ground, where it must have hit instead a rough stone wall that divided the garden. Robert looked at the old wall, made of large irregular flints, dragged by stonepickers from the chalk fields. Amongst the large flints, in the now rebuilt wall, were a few pieces of heathstone, one large piece sat as a top cornerstone, where the wall changed direction, to run back down towards the parsonage. Robert felt his stomach tighten as he walked closer to look at this stone. The wall had no mortar, only earth and chalk for the stones to bed down. He placed his hands on either side of the cornerstone, his fingers working their way into the loose moist earth, to gain a hold of the large flat stone. Robert lifted it up, he already knew its weight because he had lifted this stone before, from the ditch in Dudge Lane, where it had lain upon the body of Alice Brigg. This same stone that Robert had looked for again, later on, but was nowhere to be found and yet, here it was, back in its place upon the wall. He lowered it down again and with a pressing need to piss, he began, up against the rough stone wall, thinking all the while about finding this same stone, here in the parsonage garden. Robert was certain now that Alice Brigg had arrived in the parish and had been murdered in the parish. The fallen bough of yew, the remnants since cleared, was surely the source of the yew branches that had covered the body in the ditch. The heathstone he recognised, with someone retrieving it from the ditch, to place it back upon the wall. A cart would have been needed for both the taking and disposing of Alice Brigg and the later retrieval of the stone. There were only two people in the parish who owned a cart, Henry Dowty, the overseer of the poor and John Arnold. Both Thigpen and Button borrowed carts from their brother's farms in Chauncy. But who was here at the parsonage, when the body of Alice Brigg had been concealed under a pile of yew branches and then carted down to Dudge Lane? As a wandering vagrant the troubled young woman would have surely entered the church porch, seeking shelter and charity and would have encountered the overseer of the poor, Henry Dowty. Robert recalled the look of anguish on Dowty's face when the stranger had confronted him about Alice Brigg. As his arc of piss began to weaken, Robert heard a noise behind him.

"Father," said Samuel, approaching with alarm in his voice.

"Christ's teeth boy, you did make I jump," said Robert, turning around.

"Why do you piss in the parson's garden?"

"I needed to piss, why are you here?"

"I was looking for you, you did not come back."

"How did thee know where I be?"

"I did think that you might be here, Mr Bonner said about the yew tree that was struck."

Robert had thought that Samuel had been too distracted by the thunder and lightning to hear Mark Bonner say about the yew bough falling in the parsonage garden. He looked at Samuel.

"You do know me better than I know myself," said Robert, "we may yet find who murdered Alice Brigg, you and I, from now Samuel, we shall only speak the truth between us?"

"Yes father."

"Tomorrow I shall leave to search for Joan and Rose and when I find her, we shall marry. If I do not now seek the murderer of Alice Brigg, then I can never be truthful, to Joan, to my wife and that I cannot bear. You will help me Samuel?"

Samuel nodded but then looked about uneasily. Robert showed his son the heathstone, upon the corner of the wall.

"It is the same stone that lay upon Alice Brigg, when I found her in the ditch. It is now placed back upon the wall. Somebody did bring it back."

They both heard voices approaching and Samuel quickly grabbed his father's arm and pulled him along, to the rear of the parsonage where they hid behind a corner of the building. It was Augustus' voice that they could hear.

"They are old but they will serve us for this year, they are kept at the bottom of the apple store" said the parson's brother, to another person whom Robert could not see.

A door squeaked open and Robert and Samuel exchanged glances and waited. A sudden thwack made Robert start as an arrow hit the trunk of the yew tree with a solid thud. He and Samuel would be seen as soon as someone walked across to retrieve the arrow from the tree.

"Leave it be, the fletching needs to be done, we have enough, carry the bows and I shall manage the quivers and braces and let us see if you cannot topple Dowty from his perch. I shall not take part for my eyes are not what they once were."

"You hit thic yew well enough zur? I did hear that a great bough did fall from thic same tree, but none were saved for the making of new bows?"

It was Philip Skutt, the blacksmith's eldest son who was accompanying Augustus Crouch and now carried the bows.

"Ah, you heard of this? Alas, it was indeed my brother, your parson, that did state that the yew should all be burned, placing greater import upon the wandering beast from the pound, least it be poisoned. Your parson, he does place no virtue upon our traditions, as do I," said Augustus Crouch, closing the apple store, "now, the sexton, he has the targets, they shall be hung from the old elm, as is the custom. The boys, they must climb up to tie the ropes. The Good Lord has blessed us on this day, now that the tempest has passed."

Robert and Samuel waited until they could no longer hear voices.

"Father, come, we must go," said Samuel, dragging his father by the hand.

Robert resisted and instead walked across to the yew tree to tug at the shaft of the imbedded arrow but it stayed firm.

"Who was here?" said Robert, "at the parsonage, who cleared the tree and who did build the stone wall back up?"

"Mr Arnold do sometimes come, it is his sister that is the old maid at the parsonage."

"Then I needs speak with John," said Robert, "but first I must speak with Dowty. Who was here at the parsonage, after the storm, after the yew were struck?"

"Mr Augustus, he did just blame the parson for burning the yew, but the parson, he was not yet come to the parsonage from Oxford. It were not his doing father, the parson he did not do murder. You will not say so father?"

"I did not say so boy, I had not thought so."

"Come father, we must go. The parson he has now left the church to attend to Sarah Crust, they say she will die today."

Samuel pulled at his father's hand again and Robert followed.

Augustus Crouch's voice could be heard across the Green, making arrangements for the archery contest. The two plump straw filled sacks were being hoisted up and boys scrabbled into the old elm tree to tie off the ropes. A small white circle had been pinned to the middle of each and the parson's elder brother was now pacing away from the tree, counting as he strode across the wet grass.

"Fifty paces, a mark, quickly, get a stick."

Augustus Crouch dug in his heel to mark the spot and then pointed at Samuel.

"Penny, boy, you stand there until a stick is found, do not move."

Samuel quickly ran across and stood still at the fifty paces mark. A further fifty paces was measured with more demands upon other children to mark the spot and a final fifty paces was added which concluded beside the whipping post.

"Where is Dowty?" called out Augustus Crouch, "get Dowty to come, he must defend his title."

The overseer had not been seen all day and a clutch of children ran to Dowty's farm to bring him to the Green.

"Penny boy, you recover the arrows that have missed their target, conceal yourself behind the elm."

Samuel frowned and looked towards his father before turning and running back down the open Green, towards the lone tree at the bottom, glancing behind him to ensure that no bows were being raised or arrows already aimed at the hanging targets. Once at the tree, he concealed himself behind the broad trunk and only his head could be seen, popping out and then disappearing again. A ladder had been propped up against the tree to enable the sacks to be reached and the arrows pulled out.

Robert caught sight of John Arnold who he had not seen throughout the day and was now standing by the whipping post, awaiting the archery competition.

"John," said Robert, as he approached.

"Ah, Robert, the thunder did clatter bad but tis fair

now."

"Will you pick up the bow?" said Robert.

"No, tis for sons to take over, my son Luke be good but the blacksmith's boy, Philip, he be better. Dowty he do allus win, he did allus beat I, for a man that can stumble on his own words, he do have a strong and steady arm and a good eye. T'were his father Hugh Dowty that did make him good with the bow, he did beat him if ever he missed the mark. Robert, I am main glad that your sister, she be alive. After the letter be read in church...I could not sleep the whole night, thinking of Thigpen and how he did...I cannot speak of it Robert. The parish must gather, tis the worst of things, he that is the churchwarden..."

"He shall not be John, I wished Loper to act but Loper be near dead in a chair. John, can I speak of when you did clear the yew in the parsonage garden?"

"That I did, my sister Hester be the old maid at the parsonage, Augustus he did want it gone, said the animals from the pound do wander onto parsonage ground. He d'int want no timber to be kept neither, none for new bows and the broken wall we did build up," John Arnold looked about him and then lowered his voice, "cause I did store the trunkwood in my barn and it shall warm us in a couple year or more, they say it be bad luck to burn yew but it be worse luck to be cold in winter. Luke do have some good lengths stored for to make new bows. Robert, we cannot burn good wood, we did burn the brash, like he did say."

"And was not William Crouch at the parsonage?"

John Arnold shook his head.

"The parson? He had not yet returned. Augustus, he did stay not two days. T'was only weeks after old Nathaniel's burial and the older brother, he had bin to Exeter or some such place and did stay not two days in the parish, as I did say. Why does thee ask Robert?"

"No, I did hear from Mark Bonner that the yew be struck, just that it be an odd thing that Augustus did not wish for some yew to be kept, as the parish bows, they now be old?"

John Arnold shrugged. He cupped a hand to his mouth and called out that the archery should begin before it got dark or the rain came back. A small group of children had found Henry Dowty and he was being noisily ushered to the Green.

"Shall thee pick up a bow Robert? You have been away from the parish."

Robert was about to shake his head but then changed his mind.

"Yes, I shall, but I had not thought so before today."

John Arnold had a flagon of cider at his feet and he picked it up to remove the stopper and passed it to Robert.

"Then thee'll be needing a drink Robert, the barrels do allus run dry before the archery do start."

Robert accepted gratefully and took a couple of long swigs before passing back the heavy flagon.

"Thank ye John," said Robert, "now to war."

Those entering the competition stood together and a huddle of twenty men had mustered at the first stick, fifty paces from the targets hanging from the tree and Robert joined them. Robert picked up the oldest looking bow from the grass and turned his back from the group to bend the narrow strip of yew until he heard it split towards one end. He then affixed the string into the notch, the fractured bow holding firm with the horsehair string now taught. Some men had their own bows and fitted their own thick leather wristguards, Philip Skutt then produced a small pot of grease and dipped in the two draw fingers on his right hand. Henry Dowty was summoned by Augustus Crouch to join the first round and he walked slowly with bowed head to stand unspeaking beside the group. The parson's brother surveyed the cluster of participants and frowned when he saw Robert's face but said nothing.

"Commence," called out Augustus Crouch whereupon nobody moved, he then clapped his hands and pointed at the elm tree and then at Mark Bonner, "you, you go first."

Mark Bonner disregarded the offer of a wrist guard and with his bow strung, he picked up an arrow from the selection upon the grass, the broad iron point now a rusty brown, the shaft of ashwood dull and the goose feather fletching curled with age. With no great preparation of stance, Mark Bonner held the bow flat, on its side and lay the arrow in the middle, securing the notch of the arrow into the string as he brought the bow up straight whilst also drawing back the string with two fingers, hard bending the bow and quickly releasing the arrow, all in a single movement. The arrow hit within the white disc and a cheer went up from the observing crowd. Augustus Crouch stood opposite each bowman and declared in turn which of the two sacks targets to aim for and also whether the arrow had missed altogether or struck the straw stuffed sack or the small white disc. John Arnold's son Luke, Philip Skutt, Michael Chant and Mark Bonner were the only archers to strike the small white circle, with only Robert and Henry Dowty to draw.

"Dowty next," called out the parson's brother, "the target away from the church."

The overseer of the poor shuffled forward reluctantly, stooping to pick up a bow to string it, before taking an arrow and with no wristguard or grease pot, he released with ease, sending a ruffled feather arrow into the centre of the white spot.

"A hit, a hit," called out the children who had edged forward to see the contest.

"Penny next," called out Augustus Crouch, scowling at

Robert, "to aim for the target nearest our church."

"Where be thy wife Penny?" called out a voice from the crowd that Robert recognised as Jacob Difford, "has thee lost her already, praps she be in that sack hanging from thic old elm?"

This caused a murmur of laughter from the crowd and made Robert bristle. He disregarded the leather wrist guard and picked up an arrow before taking up his position. Upon drawing the string, the bow that he had purposefully fractured, buckled in his hands and he threw the bow down upon the grass at Augustus Crouch's feet, with a grunt of disapproval.

"Another bow Penny," demanded the parson's brother, impatiently, "there, take one that is strung and has been already drawn."

Robert picked up the bow that Mark Bonner had used.

"Tis a shame that new bows cannot be made," said Robert, preparing his stance and speaking so that Augustus Crouch could hear him from where he stood, opposite to each archer in turn.

Robert paused as he levelled the bow and placed the bowstring into the arrow notch. The cluster of archers were standing back and Robert kept his voice down.

"Did not a great yew bough fall? In the parsonage garden?" said Robert, looking up at Augustus Crouch, to emphasize his words,

"Get on with it Penny," said the parson's brother, "you'll not win, even with the best bow in the land."

"And the wall, it be rebuilt, I do hear" said Robert, purposefully dropping the arrow and having to retrieve it from the grass, "but tis a pity that all that good yew be burned up."

"My brother, he did ask for it all to be gone, so that the animals may not be poisoned, now draw or stand aside Penny," said Augustus Crouch, with a growl, his eyes widening.

"That be strange," said Robert poised to draw, "William, your brother the parson, he had not yet returned from Oxford, but I did hear that it were you that did say to burn the yew and it were not the parson. That thee were at the parsonage, after the yew did fall?"

Robert drew back the bow string and sent the arrow arcing towards the elm tree where it seemed to hit the very bottom of the white spot. He paused to wink at the parson's brother before tossing the bow down upon the grass and sought out John Arnold for another pull on his cider flask.

"A miss," said Augustus Crouch.

"It has hit the spot," Robert called back.

"No, I do think," said Augustus Crouch who called out for Samuel to put up the ladder and pull out the arrows, so that they may be returned.

Samuel's head could be seen peering out from behind the elm trunk and he quickly leaned the ladder up to each target in turn, pulling out the arrows that had hit the sacks but had missed the white spot, then declaring that Robert's arrow was just within the white spot. Augustus Crouch, turned on his heel and strode back fifty paces to the second mark, ordering that the bows, wristguards and arrows be brought. One of the smaller children collected the arrows from Samuel, including the ones that had missed their targets altogether and had buried themselves in the turf upon the Green. Six men were now required to draw again, including Robert. The same order was kept, but with Mark Bonner and Michael Chant hitting the sacks but missing the white spot. Henry Dowty again drew with ease and certainty, hitting the centre of the white spot before Robert again picked up the bow.

"You'll miss Penny," said Augustus Crouch, so that only Robert could hear.

Robert levelled the bow and lay the arrow, bisecting the undrawn arc of the bow and then secured the arrow notch in the string.

"Alice Brigg," said Robert, bringing the bow upright, "a troubled young woman of good family did come to our parish, just after the yew fell and here she did die. I did find her, with a piece of heathstone to sink her in the ditch, covered over with boughs of green yew."

Robert drew the bow and released the arrow, the target now a blur but the white spot still apparent.

"A hit, a hit," cried out the children who possessed the better sight.

Robert smiled at the parson's brother as he tossed the bow down.

"Penny, the arrows," roared Augustus Crouch, his nostrils flaring in anger and he then began to mutter under his breath, as he had done at Robert's door.

Samuel peered again to make sure that no arrows were sailing toward the old elm and used the ladder to reach the targets. The sack targets now swung upon their strings, as Samuel descended the ladder. Augustus Crouch suddenly bent to grab a bow and arrow and with a loud thwack the released bow string struck the heavy cloth of his sleeve.

"Samuel," shouted his father, in alarm.

Samuel, with more than half an eye on where the arrows were coming from, leapt behind the tree just as an arrow splintered into the very edge of the elm trunk beside his concealed position.

"There, that is why I do not now join the contest," said Augustus Crouch, turning to Philip Skutt, "see, I cannot now even hit the sack. Time was, when a man could be excused when accidentally killing another, when practising upon the archery butts, such was the standing, when England's glory did so depend upon the long bow."

Samuel's head peered out briefly again from behind the far side of the elm trunk as Augustus Crouch turned and marched a further fifty paces away from the targets.

"He be riled by summat," said John Arnold, passing Robert the cider flagon, "when did thee learn to handle a bow then Robert, it not be in this parish?"

"In Chauncy, my sister Ann's husband Richard, he be a good bowman and did make I pull a lot of bow strings till my arm were sore, Samuel, he can hit the mark, he would be a better archer than I, as he do grow," said Robert, taking another swig from the cider flagon, "your boy Luke, he be good."

"Ah, he be good but Francis' boy, he'm better still but doubtful he do win, tis Henry Dowty that do reign."

Augustus Crouch clapped his hands together to muster the remaining archers to compete again. Luke Arnold drew first, from one hundred and fifty paces. It was now too far for many to see whether the white spot was hit or not.

"Penny boy," roared the parson's brother, "a hit?"

Samuel tentatively peered out from behind the tree and then ran before the tree to where he could see the target. He shouted back that the arrow had just missed the white spot.

"You, Penny next to draw," said Augustus Crouch, stabbing a long finger towards Robert, "the target nearest the church."

Robert said nothing as he raised the bow, he could feel a gust of wind on his cheek and aimed accordingly. The arrow hit the sack, but Robert could not tell whether he had hit the white spot. This was declared a miss by Samuel before he ran back to hide behind the trunk.

"Defeated Penny?" said Augustus Crouch, "Dowty

next to draw."

Robert stood back as the overseer of the poor shuffled forward and picked up the bow that Robert had cast down upon the grass. Robert remained close enough behind Henry Dowty, so that he could be heard by the bowman.

"She did come to the church porch, Alice Brigg," whispered Robert, "what did you do Henry, did thee touch her where it be soft, did she cry out?"

The overseer remained motionless, with bow in hand and arrow primed but looked down at the ground.

"Come Dowty," shouted out Augustus Crouch, "think it for king and country."

"She did die by your hand Henry," whispered Robert, "be that why you do pray so? For God to forgive?"

Henry Dowty suddenly raised the bow, the arrow tip trembling, he then drew and released, casting down the bow even before the arrow had reached its target and turning to walk beyond the whipping post and the parish stocks.

"A miss, a miss, Mr Dowty did not hit the sack," declared the children, jumping up and down in excitement.

"Now Philip Skutt to draw," said the parson's brother.

"I await my father to return," said Philip Skutt, "afore I do draw."

Robert was close behind the overseer, walking from the Green, upon a twisting and narrow, high banked footpath that led to Flower Lane. He hastened his pace to catch up with Dowty, grabbing him by the shoulder and pulling him back before striking him across the face.

"How did it go Henry? Like you did touch Joan Young when she did seek sanctuary in our church porch? Like thee do to all women who do stray to our parish?"

The overseer's eyes were darting from side to side, a

bead of blood trickled from his nose, dispersing amongst the whiskers upon his top lip. Robert pushed him back further, into the dripping hedge and raised his fist again.

"Sh..sh..she d..d..did f..f..fall."

"Did she die there on the stone floor or did thee ravish her first. The girl, she were no vagrant, but dressed as a maid, she was of good family Henry, she was troubled is all."

"Sh..sh..she w..w..were no..no..no m..m..maid. Sh..sh.. her c..c..clothes were once f..f..fine."

"I did find her Henry, Alice Brigg, laid in a ditch at the bottom of Dudge Lane with a lump of heathstone to hold her down, when I did take your cart to bring her back, she wore not fine clothes but was dressed as a maid."

"Huh, huh, huh," the overseer panted, panicking and Robert shook him again, "o..o..only a..a..after, w..w..was she.. she dr..dr..dressed as a m..m..maid."

"After? After what?"

"A..a..after h..h..he..he d..did c..c..come."

"Who did come?"

Henry's eyes flicked back fearfully towards the Green just as Francis Skutt the blacksmith rounded the corner and appeared upon the path before them, carrying a cider flagon and stopping at the sight of the two men.

"Robert? Henry? What be this?"

Robert released his hold and the overseer of the poor slipped from Robert's grip, to scuttle away, beyond the blacksmith who then blocked Robert's pursuit of the disappearing figure.

"Tis a vestry matter," said Robert, "let me pass."

"I shall not, Henry be my own cousin, thee shall say the cause of it Robert Penny."

Robert did not wish to entangle with the iron forearms of the parish blacksmith and so turned back towards the Green with

Francis Skutt, following close behind. The blacksmith placed his flagon upon the grass and then advanced, keen to see his son win the archery contest. Robert picked up the blacksmith's flagon and took two or three long swigs of cool cider, replacing the bung and putting the flagon back down.

"A hit, a hit," proclaimed the keen eyed children, as Philip Skutt held his bow aloft, to cheers from the scattered crowd.

"We have a new champion," declared Augustus Crouch, "there is a haunch of venison as a prize, back at the parsonage. Now the younger boys may compete, bring the bows and arrows."

Samuel had crept away from his target duties and looked to be leaving the Green. Robert walked down towards the church to intercept him.

"Mr Crouch, he did near strike me with the arrow" said Samuel, "I do not wish to join the boy's contest."

"He be angry with me Samuel, not thee, I needs return to the parsonage."

"No father, you cannot, let us go home now."

"The parson, he still be visiting the dying girl?"

Samuel nodded.

"Till she be dead," he said, quietly, "and then he will pray more, with the family."

"Go, go join the archery Samuel, if there is meat to be won?"

"No, I shall come with you father."

Amongst the cluster of children the youngest Difford boy then aimed an arrow directly up into the sky, causing the children to scream and run in all directions. The arrow stuck into the Green, not ten paces from Augustus Crouch who let out a roar, the enormous figure in black, snatching the boy as an eagle might pluck a helpless rabbit from the turf, shaking him violently and throwing him to the ground. In the ensuing disturbance, Robert hastened towards the parsonage, emboldened by cider and a seething rage towards the parson's brother who had said enough in church to make Joan and Rose leave the parish, to leave their life together as man and wife. Walking back through the open gateway, towards the rear of the parsonage, Samuel kept looking back across towards the Green.

"Come, Samuel, you have been inside," said Robert, walking up to the back door and lifting the latch.

Samuel looked pale and shook with fear as he moved before his father, reluctantly pushing open the door.

"Father, we should not..."

Robert urged Samuel on from behind, until they were both inside the house, closing the door behind them.

"Are you there?" Robert shouted out loudly, causing Samuel to turn and try to run from the house, with his father grabbing his arm, "stop boy, it is as well to call out, we needs be sure that none is here. Samuel, you do know this house. Where would the clothes be that Catherine was to wear, when she was to enter service as a maid, here at the parsonage, the clothes that she never did wear but parson Crouch said were kept? Clothes that were kept as if they themselves be saintly."

"I do not know," said Samuel, obstinately standing still and not moving.

"Boy," said Robert, growling at his son, "you should be afeared of me, not afeared of this house, I shall see this thing through and you are due a beating for what you did do, I have not forgot. The old maid, she has a room?"

Samuel nodded.

"Up the stairs, on one side, there is the maid's room and others that I have not seen," said Samuel.

"Then move, be quick."

Each step upon the stairway creaked, causing Robert and Samuel to wince at the protesting groans of their intrusion.

"Come, hurry," said Robert, his own heart pounding, having never before climbed a flight of stairs inside a house.

Upon reaching the hall at the top of the stairs, Samuel turned towards a narrow and dark passageway with three closed doors along its length, but then stopped.

"Father, we must go from here, now," whispered Samuel, turning wide eyed towards his father.

"Do not be afraid," said Robert, drunk from drinking other people's cider on the Green and pushing his son from behind.

Samuel stopped at the first door.

"It be the old maid's room," said Samuel, "the parson's brother do think she will set fire to the house and does take all the candles. She brings a pot for they to eat but will stay at her cousin's, until he be gone. The parson, he will make his own fire."

Robert urged Samuel onwards and rattled open the second door, having to stoop down under the low door frame to enter the room. It was dark and Robert opened a small wooden shutter to throw light into the room, causing a breeze to enter through the open frame and Robert briefly peered down upon the parsonage garden. Inside the room was a simple unmade bed and a wooden chest. Upon the chest, a small wooden cross lay next to a book. Robert picked up the book and opened it at the beginning, holding it up to show Samuel.

"What does it say, what is writ there?"

"It says Catherine Penny," said Samuel, "it be a book of psalms."

Robert lifted up the small wooden cross and opened the chest. Inside were a pair of simple shoes.

"The young woman, Alice Brigg, she wore no shoes, when I did find her," said Robert, "these be Catherine's shoes, that she never did wear as a maid, her clothes, they are gone."

Samuel edged towards the door and then fled down the passageway.

"Samuel," shouted his father, "get thee here."

"I cannot. Father you must leave," said Samuel, calling back as he ran down the passageway and staircase and then there was silence in the house.

Robert belched, the cider on top of the beer was clawing at his throat and he wanted to spit out the mouthful of rising bile but instead he held it in his mouth, until he could bring himself to swallow. He quickly closed the chest and replaced the book and small cross. Every step creaked as he walked from the room, into the narrow passageway. His stomach churned and he hurried his step, the house creaking all the more. He began to descend the staircase just as a great figure darkened the foot of the stairs.

"Penny?" said Augustus Crouch, "I heard the creaking boards. Now it is stealing? Breaking into houses?"

Robert froze, gripping tightly the dark wooden bannisters on either side.

"Shall you come quiet, to the constable, or do I haul you there?" said the parson's brother.

"The constable be sat in a chair, night and day, he says nothing, he will be no use to thee," said Robert.

"The justices then. I shall take you to the city myself, we shall leave in the morning."

"I should wish it," said Robert, swallowing again to keep the bile from rising, "I shall then say how a woman did die in the parish. A young woman with long black hair, by name of Alice Brigg. Between thee and the overseer, Dowty, she did die and was cast into a ditch."

"What do you say to me Penny? That I should know of such a woman, when I have just found you as a thief and yet you accuse me of some...murder?"

Augustus Crouch began to charge up the staircase just as the liquid content of Robert's stomach could no longer be contained and a bile rich flow spattered onto the dark wooden stairs, splashing onto the long dark cloak of his assailant, causing the parson's brother to stop and recoil.

"Penny, you...you...vile drunkard, you shall spend the night in the stocks, where you can spew upon yourself."

Robert spat to try to expel the taste of vomit and then wiped his mouth upon the sleeve of his damp coat.

"Dowty do still think it were he, that did murder Alice Brigg," said Robert, now feeling weaker and bent almost double after the act of being sick, "but you went to the church and did find Dowty and the woman, you had a lantern?"

Neither moved from their positions, with the staircase of slippery vomit between them. The parson's brother glowered up at Robert. Robert was feeling weak but kept telling himself that he must now see this thing through. He had been drunk when he had entered the parsonage but the act of spewing had straightened his senses.

"Alice Brigg, she was of good family," continued Robert, "she were no vagrant, she were troubled is all, forespoken so I were told, by one who did know her. She came to seek charity and shelter but she did die here. She were not buried in our parish, like a good Christian should be buried, she were just cast into a ditch...where I did find her."

"Does any other person know that you are here?" said Augustus Crouch, "here, inside the parsonage at no person's invitation?"

Robert shook his head slowly, not knowing where

Samuel had gone.

"Come, Penny, come down that we may sit and talk... and you may repent and return what you have stolen."

"No," said Robert, gripping the bannisters to hold himself upright, forcing himself to shout, "I have stolen nothing. After the storm that struck the parsonage yew, did you not find Dowty and the young woman Alice Brigg, in the church porch? Dowty says that she fell."

"Dowty," scoffed Augustus Crouch, "what is he to me? That stuttering fool. I have not been in the parish since my father was buried, my home it is in London, you are making a very grave mistake Penny."

"You were here long enough," said Robert, trying to gather his thoughts, what he knew to be true, yet there was much that he did not know, about which he was doubtful, "after the yew be struck. I know not why you did come and then go away and I care less, but you did send word to John Arnold, to clear the tree and build up again the wall. I have spoken to Dowty and John Arnold also. And yet you blame the parson for having the yew burned, when it was he, your brother, that had not yet returned to the parish."

Augustus Crouch shook his head and then slapped his great hands upon the bannisters, as if he were about again make a charge, regardless of the vomit slowly dripping from the lip of each bare wooden stair, between top and bottom.

"Stop...hear me out," said Robert, now breathless, holding up the palm of a hand, "her clothes, Alice Brigg, Dowty did say that they were once fine clothes, not the rags of a beggar. But when I found her in the ditch, in Dudge Lane, she wore the clothes of a girl in service. The same clothes that were got for Catherine Penny, when she were to begin in service, here at the parsonage. They are now gone from the place where they were kept. I have looked in the chest...only the shoes are there."

Robert still held the gaze of the man at the foot of the staircase, not looking away. The figure in black began to climb the stairs.

"Who did change her clothes?" shouted Robert, but with fear in his voice, "was it thee that did strip her? You saw the mark, upon her breast? You did touch that mark?"

Augustus Crouch stopped on the stairway and suddenly retreated, as if, by the words uttered, the looming figure had grown smaller. Robert could now hear a muffled sobbing and he stood slowly, beginning to descend the staircase, now holding the bannisters on either side, picking his way over the dim gleam of wet vomit, lest he should slip and fall. The stairs creaked and Robert stopped before he reached the bottom step. He strained to listen, easing forward from the stairs, slowly peering around the corner where the parson's brother had dropped to his knees upon the bare floorboards, his head bowed.

"You brought her here," said Robert, in a whisper, "to the parsonage? Did you wish to save her, Alice Brigg?"

The crumpled black figure raised his head towards Robert, his eyes unseeing, as had happened on Robert's own doorstep and then later, during divine service in the pulpit.

"Yes, yes, her poisoned lips, her poisoned lips," muttered the parson's brother, now hunched upon the floor, "she did poison me, she...she herself was tainted, father, she was not...not."

Robert leant against the wall, beside the staircase and then slid down upon his haunches.

"It did rain? On that night?" prompted Robert, quietly.

Augustus Crouch's continued to stare beyond Robert, causing Robert to shiver as though there were another presence in the hallway at the foot of the stairs, the presence of the dead parson Nathaniel Crouch.

"I had returned from Exeter father, stopping on my way to London, the storms they brought down many laden trees. I wished for the wind and rain to cease. I did go to the church, with the key. You did never let me take the church key, not after I did once spill, as Onan did once spill his seed, but none did hold our beloved saint so dearly as I, so preciously kept in my heart. You did not trust your son, your eldest son?"

"Speak, Augustus," said Robert, softly, "speak to your father of that night,"

The parson's brother remained silent, now looking down at the floor. As he began in whisper, Robert drew closer to be able to hear the words uttered.

"I...I there found...Dowty, Dowty, the weasel, father did you not call him so?"

"Yes, yes," said Robert, quietly urging, "but what of the young woman, what of her...my son?"

"By the lantern, I could see her, lying as if she slept, upon the porch floor. Dowty, I did shout, what have you now done? I struck him and he cowered. I told him that he had caused her murder, this woman, she our very own Saint Catherine, come back to the place where her altar was once blessed in holy light... but was then...desecrated. The weasel, he stammered that she did fall, I...I...I took no time in lifting her, that I might yet save her. Her clothes they were sodden, I took her to her room, so that she might yet begin in service, as you had decided father, so that she might not be drowned by ignorant men, for a witch."

"Did she look saintly, Alice Brigg?" said Robert, trying not to break the thread of the confession, "did she look as Catherine Penny did once look?"

Robert waited before prompting further.

"Augustus, tell your father, tell me, Nathaniel Crouch, what did then happen?"

"You...you said that the girl would enter service, here at the parsonage, her clothes they were kept. I did pray that she might yet return...and...by the grace of God..."

"But she were now dead? Lain in maid's clothes?"

"Dead? No, father she was not dead, how could you say so? First, I did talk with her. Did straighten her hair and read psalms over her, from her very own book."

"You did say that her lips were poisoned?"

"No, no father, she was pure, untainted, she is our own saint, she who did die at the hands of her torturers?"

Robert wanted an end to this twisting of stories.

"Augustus, I will beat you, so help me God," roared Robert, unable to contain his rage, "tell your father."

"Father, I do deserve to be beat..."

Robert slapped his hand upon the cold stone floor.

"I...I carried her down to the buttery and laid her there. She spoke not. I then went to raise Dowty, to say that he had caused her murder and that I would now call the constable. Father, oh how he did plead and spit his words, he said he would bring the cart. He came as the wind did howl and he did not awaken us, father you were not woken?"

From where he had slumped down against the wall, Robert thrashed out with his legs, at the prostrate figure of Augustus Crouch.

"Speak," shouted Robert.

"Yes, yes..." said the parson's brother, his voice rising from, the whispered utterances, "I knew not what his intentions were, but with her body gone, in the early morning, I sought him again amongst the fields, where he spat out the words of his foul deed. That he had taken a stone from the broken wall and also cut branches of fallen yew with his billhook from the cart, to cover...so that none might see his work. He went by way of the common, away from the eyes and ears of the man Poll and then on towards Clay Pond, where he was to sink her, beyond the parish bounds. The weasel, he then heard the bells of the packhorse train as they prepared to leave their camp beside the deep pond, before the dawn. The body, it was heaved into a ditch, the stone thrown down upon her and all covered over in fresh yew. Father, I did implore Dowty that the stone from our wall, it must be got from the ditch at once, brought back here and the broken wall rebuilt. Even the fallen yew, must be gone from the parsonage, all association with Dowty's deeds must be expunged from this Christian house. The parish man Arnold was to be engaged straight away and Dowty was to arrange this. I wished to attend the justices in the city, to say what fate did befall dear Catherine Penny, but...but...you...you did say fiercely...no, it is now ended...that she was a witch, that she were tainted."

The parson's brother turned his head to look directly at Robert.

"Penny, you have been stealing apples?"

"No," said Robert.

"From the parsonage garden, father, the boy he steals our apples."

Augustus Crouch swung an arm at Robert, striking him hard upon the side of the head and knocking Robert sideways. In a daze, he found himself being hauled from the stone floor and dragged about, unable to breathe with tightening hands at his throat. As he gasped for air his head was plunged forward into water, water sucked up his nose and down his throat, the strength of the hands that held him, forcing Robert's head downwards, his arms thrashing helplessly behind him but finding nothing to clutch, his eyes wide open amidst the darkness of the seething water. He felt himself weakening, a whiteness burst inside his head, it would soon be over, he need struggle no more.

The weight was lifted and Robert fell backwards, heaving water from his chest and nose, gasping, his eyes blocked with water, he flailed his arms before lurching over onto his stomach, coughing water onto the cold stone upon which he lay. He could hear a voice, many times saying the same thing.

"Father, father, father, father..."

Robert rolled over, rubbing his eyes to see. Samuel was there, standing above him, holding something in his hands. He sat up with a jerk, where was Augustus Crouch? How had he been near drowned? Not outside, not in a water trough but in a parlour, in a large tub of water? Robert gasped for air, dribbling.

"Samuel?"

Robert could barely hear his own voice with his ears still blocked with water.

"Father, get up," said Samuel, placing one hand under his father's armpit, to urge him to his feet.

"Dear Christ..." said Robert, rubbing his eyes and looking about him.

Against the door of the parlour, the parson's brother was slumped, his head hanging down, his legs splayed out across the wet floor.

"Samuel, what have you done?" spluttered Robert.

"He cannot move," said Samuel, "he is not dead, I did take the parson's crossbow. He is pinned to the door by his coat. I did first hit him with the stool, so that he would let you go."

"Where...did you...where were you?"

"I did hear all father, I did not leave the parsonage. When you were dragged to the parlour, I did get the parson's crossbow, I feared you would be dead."

Augustus Crouch raised his head.

"Penny? And the Penny boy? Breaking into the parson's own house? The justices shall deal with the both of you, so they shall. A family of verminous thieves."

Robert clambered to his feet to stand before the parson's brother, now helpless with two crossbow bolts pinning tightly the heavy black woollen cloth of his garments, holding the torso upright. Robert clutched at the door, heaving it slightly open, forcing the black figure to shuffle forward on his backside. He peered at the two iron points on the outside of the parlour door that had penetrated the thick oak.

"You have another?" said Robert, "another bolt?"

"Yes father, but he cannot now move."

"Give me the..thing...the bow, first place the bolt."

"No father, I shall not."

Robert turned and snatched the crossbow from his son and he then held Samuel's coat.

"Give it me, I shall set it," said Robert, prising the short bolt from Samuel's hand, "you must go to Loper's, get the parish constable to come."

"Father, but you said that he does not move and is sat in a chair...."

"I hear he is stirred and now walking, go," shouted Robert.

Robert heaved the door open further, dragging the weight of the parson's brother with it. He then pushed Samuel through the narrow gap, out into the parsonage garden.

"Go," shouted Robert again, "and return with the parish constable."

Robert then picked up and righted the stool that Samuel had used to hit Augustus Crouch across the back of the head. The large tub of water that Robert's head had been plunged into was now upturned with its contents pooling across the stone parlour floor. Enough dusky light seeped into the parlour for Robert to be able to see and he sat down upon the stool, breathing heavily before setting the bolt into the primed crossbow and he then levelled it at where he thought Augustus Crouch's heart might be.

The front door of Robert's house rattled open, waking Robert, where he had been leant forward upon the table, his clothes still wet from his near drowning at the parsonage.

"Uh? Samuel?"

"Mr Loper is dead," said Samuel, breathlessly, "you said he were walking again, but he be dead? I did then go to Mr Arnold's who had not yet returned home, but he will come. I did not speak with Mr Jess, for you do not trust the beadle. The parsonage it is empty, the parson has not yet come from when Sarah Crumb did die. Father what did you, where is Mr Augustus?"

Robert rubbed his face with both hands in the darkness.

"Loper dead? Then a new constable is to be got. The vestry, it must change, Mark Bonner, he shall be overseer, Tetty has said so."

"Father? What did you?"

"Thigpen, he must be punished and not be churchwarden, only Button and I are left. Button it was who did come to this door, barely a man, when they came for Catherine Penny, to drown her as a witch. None has said so...but it were he...I do know...and it shall be spoken of, he shall be challenged."

Robert could see Samuel's shape in the open doorway.

"Shut the door," said Robert.

"Father, what have you done, you did send me to Mr Loper, when you knew he could not be got, so that you could be alone with Mr Augustus? What did you?"

Robert's head slumped forward back onto the table. Samuel entered the house, closing the front door.

"Father?"

"Let me shut my eyes, boy."

"Is he dead?"

Robert lifted up his head, looking into the darkness.

"In the morning, I leave for the city. I know that I shall find Joan and Rose there. I will bring them back and we shall marry. It is done."

"What is done?" said Samuel, "father, what is done?"

"He is to write to the bishop, that I should marry Joan, here in the parish. He will not stand in our way. He is made weak by the telling of all that did happen, he pleaded that none might know of his deeds. The woman, Alice Brigg, what did happen here in the parish, it shall be forgot."

"Forgot? But he is to be punished…Mr Augustus…and Mr Dowty… father, it cannot now be forgot."

"It shall be forgot, boy. Who shall it serve, not the dead woman? Do not speak of it again."

"The brother, he cannot stay, to again beat the parson, to break his experiments? No father, it shall not be, he must be gone from the parish."

Robert heard the door latch rattle and leapt across the room, upturning the table, fumbling in the darkness for Samuel, he grabbed a sleeve and hauled his son back into the house, slamming the door.

"So help me boy, you shall now be beat for what you have done, things done behind my back, you do too much, you think you do know right from wrong, I shall show you what is…"

In the darkness, Robert witnessed a sudden light, a flash of light inside his own head and then the taste of the earth floor. He lay face down, groaning. He heard a bell, the church bell. The bell kept ringing, ringing with purpose and urgency.

"What is...?" said Robert, lifting himself from the floor and then rising slowly to his knees, "what did you do Samuel? You did strike me?"

The church bell continued to ring, jangling in Robert's head.

"There is a fire? Or else the sexton, he is drunk? Samuel? Open the door, look for fire."

Robert heard the front door open, as he struggled unsteadily to his feet.

"We must go. Samuel, help me walk."

Robert felt Samuel's arm around his waist and then held on to the door frame to steady himself, before stepping out into The Street. He could hear other voices, between the tolling of the church bell. Robert did not have the strength to call out to those already gathering in The Street and Samuel caught him as he stumbled forward and pushed to keep his father upright, until Robert was able to walk on his own. Robert then held his son by the arm to prevent his running away. The sky had cleared and a full moon showed dark figures moving downhill, towards the church, towards the frenetic ringing bell, the wet and slippery chalk surface of The Street glowing with a pale light. Robert steadied himself, held upright by pulling against his son. The ditch at the bottom of The Street gleamed with water and Samuel steered his father towards the culvert bridge with Robert touching his breastbone as he passed over the stone slab. He sensed the time when his own father had dragged him to church, dragging him across the altar slab culvert, after they had fought, he was older than Samuel is now, his father wanting to display to the parish a broken nose and his swollen eye, to shame his son.

The ringing of the church bell was slowing and the parish were gathering with questions being voiced and answers speculated upon. Robert pushed his way to the lych gate, dragging

Samuel behind him. At the church porch, more members of the parish were clustered and Robert elbowed his way through, towards the church door. John Arnold was standing before the closed door, holding aloft a lantern and shaking his head, calling out that none may enter.

"John," shouted Robert after the bell had rung once again, "be there a fire?"

John Arnold gestured for Robert and Samuel to come forward.

"Mr Arnold," shouted Samuel, before Robert could speak, "the parson, he is here, at the church?"

John Arnold nodded.

"The parson he be here but I do reckon that it be the sexton who be ringing thic bell, when he be too drunk to stand on his own. Robert, Samuel did say for me to come to you? But I did hear the church bell ring and the parson did hail for me to come."

"The thing that Samuel came for, it is done, it is passed," said Robert.

"Robert, what has thee done to thy face?" said John Arnold, holding up the lantern.

At that moment the church door began to open and John Arnold stood to one side. Parson Crouch looked pale in the lantern light, as his face appeared.

"John, I thank you for attending at the church door, tell the parish that they should return to their beds, the bell it may yet ring more, but there be no fire. Robert and Samuel, you may enter and John also, once the porch is cleared, but you must lock the door from the inside."

Just at that moment Isaac Button, the parish clerk appeared in the church porch, demanding to know why the bell did ring. Robert and Samuel slipped through the partially opened door, with John Arnold remaining in the church porch, pushing the door closed as the parish clerk's protestations could be heard. The bell had now silenced as Robert and Samuel followed in the light of the parson's own lantern, walking quickly through the interior of the church.

"It is my brother Augustus," the parson called out behind him, "I know not how...but there did become some entanglement... and now he...he...he does hang amongst the bell rope. I ...he is...he must be released. Be quick but I fear that he is... already...there."

The parson held up the lantern at the base of the tower. A black shape like a great dead rook on a gibbet, hung from the single bell rope, with arms like lifeless wings sticking out to the sides. The narrow rope encircled the neck, forcing the face to bulge out with the tongue lolling to one side, the popping eyes staring down as the body swung gently, the feet dangling just within the parson's reach.

"By God..." said Robert, then clamping a hand over his mouth least he swore again.

The belfry ladder had been moved from its place and now leant against the wall, within reach of the rope and the dangling bulk of Augustus Crouch. Samuel steadied the foot of the long ladder whilst Robert climbed with the ladder bending under his weight. The rope had been made to loop tight around the neck of the parson's brother but Robert could not lift the body or unentangle the rope.

"Get John," called down Robert, "it will take more than I to lift him down."

The parson moved quickly, down the aisle to the church door. Robert could hear the heavy door being opened and closed and then the key being turned in the lock. Surveying the scene, John Arnold acted quickly.

"Robert, let I go up first, be he living?" said John Arnold.

A look at the face of the parson's brother was enough to answer his own question. Once Robert had come back down the ladder, John Arnold swiftly climbed the rungs. Robert then followed up behind until he could hold and lift up the legs whilst John Arnold grappled and lifted under the arms of the hanging figure with one arm whilst trying to unloop the rope from around the neck with the other. The church bell clanged deafeningly just above them, with each movement upon the rope. Suddenly the weight of Augustus Crouch slipped from their grasp, dropping to floor of the church, with neither John Arnold or Robert being able to keep hold of the body. Samuel was kicked to one side by the parson's brother's boot as the dead weight slumped down, the limbs spreading out with the impact of the fall. John Arnold slowed the rope as it passed through his hands, taming the motion of bell, eventually coaxing the rope to stillness and quietness settled within the church. Robert and then John Arnold descended from the ladder that creaked under all their weight but had not broken. They gathered around the huge black figure upon the floor. None spoke at first until the parson knelt down to close the staring and bulging eyes of his elder brother. He then stood and they all bowed their heads as prayers were said. A further silence followed as all considered the consequences of this death until the parson spoke again, broadcasting the circumstances of this tragedy to himself, to those present, John Arnold, Robert and Samuel and also, in turn, to the parish, once the new day had dawned.

"I was near returned to the parsonage, when I did first hear the joyous ringing of the bell," said the parson, "calling an end to Saint Catherine's day. None felt the occasion of our saint's day more than he, my brother Augustus and it is but a dreadful tragedy that has happened here, on this eve. By his own…devotion to our own dear saint…by his dedication … to celebrate our special day...by his exuberance in ringing the church bell, so that all might know that our saint's day has ended. Yet on this day, three lives within the parish are ended and blessed shall be their journey to heaven. Sarah Crust, our parish constable Edward Loper, and now... my own...dear brother. It is a day that shall not easily be forgot and indeed we must ensure that every next Saint Catherine's day, be a day where we do remember the parish past and the parish that now is."

"Amen," said John Arnold, Robert and Samuel together.

With the parson, standing before them, forming his own public explanation for the death of his brother, Robert wanted to talk to Samuel about the crossbow bolts, still in the oak door at the parsonage and the tub of washing water emptied across the parlour floor.

Robert called to Samuel to help move back the ladder to the hatch into the belfry. They began to lift the ladder, wavering upright in the space above them.

"The parson, he must know nothing of what did happen at the parsonage," said Robert, into Samuel's ear, as quietly as he could

"I did hammer back out the bolts in the door," whispered Samuel, in response, "there are still the holes, the water it has drained from the floor. The puke on the stairs is brushed, I did sluice water after."

"Parson," said John Arnold, "where is your brother Augustus to lay tonight? Shall he be carried to the parsonage?"

The parson shook his head.

"He shall remain in the church, for tonight, Saint Catherine's church that he did love so well, he would wish it so. The vestry table, it is big, let us lay him there."

Once the body had been heaved and carried between them to the vestry table, the parson thanked John Arnold, Robert and Samuel. He then looked at Robert, questioning the blood upon his face and his swollen nose.

"I did fall bad, tis all," said Robert, reaching out and holding Samuel by the shoulder.

"John," said the parson, "now is not the time to speak of such things, but would thee become our churchwarden? I can think of no parish man more able or deserving?"

"Well, t'wud be an honour," said John Arnold, looking taken aback, "but it be not the day for such things, as thee does say parson."

"Then go to your homes and sleep," said parson Crouch, "I shall remain here to pray. Of late I have lost my father and, on this eve, my own brother Augustus. The parish, it is now my family and I shall serve you all, as best I am able, until it is my time to join the life of heaven. God bless you."

"Amen," said John Arnold, Robert and Samuel as one.

Once outside the church, Robert halted under the yew tree to speak quietly to John Arnold whilst Samuel waited at the lych gate.

"John, t'was not as it do look, what we did see. The brother, he shall be buried here in the churchyard, not buried somewhere in unholy ground."

"Tis troubling Robert, tis troubling for the parson, he be a good man, to lose his brother so...what ever do make a man..?"

"We can never know John, but we must follow the parson, in what he do wish. Tis done and we cannot right it now by the saying of it."

"But Robert, before God...I cannot speak an untruth and if any do ask in the parish..."

"I shall not say, nor Samuel and none in the parish needs know. John, thee shall now be the churchwarden, with the glebe land, tis a thing you wished for. The parish, it must settle after all that has passed, let it be so."

John Arnold sighed.

"Then I do swear not to speak of it Robert, as you do say, tis for the parson to speak for all."

After parting from John Arnold, Robert and Samuel walked home in silence. Robert thinking over and again about the self murder of Augustus Crouch. Samuel too would know that there had been no accident, the belfry ladder having been moved to enable the coiling and placing of the rope around the neck, before the body swung freely. The clashing above of the solitary bell, the bell of his beloved church, the church of Saint Catherine, would quieten and cease to the ears of the parson's brother, whilst the parish mustered in alarm at the lych gate and the church porch. The parson's words would cleanse the dread circumstances for the parish, but Dowty would know. Dowty was as guilty as Augustus Crouch. Robert vowed that, Dowty would pay dearly and there would be retribution. Robert's words to Samuel, back at the house after his near drowning at the hands of the parson's brother, were spoken falsely and now nothing would be forgot. Samuel had been right to question his father, before they had fought and Robert was struck, before the tolling of the bell. Thigpen also would be made to pay the severest price, for his deeds done in Watery Lane to his sister Catherine, all those years ago. Nothing would be forgot. Robert's head and face ached as he crawled onto his bed, fully clothed.

Robert jolted awake. The poisoned ox had just risen up and clambered from the earth, where it had been buried but the beast wore the head of Augustus Crouch. A paleness could be seen under the front door. He felt his face and touched dried blood about his nose. The side of his head was sore and he heard himself wince with the pain that his own probing fingers had caused. He wanted to go back to sleep but the dream now kept his eyes from closing. Augustus Crouch was dead and that was no dream. He pictured again the large feet overhanging the vestry table by some distance, the dark blood colours and bruising from the bell rope about his neck, covered up carefully by his brother, the parson. Loper was dead also and the young girl with the long black hair, David Crust's daughter. Robert could now see the upturned chair and table across the room that he had managed not to stumble over when they had returned late from the church. He lifted himself up very slowly, turning to sit on the bed before rising. He had slept with his boots on. He was stiff and sore and stood up unsteadily before crossing the room to pick up something laying on the floor, by the front door. It was a freshly cut length of thick hazel, a dog stick. He had thrown the old dog stick at Peter Thigpen, hopelessly missing his target and Samuel had now replaced it. It was this stick that had struck Robert across the face, sending him to the floor. He moved slowly to the back door, not disturbing the steady breathing of Samuel in his bed as he went out into the yard, leaving the door ajar. He visited the privy and then drew a full pail of water from the well, drinking deeply from the bucket and pouring the remainder over his head. He refilled the pail, tipping it into Katy's trough which she ignored, waiting until Robert had gathered her fresh hay from the barn. His dream was not yet forgot. He walked around to where the old ox remnants had been buried, upon which Samuel had burned the remaining yew branches. The chalk and soil filled hole had now been disturbed, with the covering turves heaved to one side. As he stood above the filled pit, he sensed the slipperiness of fat and decayed flesh upon his fingers. He looked down at his hands. Robert now realised that it was he that had delved into the pit of entrails, skin and ox head, to disturb the fill of the pit and it had not been the diggings of a badger or a fox. On the day he had failed to make a barrel stave for Will Feather, the old cooper, Robert had returned home badly drunk on cider. Joan had then moved to sleep in the barn so that she and Rose could no longer hear Robert's drunken singing of bawdy songs. Robert could remember nothing of that night but before he had collapsed onto his bed, had he taken the tied leather bag from above the privy, to bury it where none would ever find it? Knowing, even when drunk, the importance of the bag that would provide certain proof to those that wished to accuse him of the murder of the man who called himself Jonathon Brigg? Robert dropped to his knees before the pit, his empty stomach filling with a rising stench as his hands broke into the sticky chalk soil. He turned his head to the side to breathe deeply before wrestling with the ox head, turning it over, feeling below into the slippery hollow where the head had settled. From amongst the entrails, he pulled out a small but heavy bag, now coated with slime and he wiped his hands upon the dewy grass before clawing at the fine drawstring with rough, wet fingers. He finally loosened the drawstring and felt inside. The first object that he took from the bag was the tailor's scissors, once belonging to Jonathon Brigg. Robert explored further and amongst what must have been a threaded necklace he felt the unmistakable heaviness of gold coins.

"Father?"

It was Samuel, calling from the back door.

"Father?"

Robert quickly took a gold coin and slid it into the top of

his boot, before drawing the string shut and stuffing it back down into the putrid hollow, dragging the ox head back on top.

"Samuel?" Robert called back in reply, standing up and kicking the earth and ragged turf back into place, "I'm at the well."

He quickly drew another pail of water, tipping it over his hands and then scraping at his fingers to remove the slime, before wiping them on the grass. Samuel was now inside, picking up the table and chair and his stool. He looked up at his father and seeing the bloody mess on Robert's face, he lowered his head.

"Father, I do deserve to be beat, for all that I have done. I shall not run from you."

Robert sat down heavily on his righted chair.

"Come," said Robert.

Samuel moved within reach of his father and Robert placed a hand on his son's head, but then removed it when he thought that his son might still smell the rottenness of the ox.

"Something had been digging at the ox pit, it should be filled more, a badger, or a fox?" said Robert, who then coughed and cleared his throat, spitting onto the earth floor, "I am to leave for the city. Joan and Rose, I will find them and bring they both back, and then we do marry. None shall now stand in our way."

Samuel looked up and nodded.

"I will light the fire and boil water, thy face it is bad and must be cleaned."

Once the fire had been lit and the water steamed, Samuel then began to attend to Robert's nose and cheeks, carefully washing away the dried blood.

"Father, I would cut your hair and whiskers..."

"No," said Robert, abruptly, "there be no scissors here. I will stop at Chauncy. My sister Ann, she do have scissors."

Robert closed his eyes as Samuel dabbed with the old

cloth. He then looked up before gripping his son's wrist, the stayed cloth dripping pale bloody water to the floor.

"Samuel, you do promise on your life that thee shall never say to another, what we did see in church?"

"I do promise father."

"John Arnold has sworn not to speak of it to any and nor shall we speak of it. If the parish did know then it would do unto the parson a great harm. It shall not be said, not to Joan, not to Ann nor to Catherine."

Samuel nodded, and their eyes met, to confirm this bond of secrecy. Robert kept his grip of his son's wrist and spoke again.

"Will you now say to Tetty that Catherine, she must be written to, not to tell all, but to say that her letter it be read, as she did wish. Say that we shall meet again, after all the years that have passed. Say that I be main glad to know that she do live. Let the fish ponies carry the letter, when next they come. Will you do this?"

"Yes, I shall go to Tetty."

Robert released his son's wrist and Samuel continued, finishing the task. He took a step back to view his father's face before speaking.

"Father?"

"Yes Samuel," said Robert, gently touching the bridge of his nose.

"We must always now say the truth, to each other, none shall speak a lie or keep secrets, for it does bring great trouble?"

Robert nodded.

"Atrox melior ...dulcissima...veritas...mendaciis," said Samuel, slowly and with a half smile.

"Christ's gob," said Robert, looking up at his son, "and now the parson, he will learn thee more damned Latin?"

"And you shall build your windmill?"

Robert had forgotten all about building his windmill, his post mill.

"When I return, with Joan and Rose," said Robert, "then I shall build the mill and be an honest miller, to the parish."

Robert stood and the gold coin had slipped further down inside his boot, the edge of the coin now pressing into his heel, causing him to limp as he moved from his chair.

"Father, shall you be able to walk?" said Samuel, watching as his father opened the front door to pass beyond the threshold.

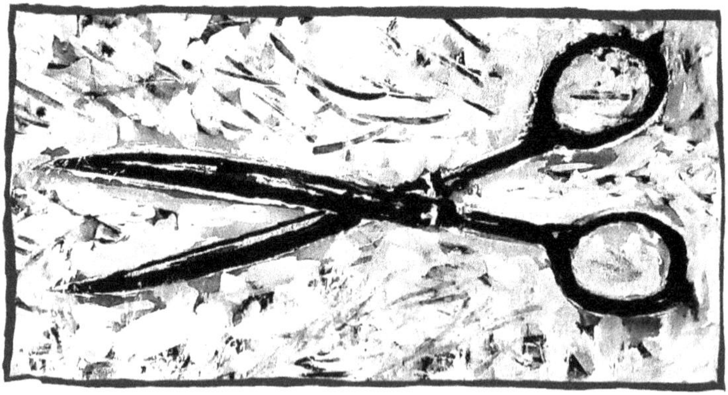

With gratitude to Leah and the Heytesbury Readers book group for their very honest and invaluable critique during the final stages of this book. Thank you.

"The Parish Waywarden" is the first of a planned trilogy, plotted but as yet two-thirds unwritten. The next in the sequence is titled "The Post Mill" and the fate or fortune of Robert Penny and his son Samuel conclude with "The Parish Constable". Encouragement to this end may be channelled through the e-mail address at the front of this book. Something in the vein of "Get on with it" will probably suffice.

Other books by Nick Cowen;

The Complete Adventures of Henry Chalk, Pedestrian Tourist

Trust Harrison

This Way Not That Way

Details available at the Hobnob Press website.

Milton Keynes UK
Ingram Content Group UK Ltd.
UKHW020802311023
431653UK00014B/368